OUT OF THE *Blue*

Out of the Blue

By E.L. Irwin

www.elirwin.com

To my daughter, Lindsay—you still inspire me, and I'll be eternally grateful you're in my life. Also, I'm thankful, and beyond thrilled you were smart, and waited, and found your own Asher.

And to those who believe in true love, or are still seeking it, this one's for you.

Contents

CHAPTER ONE
A Chance Meeting

Katy-

In my rearview, I took note of my blackening eye. *The bleeding's stopped, at least.* Gently, I dabbed at the blood crusted at my brow, thankful the adhesive sutures held. *Is this really worth the effort?* Dabbing at my eye again, wincing as I did, I glared out the windshield at all the vehicles in the parking lot.

Suddenly my truck shuddered with a loud bang, drawing my attention back to the rearview and the attached horse trailer. This morning hadn't gone according to plan, *at all.*

To start it all off, I'd overslept, which I *hate* doing. Then, in my mad dash to get ready, discovered I'd started my period a week early. And to top it all off, I'd forgotten to set the timer on the coffee maker last night. This resulted in me making the four-hour drive from Cody to Casper dry. Miserable was putting it mildly.

The morning might have been salvageable, if not for that colt. Closing my eyes briefly, I thought back to when it'd all gone sideways. I turned my gaze to my palms lying face up on my thighs, and considered the angry marks. The rope burns stung; thankfully the one had stopped bleeding. Slowly, I flexed my fist, not wanting my hands to stiffen. Each movement though, brought a new level to my discomfort. Of all the horses I'd selected, it was the colt who'd put up a fight. It had taken some doing, and I was bruised and banged up as proof, but eventually I'd gotten him loaded in the trailer. The rest of the horses would be delivered in a couple weeks.

The colt squealed, kicking the side of the trailer again, bringing me out of my thoughts.

Ah, to heck with it—I still had the colt to deal with and another four-hour drive ahead of me—I wanted my danged coffee. Blowing out a breath, I shut the engine off, and stepped from the truck, feeling far older than I was as my body complained descriptively.

It was the end of April; the ground no longer frozen here in Wyoming, though we did still get temperatures below freezing at night. As I stretched, my breath clouded the space in front of me, and I shivered, estimating it was barely above freezing now. The colt kicked the side of the trailer again, rocking the rig around some.

"Yeah, yeah." I grumbled before heading towards the Café Palace.

Nearing the entrance, I passed a sleek black motorcycle and gave it a cursory look. I've never been on one, but always thought they looked cool and edgy. This one had a certain rough sex-appeal to it, and I was momentarily distracted as my eyes roved over its frame, noting the Harley-Davidson insignia on the matte black finish. The bike reminded me of something out of one of the Chris Nolan Batman movies, and I felt an appreciative grin tug at my mouth.

That grin quickly faded however, as I caught my rumpled reflection on the glass front of the café. *Ugh.* Not much I could do about it, though, so I squared my shoulders and stepped inside, breathing in the wonderful scent of brewing coffee.

Three people were in front of me when I stepped into the Palace. Way less than I'd expected. Recognizing Jeff, this morning's barista, I gave him a half-hearted friendly wave as I got in line.

Waiting patiently for my turn, I gently tapped my finger against my thigh to the rhythm of the music playing in the background. I listened to a couple songs play through while my patience slowly ebbed away. As I was reaching my limit, thinking the woman in front of me needed to make her decision—she'd changed her mind now *three* times—I heard, from off to my right, the door to the restroom open. Simultaneously, the woman ahead of me *finally* settled on her choice and stepped away from the counter.

A new song began to play, an old 80's classic, Bryan Adams' *Can't Stop This Thing We Started.* Jeff smiled as I stepped forward.

And hit a brick wall.

Or, more accurately, the brick wall hit me.

I deal with large animals all the time so I'm used to being jostled by them. *This* one was huge—a virtual giant.

He was male—undeniably, obscenely, irresistibly male.

That was my first impression of him.

I couldn't rightly put my finger on what it was that so appealed to me but, whatever it was, this fella had it in spades. Everything feminine and womanly in me suddenly woke up and stood at attention. Fireworks exploding inside the Café Palace couldn't have given me a bigger jolt.

This was more than the simple acknowledgment of someone of the opposite sex, or even one who is exceptionally good-looking. I live in Wyoming for crying out loud, on a real working ranch, surrounded by cowboys.

In Wranglers.

I'm used to men. I'm comfortable around them. Honestly, I find myself more comfortable with men than I do with most women.

With a man, I always know where I stand. Whether they're angry, tired, hungry, frustrated, in pain—I can always tell. And act accordingly. A woman? Well, it's been my experience a woman can smile in the most inviting, friendly manner and hate my guts all at the same time.

Gina, one of my two very best girlfriends, says women tend to be uncomfortable around me because they're insecure. Though I've taken her words into consideration, I still end up guarded. Because I'm either myself and their insecurities come out, or I'm reserved and they call me stuck up—it's so unfair.

I mean, I get it, okay? I'm tall, blond, and fit. I have a woman's body. I have appropriately rounded parts where it's appropriate to have rounded parts. *So what*? I still get PMS (like today), just like the rest of them. I get zits. I have bad hair days. Bad breath. I try to watch my weight and nutrition. We're not that different.

Which brings me back to my original statement. As I said before, I'm way more comfortable around men. Generally, I don't have to wonder if they like me or not; I can just tell. Not so, with this one. He made me very uncomfortable. Bryan Adams kept singing about coming to get me and how I couldn't stop him, which somehow made me feel hunted and prey-like.

He was more than masculine, my giant. He was like...I don't know...an alpha male. The kind other men, tough men, give ground to. The kind they'd look up to, defer to, or even be envious of, which brought about my second impression. Irritation. For the first time in a long time, maybe the first time ever, I felt a frisson of uncertainty and unease course through me. Something quivered in my stomach, curled, and writhed there.

When a woman meets a man like this, she doesn't want to meet him under the circumstances I found myself in. She wants to be attractive and presentable, not dirty, sweaty, bleeding, and grumpy. So, I hated him. Perhaps it was the circumstances I really was hating. I know it was probably completely irrational, but I felt a flash of anger flood through me. I was mad clear through. I was mad at him for being so thoroughly male and attractive. I was mad that I was attracted to him. I was mad that I was mad.

It's been my experience that I'm typically taller than most gals I meet—I'm five-foot-ten. This fella topped out well over six foot. Other than his size and possible weight—he'd stepped on my toe and even with my boots on, I could easily tell he weighed more than two hundred—I couldn't tell a whole lot more about him. The breadth of his shoulders suggested strength and mass, but it was hard to determine the extent of it.

He wore a black hooded sweatshirt with the hood up. His jeans were slung low on his hips; he wore some kind of utility boots in black leather.

A black leather jacket was under one arm and a black motorcycle helmet was under the other. *He must like black.*

Seconds only had passed during my silent analysis.

Shooting a look of intense anger and disgust up at the hooded-head, I found myself looking into the brightest blue eyes I'd ever seen.

Bright.

Brilliant.

Blue.

They were amazing; so amazing, in fact, I forgot my pique for a moment. It was like looking into the depths of a deep, cool mountain lake, or a rare gemstone; the color was incredible. Briefly, I saw curiosity flare in those eyes as they quickly scanned my face, momentarily hesitating on the cut above my eye. "Excuse me," the giant mumbled before turning back to the counter.

Taking *my* spot at the counter.

The intriguing blue eyes were forgotten; irritation blazed once more.

"Don't worry about it," I stated succinctly. "You go ahead; *ladies* first, right?" Two people stepped into line behind me. His shoulders stiffened and I felt another aggravating moment of unease.

Slowly, he turned back around, his eyes easily seeking and holding mine. "I'm *sorry*?" he asked, as if he wasn't sure he'd heard me correctly.

I narrowed my eyes, then asked, "Are you really?" Still not cutting him any slack, I continued, "You're holding up the line." I knew my smile was sarcastic, but couldn't seem to help myself.

"You just said, 'ladies first', so please, you go first." With a jerk of his thumb, he indicated I precede him. Mutely, I shook my head and felt my right eyebrow rising. "I insist." His voice was a tad firmer than it had been before. "And to prove I'm a decent guy, I'll even buy your coffee."

"No *thank* you." I leaned around his shoulder, trying to ignore the tension continuing to build inside me, and saw Jeff had my coffee ready; *bless him.*

"Nice shiner." Jeff nodded at my eye. "Figured iced would be best." He spared a quick glance at the large man before refocusing on me.

"Yeah...you should see the other guy." I jerked my chin toward the horse trailer and offered a small grin. "Thanks, Jeff, see you later." I paid him as I took my cup, and without a further look at the giant or the other poor folks still waiting, I left the Café Palace.

Asher-

Asher watched the young woman, his curiosity flaring. He'd simply been passing through Casper; his last assignment had been taxing, and Asher had taken a couple weeks off to ride and clear his head. He'd chosen this part of the country because it was open and remote; he'd spotted the Café Palace sign from the highway, and decided to swing in for a quick stop.

Asher'd had his head down when he exited the bathroom. Being a tall man, he's easy to spot in a crowd, and he'd only wanted to get in and get out without any hassle about recognition. So, he'd kept his head down, hood up, and simply hadn't seen the girl until he'd literally bumped into her. He was embarrassed that he _had_ knocked into her, but felt simultaneously annoyed she hadn't given him a break when he'd tried to apologize—it wasn't like he'd meant to do it.

Then again, this _was_ coffee they were talking about, he grinned. Her quick comeback to his mumbled, embarrassed apology had surprised him.

Asher noticed her now. She was taller than most females of his acquaintance; still, she was nowhere near to his six-foot-five frame. Ash weighed over two hundred and forty-five pounds and virtually all of that was muscle. To be honest, he was impressed by the way he hadn't sent her sprawling when he'd accidentally knocked into her.

The girl had strength.

And spunk; he watched as she glanced back over her shoulder, irritation still evident in her eye. Asher couldn't keep the grin off his face at her annoyance with him. It was like watching a cute, fluffy kitten hiss and carry on—adorable and *thoroughly* non-threatening.

She wore a pair of worn, flat-heeled, western boots. Her jeans were faded and she looked good in them. Her threadbare flannel shirt hung loose around her frame; it was a testament to her physique that the flannel did not deter in *any* way from her shapely form.

Asher had noted her mild tan; the flannel had been unbuttoned enough to view her collarbone; her skin was beautiful. He could tell her legs were long, hips appropriate, her waist narrow. She wasn't skin and bones, though. He'd not even have said she was slender.

Healthy.

She was healthy, vibrant; she was *alive*.

He liked the way she moved. Purposeful, yet feminine, womanly. She had a sensual mouth; her bottom lip fuller than the upper, with maybe a slight hint of a pout. That pout emphasized with the angry look she'd shot over her shoulder. He liked her mouth. If he had to pick a favorite feature, he'd have chosen her mouth. Asher had no idea what the length or cut of her hair was, but from the amount coming through the back of her baseball cap, he could see it was blond, with possible hints of red. The sun had caught it, just so, as she'd stepped up into the truck, making him think of red.

When Asher had first seen the cut above her misty-green eye, he'd felt a surprising flash of anger spark through him at the thought that someone might have harmed her. He'd almost asked about it, then he'd looked more closely at her clothing and noticed the dirt and dust, her boots, and deduced it had been an accident involving animals. His suspicion was confirmed by the girl herself as she spoke with the barista.

His sharp eyes quickly noted the name inscribed on the door of her battered truck. "The Blues Avenue" it read in western-type script. He committed the name to memory.

Asher paid for his coffee. "That woman...that was just in here? You wouldn't by chance know her name, would you?"

"I do." Jeff looked at Asher and waited.

"See, I wanted to apologize to her for my rude behavior."

Jeff nodded slowly. "It's KatyBeth. She comes in every-so-often. And that's about all I know."

Asher was willing to bet Jeff knew more than that, but he considered, Jeff didn't know *him,* and Asher knew people tended to find him intimidating. He could respect Jeff's stance. "Thank you." Asher offered, as he turned to leave.

Asher decided to stop in Casper for the night. After checking into his room, he quickly found the phone book, attempting to find the name on her truck door. Having no luck, he did a search on his cell. When that produced nothing, he speed-dialed a number. The phone rang several times, without answer. Tapping End, he quickly redialed. After about the tenth ring, someone finally picked up.

"*What*?" the gravelly voice said, still thick with sleep.

"Get up," Asher said.

"You might say please, Ash," the voice grumbled.

"Sammy," he warned, impatient. "I need you to find someone. Please."

"*Interesting,*" Sammy replied, sounding intrigued. "Who is it I'm find-ing?"

"A woman."

"They have agencies for that, with professionals, no attachments."

"Not that kind of woman. Idiot. Are you up yet? Get something to write this down." Asher heard sounds coming from the background indicating his request was being complied with.

"What's the name, Bwana?"

Asher chuckled. "KatyBeth is the woman's name. She was driving a truck with the name 'The Blues Avenue' on the side. I've looked in the phone book already and came up empty..."

Sammy chuckled dryly. "What'd she do, scratch the bike?"

"I just need you to find her, Sammy." Asher tried to keep any feeling out of his voice, though he was sure Samuel picked up on his interest.

"Ah...it's nice to be needed," Samuel replied lazily. "What's so special about this woman?"

"Call me when you have the information. I'll be waiting." Three hours later, Asher received the call. "It took you long enough."

"I was sleeping when you called. I had to wake up. That meant a meal, a shower, and caffeine, not necessarily in that order."

"Do you have the information?" Asher tried to rein in his agitation.

"I had to pull some strings, but I believe I do. Your young lady is a third owner in the dude ranch named, 'The Blues Avenue', which is located way out in the sticks a little way south of Cody, Wyoming. Where are you now?"

"Casper, Wyoming."

"And what's your interest in this girl?" Samuel tried again.

"What else did you get on her?" Asher ignored his attempt.

"You want everything?"

"I always do."

"Very well," Samuel said in a business-like voice. "Her name is Kathryn Elizabeth Reilly. She's twenty-two years old; her birthdate is March 30th. She's an only child. Her parents are Jackson and Naomi Reilly, both in their late fifties. As you said, KatyBeth is how she's referred to. She's a wizard with horses and can apparently hold her own against the gents when it comes to cattle. She's single, no previous marriages or children. Her political leaning is conservative and she and her parents are members of the Wind River Baptist Church.

"Miss Reilly graduated from Cody High School with a 3.92 GPA, her strongest subject being Mathematics. Their dude ranch... You understand what a dude ranch is?" Samuel asked.

"Yes. Continue."

"Their dude ranch sits on about 2500 acres, just southwest of Cody, between Highway 14 and Interstate 120. They run a small herd, and by small, I mean about four hundred head of Angus and Hereford-crossed beef cattle. They've been in business for the last twelve years and have either broke-even or sustained a profit. They rent out rooms on their ranch from April 1st through October 31st. You can book a private cabin, designed more for larger groups, or a room in the main house. During your stay at the ranch, you can fish, hike, get equestrian lessons, go on cattle drives, and other such fun. Does this meet with your requirements, Great Bwana?" Samuel finished dryly.

"Good job, Sammy. Do you by chance know whether they're booked yet for this coming season?"

"There are a few minor bookings in July and August, nothing so far in September and a week for a church group in October."

"Text me the number, will you? Thanks, Sammy, I'll be in touch." Asher ended the call, then sat quietly for a moment, contemplating. It had been a *very* long time since he'd felt this kind of interested excitement about a woman. Normally, they weren't hard to come by; in fact, it was generally quite effortless. Was it the challenge then? *Maybe.* Partly. *Probably.* Asher pursed his lips, his eyes focused, his fingers steepled across his chest. Suddenly, he leaned forward and dialed his cell phone again.

Samuel-

Samuel Darrante ended the call and sat back in his chair, a faraway, contemplative look in his eye. Asher was interested in someone. Enough to send Samuel after information on her. How long had it been since Asher's last relationship? At least two years. Maybe longer. He hadn't been celibate during that time, though. Not at all. But he hadn't allowed anything deep or lasting to even hint at growing. And, *he* hadn't chased anyone. No, they'd all thrown themselves at Asher. Relentlessly.

Samuel sometimes thought that was the reason behind Ash's life choices. The risks he continued to take. Unnecessary risks. Samuel scratched his chin, his mind whirring. He'd have to keep an eye on this. This woman. Asher's interest in her. Samuel'd been after Ash for years to step back, settle down. Maybe he would; Samuel would have to wait and see.

CHAPTER TWO

Oh, I Just Love Surprises

About two weeks later.

Katy-

The phone began ringing a little after eight as I came in from the morning feeding. Mom answered after the third ring. I listened to her quiet, steady voice as I made my way down the hall to the kitchen; it was a sound that always gave me peace. Nothing ever seemed to ruffle Mom's feathers.

Today would be the exception to that rule.

"Who was that, Mom?" At the shrill tone of her voice, I'd turned and headed back to the office.

Mom sat silent for a moment; her eyes wide, lips slightly parted. I'd had to ask the question again before she heard me. She took a deep, steadying breath and said, "His, his name is Rupert Bosworth. He represents Black Hills Entertainment. They're a *movie* studio. They want to hire the ranch...and *you*, for their next project. They want to begin filming next month..."

"What? Next *month*?" I stammered. "That's...that's kind of short notice, isn't it?"

"They said they were under a time crunch and needed to get going as quickly as possible."

The fax machine rang.

Twenty pages in all came through in crisp, black and white print. I picked it up and began reading the proposed contract. After a moment I had to sit down, suddenly feeling lightheaded. Despite the number of pages in the contract, it was pretty cut and dried.

Black Hills Entertainment wanted to use our ranch. The land mainly, but the cattle and horses as well. And they wanted to hire *me*. They named me. Their star actor would need my expertise for the lead role he was portraying. For a thirteen-week period, I was to be his personal assistant and personal trainer, educating him in all aspects of horsemanship and cattle ranching. From all the details and possible scenarios listed, we'd be nearly joined at the hip for those thirteen weeks. The studio was offering an astronomical amount of money, most likely to compensate for the short notice they were giving us—more than I was able to fathom. All travel expenses for me would be covered.

"When will Dad be home?" I asked quietly, my heart thudding in my chest.

"Lunch."

"He should read this," I paused, then continued. "What do you think?"

"I'm not sure... It's *a lot* of money and the ranch could use it, no doubt. What they ask for with regards to the ranch isn't much. But what they're requesting from *you*, that's another thing altogether. That decision rests entirely on you, sweetie."

"When do we have to respond?"

"By three tomorrow afternoon. This Bosworth said we should have our attorney read it. I'll call Dave Laney and see if he's available today—I can fax it over. If he thinks this is safe, then, if *you're* willing, we sign and fax it back. Their actor should arrive sometime next week."

Standing, I put my hat back on. "Holler when Dad gets back. I've work waiting." I had a handful of horses to collect from one of the out-pastures, and couldn't sit around worrying over this momentous new development. When I came back inside, Dad was seated behind the desk, his reading glasses on, completely engrossed in the contract in his hands. Quietly, I passed through on my way to the kitchen.

As I finished eating, Dad took a seat at the kitchen table across from me. "What do you think?" I asked. "Have we heard from Dave Laney yet?"

"Not yet." Dad's calm eyes searched mine. "As far as I can tell, it looks like a legitimate contract. It'd be nice to have the security that money would offer," his eyes roved over mine again, no doubt trying to gauge my mindset. "But like your mother said, the largest aspect of the agreement has to do with you. Three months is a long time. It's not that it would be hard on us, we'd certainly have enough to hire out extra help, but, regarding you... You need to make up your own mind on this. We've no idea what this movie star is like; he may be a world-class jerk for all we know. I've heard some of them can be very demanding. And *you'll* be the one having to deal with him."

"True," I agreed with a nod. "Though, even if he is a creep, as long as he's not abusive, I think I can hack three months of being his assistant. I'll wait to make up my mind until after I've had a chance to speak with Dave. I'll try him again shortly."

After I'd helped Mom clean up, I went back to the office and dialed Dave Laney, attorney at law. The receptionist answered after four rings. "Law Office," she said, in her professional voice.

"This is KatyBeth Reilly. I'm trying to reach Mr. Laney. Is he available?"

"Just a moment, Miss Reilly, and I'll check for you." Music was playing, so the hold wasn't a tedious one. As I waited for the receptionist to pick up again, I quietly sang along with the sultry-voiced woman who 'set the rain on fire.' After a minute or two, Dave Laney himself got on the line.

"KatyBeth? Hey, Hon, it's Dave. Listen, I've vetted this company and finished reading through this contract—it looks good to me. This is legit."

"Dave, I noticed the name of the actor wasn't given, is that a problem?" I rubbed at my chin, trying to settle my thoughts.

"Not unless you want to make it one. What's on your mind?"

"Well, not knowing what caliber of person I'll be catering to for the next three months gives me a slight pause." I exhaled fast and asked, "How difficult would it be for us to get out of the contract if this guy is absolutely horrible? I mean, if he's the type to pitch a fit over every little thing and go into verbal tirades, then I want the reassurance I can back out, legally."

"It's not watertight. They've left you some breathing room." I heard the clink of ice against glass, then Dave swallowed, before continuing. "I'd say it's up to you, Katy. You'll have the hardest job here. However, the payoff for you all would be immense—I mean, I don't have to tell you that. There're *a lot* of zeros in that figure. I can't see any way you all would be taken here. And if their big-name actor *is* a real creep, well, I'm confident I can break this contract without loss to you or the ranch."

The tension in my shoulders eased at his announcement, and I nodded to myself. "Thanks, Dave, that's what I needed to hear. We'll go ahead and sign then. Send me the bill and we'll get you a check. Take it easy." I made my way back to Mom and Dad. Their heads were together, obviously talking. "Dave says it's a good deal. He reassures me if this turns sour, he's confident he can break the contract without loss to us. So...I think we ought to run with it; that's a lot of money and I'd hate to pass on it when it's landed so neatly in our laps."

At my entrance, my parents had leaned upright and exchanged a look. Dad nodded at Mom, "Okay." Mom handed him a pen. He signed, then Mom, then she handed me the pen. I stared at the spot for my name for a long moment, then leaned down to add my signature.

Picking the documents up, I stacked them neatly, willing my heart to remain calm. "I'll wait until tomorrow to fax these." Pausing at the door, I turned back toward my parents. "I was thinking about having a barbeque on Friday. It's supposed to be great weather and if I'm going to be busy for the next three months...well, a barbeque sounds nice."

"It does," Mom agreed. "First barbeque of the year. We've got several of those tri-tip roasts in the freezer. I'll get them in marinade and by Friday they'll be perfect."

Katy-

Three of the horses would need new shoes. I'd have to call Calvin and have him out. Maybe I'd have him come on Friday and he could stay for the barbeque. I reminded myself to check the date and time the horses I'd purchased a couple weeks back were coming in. Hopefully, it would work out and they'd arrive before Friday.

Every day for almost three weeks, I'd been working with that young colt. The first few days were the toughest; he didn't trust me at all and thought the whole world was his enemy. I named him Jet for his jet-black coat and because he took off like a rocket. I'd been riding him now for the last four days and was pleased with the progress he was making.

After I'd finished my afternoon chores, I sat on a bale of straw, allowing my mind to wander. Despite my initial apprehension, I was thankful we'd been given this opportunity and made my mind up that, short of physical abuse, I'd stick this out no matter how difficult I found my client. I'd give him no reason to find fault with me. He'd walk away a master equestrian.

I closed my eyes for a moment, simply breathing, letting my resolve fill me entirely. One of the tame barn cats jumped into my lap and began purring. Absently, I stroked its fur, my thoughts lost in a daydream.

Out of the blue, I found myself thinking of the behemoth, I mean the giant of a man, who'd bumped into me a few weeks ago in Casper. I'm not sure why *he* came to mind. Perhaps it was the blue his eyes had been; they reminded me of the night sky. It wasn't fully dark yet, just a light shade of twilight, but the blue the sky had become was a close match to his eyes. I remembered that moment of unease I'd felt when I'd spoken to him.

I thought about that. It hadn't been fear, exactly, just...I don't know. Unease, I guess? Maybe excitement? I considered that emotion and my body's response to him.

My pulse had quickened.

My heart had skipped.

My throat had been tight; I'd found it difficult to swallow. Possibly it had been excitement, then. Whatever it had been, that feeling was a first for me.

Mom called from the house and I knew dinner was ready. I eased the cat off my lap, turned out the lights, and closed the barn door for the night.

After dinner, I showered, then lounged in my sweats on the couch as I made a few phone calls. I verified the delivery of the new horses from Casper. They'd be here Thursday afternoon. Both Deken and Derek were available for those summer months and thought my three-month project would be awesome.

I called Calvin, my very best friend, and our ranch farrier, and scheduled him to shoe for me on Friday. And, yes, he'd stay for the barbeque. Everything seemed to be aligning. Now, we just had to wait for the actor's arrival.

Asher-

"Well, for better or for worse, all parties have accepted your terms, Ash." Cory settled comfortably on the sofa. "Rupe received the signed contracts from the Reillys at 2:57 this afternoon." Cory jerked his chin at Asher, a glint in his eyes. "Your girl was cutting it kinda close, don't you think? Maybe she's not as interested in you as you think, huh?"

"I'm sure she was simply letting us know she would agree to do this, but only on her terms. And *she* wasn't interested at all, Cory. She doesn't even know it's me." A sparkle of excitement flashed in Asher's bright blue eyes.

"I've seen that look before," Samuel stated from across the room where he'd been studying Asher. "You're in hunter mode."

Asher gazed back at him mutely, his face closed off, his eyes now guarded.

"Sammy's right, Ash." Cory reached for a handful of mixed nuts on the coffee table, popping a couple in his mouth. "I can't figure it. You just took a *huge* cut in your fee to practically guarantee the Reillys' acquiescence to the studio's request—a request on your behalf, I might add. In addition, you didn't want to do this film in the first place. Black Hills was on the verge of signing with that British pup and you swoop in after doing a complete one-eighty. What gives?"

"Actually, he's from Down Under." Asher tossed over his shoulder in a perfect Australian accent. He angled away from the window and the mountain view, to run his gaze over the room.

"All right, he's an Aussie." Cory shrugged as if to say *so what*. "Still...?"

"As you say...I'm...*hunting*."

Samuel silently noted the gleam in Asher's eye and the feral smile playing on his mouth.

"You could wink at any given moment and have your pick of women and you want nothing to do with them. Why this woman?" Cory asked again.

"You'll have to wait and see, the both of you," Asher replied. "Be ready to leave on Friday."

"Sammy says she's a church-girl." Cory jerked his chin at Asher, unwilling to let the conversation end. "Either she'll be a bigoted Bible-thumper or she'll be one of those hypocritical ones who're hot to trot for everything. Come on, Ash, you can do better."

Asher narrowed his gaze at Cory; his jaw tight with suppressed irritation.

"Cory." Samuel warned in a soft voice.

Cory shrugged; he wasn't worried. Asher would never hurt him. "Maybe you'll get lucky and she'll be..." he trailed off, suddenly registering the look on Asher's face.

"Be careful how you speak about her." Asher's voice was low, cold. "She's...just be careful."

Asher-

The drive to The Blues Avenue Ranch was a picturesque one. The landscape was rugged; large crevices struck through tall jagged cliff tops. Pine trees, Aspen, and Birch dotted the land in clusters here and there. Despite the unseasonable warmth of the day, Asher spotted snow in shadowed and shaded areas. He'd carefully studied the map Samuel had written for him earlier and knew his turnoff would be coming up soon. He checked his mirrors; only Samuel and Cory were behind him.

He was still angry with Cory for his words about KatyBeth Reilly. Cory quite often spoke before thinking. Asher had always chalked it up to immaturity and never let it get to him before. *In all honesty, Cory could be right.* After all, Asher really didn't know her. Somehow, though, he'd be willing to bet a fortune on the idea that Cory was completely wrong in his assumptions.

A long, winding dirt road appeared in front of him off to the right. The wooden sign hung over the entrance read, "The Blues Avenue" in the same western-styled script he'd seen on the side of her truck. Excitement at seeing her again sparked through him.

Tall Blue Spruce pines—the source of the ranch name, he fig-ured—and various types of Cypress lined the long driveway. A split-rail fence, painted white, was a nice backdrop for the colorful trees. After a couple of minutes cruising slowly down the dirt lane, the foliage broke and the ranch house came into view.

Asher barely noticed the house.

What he noticed was the girl.

In a large open field just south of the big house, something had caught his eye. A raucous game of flag football was in full swing. They were playing three-a-team. KatyBeth was among the players; he recognized her by the color of her hair, which was longer than he'd expected. Asher stopped his bike in the shade of a large fir tree and shut the machine down. Samuel and Cory stopped beside him. They, too, turned their bikes off, then removed their helmets.

Asher was focused on the game, or rather, the girl; she was in the quarterback position. He felt his lips lift, his eyes sharpened in anticipation. A stereo up by the house boomed some type of rock music, and he watched as she dropped back. One of her teammates, a male, was her blocker. The other teammate, a female, ran a simple pattern.

Asher felt his smile widen as he took in KatyBeth's touchdown dance. She knew what she was doing; he had to give her that. He wagered the distance she'd thrown the ball had been at least thirty yards and there'd been plenty of zip in that tight spiral. She'd thrown it right in front of her receiver in a perfect execution.

Katy-

My teammates and I celebrated our touchdown with a little air guitar in the end zone. One of my favorite rock groups, Kutless, blared from my stereo speakers. After completing the one-legged guitar hop, I huddled my team and planned our defense. I was just assigning the coverage when the music abruptly cut off. Looking to the patio where Dad was manning the grill, I hoped he'd be waving us in to eat. Jack and Jill, our dogs, were seated beside Dad in their favorite strategic position for getting any scraps—staring away from the house in the direction of the driveway.

Mom was beside the stereo, looking in the same direction.

Deken said something and, as I turned towards him, he picked me up, flipping me over his shoulder, declaring his team the winners.

"Put me down you idiot!" I laughed, smacking his shoulder. After I had my feet on the ground, I turned to see what Mom had been looking at.

Anyone know them?" Derek asked. "Might just be lost."

"I'd be happy to help them," said Candi; her interest obvious.

Candi was one year older than me and Native American, from the Northwest Shoshone Indian tribe. She was beautifully exotic, with large, deep-brown slanting doe eyes, golden-brown skin, and dark shoulder-length hair.

Grinning at her, I shielded my eyes against the glare of the sun. There were three of them, all standing in shadow, so I couldn't identify anything specific. I headed in their direction, still smiling from Candi's comment.

I had a hunch one of these men was my new client. Though, I hadn't expected him until sometime the following week. If this was indeed my new client, he was rather early. I thought about that. If it *was* him...well, my job as his official, *whatever my title was,* didn't start until the 1st of June—I had that in writing.

I'd gone about ten feet when Deken called to me. I turned in time to see him toss me the football. Though he'd tried to catch me off guard, I caught it easily, my smile deepening.

As I turned back to the three still unknown men, I heard one of them—the shorter, beach-blond one—say something casually over his shoulder. He'd been facing away from me, was talking to a tall, thinner man, whose hair, at this distance looked black. "...Lucky toss, no girl can throw a ball like that with any kind of consistency."

Irritation flashed through me, and without thinking, quickly threw the football, aiming for his shoulder. I put a lot of punch in that ball and waited for it to smack him. The third man, who'd been leaning against his machine, farther still in the shadows than the other two, suddenly moved, catching my ball one-handed, right before it hit its mark. Gritting my teeth at that, I felt only slightly mollified to hear the loud *smack* the ball made when it hit his palm.

I noticed he hadn't dropped it, was still holding the ball, and was now facing in my direction. Mentally, I shrugged off the small shiver of...*something* I felt, and wondered if he was some kind of bodyguard for the blond.

Moments later, chagrinned, I hoped the one I'd thrown the ball at was *not*, in fact, my new client. I shouldn't have acted so foolishly. Taking a deep, steadying breath, I felt someone come beside me. Without turning,

I knew it was Calvin; he always seemed to know when I was upset about something.

Asher-

Asher saw her eyes flash in anger when she'd heard what Cory had carelessly said. He'd had a split second to act before the ball she threw hit Cory's back. His palm stung slightly with the impact. He could feel his lips struggling to keep a full-blown smile from erupting at her show of irritation. Pleasure coursed through him as Asher watched her approach, noting the seductive sway of her hips. When the young man, one of a pair of identical-looking twins, picked her up, Ash had felt an intense and unwarranted surge of anger.

Samuel had seen.

Samuel always saw things. That was why he'd commented on her passing skill; he'd been trying to distract Asher, give him time to cool down. His ploy had worked. Of course, then Cory had to smart off about her. Asher shot a look of irritation at Cory that he missed by a mile. Quickly, Asher refocused his attention back to her.

Today she was wearing a pair of cut-off denim shorts with a bright white tank top underneath a cut-off green and gold football jersey with a barely discernable number four on the front.

Legs that had only been hinted at before in her faded jeans were now on full display. Her tan was beautiful. *She* was beautiful. And barefoot, he saw, to his amusement. Even her feet were attractive; her toenails painted a shimmering shade of red.

Asher gave a moment's attention to the man walking beside KatyBeth. He sensed a bond there. What type of bond it was he didn't know, but intended to find out. Ash leaned back against his motorcycle; his eyes trained again on KatyBeth as she approached. He spun the football absentmindedly in the palm of his hand, and waited for the moment she'd recognize him, wanting to see her reaction.

Would she recognize him?

He was certain she would.

His eyes narrowed slightly in anticipation.

CHAPTER THREE
Dazed, Confused, and Annoyed

Katy-

I was still about thirty feet away, when the big one, the one with the football, casually underhanded it back to me. There was something about him...

"You guys lost or somethin'?" Deken hollered from behind me. I could tell by the sound of their voices my friends had followed us.

The thinner, leaner man responded. "We're looking for Miss Reilly." I got a distinct impression this man could be lethal. Something in his tone of voice maybe, or his stance, I couldn't decide exactly, but he definitely seemed to have an aura around him that stated "danger." The younger one, the beach-blond egotistical one was simply carefree, like any two-year-old over-confident colt. He wasn't a problem. Highly annoying certainly, but not a problem.

The big one suddenly shifted his weight, no longer in the deep shadow, and I was able to see him more clearly.

I stopped walking; just stood there, staring, like an idiot. I had good reason, though. He had to be one of the most attractive men I had ever seen. All sorts of alarms were going off in my head, but I was so caught up in the confusion of tension and attraction that I wasn't paying any attention to them. I should have paid careful attention. Ask any of my friends—I don't react like this to men. Other than the virtual giant from the coffee shop,

I've never, ever had one affect me like this guy was doing. Which irritated and perversely excited me at the same time.

My eyes traveled slowly up his big frame. I couldn't say for certain how tall he was, but I knew he was well over six feet—he was massive. A lot of tall men look over-lean and lanky, and tend to stoop and hunch over, subconsciously trying to minimize their height. Not so with this guy. His shoulders were square, his back straight. There was nothing lean or lanky about him. He was unapologetically *male.*

Heat stained my face, and I hoped it wasn't too noticeable. I simply couldn't seem to force my eyes to move any faster, and the rest of me wouldn't move until my eyes had finished with him.

His jaw was firm and squared off, with some slight stubble around his mouth. His lips were full, but so ridiculously masculine there was no way under heaven to call them feminine. I focused on his mouth for a moment, almost mesmerized, and his lips parted in a small, possibly knowing, smile. White teeth flashed at me and I swallowed. Disappointment flooded me when I reached his eyes however, as he wore dark aviator sunglasses.

Suddenly, I remembered I'd been spoken to and needed to provide an answer. "I'm...KatyBeth, and you are?" My reaction to the big, dark man unnerved me, and I hoped I didn't sound as breathless as I felt. Gratefully, I directed my attention to the leaner one, the lethal one, and wondered why I felt safer addressing him than the giant. I didn't even consider the two-year-old "colt."

"I'm Samuel. Samuel Darrante," the dark, lean one answered. "We're here from Black Hills Entertainment. I believe Rupert Bosworth may have informed you we were coming."

"He said you were coming, but not until sometime next week. Are you my client then, Mr. Darrante? I'm sorry, Mr. Bosworth didn't provide me a name for my contact." For many obvious reasons, I didn't want the young, obnoxious one to be my client. And the big one, well I found him too disturbing for my piece of mind.

"Ah...sorry, no," he replied, almost with a touch of humored sympathy. My heart sank. Possibly my stomach right along with it. Taking a deep breath, I looked at the young one, my eyebrows raised, in hopeful question.

He grinned and shook his head, then jerked his chin in the direction of my worst fears. I closed my eyes for a moment. *Dang it!* My breath seemed to be getting stuck somewhere in my throat.

When I opened my eyes again, the big man was smiling. He stepped entirely from the shadows, quickly closing the distance between us until he stood but an arm's length away. Calvin stiffened beside me—it was a normal reaction. I watched as the man's arm lifted, his muscles bunching as he grasped his sunglasses and removed them carefully from his face.

Blue!

Brilliant blue eyes gazed down at me in happy anticipation. This time, I knew my heart stopped for a moment. When it restarted, it was pounding. In disbelief. And anger. And if I'm being honest, I felt pleasure also. This was the second time the man had unnerved me simply because he was so attractive and *masculine.*

I shook my head. What were the odds the giant who nearly knocked me over and had caused me such unease would be the same man standing before me now, still stirring unwelcome feelings?

"Is this a joke?" My heart pounded, and I hated he'd caused that reaction. Knowing he was my client, I dared to let him feel the full weight of my anger. I wanted to be violent; I wanted to scream. The sudden rush of powerful feeling coursing through me stole my breath, paralyzing me.

"No." His voice was calm. In some perverse way, I found the strong timbre of it soothing, which increased my irritation with this whole mess—with him—that much more.

"What's the matter, Katy, you know this guy?" Calvin placed a comforting hand on my shoulder, giving me light squeeze.

"We've met before." I continued glaring at the man in front of me.

"Actually, that isn't correct," the giant said, his gaze narrowing on Calvin's hand still resting on my shoulder. "You really can't term what happened back in Casper as 'meeting' someone."

"Maybe you'd better explain, mister." Calvin's tone was firmer.

"I'm ashamed to admit that I did the, apparently, unforgivable act of taking this young woman's place in line, not to mention, nearly knocking her to the ground in the process." He didn't sound the least bit ashamed. "Imagine my surprise to find her here." His blue eyes were now looking into mine.

"And you are?" Deken asked, stepping to my other side. As I was still glaring at the large man in front of me, I was clearly able to see the flash of irritation in his eyes, when they landed on Deken. *What's with this guy? He glares at Calvin, now he's glaring at Deken.*

Before he could respond, Candi sucked in a deep, excited breath. "Oh...wow, this is SO cool. Deken, honestly! This is Asher Fitzpatrick." She flapped her hands excitedly. "He played in that submarine movie you like so much."

"It's a pleasure to meet you. I am Asher Fitzpatrick, but please, call me Ash." His voice still quiet, still somehow alluring, he turned his blue eyes back on me. "You wouldn't accept my apology before. I sincerely hope you'll accept it now. I am, *truly*, sorry for virtually trampling you. Forgive me?"

"How...?" Unable to fully frame my question, I knew he'd understand all the same.

"Did I get here? How did this happen?" he clarified.

"Take your pick."

"Would you believe me if I said, 'Fate'?"

"*What* are you doing here?" I tried again.

"In twelve days, I'll begin training for my role in my new movie. I understand the studio has hired you as my assistant and personal trainer. I called a week or so back to arrange for an extended stay prior to the start of our work association."

"We begin training on June 1st," I replied.

"I understand you're the best there is in the field," he agreed with a nod.

"That's a load of crap." Asher simply stared at me; challenge clearly evident in his eyes.

"You're saying you *aren't* any good?" Cory asked.

"I'm good, just not the best."

"*How* good?" Asher asked, a challenge in his voice now.

"Good enough for who it's for. *Satisfied*?"

"Not nearly," he replied, his lips curled slightly. "Not yet, at least."

"What more do you want?" Calvin asked. Challenge now rang in his voice as well.

"Many things." Asher's gaze held steady to mine.

I took a deep breath. Then another. It was as I feared; the only thing bigger than him was his ego. Well, I've tackled bigger broncs, I could take his ego, too. "Who're your friends? They weren't mentioned in the contract."

"Only that. My friends. You've been introduced to Samuel already and Cory, I believe, owes you an apology." Asher was still watching me, seeming to absorb my every response.

Mentally, I gathered myself. He'd get the reactions I wanted to give and nothing more. "Will you both be staying for the duration of the filming or are you here only for a few days?" I was proud of how calm I sounded now.

Asher's eyes flickered as he took in my changed demeanor. Internally, I gloated that I'd affected him. Meeting his gaze levelly, I waited for his response.

"Sammy and Cory rode along simply for moral support. They'll be leaving in the morning. Then you'll have my undivided attention. For thirteen weeks."

"Not for twelve more days, Mr. Fitzpatrick. I'll accept your undivided attention on June 1st. Until then, you're a paying guest, same as any other. Any one of these friendly people you see standing here can assist you with anything you may need. Now, I'll introduce you to my parents," I nodded in their direction. "We were just sitting down to eat. You're welcome to join us."

"Great, I'm starving," Cory said, a cocky grin still on his face. "By the way, sorry if I offended you."

"You didn't," I replied. "If you'll follow me, I'll take you to your room so you can freshen up." Turning away, I told my friends, "Let's call it a game, okay? I'm sure dinner's ready. Go eat. I'll be there shortly."

They gave me a quick, collective smile, everyone except Calvin. Concern was clearly stamped on his face. I looked to the patio, noting the curiosity on Dad's face from all the way over here.

"Lead the way," Asher said quietly as he stepped to my side.

Ignoring the heat that swept through me, I led them to where my parents waited. "Dad, Mom," I said as we stepped onto the patio, "this is Asher Fitzpatrick and two of his friends, Samuel and Cory. Asher is from Black Hills Entertainment. Gentlemen, these are my parents, Jackson and Naomi Reilly."

"Welcome." Dad stepped forward to shake hands with our guests. "It's a pleasure to meet you all. Have you eaten yet? If not, you're more than welcome to join us. We were just sitting down."

The size of Asher struck me anew as I looked at him next to my father, who'd always seemed tall to me; Asher was several inches the taller of the two. Mom moved forward next and shook hands with our guests. After the introductions were out of the way, I led them through the side door into the kitchen.

Calvin-

Calvin watched Katy lead her new client and his guests away and felt as if the ground had disappeared from beneath his feet. Mentally, he scrambled, trying to find his footing. Thoughts ricocheted. His heart throbbed, and he needed to sit down. Fearful thoughts. Lost thoughts. This man meant something to Katy. He could see it. Feel it. Was she even aware? He couldn't fathom the extent of what he'd just witnessed. The tension. He simply knew it would be far-reaching. Swallowing his heart back, he silently prayed for strength.

Katy-

"Obviously, this is the kitchen. Unless we're eating on the patio, this is where all meals will be served." I tried to sound brisk and business-like and unaffected. "Please, follow me."

Next, I led them into the great room, then down the hallway to the guest quarters. Asher's room was at the very end of the hall on the left-hand side, furthest from the main house, for added privacy. One of the three guest bathrooms was directly across the hall. I pointed out the bathroom and showed them where the towels were kept and where to place soiled ones for washing.

"Feel free to clean up while I get the sofa-bed ready and bring in a cot. The dressers and closet are empty, so you may store your clothing in there, if you wish. Where are your bags?" I asked, looking around. Other than a backpack each, they didn't have any other bags with them.

"Samuel and Cory aren't staying long, so they didn't need much." Asher replied.

"And you? Are *you* not staying long, either?" I was aware of my sarcastic tone.

Asher shot me a grin, acknowledging my snappy question. "I had no idea what I'd need for this training or whatever we're going to call it and thought it'd be easier if you assisted me with this and took me shopping. That way, I know I'll end up with appropriate attire."

"I... You want me to take you *shopping*?" I asked. *How does that qualify as equestrian training?*

"I do," he nodded. "This is definitely one area where your experience will benefit me. Is this a problem?" Those dark brows rose in question.

Fine. Whatever. "Not at all," I said, recovering quickly. "You do have enough, though, to last for twelve days? We don't allow nudity here." I had no idea where that came from, but I could feel the heat flood my face.

The grin flashed across Asher's face again as he contemplated me. Then he said, "I have enough to make do and avoid nudity. Thank you for...making me aware of your preferences."

"I can take you out next weekend, if that suits you?"

"It does, thank you. I'll wash up and change now."

"I'll turn the sofa out and get sheets—" I said turning away.

"Miss Reilly? Don't worry about bringing another cot in; Cory and I'll bunk together for the one night," Samuel said.

I turned towards them. "KatyBeth, please. Are you sure? It won't be a problem at all."

"I'm sure. Thank you, kindly, for your hospitality."

"You're welcome." I turned, leaving the room to gather linens from the hall closet. Cory and Samuel went past me and out to the patio. They were apparently hungry and didn't want to wait for Asher. I returned to the bedroom. Asher was still in the bathroom, so I opened the sofa and fluffed the mattress. Quickly, I put the sheets on, then tucked the blankets in. I was putting the pillowcases on the pillows when I heard the bathroom door open. With one pillow tucked under my chin, I glanced toward the doorway.

And dropped the pillow, where it lay forgotten at my feet.

Darn him.

Asher casually leaned against the doorframe as he put his watch back on. He wore the same pair of jeans as before, faded denim that looked soft to the touch. His hair was wet, and he was barefoot. His shirt...was tossed over his shoulder. I could only stare, thoroughly stunned. He was like a physical work of art...so much to appreciate. His shoulders were a huge expanse of blatant strength; I noticed the matching barbed-wire tattoos encircling his biceps. He must go without a shirt a lot, because he was tan all over, no lines.

My mouth felt dry and I was vaguely aware that my pulse was pounding. *Come on, Katy. Turn around, girl. Stop staring.*

Of course, Asher caught me looking my fill. And no, he didn't let it lie. "Is this permitted? I'm not nude." I heard the amused mockery in his voice.

Nodding mutely, I tried to remember if I'd ever seen anyone with more than what is commonly referred to as six-pack abs. If I carefully counted the ripples on the smooth skin of his torso, I was sure I'd find more than six. I kept losing track, however. Which was ridiculous; I can count, *way* past six, for crying out loud.

To be honest, he wasn't entirely smooth; he had a sprinkling of dark curly hair across his chest. It trickled downward, thinning, and disappearing just above his waistband.

I watched, in dazed fascination, as Asher pulled the white t-shirt over his head. Was he deliberately trying to be sexy? Because it was very sexy, the way his pectoral and abdominal muscles stretched and flexed like that.

It's possible this was the source of my tension. As irritating as I found him, or maybe it was my reaction to him that I found irritating, I couldn't deny he was monstrously attractive. Any female would have found him so. Being a woman, there was no getting around the fact that this was a man.

I'm not sure what look was on my face and a small cognizant part of my brain desperately hoped it was blank, revealing none of my inner turmoil. I was hoping that I'd be able to speak. Or move. Moving would be good. *Looking in another direction would be good!*

Asher stepped closer. I watched as he sinuously bent, catching a faint trace of his scent—*wow*—as he picked up the forgotten pillow and its case. Holding them out to me, his eyebrow quirked up in silent question.

"Are you alright?" he asked after a moment. His voice was warm. I noticed a very slight brogue in his speech.

"Yep," I said, barely above a whisper.

Asher raised the pillow a bit higher to catch my attention. My face flamed as I grabbed it from him, whipping around to finish the job. My heart was racing, my throat dry. I blinked my eyes a few times, trying to dislodge the image emblazoned upon them.

"You almost done?" Asher asked. I heard him moving around behind me; it sounded like he was putting on shoes.

"Almost. Did you need something?" My voice sounded rough to my own ears.

He chuckled at some private joke. "Not right now. I was going to wait for you."

"Uh, you go on ahead. I'll be out in a minute." I heard him turn away, pausing at the door, before continuing down the hall. After a moment, I distantly heard the back door open and close. My trembling legs gave out, and I was grateful the sofa bed was there as I dropped down on it.

Why, oh why did this have to happen now—with him? It seemed odd and yet somehow inevitable, that I'd bumped into Asher at The Café Palace only a few weeks back and now he was staying in my home. For three months. It was fantastical, really. Things like this, common everyday people rubbing elbows with movie stars, just didn't happen in the real world. Certainly not to me.

I hadn't gotten a very good look at him in the coffee shop. Other than his size and his bright blue eyes, I hadn't seen much of him. His blatant masculinity was the only pertinent impression I'd received that day. I saw a whole lot of him today, though. And *boy* did I like what I'd seen.

Candi is the movie junkie. If I asked, she could probably name every movie Asher had ever been in, as well as the characters he played. Heck, she probably knew his birth date. I recognized him now. Being in his profession, I was certain that having fans, female fans, was something he was used to.

I wasn't a fan.

Just because I found him physically attractive didn't mean I was a fan of his work or that I liked him personally.

I didn't know anything about him. Other than he was a virtual giant. And enormously attractive. And he unnerved me. That was it; that was all I knew of him. It was precious little.

I didn't doubt he was experienced where women were concerned. You could see it on him—that confidence and self-assurance. I couldn't afford to be dishonest with myself right now. Pretending I wasn't attracted to him, pretending I was naïve about certain possibilities, would not help me to avoid dangerous pitfalls. I had no intention of falling prey to temptation. I'd remained untouched to this point in my life and intended to continue in this status until the moment I wed. Of course, after I wed, very shortly after, my husband and I would be busy exploring this realm to its fullest.

I wondered now if the only reason I'd remained untouched to this point was because I'd never been tempted in the first place. That thought gave me pause.

I was sorely tempted now.

I prayed I was strong enough to withstand the temptation he presented. Then again, I thought, *like a dousing of ice-cold water*, it took two to fall into temptation like this. Perhaps I would have nothing to worry about. Maybe he was unaffected by me. Just because he was experienced with women, did not mean he would be open to a flirtation with me or anything else of that nature.

And wasn't I jumping the gun here? Hello? Had he made *any* moves? Had he indicated at all that he found me as attractive as I found him?

The short answer: No. He hadn't.

My stomach growled, reminding me I needed to eat. Blowing out a breath, I left the room.

Asher-

When Asher stepped outside, his thoughts were still in the room down the hall. He was aware of the conversations taking place around him, and replied appropriately when called upon; but in the background of his mind, he was reliving the memory of Kate—KatyBeth was simply too juvenile a name for a woman such as her—as she had unwittingly caressed him with her eyes. His muscles clenched thinking about the heat that had coursed through him. The desire it had ignited.

Asher considered his reaction to Kate. Certainly, he'd been intrigued by her when they'd first met. She'd not displayed any of the typical responses he was used to receiving from women. It had been a long, long time since he'd had to put forth any effort at all to get to know one.

And he wanted to know her, very much.

Was that the attraction? The chase? In part, maybe; Asher didn't feel that was the only reason though. There was something...more. What was it? The answer seemed just out of reach. Elusive. Aggravating.

He'd been annoyed in the coffee shop that she hadn't turned on the charm or flirted with him, trying to attract his attention. This was the response he was used to. If anything, she'd dismissed him entirely back there. He hoped he wasn't so petty, so egotistical, that an apparent snub would cause him to go on the attack. Asher knew he was a competitive man. So, was he simply keeping score? Evening up the score? Somehow that idea wasn't jiving right now either.

He looked up as the door opened and Kate stepped out. Her eyes were bright and there was still some color in her cheeks. Other than that, she had regained control over herself once more. She didn't look in his direction; she seemed casual and nonchalant. Again, he was struck with admiration at her determination not to stumble, physically or metaphorically. And he admired her more for it.

Closer, he thought suddenly. He wanted to get closer to her. Be closer to her. He had three months. Asher unconsciously angled his body in her direction, feeling the willingness to engage in the challenge she presented rise inside him. Hungry to begin, to succeed; he considered his objective with the cool, calculating mind of a military strategist.

She couldn't be forced; the thought turned his stomach. He'd have to carefully draw her out. Get her not to see him as an antagonist. Entice her so she wouldn't fight him. It would take time. He had only thirteen weeks.

CHAPTER FOUR

Sarcasm and Other Necessary Defenses

Katy-

Sleep eluded me Asher's first night here. I'm not sure if it was still my over-heated body or tension or what. I tossed and turned for hours, pounding my pillow into various forms, trying to get it just right. Finally, I decided maybe a run would clear my head. It was warming up enough now that I probably wouldn't freeze.

Fifteen minutes later, I was slipping quietly out the back door. After locking it, I tucked the key into my bra and headed west. Jogging away from the house, the moonlight illuminating the dirt road, I thought about all that had recently happened.

Asher and his friends had been good company; they weren't what I'd expected. They seemed normal, not at all like the entertainment industry tends to portray them. If I hadn't known who they were, I'd have taken them for just another set of guests come to stay for a break from the norm. Asher spoke with my parents and Samuel about various topics. For the most part, I succeeded in remaining in the background and unobtrusive. Though, I nearly fell out of my seat when Calvin casually asked again about our meeting in Casper. Mom and Dad looked at me in surprise. Asher came to the rescue by relaying the events in detail, of how we'd literally bumped into each other only weeks before in The Café Palace.

I'd thought Candi was going to have a coronary when she'd heard this. After squealing and sputtering excitedly, her hands flapping in agitation, she'd demanded to know why I'd never mentioned before I'd met a famous movie star.

"I guess it's because I didn't know he was a famous movie star. I didn't know he was a movie star at all. No offense." I'd tossed in Asher's direction.

I'd been aware of him, though.

Like a heated, gentle caress, I was physically aware each time he looked at me. The closer I was to him the more intense the sensation. I'd tried moving away, staying away from him. It hadn't helped.

Shivering in the cool morning air, I inhaled deeply. Relishing the crispness, the scent of pine, the sweetness of the blooming Russian Olive. My head cleared with each breath, of everything but him. He, Asher, was still there, as though he'd taken up permanent residence.

I didn't want him there. Couldn't afford to have him there for my own peace of mind.

Asher Fitzpatrick was a client same as any other. Granted he'd be here longer, much longer, than any other and he affected me more than anyone ever had. But, like our other guests, he too would leave. That thought hit me in a two-fold way. On the one hand I felt relief, I'd finally be free of him and the tension he brought. On the other hand—and this hand concerned me—I couldn't deny I felt a sense of emptiness about him leaving.

Mentally, I shook myself.

I'd gone about a mile, maybe more—I wasn't truly running, more slow-jogging than anything—when I decided to turn around and head back. As I approached the ranch yard, I noticed the barn door was open. Frowning, I headed in that direction. *Had I left it open last night?* I didn't think I had, but wanted to check, regardless.

Red nickered a friendly greeting as I entered and I rubbed his nose with affection. Everything seemed in order, so after a quick look around, I left. As I closed and latched the barn door, a huge, dark shadow loomed up next to me. Unable to stop myself, so startled by the suddenness of it, I screamed. Instantly, a large, warm hand clamped over my mouth, cutting off the sound.

"Shhhh...it's only me," Asher's deep voice rumbled in my ear. I could taste the salt from his palm on my tongue.

I found my back pressed against a wide expanse of solid muscle. His warm breath tickled my neck and I shivered; it wasn't from fear or cold. Holding very still, I felt Asher's grip loosen a little on my mouth. His other arm still held me tightly to him, the heat of his hand where it lay flat against my stomach sent a pleasant thrill through me.

No! My head jerked in defiance and irritation; anger bubbling up. At him, at me. Asher finally, slowly released me, his thumb lingering against my lips. A curious flash of disappointment moved through me as I was released. Not allowing myself a moment to wonder about that, I spun to face him and caught his flash of white teeth. Asher chuckled softly, "Sorry about that, didn't mean to scare you."

I'm not sure *why* I did it exactly. I think it was simply nerves, but suddenly I kneed him in the groin as hard as I could. He didn't drop, only doubled over in pain with a groan. Shock from what I'd just done and *who* I'd done it to stole my breath. The blood drained from my face as I weakly sank against the barn, my hands coming to rest on my thighs as I leaned forward and tried to breathe again.

Asher moaned quietly.

I winced silently.

Suddenly, he jerked upright, his face instantly in mine, anger clearly evident in his features. "What the *heck* was that for?"

"Because...because you grabbed me!"

"I grabbed you because you screamed."

"I screamed because you startled me!"

Asher silently stared at me for a moment or two, then calmly replied, "I said I was sorry for scaring you."

"I wasn't scared," I said through gritted teeth. "You startled me."

"You sounded pretty scared to me. I was simply trying to reassure you; I didn't mean anything by it."

"Why do you keep doing that?"

"Doing what?"

"Just... Next time watch where you're going. That's twice." I turned towards the house. After a few steps or so I said over my shoulder, "I'm sorry for kicking you."

Thankfully, I made it to my room without running into anyone else. Closing the door with near-silent force, I undressed in jerky movements, throwing my clothes in the hamper in vibrant frustration. Still shaking, I silently stomped into my bathroom, and turned the shower on. So many feelings were rushing through me. Anger, fear of the unknown, excitement. Even as I tried to calm myself, a tremor shook me. I was a jumbled mess of raw nerves—still on edge from being...startled. A trace amount of pleasured provocation over the feeling of Asher's arms around me lingered, and I was furious because he'd managed to unnerve me yet again.

By the time I was out of the shower, I'd begun to feel truly guilty for kicking him the way I had, and knew I'd have to apologize properly. Trouble was, I didn't see him until later in the day. I was in the kitchen, helping Mom get dinner ready, when Cory came in. His eyes were on me and seemed rather direct, almost accusatory. But maybe that was only guilt talking. "Can I help you?" I asked.

"We're gonna need some ice."

My face flushed. "Okay, yeah, sure. How much do you want?"

"Gallon-sized Ziploc should do. And...uh, Ash asked me to let you know Sammy and I are sticking around a few days longer."

Now I felt truly bad. Silently, I took a disgruntled deep breath as I filled a bag with ice, then sealed it tightly, and handed it to Cory. "Is everything all right?"

"Yeah..." Cory's demeanor seemed almost somber as he turned away.

I stared after him for a moment, then, feeling as if I was coming out of my skin said, "Mom, the bread's in the oven, I'm going out to feed."

"Okay, we should be ready to eat in about an hour. Will you let our guests know before you head out?"

Mentally, I shook myself, squared my shoulders, and made my way down the hall. For several lengthy moments, I stood before Asher's door trying to think of something appropriate to say. *Stop being such a coward! Knock on the blasted door already.*

I raised my hand, but before I could actually knock, the door opened, and my breath stuck in my throat. Though Asher didn't seem surprised by my presence, his eyebrow quirked up in silent question.

Clearing my throat, I said, "My mom wanted me to relay that dinner will be ready in about an hour."

"Thank you."

I nodded, turned, and started to walk away, then remembered my intention to apologize and spun back around. "Did I... I didn't hurt you...earlier?"

Asher studied at me quietly. I couldn't quite discern the look on his face; he didn't strike me as angry. "I'll live." His tone was definitive.

"Cory came to get you ice." *As if he didn't already know that.*

"The ice wasn't for me."

"You've been in your room all day." I pointed out. *Again, I'm sure this is something he's already aware of!*

"I've been on the phone and doing some reading."

What's he reading, I wonder? "Oh," I said. "Okay. I am sorry about that. It was...you startled me. I wasn't expecting to see anyone."

"What were you doing out that early?" He leaned against the door-jamb.

"I'd decided to go for a run."

"You always run that early in the morning?"

"No. Not always. I just needed to clear my head and wasn't expecting to see anyone."

"I gathered." Those piercing blue eyes drifted over my face for a moment, then he said, "Well, at least you know the move works."

"Yeah...well...see you at dinner."

"See you."

After dinner, as I was washing dishes, the phone rang. Dad answered. "Just a minute," he said. "Katy, it's for you." Asher, still seated at the table enjoying another glass of iced-tea, glanced in my direction at dad's announcement.

"Hello?" I wished I could simply stop being so darned aware of nearly everything Asher Fitzpatrick did.

"Katy? It's Lindsay. D'ya have any time to spare for my gelding?"

"Yeah, Lindsay, I can do that for you. Can I bring Ned here?"

"Sure."

"I'll come by tomorrow evening then, and pick him up."

"You're a lifesaver, KatyBeth."

"Not a problem, Miss Lindsay. See you tomorrow."

"Lindsay Bell having problems with Ned again?" Mom asked as I hung up the phone.

"Yeah," I smiled, thinking this was exactly the distraction I needed to get my mind off my new client.

"Who's Ned?" Cory asked, his voice sounded almost accusatory.

"Ned's a horse a friend of mine is training," I replied.

"What're you going to do with him?"

"Ride him."

"She can't ride her own horse?"

"She can. I'm simply going to smooth him over for her."

"You mind if I tag along tomorrow?" Asher asked.

I blinked in surprise, then said, "Yeah, sure." *Super.*

Katy-

Glad this thing is a crew cab, I thought as Asher climbed into the truck. He was so big he made the cab seem small and closed in, almost intimate. So much for having a distraction to keep my mind off him.

"How long does it take to get there?" Asher asked as he buckled his seatbelt.

"About forty-five minutes." I put the truck in gear, heading down the driveway.

"When you're not teaching movie stars to ride horses, what do you do to stay busy? Describe your typical day for me." Asher leaned his shoulder against the door, angling his body in my direction.

Darting a quick glance at him, I adjusted my grip on the steering wheel. Touching the brakes, I turned my signal on before pulling onto the highway. "Between clients, training horses, working with the cattle. Seems there's always something that needs doing."

He continued asking questions, seeming curious about the running of the ranch, how many animals we had, and what a normal day for me looked like.

After a minute or two of silence, Asher reached over, gently grasped my right forearm, and pulled my arm slightly in his direction, turning my palm upward. I remembered the feel of his touch. The heat, the strength, the callouses, and shivered. "I see your hands have healed." I shot him a look as I withdrew my hand, trying to decipher his statement. "I noticed the abrasions that day in the coffee shop." He answered my unspoken question. "How'd it happen?"

"Young colt. I forgot to put gloves on before I roped him."

"And your head?"

"He knocked into me." I shrugged. "I fell and hit the fence."

Asher stared out the windshield. "What happened to the horse?"

"I bought him."

"You did?" he sounded surprised.

"I did. He's turned out to be a great cow horse."

"I see." Shortly after, we pulled into Lindsay's place. Asher had elected to observe from the truck. After I had Ned loaded and we were on the road and headed home, he asked, "Why'd you buy the colt?"

"He had great form. And I liked his personality; I work well with horses like him."

"You tend to go for the bad guys then, the ones with the bad rep, huh?" His tone was teasing.

"Hardly. Let's just say I try to not judge a book by its cover. I know how that feels and frankly, I don't like it."

"How have you been unfairly judged?"

I blew out a breath. "Folks tend to think I'm one kind of girl...and I'm not."

"Because you're attractive, you mean?"

Wait. He thinks I'm attractive? "Yeah...I guess." I shrugged, my mind still trying to fathom Asher saying I was attractive.

"But, that's not all there is?"

"It's a bit more than that." I brought myself back to the conversation at hand. Checking my mirrors, I saw the red and blue flashing lights pulling up swiftly. "Crap," I muttered, signaling I was pulling over. My tires found the gravel and I brought the truck to a stop. Turning off the engine, I closed my eyes briefly, exhaling a frustrated sigh. "Ash, I'm really sorry about this."

Rolling down my window, I waited for the officer to approach. A flashlight shined in my eyes and I blinked, turning away a little.

"License and registration, please."

"Sure, Andy." I handed him both items. The officer took them, then shined the light on Asher as he briefly surveyed the interior of the truck. "Is there a problem, Andy?" I asked.

Andy looked everything over carefully, then handed the items back to me. "Everything looks in order."

"It always does. Are we done here?"

Andy shined his light back on Asher. "You new in town?"

"You could say that." Asher replied, a tone in his voice that somehow conveyed impending violence.

"This fella causing you any trouble?" Andy asked me.

"He's one of the ranch clients, Andy."

"Hmm... I guess you can go, then. Just be careful."

Once we were back on the highway, Asher asked, "What the heck was that all about?"

Laughing quietly, I shook my head. "Who knows? I swear if he's on duty, it never fails. He pulls me over."

"Maybe he's after your number." I snorted. "Could be he's shy and doesn't know how to ask." Asher nudged my shoulder, "You *can* be intimidating, you know."

I snorted again, then grumbled under my breath, "More like he has a fetish for handcuffs and would like to see me in them."

"I can see the draw in that idea..." He chuckled, and I glared at him. "Ah, come on...it's not that bad, is it?"

"It's really annoying is what it is."

"Maybe someone should explain this is not the way to a girl's heart?"

"I wish someone would."

"Have you lodged a complaint with his captain?"

"No, I haven't. For the most part, I don't think he means anything by it."

"So, one of those unfair judgments...might it be that some people think you're the type of woman who'd want to be taken advantage of?"

"You're getting warmer."

"And you're not."

"No, I am not."

"I think I can relate to that."

"Really?" I chuckled. "You often get mistaken for a woman?"

Asher chuckled with me, "No, I've never been mistaken for a woman. I have been mistaken for easy, though. I didn't like it."

"Exactly." I agreed, then added, "So, you're not easy, then?"

"Nope, so don't go getting any ideas about me, Kate. I'm not that kind of guy."

I chuckled again as I thought about what he'd said. Then it occurred to me exactly what he had said. "Kate?" I asked.

"Kate." Asher nodded.

"Huh. What's up with that?"

"I don't see you as a KatyBeth." He made quotation marks with his fingers. "It sounds too juvenile. You don't mind, do you?"

"No, I guess not. Wait, how old do you think I am?" How awful would it be to learn he thought I was in my thirties or something? I shuddered.

"Not that old, relax. I'd say you were in your early twenties...am I close?" he grinned.

"Pretty close. I'm twenty-two. You think that's too grownup for my name?"

"Age has nothing to do with it. KatyBeth makes me think of pigtails and high school—juvenile stuff. I don't see you like that. If it bothers you, I won't call you that. It's just, I see you as a woman and Kate fits that image better in my mind."

Asher thinks of me as a woman. What does that even mean? I realized then that he was waiting for a response. "Sure, I guess; one name's as good as another." I glanced over and found his gaze already on me. My pulse shot into high gear and suddenly I was all sorts of warm. Jerking my eyes away, I focused intently on the driveway in front of me, though I could navigate it blind-folded, no problem. In silence, I parked the truck and shut it off. Before Asher had his seatbelt off, I was out the door, slamming it behind me. I opened the back gate of the trailer, stepping up next to Ned and felt comforted by the big spotted gelding. I took a moment, simply petting the horse, to catch my breath and calm myself.

Asher remained quiet as I settled Ned in for the night, seeming to sense I needed space and quiet. We stepped inside and found Calvin seated at the kitchen table playing cards with Samuel and Cory.

"Finally," Calvin said. "You two get lost or something?"

"Had a run-in with Andy, again."

"Guy never gives up, does he?"

Asher followed me to the sink. His body heat radiated out, covering me in a warm, almost intimate caress. I felt constricted, my pulse racing. Keeping my eyes firmly down, I stepped around him and threw a quick glance in the direction of the table. "'Night, everyone; I'm calling it early. See you in the morning." I could feel their eyes on me as I left, and was thankful when I entered my room and all I heard was silence.

Leaning against my closed door for a moment or two, I simply breathed. Once calm, I headed for the shower. After drying off, I pulled on my PJ's and was just climbing into bed when I heard a soft knock on my door. For a second, I froze, then as I recognized the sound and who made it, my heart restarted. "It's open."

Calvin leaned his head in. "You alright?" Concern thickly coated his voice.

"Come on in." I scooted over to make room for him on the bed, then reached for my brush to begin working on the tangles in my hair. Calvin stepped inside, leaving the door open, careful not to put us in a compromising position. Calvin was like that, completely trustworthy. He leaned back against my footboard, one leg extended in front of him on the bed, foot dangling off the side, the other rested on the floor.

I combed through my hair in silence, not looking at him, simply lost in thought. For about the thousandth time, I wished I could fall in love with Calvin; I knew he'd been in love with me for years. He would be so easy, so comfortable to love. He would never cheat on me, would never treat me badly, and would always put my needs before his own. My eyebrows creased as I focused on the thought of loving Calvin.

Nothing happened. No light came on. No sudden inspiration or intuition. Calvin remained, as he always had and I saw now, always would be, someone I loved, just not the way he wanted. Not the way a woman loves a man. Not the way a man wants a woman to love him. Briefly, I considered the idea of accepting the unspoken offer Calvin issued. There would be safety in loving him—that I knew—but I truly felt I'd be cheating him of something, some*one* else. Someone who would love him passionately and unconditionally. I'd be cheating myself of the same thing.

Suddenly a pair of bright blue eyes shimmered in front of me, and I inhaled sharply.

"Katy, are you alright?" Calvin asked me again. "Did Asher say something, do something to you?"

"Yes," I whispered.

Something in my tone of voice must have alerted him. Calvin sat silently for several long moments, before asking, "You want to talk about it?"

"I don't...know...?"

"Has he threatened you or something?"

"Not in the way you mean." I admitted.

Calvin gave this some thought. "I see," he said after a moment.

"He unnerves me." I said with a slight shrug of my shoulders, feeling foolish and weak.

"You like him." He stated.

Shrugging again, I shook my head. "I don't know, Cal. He makes me feel things I've never felt before. Oh, it's not love. For crying out loud, I hardly know the man."

Calvin lifted his mouth in small smile that didn't reach his eyes. "He is a man, though, isn't he?"

"He is," I whispered, nodding.

"And that's the problem...you see him as a man."

"Yup." I made the "P" pop as I spoke.

Calvin blew out his breath in a rush. I wasn't being insensitive to Calvin's feelings; we've always been close like this. He was like a brother to me, a male best friend. I told Calvin all my secrets, more so than Gina or Candi. "I guess I can see that happening. Asher's...a different breed of male from what you're used to."

"You think?" I chuckled.

"Will you be alright? I mean you're signed on for this project..."

"I know. Trust me, I know." I nodded. "I don't have any feelings for him. At least not the emotional kind, and I have no intention of being his summer fling. So...I guess I'm done bellyaching, now. I'm simply going to have to suck it up and finish this job and send him on his way."

"Has he indicated he wants you to be his summer fling?" Calvin sounded annoyed now.

"No. At least, I don't think so. No, I'm sure he hasn't. Like I said, he's just getting under my skin. A lot."

"So, he's been flirting with you?"

"I... No, I don't think so. He's just, I don't know...intense. Friendly? Maybe too friendly?"

"And you feel his friendliness is a problem because of your attraction to him?"

"Yeah, that's pretty much it in a nutshell." I felt better for having acknowledged it.

"Well then, make sure you keep your interactions in a strictly professional realm. You're not afraid he'd take advantage of you, are you?"

"No. No, not really. I don't believe he'd force himself on me or anything. And besides, he may not even like me like that. Just because I'm feeling this surge of hormones around him doesn't mean he's getting the same rush."

"Maybe. Maybe not. I think I'll keep an eye on things." I tried to stifle my yawn, but Calvin saw. "'Night, Katy. Get some rest." He stood and kissed me lightly on the forehead before turning towards the door.

"Thanks, Calvin, for talking and all."

"It's what I'm here for."

Asher-

Asher lay in bed, hands clasped behind his head, contemplating his next move. After yesterday morning, and he had to fight to keep the smile off his face, he felt the need to regroup. He hadn't meant to frighten her. Asher himself had awoken early, intending to run; he did so quite often. He'd taken a few strides down the lane and suddenly stopped, lifting his head, searching.

He'd caught a whiff of Kate's scent. Whether it was perfume, her body wash, or lotion, he found it memorable and intoxicating. One of the horses gave a shrill neigh and he swiftly focused on the barn, wondering if she was there. Asher hesitated, not sure if he should intrude upon her solitude. His desire to see her outweighed his thoughts of consideration.

When she'd screamed, he'd reacted instinctively. He remembered how she felt against him, the feel of her mouth under his palm. He remembered how much he'd enjoyed the feel of her. Enjoyed having her in his arms. How easy it would have been to turn her head and have his mouth on hers.

Then he remembered, with startling clarity and cruel discomfort, what she'd done next. At least he knew she wasn't afraid to defend herself.

As Asher lay in bed, he considered every aspect of the situation as it currently stood. There were so many underlying emotions running around. Attraction to Kate seemed a common theme. He'd easily been able to detect the looks of envy and desire on the faces of those around her. Not all of them, but enough to cause a strong stirring of his protective instincts.

Calvin, Asher was convinced, was in love with Kate. And most likely the twins were as well. Though for them, it seemed more infatuation and flirtation than honest emotion. Asher had detected the attraction Gina had for Calvin and wondered if the man was even aware. He decided he'd have to be careful about Candi. She was jealous of Kate; he'd picked up on that. Candi's flirting with him was more what Asher was used to; still, he harbored no interest in the woman.

Asher knew he'd have to tread carefully in his pursuit of Kate Reilly. He wanted to entice her, not scare her off. He wanted her to acknowledge him as a man, not a movie star. Asher wasn't sure yet how he hoped to accomplish that desired outcome. Once she saw him as a man, what would the next step be? Where did he intend to take them? He didn't know yet; Asher simply knew he wanted her.

Katy-

I slept as poorly the third night as I had the first and second. Sleep-deprivation took its toll, increasing the irritation simmering inside me. Samuel and Cory would be leaving this morning, so I dragged myself out of bed and took a hurried shower.

I'd decided last night before finally falling asleep that today I would do my best to avoid Asher. I planned to get to work on Ned, which would keep me busy all day, thereby keeping me away from the house. I swallowed down any guilt and reminded myself that Asher had plenty of others here at the ranch who were able to help him if he needed it. I still had over a week before I was scheduled to begin work with him. I said goodbye to Samuel and Cory, then without a word to Asher, saddled Ned and was gone.

Samuel-

Samuel studied Asher as Kate rode off on the spotted horse. The look in his friend's eyes had moved beyond interest and into uncharted territories. He wondered if Asher was even aware. When Asher met his gaze, Samuel said, "Be cautious."

Asher blinked. "About what?"

"You've never been over this ground before. Have a care; that's all I'm saying."

Asher stared at Samuel for a moment, then shifted his gaze to the woman and horse already topping the rise. "Duly noted."

Cory revved the engine, ever impatient to be off. Samuel chuckled and turned to the car, saying over his shoulder, "This will test you; call if you need me."

Katy-

I rode the appaloosa gelding all day through various types of terrain, working him through water, over fallen trees, through thick brush until he acted sound and no longer skittish. I arrived back at the ranch around four-thirty dirty, sweaty, and tired, but pleased. My back and shoulders were protesting the workout they'd had today, but it was a good pain.

Gingerly, I climbed down from the saddle and ambled to the barn, leading Ned as I stretched slowly. The sun was setting, painting the sky in breathtakingly beautiful shades of orange, violet, and pink. Unfortunately, all I noticed was Asher seated on the back patio. In a seemingly relaxed position, his booted feet were extended in front of him, crossed at the ankle. His face was angled slightly in my direction, his sunglasses preventing me from knowing if he saw me or not.

I hesitated, unsure, chewing my lip and weighing my options. I could try and walk past him and go in the back door, or, I could walk around to the front and avoid him a bit longer. *When did you become such a coward?* Shaking my head, I made my way to the back door. If he was aware of my presence, he never indicated it. After I set the eggs by the sink for rinsing, I tiptoed to the window and peeked out; Asher hadn't moved. Maybe he'd been sleeping after all? *And maybe you're being an idiot?* Okay! Time for a shower.

In less than twenty minutes I was back downstairs, still a little sore, gingerly rolling my shoulders, and rotating my neck as I entered the kitchen. Mom wasn't there yet, but as if he was waiting there just for me, Asher was seated at the table.

His elbows were bent, hands clasped, index fingers steepled, and resting against his mouth. He moved his head slightly back and forth, lips lightly brushing against fingertips. Asher's blue eyes were thoughtful as I met his gaze. Heat climbed up my neck. "Hey," I said. Asher nodded without speaking, his eyes still on me.

Turning, I went to the fridge. A pan of lasagna sat on the middle shelf. Taped to it was a note from Mom. I needed to make the garlic bread, the salad, and throw together a dessert; Mom had run to town for a couple things and wouldn't be back until after dinner. *Super.* I wasn't disgruntled about Mom asking for help with dinner; that was no big deal. In fact, I was glad to do it. No, what bugged me was being alone with Asher. Especially as he was right now, so focused and intent on me.

Still ignoring him, or at least trying to give the impression I was unaffected, I started the oven to preheat. When it was ready, I slid the lasagna in and set the timer. I went back to the fridge and began pulling items to make the salad. During all this time Asher had remained a silent yet poignant presence behind me.

The tension could nearly be cut with a knife; I wished Calvin or Dad would get back soon. Little sounds were beginning to make me jump. When I couldn't take the silence any longer, nor the tension, I blurted, "How... Did, uh, did you have a nice day?" *Wow, aren't you the articulate one?* When he didn't immediately answer, I glanced over my shoulder at him.

"Passable." Asher finally said. His voice was low and seemed controlled. "And yours?"

"Fine. It was fine." I nodded as I sliced the cucumbers.

"Really?"

"Um, yeah...why?"

"You seemed in pain when you came in."

"It's nothing a couple Ibuprofen won't fix."

"What have you been doing...to become so sore?"

"Just working with Ned, nothing too exciting."

"You weren't hurt anyway, at least." His eyes did a slow once-over on me. I couldn't figure out exactly what his problem was. Was he mad I wasn't here to wait on him hand and foot? I'd told him that Calvin or Mom could help if he needed something. What more did he want?

"Do you have anything in mind...to do, I mean, while you're staying here, before we start your training? I could make some arrangements for you, if you want me to."

"I have several things in mind." Asher's eyes were hooded by his dark lashes; his tone seemed lazy and yet full of meaning. Barely suppressing a shiver, I asked, "And, what might they be?"

Asher was spared from answering by my dad's arrival. Dad came in with the mail under his arm, his jacket and gloves in one hand, and his coffee mug, keys, and cell phone in the other.

"Hey." I kissed his cheek as I reached for the mail.

"Hi, sweetheart. Forecast is calling for possible snow tomorrow, or the day after. Wind is supposed to pick up tonight with a cold front moving in from the north."

"I should check out the herd. I might move some of them lower. I'll have Calvin ride along with me tomorrow."

"I can come, too, if you want," Dad offered.

"No, don't worry about it. If the temperature's dropping, you don't need to be out in it—you know your arthritis will begin acting up. Cal and I can handle it. Though, if you want, you could feed in the afternoon for me."

"Deal." Dad grinned, then left the kitchen, heading upstairs to wash before dinner.

"How many cows are you planning on moving?" Asher asked. The oven beeped indicating the lasagna was almost done.

"Not sure really." I pulled dinner out of the oven and shut it off. "I'll have to see what we have and what the grazing looks like. Once I can get a better idea of where everything stands, I'll be able to make a decision."

"And you and Calvin are going to be able to handle this, only the two of you?" Asher's eyes were narrowed slightly.

"Cal and I can handle this just fine."

"I could come along, you know, to help," he offered.

"Oh," I said. "That's really nice of you, but I can't take you up on it. See, it's a decent ride and I have no idea what your skill level is. It would be rather irresponsible of me to place you in that kind of situation. Besides, you still need proper gear, remember?"

Asher locked eyes with mine. I could see he wasn't too keen on staying behind again tomorrow, but hey, *them's the breaks*. After a moment, Ash nodded.

Calvin came in as I was placing the salad bowl on the table. "Hi, y'all; KatyBeth, that smells amazing."

"Hi, yourself. Get washed up, it's about done."

Katy-

"Dad told me about the plans for tomorrow, Katy, and I don't think I can make it. Can we go day after tomorrow?" Calvin leaned back from the table.

"Sure, I guess. What's going on?"

"My neighbor has me helping him shoe. He threw his back out again. That's where I was today. He called after you left and I just got back. He went to the doctor and they gave him some muscle relaxants, but they insist he take one more day off."

"I hope he gets to feeling better." I felt a tiny amount of guilt at the idea that Asher had, in fact, for all intents and purposes, been left alone all day. I reminded myself that, for seven more days at least, Asher was not my personal responsibility and therefore did not need to feel guilty.

Then Dad, my blessed own father said, "Hey, why don't you take Asher along tomorrow? You've got to train him anyhow. Wouldn't hurt to start early, would it?"

The weight of Asher's stare settled over me. I didn't look at him and fought to keep the heat from spreading across my face. "Asher doesn't have any riding gear; I need to take him to town and get some before we can start."

"Hm...take him shopping tomorrow. Then he can go with you and Cal. At the very least he can drive the truck for you." Dad turned to Asher. "How's that sound?"

"Works for me." Asher nodded, humor lurking in his voice; my eyes closed for a moment, trying to remain calm.

"Sure." I said, opening them again. "We can go in the morning. What time?" Being the chicken that I suddenly found myself being, I kept my gaze on Ash's forehead, not wanting to meet his all-too-knowing bright blue eyes.

"You name it, I'll be ready."

"Will nine-thirty work?"

"It will." The humor was still evident.

"There." Dad said, seemingly happy to have *helped*. "That's all settled then. Between the three of you the work will go faster."

In a flat voice, I answered, "Yeah, Dad, it's a great idea."

Katy-

As I pulled onto the highway at about a quarter to ten, I asked Asher, "Other than riding gear, what else are you going to need?"

Asher adjusted his sunglasses. "Virtually everything. I really didn't bring much with me."

"Okay...so are we talking from bare skin on up?" I heard sarcasm in my tone of voice.

Thankfully, Asher kept the grin off his face as he replied, "Bare skin on up, yes. Exactly."

My eyebrow rose like it tended to do when irritation was setting in, though I recovered quickly. "We'll go to The Boot Barn first. They have a decent selection. Then, if Wal-Mart is all right, I can run you by and you can get any other items you might need. How's that?"

"Sounds fine." Asher looked in my direction, but I kept my eyes on the road. Despite my best efforts to ignore him, I simply couldn't. I was far too aware of him. Constantly, almost excruciatingly aware of him.

"What?" Asher asked. When I glanced in his direction, I caught his mouth curving in a grin. Reminding myself to watch the road and not his mouth, I shifted my gaze back, then raised my eyebrows in silent inquiry at his question. "You looked like...like you had something on your mind."

"I have many things on my mind, Mr. Fitzpatrick. None of them concern you," I lied to us both, hopefully putting him in his place. I might be employed by him or for him, or whatever, but that didn't mean I had to spill all my thoughts to him. Those were private.

"Ash," he said after a few minutes of silence.

"What?" I said, exasperated.

"Please, call me Ash. Mr. Fitzpatrick is a mouthful and it'll get old real quick."

Adjusting my grip on the wheel, I took a deep breath and said, "Fine," knowing I sounded sullen.

About thirty minutes later, we drove into the town of Cody. It had a touristy western appeal that I'd always liked. The Boot Barn opened at 10:00 a.m. so we arrived right after the first wave of early birds had made it through. We pulled into the parking lot and I found a space easily. Thankfully it wasn't packed; it'd make shopping easier and faster without a crowd.

Snagging a cart on the way in, I went directly to the boot section, Asher following me. I waved at Janie, one of the cashiers at the front counter, who eyed us in curiosity. Well, not me so much as my companion. I could feel the gossip and speculation coming on.

When we arrived in the men's section, I stopped and turned to look more closely at Asher's feet. They were big. "What are you, about a thirteen? fourteen?"

"Thirteen and a half, extra wide."

"How much are you willing to spend?" I turned back to the boot selection. "Do you want quality or just something to get you by?"

"Quality. I only go for the best."

"Super. Have a seat there and I'll bring you a few pairs to try on." Asher sat on the bench I indicated and slipped his shoes off. In short order, I found three different pairs of boots, all good quality leather and craftsmanship.

Asher tried them all on and ended up taking two pairs. Next, we went to the jeans department. When riding, I always, always wear Wrangler. Other brands have the large seam to the inside of the leg, which will rub after a while in the saddle. Wrangler doesn't. Their large seam is to the outside of the leg. No rubbing.

I turned to Asher, about to ask what size pants he wore. Beating me to the punch, he said, "I'm a 34 or 36 x 40."

"The dressing room is right there," I pointed. "I'll be right back."

I brought him several pairs and explained that a couple were unwashed and would be stiff, but with a good washing would be more comfortable, the others had already been washed to have that worn-in feel. I sat down on the bench to the right of the dressing room to wait for him.

"What do you think?" he asked as he stepped out wearing one of the new pairs, as if somehow my answer was pivotal in his decision making.

"What I think doesn't matter." I tried to be polite. "You're the one who has to wear them, not me."

"I meant, are they long enough? Will these work for me?" he corrected.

"Oh." I felt dumb. "Yeah, those are certainly long enough. Squat down and make sure you have room to move comfortably in them. That's what I do," I finished, lamely.

He did. He squatted. He bent over and sat down next to me. He stood next to me and raised his leg up to rest his foot on the seat, simulating the motion he'd make to mount a horse, I guessed. He stood in front of the mirror, looking at the reflection he saw there, turning this way, then that way. And, as God is my witness, I tried to keep my gaze high. Tried not to take in how well the denim hugged him, and was it hot in here? Was their AC broken, I wondered?

In the end, Asher bought four pairs of the pre-washed jeans. I suggested he buy some boot socks while we were there as well; he bought a pack of ten, as well as various other items. I left Asher at the counter, figuring my help wasn't needed to pay for it, and walked back to the truck, needing a few moments to myself.

About halfway across the parking lot, I heard the loud rumble of a vehicle approaching. I glanced over my shoulder simply to make sure I wasn't in danger of being hit. Turns out I wasn't about to be hit by the truck, only hit on by its driver. A lifted black Dodge pulled up alongside me. I heard the loud catcall, but kept walking, hoping he'd take the hint.

The driver of the Dodge parked a few spots down and came around the front of his truck. He was tall, though not as tall as Ash, and nowhere near as well built. I didn't recognize him as a local, but he was at least dressed the part of a cowboy. I tried to remember if there were any rodeos or riding events in town this weekend, but couldn't think of any. At any rate, this cowboy approached with an overabundance of confidence and swagger.

"Hey, there." He grinned, eyeing me in a suggestive manner. "My name's Tim. What's yours, Beautiful?"

Blowing out a breath, I kept right on walking. I was almost to the truck; I had my keys out and pushed the button to unlock it. Suddenly, Tim was beside me; I turned to face him as he crowded me up against the door of my pickup. "Hey, where're you going? I'm talking with you."

"Back off. *Now*," I snarled low and furious. Tim chuckled as if I were being cute. Before I could blink to clear my vision and refocus, a massive dark blur appeared between us and Tim was on the ground, having landed flat on his butt. He wiped his mouth with the back of his hand, smearing blood.

"Kate, get in the truck, please." Asher spoke calmly, angling his face toward me, but kept his eyes squarely on Tim, who was at that moment getting to his feet.

Still angry and wanting a piece of the jerk myself, I stepped around Asher and faced Tim. "I don't need you to fight my battles for me."

Asher remained silent, though I could clearly see the tension in the set of his shoulders. Catching a glimpse of his face had me second-guessing the situation. Seeing the fury clearly written there, I figured it was best to get Asher out of there before he could do any more violence—he was my responsibility after all. Stepping back, I laid my hand on his arm. "Let's go."

Never taking his eyes off Tim, Asher reached over and opened the door of the truck. Silently, I stepped up into the cab, and he closed the door quietly, but firmly. After he picked up his dropped packages Asher walked around to his side and climbed in beside me. Moments later, we left.

After driving for a couple blocks in silence, I glanced at Asher. "You shouldn't have done that, you know."

"You mean I should've let him paw all over you?" His voice was quiet, but I heard the anger.

"No, I don't mean that at all." My tone was a little short. "I just meant you should've let me handle it."

"Speaking of, where was that handy move you used on me? If ever there was a time to employ it, let me tell you, that was it."

"I didn't feel the need." I shrugged.

"I see." He chuckled darkly. "I guess it's only me you like kicking."

"Don't be an idiot, of course not. I wasn't scared of him. He just ticked me off." Pulling the truck into the Wal-Mart parking lot, I parked at the back where I normally do.

"Why do I scare you, Kate?"

"You don't scare me, Ash. Not much does."

"Uh-huh." Asher grinned; his blue eyes sparkling. He shook his head, letting me know he wasn't buying it, then, he suddenly got a serious look on his face. "I should have asked sooner; are you alright? He didn't hurt you or anything, did he?"

Warmth bloomed in the pit of my stomach, and I waited a moment for my heart to slow before answering. "I'm fine."

"Yes," he replied softly, "you are."

"You know, you might want to wait here and let me do your shopping for you." I turned the truck off. "You're much more likely to be recognized here, and if you're trying to lay low and keep your mass of female fans at bay, you might not want to be flashing your mug all over town."

"You think you can keep out of trouble if I wait here?"

"What are you? My babysitter?"

"I certainly hope not," he said dryly, then muttered under his breath, "*That* would be awkward."

"Do you have a list or anything?" I ignored his last comment.

"You have a pen and paper?" Lifting the lid on the center console, I pulled a leather binder out, opened it, then handed it to him. Asher removed the pen from the binding and quickly wrote his list, then tore the paper from the pad and handed it to me.

"How about a cell phone?" he asked. I glanced at him in question. "I could call you if I remembered something else I needed. And here's mine in case you have any questions about what I wrote down." He took the list back and wrote his number. When he handed the paper back to me, I asked how I was to pay. "Here's my credit card. Just sign my name; you shouldn't have any problems."

"I'll be back shortly." I opened my door and Asher reminded me he still needed my number. "It's on the business card inside the binder there. Mine's the one ending in 7211." I didn't look at the list until I was inside and had taken a shopping cart. Now, I began scanning it; *typical stuff.* Deodorant, shaving cream (sensitive skin, he'd written next to it), razors, toothpaste, mouthwash, chewing gum, mints, lotion, aftershave, sunscreen, lip balm. He'd said to use my best judgment in choosing a scent or flavor, whatever appealed to me.

Huh.

Then I got to the last item. And, there was simply no way, *at all*, not to have blushed here. And I did. I could feel it. I was beet-red.

Underwear.

He needed underwear.

And I had to pick them out for him. He preferred the boxer-brief style. The color didn't matter.

Asher-

Asher had his cellphone in hand waiting for her call, grinning in anticipation. Maybe he shouldn't have written the list exactly as he had, but he figured there were times for subtlety, then there were times to take whatever advantages one could get. He genuinely wanted to know what her preferences were. Kate puzzled him, but he enjoyed the puzzle. And right now, he could use the distraction she presented. His anger still simmered under the surface. Absentmindedly, he rubbed the knuckles on his right hand; one felt a little bruised. The bruising felt good.

Asher had seen the pickup, seen the driver's interest in Kate through the window from inside the store. He'd kept his eyes alert for trouble, though he honestly hadn't expected anyone to bother her at this time of day. Of course, Kate was a beautiful woman. One men were naturally attracted to. Most, he was sure, would be respectful and keep their distance, though there always seemed to be a jerk in every group.

Back at The Boot Barn, Kate hadn't looked afraid at all. In fact, he would have said the look on her face had been one of contempt. Her stance hadn't been a defensive one, but rather an offensive one. *She'd honestly intended to fight that guy.* He shook his head. *What was she thinking? Didn't she know she could get hurt? Why hadn't she yelled for help?*

Asher thought he knew the answer to that—Kate was used to taking care of herself. She really wasn't afraid of anyone. Hadn't she proven that to him back there in the coffee shop? Asher looked up suddenly at the storefront. He should go inside and make sure she wasn't in any trouble again. He unsnapped his seatbelt, fully intending to find her. As he reached for the door handle, he saw Kate walking out, several bags in hand.

She hadn't called. He smiled and shook his head; she always seemed to do the unexpected. He watched her now as she walked from the store to the truck. That he felt a physical attraction for her was accurate, and yet beside the point. The physical attraction did not cover all that he felt. And he was feeling plenty.

Perhaps Sammy was right and he should be cautious. Asher mentally shrugged. The game was in play; there was no backing out now.

Through the windshield he could see the color still staining her cheeks. It gave him pleasure to see the evidence he had in fact gotten to her after all. Not that he truly thought his ploy wouldn't work; he simply enjoyed her fireworks. He enjoyed being able to get under her skin. So far, he was enjoying everything about her, and looked forward to enjoying much more.

CHAPTER FIVE
Harder than I Thought

Katy-

It wasn't difficult figuring out which horse was best for Asher's first ride, though normally I put more thought and time into the decision. I had only one option, especially for the type of riding we'd be doing tomorrow. Asher would ride George or GW, as we called him. GW was a bombproof, rawboned, twelve-year-old blue roan gelding that stood well over sixteen hands.

George isn't ridden that much anymore, mainly because he's almost too easy to ride. Most of my clients prefer a horse that will show actual signs of life on occasion. GW still has plenty of get-up-and-go, but he's just so docile folks tend to think they need to add a quarter every now and then. I'll be honest, a small part of me was looking forward to seeing Asher's reaction to the big blue horse. It would almost be like asking him to add training wheels to his motorcycle.

Tomorrow would be a long day. A full day. And I needed rest to be able to handle it. Rest that somehow eluded me. It was him. Asher. I couldn't get him out of my head. Grumbling to myself, I rolled over, bunching my pillow, trying to get it just right. I told myself that eventually he wouldn't bother me. Because eventually he wouldn't be here. The truth of that thought lacked peace. I rolled in the other direction, still seeking sleep.

The following morning, I found myself dressing with more care, refusing to even consider why. Once ready, I carried my boots downstairs.

Coffee came first, so I got the pot ready, and while that was percolating, slipped my boots on and headed out to the barn. Whenever I had an early morning ride like this, I brought Red's headstall inside the house to warm the bit.

Asher was entering the kitchen, as I stepped back in. "Morning," I said.

"Good morning," he replied. "It snowed some last night."

He looked good, and seemed wide awake in his new clothes. Clothes that did such interesting things to Asher's physique and my pulse. I turned to the coffee pot. "Yeah, I saw that. I hope it's not too deep higher up." I fervently hoped with repeated exposure, I'd eventually reach a place where he didn't affect me, at all. Saying a quick prayer for my self-control, I hung the headstall by the back door. "You slept well?" I asked, trying to be polite, as I reached into the cabinet to pull out a couple mugs.

"I did. You?"

His stare was heavy. "You take cream or sugar with your coffee?"

"Both please. Thank you."

"Here you go then, help yourself. If you want to bring it with you, there're disposable mugs in the pantry here." I showed him where they were. "I'm going to finish this, then head to the barn to get my horse saddled. When you're done, meet me out there; Calvin should be here any time now."

"Let me grab my coat and I'll come with you." Asher set his cup down and headed back down the hall. I heard his bedroom door open and the soft sounds of movement from within. While he was gone, I retrieved one of the disposable cups, and carefully poured the coffee before fitting the lid in place.

"Ready?"

Asher returned with his leather riding jacket. "Let's go."

I reached for Red's headstall, turning it upside down, slipping the bit under my arm, and caught Ash's look of perplexity. "Horses tend to take the bit better when it's not cold."

"Good to know."

The sun was just warming the horizon as we made our way to the barn. The dogs, Jack and Jill, came out from under the porch, tails wagging, and followed.

After Red was groomed, bridled, and saddled, I led him to the yard and walked him around a few times, before tying him to the trailer. "Listen, Ash..." I began, turning to him as I spoke. "Generally, I have a little more time to work with a client before actually putting him on a horse, and I *will* spend more time with you once the real training begins. But as of right now, without knowing your skill level or experience, I decided it was best to play it safe. You won't have any trouble with George. He's a nice, quiet horse."

Asher trailed me to the corral, studying me closely. I whistled softly, and GW turned his head in my direction before ambling over. I scratched his neck, then his ears. Opening the gate, not bothering with a halter or lead rope, I headed towards the barn, knowing the roan would follow along. As old as George was, he was still well muscled and had a beautiful coat. The big gelding stopped where the crossties were and waited patiently while I brushed and saddled him. Asher hadn't spoken during this time, though I knew he was there, and I wondered what he was thinking. Glancing in his direction, I found his blue eyes on me.

"Why the disclaimer on the horse?" he lifted his chin at George. "He seems all right to me."

"He is—you won't have any trouble with him."

"You said that before." His gaze was speculative now.

Hearing the rumble of Calvin's truck, I turned towards the sound, avoiding Asher's direct gaze. "And I meant it."

George followed me as I led him out of the barn to where I'd tied Red. Calvin chuckled when he saw me. "I wondered who you'd pick."

"It seemed the best bet given the circumstances."

"At least GW's the right size for him." Calvin rubbed the blue horse's nose affectionately. "Give me ten minutes. Who's in the barn?"

"Teddy, Dollar, Banner, and Jet."

"I'll take Banner. Be right back." Calvin loped off, nodding at Asher as he passed him in the doorway. I left George beside Red and went to the ranch truck. After I had it started, letting the diesel warm up, I went to the back of the still-attached trailer and opened the gate. I was reaching up for the ramp when I felt someone beside me. Asher reached around, his chest brushing my right shoulder as he lifted the latch to lower the ramp.

Through both of my shirts, the heat coming off him caressed me, making me shiver. "Thanks," I mumbled, stepping aside as he lowered the ramp to the ground.

"Sure." Asher waited for me to look at him. When I finally did, he said, "You chose the *beginner's* beginner horse." He didn't say it as a question, was simply stating a fact. Not seeing any reason to disagree, I nodded. "Will I have to get off and push him?"

That made me grin. "No. George isn't that bad. He's a good horse. You could light a fire under him or explode a bomb above him and he'd be just as calm as he is right now."

"That's good to know, at least."

"Please, don't think I'm trying to demean you or anything. Truly, I'm not. I honestly felt it was the best choice. We have a lot of rough country to cover today and cattle can be tricky and you're a high-dollar movie star and—"

Asher placed a warm, gentle finger across my lips. "I'm not questioning your intent or judgment. If you say George is the best choice, then I trust you." He stepped back, dropping his hand as he looked in the direction of the barn. By degrees, I became aware that Calvin was leading Banner in our direction. My lips still tingled from Asher's touch, and I fought to get ahold of myself. Blowing out a breath I hadn't known I'd been holding, I got Red and George loaded.

Katy-

All in all, the day went better than I'd hoped. The snow was not as deep as I'd feared, the weather not as cold. We ended up moving about seventy head of cattle to one of the lower pastures where the valley had plenty of new green growth. We took it slow and Asher survived his first cattle drive—I could only be thankful.

Being tired and a little sore, I moved gingerly, trying to stretch and loosen up. The ride certainly hadn't helped. My neck and shoulders were stiff and tight. Several times today I'd tried to loosen the muscles by rubbing them myself, but could never quite reach the right spot. Some of my tension issues may have had to do with the way I constantly seemed hyper-aware of Asher. It was exhausting trying to maintain the façade that I barely noticed him, that I was completely unaffected by him.

Waving at Calvin as he turned his truck around heading for his neighbor's place, I took a steadying breath and tried to gather the energy I'd need to complete my duties. Exhaling, I shrugged my shoulders again, and got to work.

With Asher's help, I got the untacking and feeding done quickly. He was seated on a bale of straw, straddling it, one long muscular leg on either side when I exited the tack room. Flicking off the light, I tried, unsuccessfully, to not recall how those legs had looked mounted on the big roan gelding.

"Thanks for your help." I indicated the horses he'd assisted me with only minutes before.

"No problem," he replied. "Thanks for letting me tag along."

"Sure." I rubbed my neck and arched my back a little, trying to ease the knot between my shoulder blades. Asher's keen blue eyes followed my movements, making me feel warm and self-conscious. Needing space, I said, "I'll see you later."

"Kate." His voice was low and as non-threatening as he could make it. "Sit down a moment...rest. I'll make room." Asher scooted back, leaving me most of the bale. I hesitated; sitting down beside Asher sounded much more tempting than it should have.

"Thanks," I glanced in his direction. "I should get in and get cleaned up."

"I don't bite." At that statement, my gaze jerked to his. He grinned, his eyebrow rising in a dark arch. "I promise. You look beat. Sit and relax for a moment."

His eyes held a challenge in their blue depths, daring me to prove I wasn't intimidated. A part of me flared up in excitement, the part that enjoyed the challenge.

Carefully, I made my way to him and sat down. Every nerve-ending I possessed was dancing around right now, giddy with suppressed excitement. Closing my eyes for a moment, I worked at calming my pulse. When I opened them again, I couldn't help but glance in his direction. I also couldn't help the involuntary twinge I felt when I turned my head. With the spasm of pain, I reached up to cup my neck, a small groan escaping.

"You alright?" Asher asked, concern evident in his voice.

"Yeah, think I slept funny is all." I squeezed my shoulder and closed my eyes again for another moment.

Asher scooted closer to me. "Turn around." My eyes flashed open, and I glanced at him questioningly. He motioned with his hand for me to turn around.

"What?" I asked stupidly.

"Will you turn around and stop being difficult."

"I'm not...I'm fine...I...."

"Kate. Turn around. I'm not going to hurt you, come on." Asher placed his hands gently, but firmly on my shoulders, moving me to obey him.

Exasperated and simply too tired to fight him right then, I swung my leg over so that my back was to him. I sat rigidly—the only defiance I was able to muster at the moment. Asher scooted a bit closer. He brushed my hair off my shoulder with a gentle sweep of his hand, his fingertips lightly grazing the back of my neck, causing me to shiver involuntarily. Then he placed one large hand on either side of my shoulders and began to squeeze in rhythmic motions.

Instantly, I felt little explosions of pleasure and pain erupt under the pressure of his hands; his fingers were firm and seemed to reach deep to all the places I had heretofore been unable to reach myself. I tried not to make any noise at all; tried to remain still, but there was absolutely no way to keep the tiny moan from escaping. It felt that good. My head seemed light and heavy at the same time. The tension seeped away with each movement of his hands as they flexed across my shoulders and up my neck, to the base of my skull. My head didn't want to stay upright any longer; with the release of the tension and pain, my muscle control seemed to have eased as well.

The massage could have lasted a minute or an hour; I had no sense of time, was so lost to his ministrations. Gradually, I became aware his hands were still, that I was leaning back against him and he was leaning into me. Asher's breath gently fanned my neck and my ear; his breathing sounded rough. Slowly his hands flexed in a gentle caress; his thumbs moved in a slow, circular rhythm.

Awareness snapped into me, and I stiffened, slowly pulling away. At first, Asher resisted, then he hesitantly released me and scooted back. We both seemed to hold still for several long moments, seemingly unsure of exactly what to do. Finally, I turned. "Thank you," I told him. My voice was low, but thankfully not breathless or trembling.

"How do you feel?" His voice was equally low.

"Better." I slowly got to my feet. "I'm...going inside now."

"You should go in," Asher agreed.

I spared him a quick glance as I walked out of the barn. What I saw on his face sent a flash of shock and heat through me. *Desire.* Desire was clear on Asher's face.

Asher-

Touching Kate had been a mistake, Asher decided. Though there was nothing dark or dangerous about her, he couldn't help but feel she was like an addiction for him. No matter how small a contact-high he got, no matter how good he felt afterward; she always left him wanting more, needing another hit.

Asher was still trying to come to terms with his feelings and intentions about Kate Reilly. Spending time around her, being in her presence, tended to desensitize him. Offering to rub her shoulders had seemed innocent enough. What harm could possibly be done by the act?

They'd ridden all day. She'd pulled her weight and then some. Asher was well attuned to the signs of fatigue and though she never once complained, he saw her discomfort.

So, he'd offered. And she'd enjoyed it, his touch. He could tell by the way she leaned into his grasp instead of away from it. He was helping her—that's what he'd told himself. No harm done, right? If that was truly the case, then why was he so shaken? Why did he feel emotionally and physically shattered? Why were his hands refusing to let her go? His head had begun to pound as he sat there wracking his brain for an explanation.

Suddenly his pocket vibrated. Asher was instantly, cruelly jarred back into reality. He knew he had only ten minutes to call in and report. Reluctantly he released her; his hands slowly sliding from her shoulders as he leaned back. Asher urged Kate to go inside; he needed to clear his head before he made the phone call.

He gazed after her as Kate stood and left the barn; he'd been unable to keep the heat he was feeling hidden. Kate saw it for what it was; there was nothing he could do about it now. *Focus.*

Deliberately he closed his eyes against her, forcing his mind in another direction. He sat quietly for exactly three minutes, harnessing his mind, steeling his concentration. Seven minutes after he received the alert, Asher dialed the number he'd been sent.

CHAPTER SIX

When Life Tosses You a Lemon... Throw it Back

Katy-

Last night I'd texted an SOS to Candi and Gina; we'd agreed to meet here at Glendale Park at eleven o'clock. This park, this tiny sunny, grassy knoll was *our* spot. The place we'd meet when we needed to talk. I always brought the blanket and a box of Oreo Double-Stuff Cookies. Candi brought the coffee—she worked at Rawhide Coffee, and Gina the box of tissues, just in case, because she worked at Walgreens. I only had to wait about fifteen minutes before they arrived. We took our normal positions.

We looked at each other for a moment in silence. "What's your emergency, Katy?" Candi asked as she passed the coffee out. "Does this have anything to do with your hunky client?" She sounded hopeful. I handed her a five-dollar bill as I reached for my coffee.

"Could you spot me, Katy? I get paid next Friday," Gina asked as she took her coffee. Grinning at her, I handed Candi another five dollars. The three of us girls were as opposite as could be. I'm tall, blond, and curvy. Candi is petite, or vertically challenged as we like to call it, and Native American, and Gina is somehow a mixture of many things all together. She was taller than Candi, though not as tall as me. She wasn't as curvy as I was, but not as slender as Candi. She was the palest of us. Her skin was cream and roses, with a beautiful dusting of freckles across the bridge of her pert little nose. Her eyes were a striking pale-blue color that beautifully complemented her rich ginger hair. It was always hard for me to decide what her best feature was; she had so many.

"Yeah, actually it does." Automatically taking two tissues from the box resting between the three of us, I simply crumpled them, holding them in my hand. "Something happened last night...and I'm not sure what to do about it."

"What happened?" Gina asked.

"Did his girlfriend show up?" Candi asked. "Because that *would* be disappointing."

"He has a girlfriend?" My heart thundered in my chest.

"You're *blushing*! You never blush." Gina said. Candi was quiet; the look on her face speculative and curious. I closed my eyes and took a deep breath, bracing myself. "Does Asher have a girlfriend, Candi?" My pulse pounded as I waiting for her answer.

"How would I know? But, would you think a guy like that would be single?" she replied.

"Why are you asking, Katy? What happened?" Gina asked again.

"Okay. You know Asher is...he's..." I motioned with my hand, trying to convey what I was having a hard time verbalizing.

"Hot." Gina interrupted, supplying me a word.

"Yeah. He's hot. I mean, really, really hot." I agreed.

"So, you like him?" Candi asked, her dark brown, perfectly shaped eyebrow arching up elegantly.

"Yeah. At least...I'm really, really attracted to him," I clarified.

"So, you like the man; who doesn't?" Candi said.

"Did he say something to you about it?" Gina asked.

"No, he hasn't said anything." I took a sip of coffee. "I mean, I haven't said anything to him either."

"I'm not following you. You called an SOS. How can we help?" Gina picked up the unopened package of Oreos, tore it open, and pulled two out.

"Well, I think...that is I'm not positive, but I *think* that... Asher... is attracted to me, too." I whispered.

Candi and Gina were silent for a moment, staring at me in disbelief. I could understand their astonishment; I've never seriously liked a guy before.

"Wait." Candi finally broke the silence. "You think *Asher Fitzpatrick* is attracted to *you*?"

"Yeah. I'm just...not sure...."

"What makes you—" Gina started to say before Candi interrupted her.

"Oh, *puh-leeze*. I know you're God's gift to men and all, but come *on*. Why would Asher Fitzpatrick like you?"

"That's not fair, Candi," Gina said.

"Whoa!" I said, a little bewildered.

"I knew you thought that everyone with a Y chromosome had to be in love with you, but I never expected you to take it this far." Candi stood up. "You've had Calvin following you like a puppy for years, all the while knowing how Gina felt about him and now you think the guy that *I* like, that I've liked for *years,* wants you, too? And, even if he does, it'll be for one thing only and you know it, and that just makes you a slut!" Venom coated her words as she stormed away.

Gina had her hand over her mouth, her light blue eyes wide in shock. "I'm *so* sorry, Katy." She jumped up, going after Candi, her red hair waving behind her.

The blood had left my face at Candi's words and I was glad I was already on the ground. My eyes filled with tears that soon began to slide down my face. My lips trembled. What had happened? Why would she say that to me? What had I done to her?

I sat there for several minutes, too stunned and shocked to move. Eventually, Gina came back. Her mascara was a little smeared; I knew she'd been crying. Looking up at her, I shook my head. "Gina?" I whispered. "What just happened? What did I do?"

Gina knelt beside me, wrapping her arms around me. "I don't know, Katy. I don't think you did anything. I don't know why Candi would say those things. I don't understand."

"Did she say anything to you?"

"Just more stupid stuff." Gina sniffed.

"Do you think of me that way?" I asked, my voice low and thick, braced for her response.

"Of course not!" Gina assured me. "And, I don't think Candi does either. Not really. Something is obviously bothering her, but I don't think it's you. This doesn't make any sense!"

"We've been friends since first grade," I whispered. "She's never been this mad at me before. She's never said anything like this before. I don't understand."

"Well, that makes two of us." Gina helped herself to another cookie. "I told her I'd call her tonight, so maybe I can find out what's really behind this. But enough about her; tell me what's going on with you. You needed our support and advice on something and that's why I'm here. So, spill."

Hiccuping, I dried my tears. "Gina, I want you to know...Calvin knows how I feel about him. He's like my brother and I don't love him in any other way. I've been as honest with him as I was with you. I've even talked with him about Asher. Or rather, my attraction to Asher."

"I know that. And maybe I shouldn't continue to carry these feelings for Cal, but that's simply where I am right now. I know his friendship and lack of attraction for me has nothing to do with you. I never thought it did." Gina gently squeezed my arm. "So, what's up with your movie star?"

"Candi's our celebrity expert, not me. I don't have crushes and things and I... He steals my breath and I literally can't breathe, and I can't think. And I've been telling myself, repeatedly not to get carried away. I mean, he's a movie star! I'm a small-time cattle ranch owner. He probably lives in Beverly Hills. I live in the hills outside Cody, Wyoming.

"I know once this movie is done filming, he'll be gone and I'll be alone here, nursing either a broken heart or a powerful unrequited attraction. So, I've been trying to be cautious, to ignore my attraction, but..."

When I didn't immediately continue Gina gently said, "But, what?"

"He's making it so hard." I shook my head. "I swear he must suspect and is messing with me."

"Has he said something? Done something to you?"

"Yes. No. I don't know. He watches me. Sometimes he touches me. Oh, not in a bad way. Well, like yesterday, he gave me a shoulder rub—it felt amazing, by the way. I don't know how to explain it, but I'd almost swear that he's as attracted to me as I am to him."

"Wow." Gina slowly shook her head, and took another cookie. "Is this a bad thing, though? I mean, maybe this is the start of a beautiful relationship. It could happen."

"It happens in movies, Gina. Not real life. And besides, what do I really know about him? Other than the fact that his smile is enough to curl my toes and fire my libido? What if he *is* simply looking for easy action and figures I'm it?"

"Well, then you explain to him that you're not that kind of girl and..." Gina trailed off into silence at the look on my face. "You're not thinking of doing something stupid are you? I mean, you know I'd still love you and all, but I'd be really, really upset with you. We made a pact, remember? Not until we're married. I still have our signed copies. And besides, I don't think that's what you really want. Is it?"

"No. No, I don't want that and it's not something I'm thinking about doing. I'm just afraid." I whispered. "What if I'm not strong enough? I've never dealt with this before."

"What are we told to do when faced with temptation, KatyBeth? What has Pastor Ryan always said?"

"To avoid it. To flee from it," I replied automatically. "I don't know how to do that, seeing as how I'm kind of stuck with him for the next three months."

"Okay. Let's think about this. You must be around him. You can't avoid him. Can you try not to be alone with him?"

"Yeah, that's what I'm doing now."

"Okay, well that's a start at least," Gina glanced at her watch and bit her lip.

"You gotta run?"

"Yeah, lunch is about up. Listen," she said as she got to her feet. "If you find yourself alone with him and he tries something, you simply tell him what's up and stand your ground. After I talk with Candi, I'll call you tonight, okay?"

"Thanks, Gina. Love you."

"You too, babe."

Katy-

Calvin was waiting when I arrived home a little after three. Without a word, he took me in his arms, squeezing me tight. He held me like that for several moments and finally said, "Gina called. Said you and Candi had been in a fight and you could use a hug." By this time, I had tears running silently down my face again. I wiped them on his shirt and tried to laugh a little. "You want to talk about it?"

I shook my head. "Thanks, though."

"You gonna be all right? You want me to talk with her?"

"No." I hiccuped. "She'll come around when she's good and ready, I hope."

"She will. Friendship like you three have is long lasting and tough as nails. You pray about it and be patient. I gotta run; I only swung by to check on you."

"Thanks, Cal. You're the best."

"You know I'm always here for you, no matter what." He gently squeezed my shoulder.

Sniffing some more, I said, "I know, and I love you."

When I finally made it inside the house, I found a note from Mom taped to the fridge door. She and Dad had gone out to dinner and Asher had informed her he wouldn't be back for dinner tonight either. That left me with an empty house. I threw together a quick salad for myself that didn't take long to clean up, and soon the silence was getting to me. Needing something to do, and being in the emotional state I was in, I made cookies. Lots of cookies.

I'd tried texting Candi; she never responded. I told her we needed to talk and that I loved her. Gina texted me, said she'd talked with Candi and from what she could gather, Candi was feeling insecure and tired of walking in my shadow. Confused by that assessment, I felt there had to be more to Candi's anger than simple insecurity. Something must have happened to set her off like this. But until she was ready, I had nowhere to go with my supposition.

Not sure what else I could do, I put my earbuds in and got to work. Soon, I had several dozen beautiful chocolate chip cookies cooling on the rack. When I bake, I generally triple the recipe and freeze several batches. The clock above the stove said it was nearing eight. I pulled another tray out of the oven, setting it on the counter to cool, and put the last tray in. I reset the timer, turned around, and screamed.

I'm glad I hadn't been holding anything breakable in my hands, because it would have gone flying. Asher leaned against the kitchen table, arms crossed, his eyes on me. I ripped my earbuds out and hoped to high heaven he hadn't seen my dancing or heard me singing.

"What the heck?" I fumed, stomping up to him. Slapping my palm against his chest, I tried to ignore the way he felt, all firm, tight muscles. "What is it with you and sneaking up on people?"

"I'm sorry; I thought you heard me." Asher chuckled quietly. "I didn't see your earbuds. Honestly, I wasn't trying to frighten you."

"Yeah. Well." *Miss Articulate.*

"I sincerely apologize." Trying to keep the grin off his face, his bright blue eyes flashed in amusement. Asher briefly turned his gaze to the cookies. "Are these for something special?"

"No. Help yourself. I was bored," I grumbled, turning away. He'd been watching my mouth and it was making me nervous and irritated. "Where have you been, today?" *Wait. What? Why did you ask that?*

"I had some things to do in town. Did you miss me?" Asher teased.

"Yeah, I was *so* distraught."

"That explains the need to bake."

"No, it doesn't. I was being sarcastic."

"So was I," he replied. "Where were *you* today?"

"I just had some things to do in town. Did you miss me?" I mocked.

"Yes."

Asher was so sincere in his reply that my hands became still under the hot, running water. Deciding to ignore his last comment, I said, "I'd like to start early tomorrow morning. Will eight work for you?"

"It does."

"I'm going to put these away, then call it a night. I'll see you in the morning."

"Sleep well, Kate," Asher stood still for a moment; I could feel his gaze on me, but didn't turn around. After a moment, I heard him leave the kitchen.

Asher-

Asher had hoped being away from Kate would have given him a much-needed edge, that he'd feel sharper, and more in control of himself. He'd had no contact with her for close to twenty-four hours, but instead of coming down off his high, he found he simply missed her more.

When he should have been deciphering codes, interpreting foreign messages, and maintaining his cover as a Hollywood playboy, he found himself thinking about her; wondering what she was doing. He'd been so caught up in his daydream he'd almost missed a key phrase in the message he was listening to.

Asher played the recording back a second time. Then a third. He listened intently to the heavily accented voice, trying to glean every drop of intel from it he could. There. He heard it again. A name. Was it a person? A place? An event? Asher wasn't sure. He'd have to keep listening. He felt he was close though, close to the break he needed.

CHAPTER SEVEN
Maintaining a Professional Attitude

Katy-

"How long have you lived here?" Asher asked the following morning as we made our way to the barn. I'd resolved last night, as I was going to sleep, that I would firmly contain any attraction I felt and maintain a perfect example of professionalism. Whenever Asher attempted to steer the conversation in a personal direction, I would firmly get it back on course. I would keep my thoughts appropriate. I would *not* visually appreciate my client.

When Asher had entered the kitchen, I'd taken a moment to assess myself, making sure my pulse was calm, and I was breathing normally before turning to face him. So far, so good.

When I saw him, I'd had this sudden sinking feeling my efforts were an all-encompassing lost cause. I'd known I was staring, but I couldn't seem to look away. Asher had walked past me, seemingly oblivious to my state of mind—thank the good Lord—to the coffee pot. He'd stirred the air with his passing, his scent lingering, and I'd asked myself the question I'd been repeating ever since I'd met him. *Why, oh why, does he have to affect me so thoroughly?* Why couldn't I be as immune to him as I was to every other man I'd met? Problem was Asher was the type of man who made a woman glad she was a woman. I felt womanly around him—not that I'd felt un-womanly before—he simply brought some new element to the fore.

My conscience finally spoke loudly enough to be heard over my raging libido. "I was born here, graduated high school here," I replied as we reached the barn.

"I would imagine, being from a smaller community, you're a pretty close-knit bunch, huh?"

"Yeah, we are. My friends that you met last week? We've known each other since grade school. Deken and Derek, the twins, they moved here the first year of middle school and Calvin has known my parents since before I was born. My mom used to be his Sunday School teacher."

"You and Calvin seem close," Asher commented, casually.

"We are. I'm an only child, but having Calvin around has been like having a real brother at times. We'd fight like cats and dogs growing up—I got into my first fist fight with him." I chuckled remembering that moment.

"Why does that not surprise me?" He laughed. "And, what do you mean your *first* fist fight? Do you make a habit of getting into fights? Is this something I should be concerned about?" I rolled my eyes at him. "So, you don't make a habit of getting into fights?"

"Of course not."

"You had me worried there for a minute."

"Yes, I can tell; you're just shaking in your boots." Asher chuckled, the sound rich and distracting. Refusing to be fazed, I turned to face him. "Don't take this wrong, but until I can see for myself exactly what your experience is, I'm going to proceed like you've never seen a horse before, and I'm *not* counting your ride on GW as any basis to judge your capabilities, either. That'd be like congratulating you on not falling out of your chair while seated on a flat surface. I intend to start from the ground up." Knowing I'd just spewed a ton of verbiage at him, I continued, determined to keep my mind on appropriate topics. "Knowing a horse's anatomy is important. Having that knowledge will give you an edge in confidence when you ride. After we cover that, then I'll walk you through grooming again, and tacking—that's saddling your horse. Again, this knowledge will help you while riding."

"You're the boss." Asher smiled. His gaze flicked to my mouth then back up again. "Thanks for the clarification about my previous experiences."

"I just figured..."

"What? Just say it."

"Well...you're an actor. I mean, if it were only a matter of getting on a horse and riding around, *pretending* to know what you're doing, well, any actor can do that. And then they're sure to have a horse that's well trained to make you look good. But since your studio went to the effort of hiring me to train you in equestrian skills, I figured they wanted, or maybe you wanted to do more than simple acting when you're on your horse." I finished with a small shrug.

"Excellent reasoning," Asher replied, the look in his eye a considering one. "Like I said, you're the boss. I'm all ears."

"I'd have said you were all muscle, but..." Mentally, I slapped myself upside the head. "...that's just me." *So much for keeping things on a professional level.* Face flaming, I turned away. "Look, forget I said that. I'm sorry—maybe I need more coffee."

"Not sure I can do that. My ego's taken a hit lately and this certainly helped."

"Fine. Like I said, I'm...I shouldn't have said that. You can take it as a compliment if you want." Needing to find some way to salvage this and get back on track, I said, "I'm going to grab a couple of horses and we'll begin."

When I returned, the look in Asher's eyes was heated and direct. Flustered, I said, "This is Cherry," and scratched the face of the leopard Appaloosa mare. "And this is Dollar. Like GW, we often put inexperienced riders on Dollar. He's a real teddy bear." I patted the shoulder of the big paint beside me.

"Cherry and Dollar," Asher repeated, scratching them.

We went over basic horse anatomy. I showed him how to lift the horse's leg to see the inside of the hoof. I pointed out the sensitive parts in the frog and explained why shoes helped. Asher arched a brow at the term 'frog', so I explained it was simply the softer triangle-shaped tissue at the very heart of the hoof and showed him how to clean the area and why it was a good idea to do so. Next, we covered the legs, both front and back; the cannon, hocks, how to feel for heat and swollen joints. We discussed the finer points of saddle placement, how to take the withers into account. I showed him how to safely get a horse to take the bit without losing a finger.

Ash was a bit nervous about that one and I had to chuckle at the expression on his face, but he trusted me and did everything I instructed.

"So, Dollar, I'm assuming is a boy? And Cherry is a girl?" he asked.

It was a little after noon; I wiped the sweat from my lip with the back of my hand. "Correct."

"How can you tell? I mean, looking at them, if you hadn't told me their names, I couldn't have told you their genders."

"Well...Cherry is a mare. Dollar here is a gelding. That's a male horse that can no longer produce offspring."

"So, you're saying he can't get a female horse pregnant?"

"Correct. He's been gelded."

"Gelded? What's that?"

"You know what castration is?" Heat bloomed in my cheeks.

Asher gave a pained look. "*Oh*. That's awful."

"I would imagine he thought so at the time, too. But rest easy, he doesn't remember it."

"So, where...I mean, how can you tell? I'm still not seeing a physical difference between them, to indicate gender."

My eyes narrowed in suspicion. "Are you being serious?"

"Yeah, I'm being serious. I'm trying to figure this out."

I studied him a moment, then decided he was being sincere. "Well, I'm not explaining this to you; just take a gander for yourself. The evidence of their gender is right there between their back legs. It's easier to see if you view from the direction of front to back. If you still have questions after that...I might have a book you can borrow." Asher eyed me now, and I waved him on, feeling the red creep up my face again. My mouth twitched as he bent down and looked. First Cherry, then Dollar. Ash stood up, his eyebrows raised, his lips pursed.

"Everything clear now?" I tried not to laugh at the expression on his face.

"Yeah...thanks."

"Oh, you betcha. Let me know if you need anything else." Mirth escaped then, and I was thankful to see Calvin pulling up. Still smirking, I waved to him, then gave Asher Dollar's lead rope, and I took Cherry's.

As we saddled the horses, Calvin came over to see how things were going. "Oh, I think things are going fine." I couldn't help but chuckle. "He's, uh...he's learning lots of new things."

"What's so funny?" Calvin looked back and forth between us.

"Kate just taught me the difference between geldings and mares, and is now mocking me." Asher replied.

"Cal, it was priceless." I giggled.

"*What* did you tell him, Katy?" Censure was strong in Calvin's voice.

"I didn't *tell* him anything. He asked how to tell the difference between them, soooo...I had him look for himself." Calvin's tone irritated me; I hadn't done anything wrong.

"I kind of had an idea. I mean, being a man, you're familiar with the general...but seeing...*that?*" Asher chuckled.

Calvin seemed to relax at that. "Now that you've got the anatomy down, you guys gonna ride?"

I nodded. "Yeah, we'll ride in the pen for a while, see how he does."

"Maybe take him to the back arena. I've got a one o'clock that should be here soon." Calvin suggested.

Asher might not have known much about horse anatomy, but he was a fast learner and had natural ability in the saddle. I could see him mentally filing and categorizing answers, seemingly taking this seriously. No sloughing off.

Several times, I'd caught his eye, and told myself it was only because he was paying attention to the lessons, and had nothing to do with me personally. I'm not sure I was very convincing, seeing as how my heart lurched in my chest each time it happened. After the horses were saddled to my satisfaction, we walked them around to the back of the barn.

Mom came out with a tray of sandwiches, just as we reached the smaller, more secluded riding paddock. "Thought you could use a break."

"Thanks, Mom." Asher and I tied the horses securely to the fence, then found a place in the shade to eat. Calvin joined us, his client running a little late. I think he was simply making sure we weren't all alone out back here.

After we'd finished eating, Asher ran in to use the facilities, and while he was gone Calvin asked me about the name change.

"Name change?"

"Asher calls you, Kate, huh? He doesn't like KatyBeth?"

"I don't know." I shrugged. "I asked him about it the other day when he first called me that."

"And, what did he say?"

"He said he couldn't see me as a KatyBeth and asked if he could call me Kate."

"You're okay with that?" His brows arched.

I shrugged casually. "No reason not to be, right?"

"It's different, I guess." Calvin said. "Seems a tad preferential, and...based on our previous conversation...I only thought I should point that out. Be careful, Katy."

"I am." I assured him, and wished Cal would relax; I didn't need this added stress. I'd begun to regret ever mentioning Asher and my feelings to him.

After a moment of silence he asked, "You hear anything from Candi yet?"

"No, not yet; she's still not answering my texts."

"Don't worry about it, just keep trying."

The rest of the afternoon consisted of me going over all the basics of horses and horse riding with Asher. I demonstrated proper mounting and dismounting, how to use legs and reins to give your horse guidance. I instructed him to keep his heels down and toes up. Then went over the differences between western and English saddles, and how to sit them. I started him at a walk and after a while moved him to a trot, and showed him how to post. It took him a while to master that principle, but eventually he was moving smoothly, collecting his mount.

He worked in a figure eight for a while, then brought Dollar to a stop, with me reminding Asher not to jerk the reins, but to ease them. He needed to be firm, not sharp. Sharp was for a disruptive horse who needed an attitude adjustment. We rode that way for a few hours before calling it a day.

Thursday and Friday were much the same. I covered and re-covered all the basics with Asher and had him do some light riding in the arena.

On Saturday, we spent most of the day riding, and Asher was tested on what he'd learned so far. He passed with flying colors. After several hours of continuous riding, I rode up to where he was stopped and asked how he felt.

"Pretty good, I guess. Not too sore." Asher studied me for a moment, then asked, "You do anything special on Sunday?"

"We attend church in the morning. And quite often at night, as well."

"And yet you and your family stayed home last Sunday." Asher spoke quietly, almost to himself.

"We often do so when guests are staying over the weekend—we didn't want to leave you unattended. We're responsible for your welfare, and it would've been wrong to leave you on your own like that."

Asher was quiet for several moments, seeming deep in thought. Then his eyes lifted to mine. "May I go with you, tomorrow?"

"Uh...sure."

"You sound like you're not sure about that. Would you prefer I didn't?"

"No, not at all. I'm...I guess...I'm surprised that you'd want to go, is all."

"Why is that?"

"I don't know. I guess..." I paused, then continued. "I just didn't figure you'd want to go to church." I was uncomfortably aware of the added emphasis I'd placed on him personally.

"Really?" He scratched his chin thoughtfully; his blues eyes considered me. "Isn't church the place for sinners? Or do you figure I'm so far gone it wouldn't be any help?"

"Only the dead are too far gone for it not to be any help." I blew out a breath. "You know what? I owe you an apology. I formed an opinion about you, without anything to back it up. I was wrong. I'm sorry. Please, forgive me."

"Shoe's on the other foot, now." Asher gazed at me intently, a smile playing on his lips. He dropped his gaze to my mouth before returning to my eyes. "I'll tell you what, you agree to forgive me and not hold it against me for nearly stomping you to death at that coffee shop and I'll forgive you for forming an inaccurate opinion about me. How does that sound?" He urged Dollar into a walk, moving him in a tight circle around Cherry and me.

"Agreed." This awareness was growing deeper, wider, and more potent. Asher's gaze dropped to my mouth again; my lips felt dry and I wanted to lick them. Thankfully, we called it a night shortly after that.

Asher-

Asher decided being close to Kate was infinitely preferable to keeping his distance, or limiting his contact. He found even though she challenged his self-control, he was able to focus and concentrate better when she was near. He'd been able to put to rest several pressing issues and felt he was much closer to solving numerous important puzzles on his plate.

When Asher had first arrived at Kate's ranch, he'd intentionally done so on a Friday. From what he knew of Christians—which admittedly wasn't much—Sunday was their day to honor their God. Skipping church was akin to stealing. When Sunday had come and Kate and her family had stayed home, he'd wondered about her devoutness. He'd heard, once again, Cory's assumptions about her play through his head.

When he'd asked her about it, and discovered the reason they'd remained home was for his benefit, Asher decided that was thoughtful and considerate of them. Maybe he'd brave church and see for himself what really went on there. At any rate, he didn't want to spend time away from her; going to church seemed a small price to pay for being in her company.

Maintaining his cover as a high-flying movie star had always seemed nothing more than a huge headache. He hated the act, despised the deception; both his own and what came from those around him. He'd considered several times just quitting, quietly walking away; it could easily be accomplished.

If he'd done so, he'd have never had this opportunity with Kate.

That thought caused him no little unrest.

Later that night, as Asher watched Kate when she left the table, he did his best to not allow his gaze to linger on the sway of her hips. Knowing Calvin was watching, he blinked and shifted focus, though the image of her was firmly in his head. So far, he thought, his plan was working. She was becoming more relaxed in his company, thereby allowing him to maintain the level of awareness he needed from her. He reflected on their discussions each day. She'd enjoyed his discomfort at discovering the distinguishable differences between male and female horses. Asher liked that she found humor in him.

When Samuel had dug around for him, his report about Kate had indicated she was single. *Single*, he'd assumed at the time, meant no one, boyfriend or husband. Now that he was here with her, he admitted to wondering about the connection he sensed between her and Calvin. Kate said she viewed him as a brother, and always had, but there was an underlying current from Calvin that indicated the man felt much more than sibling affection.

The emotion that fired through him at that thought was not anger or jealousy per se. It was closer to fear. Fear that he might have missed out on something important to him, something essential, that he was already, even now, too late.

Admittedly, when he'd first seen her in Casper, he hadn't been thinking about building or nourishing a relationship with her. There'd been the normal response a man feels when faced with a beautiful woman—make a sublime first impression, get her attention, and hopefully all other agreeable options fall into place. Then he'd felt his manhood challenged when she'd dismissed him and the strongest urge within him at the time had been to engage her, to take up the challenge she'd unwittingly issued. And win.

It left him almost dazed, how quickly his gameplan had evolved. It was no longer a desire to simply win, to get her to acknowledge him as a man. Kate herself had become the prize; knowing her, being with her, having her. Like every mission he'd ever been assigned, Asher knew he needed to determine who beside himself was an active player. He would need to be evaluated, then strategically eliminated.

He looked closely for any indication from Kate that what she felt for Calvin was more than friendship. There were no moments of breathlessness, no blushes that colored her golden skin. This observation gave him no small amount of satisfaction.

CHAPTER EIGHT

Didn't See That Coming

Kate-

"I was thinking," Asher stated after church. "I'm going to need to pick up a few more pairs of jeans. Riding is a bit more sweat inducing than I imagined it would be. Would we have time today to get some?"

"Yeah, let me change; I'll let my parents know, then we can go, if that works for you."

"Take your time. I'm not in any rush."

I quickly ran upstairs, reminding myself he'd said to take my time. Dressed, I opened my door just as Calvin stepped from his room. He noted the purse slung over my shoulder. "Where're you off to?"

"Ash says he needs more clothes."

"You think that's smart? I mean, you know what we talked about..."

"Cal." I tried to keep the impatience out of my voice. "I've been hired to do this. It's my job."

"Be careful. That's all I'm sayin.'"

"You know I'm a big girl and can take of myself." I pointed out.

Asher was seated with Dad at the table when I entered the kitchen. Mom stood at the sink washing a head of lettuce. "Ash says he need more jeans, so we're running into town. I'll have my cell if you need anything. I'm not sure how long we'll be; if it's later than ten, I'll call, okay?"

My parents nodded, then I headed to the office to retrieve my handgun. After checking the magazine, making sure it was full, I slid the pistol into the special compartment inside my purse. Once we were on the road, I asked Asher if he was hungry. "We could eat before shopping, if you want."

"If you're hungry we can stop, otherwise I figure we'll get something later."

Calvin-

Calvin leaned against the porch post and watched Katy and Asher drive away. His jaw clenched and he tried to calm the agitation in his chest. Changes were coming. He could feel it. Something almost inevitable loomed on the horizon and panic wanted to set in. He took a deep breath. His dream, the one he'd held to so tightly seemed to be unraveling. Naomi called him in for lunch. He took another deep breath, closed his eyes, and made a conscious decision to leave it all in the hands of the One who knew best. Asking for strength, he went inside.

Kate-

After about twenty minutes of silence, Asher nodded at my purse. "Do you know how to use that?" I shot him a look, unsure what he meant. "Your weapon. Do you know how to use it?"

"How'd you know I had it?"

He shrugged. "I know what to look for." I didn't know what to make of that. Was he trained in law enforcement? I'd never had someone spot my gun before; I wasn't sure I liked that. "You didn't bring that because of me, did you?" Asher asked suddenly, the look on his face concerned. "You're not... You're not afraid of me, are you?"

"No!" I was shocked he'd even think that. "But...as you're with me today, I made a special point of bringing it." Confusion lit his blue eyes. "Well, you're famous. Most folks, I'm sure, will be respectful, but on the off chance we run in to some nut, like last time, I wanted to be prepared."

"So...you're carrying it today for *my* protection" Asher breathed deeply. "I'm not sure how to feel about that."

"It's just...I feel responsible, and want to make sure you're safe. I suppose if it comes down to a fistfight, you'd be fine. But if it's something more, I want to be prepared."

After a minute or two of silence, Asher said, "I appreciate you taking my well-being so serious; thank you. Let me assure you, regardless of the circumstances, I know how to take care of myself." We were quiet for a few minutes. "You didn't answer my question though. Do you know how to use it?"

"I do."

"How well?"

"I hit what I aim at."

"And if someone were attacking you, if you had to use it in defense, how would you do then?"

"I imagine I'd do all right." I glanced at him.

"Would you like to be certain?"

"What do you mean?"

"If you want, I can show you how to use it defensively, how to fight off an attacker with, or without your firearm."

"You know how to do that?" I asked, skeptical.

"I do." He nodded, lightly nudging my shoulder with his fist. "So, what do you say?"

I shrugged said shoulder, mainly because it was tingling from his touch. "Sure, if we have time."

"I'll make time." Asher stated. "It's important."

We arrived in town around four. As it was Sunday, I told him we'd better get his shopping needs taken care of first, as some businesses closed early on Sunday.

As I waited for the signal to turn green, another pickup pulled up next to me in the left-hand turn lane. The driver revved his engine and I glanced over. He was young, attractive, and maybe a little older than me. He wore a ball-cap pulled low over curly blond hair and had an interested look on his face. He offered a friendly smile, and I nodded before turning back to the front. Asher muttered, "Figures."

The light changed and I accelerated through the intersection. "What?" I clicked on my turn signal.

"Another one."

"Another one what?" I asked as I parked.

"He's interested in you, probably wants your number."

"Sure, he does." I stepped from the truck.

"Well, he pulled into the parking lot. Dinner says he asks you out." Asher slammed his door.

"And if you're wrong?" I shot over the hood of the truck.

"I'm not." Asher shook his head. "I'll head in so he can make his play and prove me right. Holler if you need help."

I stared in confusion at Asher's back, and considered what he'd said. It didn't take long to realize he hadn't given me a proper bet. The way I understood it, if he was right, I had to buy him dinner; but he hadn't indicated what he'd do for me if he was wrong. Locking the truck, I started across the lot, intent on getting our terms ironed out. In a perverse sort of way, I found I was enjoying these verbal skirmishes with him.

As I reached the door, the blond driver appeared next to me. "Allow me." He opened the door in a gentleman-like manner, removing his ball-cap with a flourish.

"Thanks," I grumbled, distracted, scanning the area for Asher.

"My name's Alex." His tone was friendly. "I noticed you back there and..." He indicated with a jerk of his chin in the direction of the street.

"Hey, I know this is really forward, but do you have plans for dinner tonight?"

Hoping I didn't sound as perturbed as I felt, but *darn it,* he'd just cost me the bet, I said, "Actually, Alex...I uh..."

"Kate has plans, Alex." Asher suddenly appeared at my side; he rested one hand on my shoulder, his thumb brushing lightly over my neck. I glanced up, but he wasn't looking at me. His blue eyes were focused on Alex.

"Oh." Alex sounded surprised; he took in Asher, his eyes widening. "Hey, sorry about that. Guess I didn't see you back there. Nice meeting you."

"Sure." After Alex walked away, looking once or twice over his shoulder, I turned to Asher, who was grinning. My brow rose in silent question.

"Told you." He sounded smug.

"Shut up." I headed towards the men's section, and gritted my teeth, ignoring his soft laughter. Along the way we passed several cowboys and cowgirls; the ladies had their eyes glued to Asher, not that I blamed them. I knew a few of them from around Cody, and nodded in passing.

While Asher was in the dressing room, three bull riders walked past. One of them caught my eye and winked. I ignore most advances from guys like these, knowing they're probably only interested in a wife for a night. About three minutes later he and his companions walked by again, this time stopping a little past me before turning back.

The one who winked gave a cocky grin. "My name's Toby...and, if I could rearrange the alphabet, I'd put U and I together." *Was he for real right now?* Toby stuck his hand out in greeting so, to be polite, I smiled and shook it. He caught me off-guard as he lifted my hand to his lips. "You got a name, Beautiful?" Toby tried again.

Beautiful my big toe. "KatyBeth."

"I'm in town for the rodeo, KatyBeth. How'd you like to come along with me and see what a real cowboy does?"

I'm sure he thought I was some city girl who'd enjoy the attentions of a *real-life* cowboy, but I was about to burst his bubble. "That's awful kind of you, Toby, and if I wasn't on the clock right now, I'd be tempted. But I'm working, so I can't. You have yourself a nice evening."

He looked me over more closely. "What kind of work do you do, Sugar?"

"It's KatyBeth, not Sugar, and I'm real busy." The concept may have been hard for him to comprehend; I was simply standing here after all.

"Are you free later?"

"'Fraid not. Sorry."

"Can I get your number? Maybe we can get together sometime."

"You are persistent. I'll give you that."

"When I see something I want, yeah." He grinned.

At this point I'd run out of patience and turned my back on him, rolling my eyes as I started to walk away. Toby reached out, taking my arm. "Hey, wait a minute. I want to talk with you."

I narrowed my eyes. "Get your hand off me—right now!"

He quickly let go and took a step back. "I didn't mean nothing."

"Turn around. And walk away." My eyes were as hard and unfriendly as I could make them.

"Whatever," Toby muttered turning away.

Feeling a presence at my shoulder, I glanced back to see Asher. The look in his eyes was murderous, and I was suddenly glad Toby had walked away when he did.

Though I couldn't figure out why Asher should be so angered by the exchange, I could clearly see that he was. He hadn't been angered when Alex approached me; I chalked it up to his possibly having a normally protective-nature regarding women. It wasn't a bad quality to have, I noted. "You ready?" It took a moment for Asher to respond to my question. His eyes were focused on his target, which, at the moment, was still Toby. His eyes were hard when he finally looked at me. "Hey, I appreciate your concern and all, but I can take care of myself. So, you just calm down, okay?"

"I am calm," was all he said before moving to the checkout.

Asher-

When Kate had come down the stairs that morning, Asher knew he was in trouble. He'd been fully aware of Calvin right behind her and tried to keep his face expressionless; but there was no way to keep his gaze off her. Kate stunned him repeatedly. Just when he thought he had her figured out, when he felt he finally had her pegged, she presented a new facet for him to consider. There was so much about her he wanted to explore. It had taken every ounce of his self-control to let none of that show.

She was a walking, talking, living, breathing contradiction. He puzzled over her and felt in equal amounts frustration, admiration, and enthusiasm for the challenge she presented. At one point she came across as fearless, afraid of nothing, ready to take on the world, but then he recalled the afternoon three days ago when he'd found her standing on a kitchen chair, broom in hand, visibly shaken. Asher recalled looking around, thinking he'd see at least a snake or something similar; but to his surprise and immense amusement what he'd found instead turned out to be nothing more than a common cricket.

Kate had been mortified to have shown such fear in front of him and had threatened him with bodily harm if he ever breathed a word of it to anyone. Scared of a cricket, but not of a man. Asher wondered now if Kate was simply grossly naïve about the dangers that lurked in the world, or if she was being carelessly arrogant in her self-confidence.

When Asher had stepped from the dressing room to the sight of the muscled cowboy with his hand wrapped around Kate's arm, he'd become instantly infuriated. As he headed towards them, intent on removing the offending appendage from the cowboy's body, he heard her calm, but firm rebuke. Her voice had been cold steel, and he realized her intentions—she meant to physically engage the man if he didn't do as she'd said. By the time he'd reached her, the cowboy had released her and walked away.

Asher was furious. With the cowboy, with Kate, with himself. Some part of him knew he was being irrational, but he couldn't think straight right then. It was only through years of training and discipline that he was able to keep himself in check, when what he wanted was to rip the man limb from limb. He wanted to shake her. Why hadn't she called for him? Didn't she know she could have been seriously injured? He wanted his hands on her, to ascertain for himself she was all right. He simply *wanted*.

Asher took a deep breath and realized she'd spoken to him. Blinking his eyes, he saw they were in the truck already, and had no recollection of how he'd gotten there. He knew he had to get a handle on himself. There was no excuse to have lost control like that.

"I'm sorry, what did you say?" he asked quietly.

Kate looked at him, concern evident in her green eyes. "Are you alright?"

"Fine." Why was she asking him if he was all right? She was the one who'd been mauled back there, not him. Facing her, he gave her a thorough once over; sure enough she was calm, no evidence of excitement on her face or in her demeanor.

Kate-

Over the next several days, I continued to drill Asher on the anatomical points of the horse, and how to saddle and unsaddle, mount and dismount. I put him up on a half-dozen different horses. Each one, I felt, offered a different experience. After five more days of 'basic training' as Asher had begun calling it, I felt he was ready for an all-day trail ride, and not on a horse of GW's caliber.

Calvin wasn't happy; he had several appointments scheduled over the next few days, and was unable to accompany us. He'd tried talking me out of going, or at least postponing the ride, but I knew time was of the essence. Calvin meant well, but his constant, concerned assessment was getting on my nerves. I gently reminded him, again, that this was my job. "Just be careful," he grumbled in what was becoming his ritual refrain.

Asher and I left early on Friday morning. He rode Dollar and I was, of course, on Red. At first, we were content to simply enjoy the ride, each of us lost in our own thoughts. I led him past the Jump Off, explaining that this was where all our trails basically started. We continued up the mountain, the trail winding through the foothills. We surprised several deer, mostly doe accompanied by a fawn or two, but we did fleetingly see one large buck.

"You sure you and Calvin are only friends, Kate?" Asher suddenly asked; we'd been riding about an hour now.

I looked over at him; surprised by the directness of his question. "Why do you ask?"

"Call it...Call it curiosity." He shrugged his massive shoulders.

"Cal's like a brother to me."

"Is that all, though? You and he...never explored those feelings of affection any further?"

"We did." I said, attempting to head things off by being honest. "A long time ago."

"Explored...how?" he persisted.

"We tried dating, while I was still in high school. He was my prom and homecoming date for my senior year."

He seemed to consider this for a moment or two before asking in a low voice, "You two ever kiss?"

"Why are you asking this?" I demanded, bringing Red to a stop as I faced him. His questions were starting to annoy me. I'd been doing well at keeping things far from a personal nature. And now here he was, digging deep again; stirring up ideas I wanted left buried.

"Curiosity, like I said," he replied, easily coming to a stop next to me.

"Seems more than that." I was feeling prickly as a porcupine.

Asher took a slow, careful perusal of me, then carefully said, "There are times when I catch a glimpse of something on his face when he looks at you—it's not brotherly affection *he's* feeling."

"And how is that any of your business?" My question came out sharper than I'd intended.

"Why are you snapping at me? It's a simple question."

"I'm not snapping at you."

Asher snorted. "Yes, you are."

His humor increased my annoyance. I decided to ignore him and keep riding; at this point he could turn around and head back to the ranch for all I cared. After about ten more minutes, Asher asked if there was anything bothering me.

"Shut up." I closed my eyes in frustration, and again heard his warm chuckle, snapping something inside. "What's the matter with you?"

"Nothing," he replied. "What's the matter with you?"

"You!" I shot back. "Happy?"

"What did I do?"

The humor in his voice had me bringing Red to a stop again. "You're irritating me and you're doing it on purpose."

Asher flashed a grin and I felt it when his gaze brushed across my lips. "How am I irritating you?"

"Asking me all these questions." *Butting into my personal life.*

"Let me get this straight. I'm irritating you because I asked if you'd ever kissed Calvin?"

Yes! "You're irritating me because you're even asking in the first place!" I ground out. "What does it matter if I kissed Calvin or a hundred other men?"

"It matters." Asher stated; his voice was low and rough. "It matters. Like I said before, I've noticed the way he looks at you and speaks to you; I'm curious. What can I say?"

Asher taking such an interest in my personal life was throwing me for loop. It wasn't fitting into the carefully constructed limits I'd set for myself and our relationship. It had me scrambling to get my footing back. Not meeting his eyes, I found myself asking, "Why did you notice?"

"I'm a man, Kate," he said with exaggerated patience. *Like, somehow, I'd missed that part.* "I just can't tell if you feel the same way about him. I can tell you care about him, but I can't read you as easily as I can Cal."

I took a deep breath and said, "I love him, Ash. But he's always been a brother to me. Cal and I have been honest with each other. I know how he feels and he knows how I feel."

Asher stared; speculation evident in his eyes. "I'd like to know why. I mean, as an outsider, he seems like the perfect choice. You're both from the same area, no danger of one moving the other away or anything. You both love horses. You get along well together. He loves your family. They obviously love him." Asher continued in a careful voice, "Calvin seems like the natural course your life would have taken."

"I know he does." I whispered, feeling a desperate sadness for the love I longed for, yet knew I wouldn't find in Calvin. "I wanted to love him more than I do. I simply...don't." The words seemed to be coming faster now. "He's one of my closest friends. And I love him dearly, but he's not...I'm not...I don't love him like that. I don't feel a..." I searched a moment for the right words, "...physical attraction for him. I have no desire to kiss him or, or anything else along those lines. A married couple, they need to have that. At least, that's how I always figured it."

Asher was quiet for so long I figured he'd gathered all the information he'd been after. It was several minutes later; we were quite a bit farther up the trail before he said, "Have you kissed him, then? You did try?"

I didn't see any reason not to answer at this point; I'd already disclosed so much. "We did. I tried really hard, but there was nothing, at least from my end."

"And how would he react if you had a boyfriend? Would he object?"

"I believe he would want me to be happy. And I think he would be happy for me."

We rode on in silence for a bit longer. Around noon, we stopped next to a tiny stream and dismounted. Earlier that morning, I'd packed us a couple of sandwiches and we sat in the shade as we ate them. Up until this point, I'd successfully stamped down my own interest about Asher and his personal life, but considering the questions he'd asked me I decided I was due. "Out of curiosity—fair *is* fair—do *you* have a girlfriend?"

"Not at this time," Asher replied with a wolfish grin.

"What does that mean?"

"It means that right now, at this moment, I do not have a girlfriend."

"But you intend to have one?" I sensed something he wasn't saying, but implying.

"I do. Yes." *Lucky her.*

His confidence grated on me. "You have someone already picked out? Does she get a say, or do you keep a few spare women on the side for when you need a date?" Asher raised his eyebrows at me inquiringly, but remained silent. I stared him down, determined to wait him out. Then faltered, and decided to restate my question somewhat. "You sound certain of her. Have you known her long?"

"No...not long. And I'm *never* certain of what she'll do. She always...surprises me. But I intend to give it my best shot at any rate."

"You mean there's a possibility that *Asher Fitzpatrick* might be turned down for a date?" I was fully aware of the sarcasm in my voice. "That there's a woman out there impervious to your charms?"

Asher chuckled darkly at me. "Now you're mocking me." *Gee, you think?* I shrugged my shoulders and kept my mouth shut. "Come on, Kate," he cajoled. "Do *you* think I'm charming?" I rolled my eyes and concentrated on Big Red, who was grazing several feet away from us, adamantly keeping silent. "All right...well, you may not find me attractive, but there are a few women who do. Take your friend Candi for instance; she seemed to like me all right." I gave an involuntary jerk at the sound of her name. Standing, I dusted off my jeans before walking over to Red. Candi was not a subject I was willing to discuss right now. She still refused to speak with me and

Gina said she'd been getting a cold shoulder now as well. I leaned on the saddle for a minute before I tightened Red's girth and prepared to mount.

"You're upset. What did I say?" Asher quietly asked from right behind me, causing me to shiver slightly. I hadn't even heard him move.

"Give me a break. I'm fine." I tried to lighten the mood and redirect the conversation. "You know you're charming. You don't need me or anyone else to tell you that."

He moved around to my side, regarding me closely; I hoped he wasn't picking up any of my inner turmoil. Finally, he shrugged and said, "I might have heard that before, but I'd be curious to know what your take is."

"My take?" I gave a half-hearted attempt at a laugh. For some reason he seemed determined to carry this conversation further.

"I value your opinion."

I gazed at him for a moment or two longer, trying to detect any mockery. Instead, I found a steady calming sincerity that encouraged me to trust him. "Fine," I took a deep breath, then let it out in a rush as I began. "I do think you're an attractive man. I don't think any woman could honestly deny that."

Asher quietly contemplated me; I could see him chewing over what I'd admitted. Finally, he softly said, "That wasn't so hard, was it?"

"Define hard." Asher chuckled darkly at my words, like they were some secret, private joke. "No, it wasn't so hard. Still, I don't think my answer is anything to get all worked up over."

"I didn't think I was worked up, only curious."

"Really?" I stated in disbelieving sarcasm. "Because it was beginning to feel like an interrogation or something. Are you sure you were *only* curious?"

"Yes." He rubbed a hand over his face as if frustrated. His voice turned rough and I caught a hint of that brogue once more. "Definitely curious. Intensely curious, Kate."

"Intense is pretty accurate," I muttered. "Maybe I'm pushing you too hard, maybe you need a break..."

"You're not pushing me. I don't need a break. It's just..." He chuck-led darkly again. "It's...me."

"Well...I'm relieved," I said, knowing I didn't sound like it.

"I am, too, actually." Asher suddenly smiled. "You don't know it, but you've given me courage to act."

"To act?" I knew I sounded confused, but couldn't seem to fathom what he meant. "You mean, for the role you're playing in this movie?"

Asher hesitated a moment. "That...among other things."

"Glad I could help." I think I understood him now. "You ready to get going?"

"In a moment." He faced me. "Tell me something. I'm curious again. When you kissed Calvin, how did you know you felt nothing for him? Was the kiss repulsive?"

Regarding him closely, I tried figuring out exactly what he was asking; why he'd turned the subject once more to me and Calvin. "It wasn't repulsive, no."

"Yet, you didn't enjoy it."

"Yes."

"Yes?" Now he looked as confused as I felt.

"We need to get going." Suddenly, I was feeling strange and my lungs didn't seem to want to work. Before he could respond or stop me, I'd virtually launched myself back into the saddle. Without looking to see if he was behind me or not, I headed for home, my hands shaky and heart thundering.

Though he'd caught up and rode at my side, we didn't speak for the remainder of the ride; each seemingly lost in our own thoughts. Once or twice, I glanced in his direction; he didn't seem angry, but he was keeping a safe distance. The sun was beginning to set as we rode into the ranch yard and I breathed a sigh of relief, in desperate need to be away from Asher, to gather myself. Dismounting in the barn doorway, I led Red to the tack room, again not looking to see what Asher was doing. After Red was unsaddled, I brushed him until he was dry and his coat was smooth and shiny.

Once I'd turned Red into his stall, I prepared the hay and water for Dollar while Asher brushed him. When the silence became too much, I finally spoke up. "Are you sore at all?"

"Tight." was his terse response.

Understandable. It was a long ride. "Make sure you stretch." I paused a moment, unsure how to proceed. "Listen, about earlier, I hope you weren't offended. I didn't mean to be so abrupt. I...I'm...I didn't mean to be so abrupt," I finished lamely, knowing I'd just repeated myself.

"You don't have to apologize." He hesitated. "I'm wound real tight, Kate." Asher walked Dollar into his stall and turned him loose. Then he closed and latched it. He faced away from me, both hands resting on the half-door, his head dipping slightly, uttering a stifled groan. Taking a deep breath, he held it, the wood groaning under his hands as they tightened. He exhaled with a dark chuckle and shook his head.

My heart suddenly lodged somewhere in my throat as the air between us seemed to charge. "Ash?" I whispered. "What's wrong? Are you alright?" Whether from tension, or something else, I couldn't seem to catch my breath. As if my blood sugar had taken a dive, I felt almost jittery.

"No, Kate. I'm not alright."

He didn't sound in pain, but I wasn't sure. "What's wrong?"

Asher let go of the stall door and faced me; his mouth twisted in a harsh line. His eyes burned, heat in their blue depths.

Hunger.

Desire. Potent and heady.

"I've tried to be so...*darned*...careful." He shook his head in an aggravated manner, chuckling darkly. Stepping away from the stall, he was suddenly right in front of me. My eyes flared wide at his proximity, then fastened on his throat, my pulse throbbing. My body locked in place, unable to work around the frozen bundle of raw nerves I'd become. Who was I kidding? I couldn't have moved if I'd wanted to. And I didn't want to.

Asher reached for me, his hands warm and solid. For a moment he simply gripped my forearms, holding them down at my side, then slowly, slowly slid those hands upward. He grazed my elbows, causing me to shiver. His fingertips trailed up the back of my arms, across my shoulders, and up to my neck. His body trembled against mine and I was acutely aware of every contact point between us. He bent his head, rested his cheek against my temple, breathing deeply, then, like a cat, rubbed back and forth.

Gently, he massaged my shoulders with his long fingers, kneading rhythmically. My body trembled, far beyond my scope of control. His hands shook a little as they carefully closed around my throat in a light caress before loosening, his thumbs resting right above my collarbone. I'd never realized before how sensitive a collarbone could be, but as his fingers slowly slid back and forth there, I felt as though I might come undone. Blindly, I reached out, grasping his waist, to steady myself. Asher held me still for a minute until the tremors subsided. Then, his thumbs followed the curve of my throat, hooking under my chin, pushing my face upward, his touch still exquisitely gentle.

Lowering his head further, his mouth found a resting place in the crook of my shoulder. The pressure of his lips on my skin stole what little breath I'd gained; my grip on him tightened. In agonizing slow motion, he rolled my head to the side, nuzzling his way up to my ear. His breath tickled, cooling my overheated skin. My eyes fluttered closed as everything around me spun. One tender kiss after another he placed against my neck. My trembling grew worse, and I swayed; his hands tightened, remaining gentle, holding me steady.

Was this really happening? Had my imagination run away with me or was I really and truly here, *right now,* caught up in this intimate embrace with Asher Fitzpatrick? And...if it was real...then what in the world was I doing? His teeth grazed my ear, scattering my thoughts.

Asher moved his fingers into my hair and inhaled deeply, growling softly as he did in low, guttural tones. Roughly, he whispered into my hair, "I'm going to kiss you, Kate—right now." Trailing his lips from my hairline, he came to rest at the corner of my mouth. He seemed to gather himself as he drew in a slow breath. His lips hovered a moment before he tenderly touched his mouth to mine. As if I'd been electrocuted, my body jerked at the contact. He held me steady and continued to kiss me. Lightly at first, just tenderly pressing his lips against mine, again and again. Then he began to move his mouth, caressing, tantalizing, taking little nibbles. Suddenly he made a low sound, then he was really kissing me.

I've never been kissed like this. Ever. In all the times Calvin and I had kissed, not once did it even come close. Never had I felt this sort of earth-shattering awareness. This all-consuming emotion and *need*. Of their own accord, my hands slid up his arms, over his shoulders, around his neck and tightened, pulling myself against him, pulling him against me. Asher made a sound then, a euphoric cadence that sent a thrill shuddering through my body. Not breaking contact, I found myself lifted, then my back was against a wall. Asher leaned into me, his body striving against mine, pinning me, holding me in place. Panic fired through me, uncertainty and confusion swelling at this new and almost frightening experience.

"Asher, stop," I whimpered, overwhelmed by every sensation, as his mouth left mine and trailed along my throat. "Please, stop. I can't do this."

"Can't stop. Not yet. I...need this." His mouth found mine again, searching so tenderly, so intimately. Honestly, I didn't want him to ever stop. I wanted more. What, I couldn't say...only *more*.

Panicked, desperate, I shoved against his chest. That seemed to reach him. As he peeled himself away from me, I slid to the side out from the shelter of his body, and panted. "I can't do this! I don't know what you think you're doing, but *I* can't do this."

"Why not?" he rumbled, stepping closer.

"Because...just...because." *Wow, that sure explained a lot, Katy.*

"I want you, Kate." He spoke quietly, sincerely, and I swear my knees went a little weak.

"No, you don't." I shook my head, holding my hand out to ward him off, trying to reason with him and myself.

"I *want* you." Asher stated again, his voice soft, pleading, and intense.

"You can't." I whimpered desperately, a pleading note now in my voice.

Asher gave me a piercing look. "Why not?"

"Because I can't trust myself with you—that's why!" I yelled. It took a split second for me to realize what had come out of my mouth, what I had unwillingly admitted. Sucking in a quick, noisy breath, my hands slapped against my mouth. I caught the satisfied gleam in Asher's eyes, and did what anyone would do in this situation. I panicked. "Forget I said that. I have to go." I tried walking past, but he stepped between me and the door.

"Ah, no. You're not going anywhere."

My eyes stayed glued to the ground, refusing to look at him. "I'm not doing this with you, Asher."

"What aren't you doing with me?" he challenged.

"Psht! Just...stop talking!"

"No." He replied. His voice was level and invitingly calm, which only irritated me. "Stop ignoring this."

"Listen, you need to shut up and get back inside that little box I had you in." I growled, angry he was trying to force this conversation, angry he was making me face these desires. "And I'm not ignoring anything. Because this isn't anything."

"Are you denying there's something between us?" He sounded incredulous, almost angry; the levelness gone now.

"I'm not denying..." I shook my head, trying to clear it, and made the mistake of meeting his gaze.

"Well. That's good to hear." Asher grinned. "And I don't do well in boxes. I don't like being boxed in. It makes me irritable and I tend to break them."

"In three months, you'll be gone. You're simply another ranch client, and when this job is finished, you'll leave, just like all the others."

Asher watched me quietly for a moment, then said, a small smile playing around his mouth, his voice heavy with sarcasm, "Ah...I see. You've already written this script and know the ending." Deciding silence was the best course of action, I kept my mouth closed. "I thought God was the one in charge of everything; I didn't realize you were."

"I'm not. Look, I've known you for two weeks, Asher! Two weeks is not that long. It's a drop in the bucket. What happens tomorrow? What happens right now? How far does this go?"

Asher let me step back, but he tracked my every movement. "I thought I could take this slowly, but I..." He stopped and seemed to consider his next words carefully. "Look, I lost control. It won't happen again—I promise." He took a step toward me. Flinching, I stepped back. I wasn't afraid of him; I was afraid of myself. Asher stopped, regarding me intently. His voice was level when he said, "Tell me what you felt when I kissed you."

"It doesn't matter what I felt. I'm still not doing this with you."

"But you felt something. You did feel something when *I* kissed you." His voice now held a mixture of defiance and possession.

"I'm not sure what it was...something...I don't know." My voice came out all kinds of shaky.

"Passion, that's what you felt. It's passion."

I shook my head. "Lust, maybe. But, not passion."

"What's the difference?" He chuckled, leaning back against the barn door.

"Between lust and passion?" Asher nodded, a grin still playing on his lips. "Lust is a physical response based upon nothing but bodily desires. Passion is the physical expression of love between two people who mutually respect each other, who are fully committed to each other."

"That sounds like a textbook answer. You may have seen passion in a movie, read about it in a book, but I'd say you've just had your first taste of what passion will be for you. And I do respect you, Kate."

"Do you? Truly?" Desperately, I tried to ignore the heat and desire his words caused.

"Yes, I do."

"Then listen to me, right now, Asher Fitzpatrick. Because I mean every word I'm saying. I can't—I *won't*—deny the physical attraction between us.

You make me think things and feel things I didn't know I could think or feel. I'd be lying if I said it didn't exist. But...what I have to give, what I have to offer, what I've been holding on to is for one man and one man only." I took a shaky breath, then continued. "I don't know if that man is you. Only time will tell that. But I can't play with this fire and not get burned. I'm holding on by a thread, because I enjoyed that way too much. Please, *please*, if you respect me, if you have any regard for me at all, please don't push this." He watched me; the turmoil going on in his head evident in his eyes. When he remained silent, I tried again. "I'm willing to get to know you. I'm willing to pursue a...future...with you. I am *not* however, willing to be a temporary and convenient acquaintance. I won't sell myself short."

Asher stared at me in continued silence; his eyes were guarded as they searched mine. I had no idea what he saw there. I didn't know if he was thinking he'd made a mistake in kissing me, if he was thinking I wasn't worth the effort. I waited, half afraid of what conclusion he was going to come to.

"What are you saying?" he finally asked.

I breathed a silent sigh of relief he hadn't simply turned away in disgust and walked out. "Ash, what do you *want* from me?"

"You. All of you." He said it with such assurance.

I stamped down the heat that flared from his statement and reminded myself to be strong and persevere. "For how long, though?"

"For as long as you'll have me."

My heart fluttered in my chest. "You have no idea how much I want to believe that, or how incredible that sounds. Let's take this slow. You say you feel that way now, but," a flame of hope began to spark. "I want to be sure, Ash—no mistakes."

"Slow." Asher suppressed a shudder. "I've been trying *slow*. Slow is hard."

"But not impossible, right?" I clarified.

He closed his eyes for a moment, inhaling deeply, slowly. He rubbed his palms against his face in a show of mild agitation. Then I heard him sigh and chuckle darkly. "No. It's not impossible," he muttered. "Difficult, yes, but not impossible." My mouth curved up and Asher smiled back. "If slow is what you want, I'll do it." His eyes were strongly focused on mine. "But you've got to help me out here, okay? You can't look at me the way you have; it only makes this harder than it already is."

"Okay," I breathed.

"Look...go on inside. I'll be in, in a minute. I need to cool down."

"I'll see you later then?" I turned to open the barn door.

"You'll see me later." Asher affirmed, his voice soft and full of resolve. "We'll take things slow and work through this. Because, Kate? I'm not giving you up."

Asher-

Asher had dreamed about—fantasized about—what it would be like to finally kiss Kate. The reality was far better, and far worse, than he'd anticipated. Better, because there was simply no way to have predicted how good it really was, how truly stunning she'd feel under his hands, in his arms, with his mouth and body on hers. Worse, because now that he knew, he wanted more, so much more. Worse, because although he felt like he was literally dying from the pain of his physical need for more, he'd just promised to not rush things. It was so much worse.

As his body had registered the promise his lips had made, it had rebelled in frustration. His whole frame had shuddered. His fists had tightened, feeling like he was about to come out of his skin. Then he'd looked at her, seen the light in Kate's green eyes; saw the trust and hope there, and somehow felt himself calming down.

She'd pretty much indicated she was a virgin. He shook his head. *Was that even possible?* Did women still hold onto their virtue like that? Saving themselves for their husbands? He'd certainly never met anyone who claimed such a thing before and Asher knew he himself could not claim to be. He considered the idea as Kate walked out and he felt two emotions surge through him: lust and hope. The thought that if he and Kate ever did come together in the way he desired, he would be getting not only her body, but her faith and beliefs and ideals as well, left him breathless. He could be her first. And last. Her only. Lust and hope. He lusted for that and hoped he was strong enough to see it through. Asher chuckled to himself. If Kate could see the turmoil raging inside him right now, if she was somehow privy to the thoughts in his head, she'd not have any doubt as to the difference between passion and lust.

CHAPTER NINE

So, Sometimes They Call Me Rocky

Kate-

I spent the weekend on pins and needles wondering what Asher would do next. What I should expect. But when we saw each other Saturday, he seemed relaxed. Not at all how he'd been Friday. He attended church with us again on Sunday, but again, he was nonchalant and...casual. So casual in fact, I wondered if I hadn't imagined the whole thing, just dreamed it up in my over-active imagination. Then, in passing, he'd trail a light grazing touch across the back of my neck, or rest a weighted, gentle hand on my shoulder, and I'd *know*. I hadn't imagined any of it. This was real.

The week began with a continuation of Asher's equestrian training; he worked the barrels and did the pattern from both directions, putting in several hours in the saddle. Later in the morning, a member of the film crew called, letting us know to expect arrivals beginning the following week.

"Now the circus begins." Asher sighed as he sat down for lunch.

"Is it really that bad?" I glanced over my shoulder in his direction.

"It is. And it isn't."

"I guess this is where I'll really earn my keep, huh?"

His gaze was direct. "You've already earned it, Kate. I've learned a lot."

"I hope so. I guess we'll find out in a week or so." I smiled.

We finished eating, then after cleaning up, went back out to the barn. I wanted to ride one of the new horses this afternoon and I was going to have Asher give jumping a try.

In the tack room, standing with my back to the doorway, I searched the shelving against the wall where I kept various odds and ends. I knew we had a couple of helmets out here; where I'd stored them was the question.

Suddenly, Asher was right behind me. Leaning forward, hands gripping the shelves, he caged my body. I felt him inhale and exhale as he pressed against my back.

"Ash," I whispered, frozen. "What are you...?"

"Shhhh...I'm not breaking my word; I remember what you said." His voice rumbled deliciously in my ear as he skimmed his nose from my shoulder to my ear. "I need to feel you close for a moment. Just...give me *this.* Please."

Asher pulled his left hand away from the shelf, his fingertips trailed along my shoulder blades, my neck, stealing my breath. He rested his hand at my hip, where it lay, warm and solid. At first his grip was light, then, mouth against the back of my neck, he inhaled deeply, slowly. His hand tightened, fingers grasping, pulling me closer; my body shuddered in response. After a moment or two, he placed a single kiss where my shoulder met my neck, then his grip loosened, and he slowly pulled away. "Thank you."

I didn't trust myself to speak, so I merely nodded, hoping he could tell from the back what that movement meant.

"You know," he sounded thoughtful, "once the production crew arrives, we won't have a whole lot of time to spend alone together. Could we take tonight off maybe?" Asher reached for my hand, turning me around. "Let me take you to dinner, Kate."

My face was still flushed from the heat; my pulse still raced. "You want to take me out to dinner?"

"I do." Asher lifted my hand, ran his lips across my knuckles setting them on fire.

"Okay." I struggled for calm.

"What time works for you? I'll make some reservations."

I blinked. "I have to feed at four...I can be ready by five-thirty?"

"I'll make a reservation for seven. That gives us plenty of time. Do you have a preference as to where we eat?" I shook my head. "We'll take the bike. I'll pick you up at five-thirty, then." He winked as he left to make that call. I watched him walk away, a feeling of dazed happiness rising inside me.

Kate-

We called it a day around a quarter to four and got the animals fed in record time. While Asher was showering, I let Mom know he and I wouldn't be home for dinner. "Oh?" Curiosity flared in her eyes.

"Yeah...Asher wants to go out to dinner tonight. Is that all right?" I tried to be casual about it.

"Of course; be careful," Mom said, nonchalantly. "And have fun."

"We will," I told her.

During my shower, I wondered: Was this a *date* date or simply dinner? *I should have asked him.* What should I wear? I'd be riding his motorcycle, so definitely pants. Looking in my closet, I eventually settled on a pair of lightly faded cropped jeans. The hems had a rolled-up unfinished look, that I liked. I paired them with my favorite casual blouse, in a shade of deep midnight blue.

For shoes, I chose a pair of brown leather sandals that had a three-inch wedge heel, and tied around the ankle. Normally, I might have put my hair up, but since I'd be wearing a helmet, decided to leave it down, simply blow drying and curling it, knowing most of the curl would relax to more of a wave anyway.

On the way out of my room, I sprayed some of my favorite perfume on my wrists and at my neckline. I grabbed my light-brown leather jacket, and a multi-hued gauze scarf, figuring I could use it to stave off the ever-attractive helmet head.

Asher was waiting for me when I came down the stairs. The heat in his gaze made me glad I'd taken extra time on my appearance. His cologne, I noticed as I got closer, was intoxicating. and I couldn't take my eyes off him. Even with my heels on, I had to tilt my head back to maintain eye contact, and found myself appreciating his height even more.

I meant to compliment him on his appearance, but instead blurted, "How tall *are* you?"

Asher grinned. "Six-five."

"Wow." I blinked. "You are really tall."

Tucking a stray piece of hair behind my ear, his blue eyes searched mine, and I wondered what he was thinking. After a moment he nodded towards the door. "You ready then?"

"I am."

We said goodbye to Mom and Dad and Calvin—who said he'd wait up for us. *Thanks, Calvin.* I could clearly hear the disapproving tone in his voice, and wondered if Asher noticed it as well. If he did, he never mentioned it.

Asher helped me put the helmet on, making sure it fit properly. "All you have to do is hang on to me. I'll do everything else."

Maybe it was simply Asher, but I couldn't help thinking how sexy he looked on his bike; his muscles straining the fabric of his shirt, his tan making the white knit stand out even more. His forearms rippled as he revved the engine. I watched his hands as they wrapped around the rubber grips and remembered how those hands had felt on me, wrapped around my arms, my neck and trembled at the memory. When he turned, he caught the look in my eyes and shook his head. "That doesn't help," Asher rumbled.

A blush stained my cheeks. Blowing out a breath, I mounted the bike behind him. I had to wrap my arms around his waist and tried in vain to keep my hands in one place, to not allow them to move. The hard muscles I'd seen only once before, were under my hands, my fingertips, begging for attention. They clenched under my touch as his breathing sped up.

"Behave yourself, Kate," he growled. "I can only take so much."

"Sorry." I breathed against his back, shaking my hands out before once more taking hold of him. Forcing myself to be still. After a moment, Asher turned the big bike down the driveway.

He'd awoken something in me and I feared, should he and I not work out, I'd be ruined for other men. I was equal parts thrilled and terrified at the realization.

Asher took us to Buffalo Bill's Steakhouse. The parking lot was crowded when we arrived, and I was glad he'd thought to make a reservation. After Asher shut the bike down, I reluctantly pulled my arms back and stretched. Carefully, I climbed off and waited for him to do the same. Unbuckling my helmet, I handed it to him. Asher looked at me, one eyebrow raised in silent question as I removed the scarf and fluffed my hair.

"What?" I was pretty sure I knew where this was going.

"You want to tell me what that was about?" His voice was edged in heat.

"No." *Why do I feel like a kid caught with my hand in the cookie jar?*

"I thought you wanted to take things slowly." Yes, there was definitely an edge to his voice.

"I did." I nodded. "I do."

"Didn't seem like it to me. I didn't know if you were hungry for dinner or me back there." His blue eyes flashed and it wasn't only anger I saw.

"Look, this isn't easy for me, okay?" My hands snapped to my hips in agitation.

His eyes followed my movements, continuing along the curve of my hips, resting there. "And you think it's easy for me?"

"I'm not saying that. I'm only saying it's not easy for *me*. I've never felt this before. I don't have any experience with this sort of thing."

"Fair enough." Asher suddenly flicked his gaze up to meet mine. "Let me know when slow becomes irritating. Now, let's go eat." He took my hand, leading me toward the front doors. His eyes roved the parking lot, carefully taking everything in.

"Are you worried someone might recognize you?" I tried for a change of subject, anything to lighten the mood.

"Not at all." He looked down at me with a knowing grin. "Most times, the fans are respectful. It sort of comes with the territory, though. You get used to."

The *maître d* located the name Asher'd given—Noah Fitz—then personally led us to our table. We were towards the back of the establishment, at a corner spot somewhat hidden by a large potted palm. After we'd been seated, I asked about the name he'd used. "One of my alias's. Noah's my middle name."

"Asher Noah Fitzpatrick." I inhaled. "Noah Fitz; I like it."

"Probably isn't the tightest security-wise, but it does the job."

I excused myself then to use the restroom; mainly I wanted to check my hair. I had to walk past the bar to get to the bathroom and after I'd given myself a touch-up, I made my way back to our table. I was almost there, could see Asher's shoulder, when I felt a hand on my arm, gripping with enough force to stop my forward momentum.

Johnny Khyle hadn't changed much since I'd known him in high school. He'd graduated the year before I had, and had been on the football team. Johnny was dirty-blond, tanned, and a little over six feet tall. He'd managed to retain a good portion of his high school muscle tone, and I could tell his ego hadn't shrunk any since he'd graduated. The scent of alcohol fairly emanated from him. *Some things never change.*

"KatyBeth Reilly, look at you. All grown up." He still held my arm, his eyes traveling slowly up and down my frame, turning my stomach. "You look so good. I wanna eat you right up."

"Johnny." I kept my voice calm.

"Sit down." He tugged lightly on my arm, indicating the seat next to him at the bar.

"I'm here with someone," I said firmly.

"Yeah?" He looked around. "You still got Calvin tagging along after you?"

"Calvin's a good friend and not here tonight." Losing patience, I twisted my arm, dislodging his grip, and walked away. Asher had seen at least some part of what had occurred. Fury simmered in his eyes. Quickly, I stepped to his side. "Don't worry about it, Ash, I handled it." I waited for him to meet my gaze. Somehow, I knew his reaction to advances like these had changed after we'd kissed. After a tense moment, he glanced down at me and nodded. Turning, he placed a hand on my lower back and led me to our table.

After he seated me and sat down, not across from me but at my side, where he could see anyone coming to our table, he asked quietly, "Who is he?"

"Just a guy I went to high school with."

"Ex?"

"Not even close."

"What did he want?" I could still detect the underlying anger in his voice.

"He was only saying hello. Ash, please don't let it bother you. Okay?" Asher studied me closely for a moment, then nodded.

Our server came then and introduced herself; Megan was her name. She told us of the special that evening, took our drink order, and left us with a couple of menus, saying she'd be back to check on us.

"What sounds good to you?" Asher asked after a minute or two of perusing the menu.

"I'm thinking the seafood pasta platter sounds pretty good."

"We're in a steak house in the middle of cowboy country, and you're going to order seafood?"

"Yep."

"I see." A smile played on his lips in a thoroughly distracting manner.

"What are you getting?" I tried not to stare at his mouth.

"I'm thinking the prime rib."

"The prime rib is good here."

Megan came to take our order, and to bring us a bread basket and our drinks

"So, Asher, tell me about yourself. I know your middle name now, but don't know how old you are."

"You're not afraid of dating an older man, are you?" he teased.

"Terrified."

"I'm twenty-eight," he paused then added, "That's not too old for you, is it?"

Shaking my head, I decided to clarify something that was on my mind. "And, *are* we dating?"

"For the time being. You said I had to go slowly. I figure *dating* is a nice, slow first step."

"I did say slow." The garlic bread was buttery and flaky, nearly melting in my mouth. "Any siblings?"

"I have one sister. Jamie's twenty-six. Married. Her husband's name is Sean. They live in Arizona with my nephew Michael, who's three."

"And your parents? Are they still living?"

"They are. My father's name is Tiernan and my mother's name is Callie. They live in Ireland now."

"Ireland? Is that where you're from?"

"My great grandfather immigrated here when he was a young man. Though, my parents moved back when I was barely crawling." Asher took a drink of his soda and said, "You'd like it there. Maybe I can take you one day."

"We'll see." I tried not to get ahead of myself. "How did you get into acting?"

"It's stupid really. One day, Sammy and I were out playing ball with a couple guys. A man approached and asked if I'd be interested in some modeling shots. Sammy dared me to try it, so I did. About four months later, I was 'discovered' and the rest is, as they say, history."

"I know the film you're working on now is a western, but I don't think I caught the name of it, or the plot for that matter."

"My character's a rancher whose claim to his land is being challenged. Basically, a range-war takes place. Lots of action, a little romance. It's called *Dust Devils.*"

"Sounds entertaining." I took a sip of my iced tea. "You mentioned you didn't have a girlfriend. Are you seeing anyone, though? Even just casually?"

"Yes." His tone was serious. "You. Though, I feel anything but casual about it."

"Only me?" I clarified, a light blush staining my cheeks.

"Only you."

"And...why is that?" I'd thought about it late into the night, wondering exactly what it was he was seeing in me.

Asher silently studied me for a moment, the replied, "No one else interests me the way you do."

Shaking my head in silent disbelief, I saw Asher raise his brows in question. "I don't get it. I'm just your average girl. That's all."

"You're far from average, trust me."

I took another sip of my tea. "Don't get me wrong, I'm flattered. I guess, it just doesn't feel real to me. I'm sure you could have your pick of available women, women who are much less trouble than I am to you. Women who wouldn't set limits, boundaries, or conditions on your relationship."

He took a slow breath. "You think I'd be more attracted by an uncomplicated, unrestricted coupling than I am by the challenge you present?"

I sensed I'd offended him and felt bad, but still needed his answer. "I don't really know what would attract you, Ash. I don't really know you, or what makes you tick."

The look in his bright blue eyes was serious with maybe a touch of irritation thrown in to keep me on my toes. "You said you were willing to get to know me. Did you mean that?" My chin dipped in agreement. "Then I'm hopeful you'll soon find out exactly what kind of man I am, what it is about you that attracts me and drives me crazy, and what makes me...*tick*."

Megan returned then with our meal and while she was there, she refilled our drinks; I hoped Asher tipped her well for her efforts.

"Did you want to pray?" he asked before we began eating.

"Sure," I nodded, pleased he'd thought of that, then bowed my head, keeping it quick, but sincere. Asher and I continued our conversation as we ate. He asked me what my favorite kind of music was.

"I'm definitely a rock-and-roll kind of girl." I grinned. "But I enjoy all kinds of music."

"Who's your favorite artist?"

"Are we talking secular or Christian artists?"

"Both."

"The Christian artist would have to be Kutless—love them, and secular is definitely Foreigner." Asher chuckled gently, his blue eyes crinkling at the corners, his lips curved upward in a grin.

"What?" I tried not to stare at his mouth.

"I'm not familiar with Kutless, but Foreigner?" He chuckled again. "If you weren't sitting here in front of me, if I didn't know you, I'd have said your age was showing. Foreigner; aren't they kind of old?"

"I don't think Foreigner can ever be *old*. They're...classic. *Juke Box Hero* will never go out of style. Lou Gramm had, or has—I'm not sure if he's still singing—an amazing voice," I told him between bites. "I can easily say that his is the sexiest singing voice I've ever heard."

"Do tell," Asher's blue eyes were focused on me. "What is it you like about it?"

"What's not to like?" I challenged. "He has amazing control and range. His voice can be all growling *purr,* then full and powerful, and then hit those high notes...*Yeah*. It's amazing."

Asher gently grazed his knuckle across my cheekbone, causing me to fall silent as he watched me. After a moment he said, "I think an appropriate song might be *Waiting for a Girl Like You,* or *I Want to Know What Love is. Hot Blooded* might be another good one. I feel like Lou Gramm some days, all frustrated, pent-up tension that continues to build."

"I'm not trying to make this hard on you."

"I know that; you...get under my skin is all. I suppose you could say I'm learning a new discipline, besides the equestrian one, I mean."

"And what is that?"

"Self-control."

"That's never been a strong suit for you?"

"Not until I met you."

Megan came back to our table with a refill on the bread basket. She also had a drink with her.

"This was sent to you by the gentleman at the bar," she set the gold-colored liquid beside my plate. I didn't bother to look, knowing who sent it.

"No, thank you. Please take this back," I said quietly, my eyes on Asher, willing him to remain calm.

His gaze was gentle as it rested on me. "Please inform the gentleman he's not to bother Miss Reilly any longer. Thank you," Asher told her.

"Sure thing. Sorry about that." Megan quickly snagged the glass, immediately returning it to the bar. A moment later, I heard a crash and a yell, followed by the sounds of a scuffle. I was sure a couple of bouncers were assisting Johnny outside.

"I hope they took his keys." I muttered quietly. Asher, though calm, had fire in his eyes and I hoped we didn't run into Johnny anytime soon. "Do you like to dance?" I hoped my question distracted him.

Asher chuckled; his gaze became calculating, and he said, "I do, and yourself?"

"I don't really go *out* dancing, but I do enjoy it with my girlfriends. Sometimes we take a speaker out to the barn and dance. I guess we haven't done that since high school." I smiled in remembrance, even as pain stung my heart at the thought of Candi.

Quietly, he contemplated me, something deep going on behind his gaze. I was about to question him when he said, "Dance with me, Kate."

"Now?"

"Now. I saw a small dance floor on the other side of the bar." Standing, he held his hand out. "Come on, you mentioned dancing to distract me. I am sufficiently distracted by the idea of dancing with you."

Taking a slow breath, I placed my hand in his, enjoying the way his fairly wrapped around mine. As we passed the bar, Asher told Megan we'd be right back, then said something else to her that I couldn't hear. As we reached the little handkerchief-sized dance floor, a new song began to play. It was Foreigner's *Waiting for a Girl Like You*. I looked up at Asher and he shrugged, as if to say, "It's nothing."

Asher gently, purposely pulled me close, his left arm snaking around my waist, his right hand grasping mine, holding it between us against his chest. Then he began to sway, the room around us fading until it was only the two of us in our own little world.

When the song ended, we continued as we were for a moment or two longer. Asher moved to release me, and I resisted, tightening my grip, unwilling to lose contact with him. Hearing his warm chuckle in my ear had my face flaming. I raised my head to see we'd been joined by a few other couples and weren't the center of attention.

Asher asked if I'd like dessert as we made our way back to our seat. I assured him I didn't. "If you're ready, I'll get the ticket and we can go."

"If I remember correctly, I owed you dinner."

"Maybe another time; tonight's mine." Asher took my hand again as we made our way outside. As I was thinking the evening had been perfect, I heard a loud catcall come from off to our right, and felt my heart plummet. Johnny Khyle was standing about twenty feet away and he wasn't alone. I didn't think I recognized his companion, but I did recognize trouble when I saw it.

Suddenly, I was furious. I manage to maintain an even demeanor most of the time, but right now I was seeing red.

I wasn't the only one.

Asher, who was still holding my hand, pulled me behind him, placing himself directly between me and any perceived danger. Stepping around Asher, I glared at Johnny and said in a hard voice, "You're drunk, Johnny, go home."

"How 'bout you come with me?" he slurred, sauntering in our direction.

"How 'bout you shut up?" I shot back.

"You know you want it...can't fool me none. You been wanting this a long time now."

Asher growled something and I tightened my grip on him, still trying to keep him moving in the direction of his bike. "I just want you to go home and sober up." We'd gone maybe five feet, when Johnny cursed and threw a bottle at us. He was so drunk it went wide, not even close to hitting his mark.

"That's it." Asher growled, turning in Johnny's direction. Moving quickly—I was proud of how fast, especially in the shoes I was wearing—I planted myself firmly in Asher's path. With both my hands on his chest, I tried to slow him down.

"Ash!" I pleaded. "He's so not worth it, okay. Let's go. Come on. *Please!*" Asher slowed a bit and I pushed him back even farther. One arm slipped around my waist, ready to react should Johnny be stupid enough to continue this. Asher's gaze shifted from Johnny, focusing on the other man, and I spun around to see what was happening. Johnny's friend closed in on us; I think just trying to throw off Asher's concentration. Asher turned his body toward the new target, which gave Johnny the opening he'd been looking for.

Or so he thought.

Stupid Johnny. He'd thought the only danger was Asher. And in any normal circumstance, or with any other girl, that might have been the case. But Johnny forgot to take me into account.

Just call me the *Italian Stallion*.

Actually, I'm not Italian. I think I have Irish somewhere in my past, like Asher.

With Ash focused on Bill—I'd remembered the name of Johnny's friend—Johnny thought he'd get a clear line on a sucker punch. He moved in and, before I'd even thought my actions through, I'd formed a fist and swung. The crunch of his nose as my fist connected with his face, regardless of any pain caused to me, was highly satisfying. Johnny went down, *hard,* his head bouncing off the blacktop with a hollow thud.

In something akin to shock, I stared at him for a moment, before bending to check his pulse. While down there, I searched his pockets, grabbing his keys. Thankfully, his pulse was steady, so dusting off my hands, I stood up.

Bill had stopped cold, wanting no part of Asher, and I honestly couldn't blame him. If I'd had to fight Asher, I wouldn't have wanted any part of him either. Bill backed up; hands raised. Asher spared him a moment's glance, then turned to me, taking in the situation as it stood. "What the *heck* were you thinking?" he exploded. His anger, directed at *me,* brought me up short. What was he so angry about? Hadn't I just saved his butt? "I... He was going to sucker punch you." I explained. "I stopped him."

"Do I look like I need protection?" he all but snarled at me as he too bent and checked Johnny's pulse.

"*No,* I was...I was trying to help. Are you mad? Why?" A flame of anger began to burn. Here my hand was beginning to throb, because I'd stepped in to assist him and he was getting bent about it?

"You might have been hurt. Why didn't you let me handle it?" Anger was still quite evident in his voice. My anger, on the other hand, had shifted dramatically, as I realized his emotion was from concern on my account. Oddly, his anger pleased and touched me, giving me a warm feeling in my stomach.

And I suddenly wanted him to kiss me.

"Let's get some ice for your hand. It's swelling." Asher gently took my wrist, lifting my right hand so he could see it better, noting the small abrasion, the mild discoloring. Turning suddenly to Bill, he asked, "You got a car?" Bill nodded. "Take him and get out of here. If either of you are here when I come back, I'll finish this. Tell your pal he can get his keys from the sheriff."

Asher led me inside where we were taken to an empty table; the waiter brought me some ice wrapped in a napkin. The manager spoke with us, upset to hear what had happened, and apologized repeatedly. Asher and I both assured him we were not angry. We did not want to press charges.

About fifteen minutes later, a sheriff's deputy arrived. While I'd been giving my statement to the deputy, Asher had called my parents, letting them know we were running late. Finally, about an hour later, we were back on Asher's motorcycle and heading home. It was almost eleven. He'd been pensive, almost distant, with an irate edge still lingering. My hand was throbbing incessantly by this point, and a disgruntled feeling had settled over me. I really wanted some Ibuprofen and more ice. My head was beginning to pound, probably just a stress-reaction, but I found it difficult to hold on to Ash during the ride back. Holding him made me aware of him.

And he hadn't kissed me. I wasn't sure which bothered me more, the throbbing of my hand, my pounding head, or my strong desire to be thoroughly kissed by Asher.

Asher-

Asher was furious. Anger and irritation boiled under the surface, aching for the slightest provocation to erupt. His jaw clenched as he revved his bike, shifting gears, demanding more speed from the machine. Kate tightened her grip on him; he felt her hands, small and warm, where they grasped him with more pressure and he swallowed back some of his agitation. He forced himself to calm down, but found he was still unable to speak.

Asher blamed the man—*Johnny,* she'd called him. And he blamed Kate. She was too beautiful, too desirable for her own good. He'd been relieved to hear Johnny hadn't been an ex of hers—the guy was a pig. Asher knew there was a time, not that long ago, when he'd have destroyed the man.

But Kate didn't know that side of him—the warrior, the annihilator. Asher feared her reaction if she became aware of it, if she saw him crush another human being like that. So, he'd controlled himself. Kept that fury contained. By thinking of her, he'd managed to keep the beast tightly under wraps.

To say he'd been shocked by what had happened would be putting it mildly. Shocked didn't even come close. Asher still couldn't believe Kate had stepped between him and an enemy like that. Couldn't fathom she'd actually physically engaged Johnny. Almost as shocking, was seeing how well she'd handled herself and the situation. He smiled, remembering with grim pleasure, seeing Johnny go down the way he had. Though, it should have been worse, much worse.

Asher was snapped back into the present when, as he brought his bike to a stop, Kate virtually leaped off the machine, moving swiftly toward the house. Scrambling to catch up with her, and in gentle exasperation, he grasped her uninjured arm, turning her back around.

Right then, in that moment, he wanted nothing more than to kiss her. To get his mouth and hands on her. He just didn't know how he'd stop at a simple kiss. Too much heat, too much explosive desire roiled around under the surface for him to be certain of his self-control. He knew he was at the snapping point and wouldn't chance it. Not with her. Not now, not after all the effort he'd put forth and the ground he'd gained—he wouldn't ruin it carelessly.

CHAPTER TEN

Temperature Rising

Kate-

We arrived back at the ranch just after midnight. Asher had remained quiet and aloof on the ride home, and I wasn't sure what I'd expected, but it wasn't his current mood. Before he'd even shut his bike down, I was off it and moving towards the house, irritation simmering under the surface. He muttered something under his breath, but I didn't pause to hear. I was angry. I was hurting. I wanted some pain meds. I wanted him to kiss me, *darn it!*

I'd gone maybe ten feet, when he pulled me around to face him—from my good arm, I should add.

"What's the matter?" His voice didn't indicate concern.

"Don't worry about it. I'm tired. I hurt. I want to go to bed. I'll see you in the morning." I tried pulling away from him. Of course, *darn him anyway,* he was stronger, and I was unable to make the exit I'd desired. Asher took a slow breath and closed his eyes, pinching the bridge of his nose with his other hand. "Let me go." I tugged on my arm.

"Not until you tell me what's wrong." He finally opened his eyes to look at me.

"What's wrong?" I fairly shouted at him. "What's wrong is...is you're mad at me. My hand is throbbing. And I'd really been hoping you'd ki—" Cutting myself off, I exhaled and said, "My hand hurts."

"I'm not mad at you." Asher stated calmly.

"You were, though." I argued.

"I'm not now. I wasn't..." he began; then started again, "I wasn't mad *at* you. Well, maybe a bit. I *was* angry. I was *furious.* I still can't believe you stepped between that idiot and me. What were you even thinking?"

"I don't know! He moved and I reacted. Johnny was asking for it—I didn't do anything wrong."

"Johnny was most definitely asking for it. He was begging for it and I'd sincerely hoped to deliver." Asher had been looking away; suddenly his eyes snapped back to mine, fire sparking from their depths. "And then you! You decide to act like my bodyguard and you, my date, my five-foot-four date, is the one to knock him senseless."

"I'm five-foot-ten, thank you very much."

"Forgive me." His voice was heavy with sarcasm. "I miscalculated. You seem so short to me."

"I'm actually tall. Just because you're a moose doesn't mean the rest of us are short!" I hissed at him.

"Moose?" he asked, incredulous.

"My hand is still hurting."

Asher didn't respond, simply began walking towards the house, carefully pulling me along behind him. We went to the back door and he tried the lock, finding it open. Stepping in, he led me down the hall, without slowing, to his room, threw the door open and sat me on his bed. Asher was across the hall and into the bathroom and back before I'd had a chance to consider where I was or what he was doing. He had a glass of water in one hand, and held his other hand out to me.

In automatic reaction, I held my palm up and he placed three pills there. I put them in my mouth, then accepted the glass of water. After I'd swallowed the pain medicine, he took the glass, setting it on his dresser.

Asher turned, studying me in silence. Somewhere in the background of my mind, I noted his bedroom door was open and I was on his bed. The rest of my mind was focused on him and other needs that were reawakening.

My gaze stayed locked with his. I'm not sure exactly when the heat in my eyes changed from anger to something else, but Asher must have noticed.

"Don't you do it. I'm not strong enough." His voice was hard, gravelly. "You get up right now. Go to your room. *Now.*" The room spun mildly as I carefully rose to my feet. "Even if it kills me," he whispered, his voice raw with desire. "I know what you want. But Kate, I'm not strong enough to stop there. Not right now. And you'd hate me later; I don't want you to hate me. So, *please,* get out, now."

Undecided, I held still for a moment, need and caution warring within me. Then his words, with brutal clarity, sunk in. Silently, no longer trusting myself, I turned away. When I'd crossed the threshold of his doorway and was in the hall, he said, "I know you're feeling frustrated. You feel tight. In need."

"Yes." I whispered.

"That's how I feel, too. Every darned day. I wanted that fight, Kate. I needed that release. That's why I was angry. And that you were hurt. I hope your hand feels better and you get some rest tonight. I know I won't."

Jerking my head in assent, I headed to my room, where I tossed and turned all night.

Asher-

Asher stayed frozen for another couple of minutes, giving her time to make it up to her room. Knowing if he caught her in the hallway, he'd have her against the wall, have his mouth on hers, have *her.* Then he exploded in a frenzy of action, ripping his clothes off, trading them for a pair of sweat pants and a sweatshirt. Quickly, he tied on a pair of running shoes. Seconds later, he was out of his room, down the hall, and outside. He took off running at full speed down the long driveway. Jack and Jill ran silently with him. Asher didn't see Calvin as he stepped from the shadows. Both he and Kate had been too preoccupied with each other to notice Calvin sitting in the easy chair in the dark.

Calvin-

Calvin heard all that had taken place. His heart clenched at the thought of Katy loving someone else. Yet, he loved her enough that, if she was happy with Asher and Asher treated her right, then he'd be happy for them. Even if it gutted him. And it sounded like Asher was doing everything within his power to respect Katy; Calvin was thankful for that, at least. The realization of their budding relationship, while painful, wasn't as annihilating as he'd feared and anticipated. Calvin stood, his legs only trembling a little, as he made his way to his room. His heart was broken, but not shattered. He somehow found peace in that understanding.

Asher-

Asher returned to the house about two and a half hours later. He was dripping in sweat and shaking slightly. He patted the dogs on the head as he entered the kitchen, then locked the door behind himself. Going directly to the bathroom, he quickly stripped, then showered. The water hadn't warmed up yet; he figured the ice-cold temperature wouldn't hurt him.

When Asher stepped into his room, wrapped in a towel, he groaned in frustration; Kate's scent still lingered. It enticed him, leaving him tormented. He chuckled grimly to himself and shook his head at his own vulnerability. After dressing in a clean pair of sweats, Asher picked up his phone and dialed.

It was nearly three in the morning now, but he knew Samuel would answer.

"Yes?" came the voice on the other end. Asher was silent a moment. "Ash?"

"I need you, Sammy. Bring Cory, too."

"That was fast."

"Don't play games."

Samuel was silent as he contemplated what Asher had said. "It's that bad?"

"It's that bad."

"I'll need to track Cory down. Could be more than a week; you good 'til then?"

"I am. Just...just hurry, Sammy."

"I'm packing now."

Asher hung up and lay back on the bed. There was no point in getting beneath the covers; he wouldn't sleep tonight anyway.

Samuel-

"Ash needs us. How soon can you be here?" Samuel said as Cory answered.

"What do you mean? Isn't he doing that girl, I mean the film at that girl's place?"

"He's not *doing that girl.* This is different. She's different." At Cory's snort, he continued. "She challenges him. This is a good thing, I think."

"How is this, *she,* a good thing?"

"Because he cares for her. A lot. Maybe enough to walk away and not risk his life anymore."

Cory was silent, then said, "Give me three days."

Kate-

When I woke, my head was pounding. My hand was still slightly swollen and my knuckles were stiff and sore. The steam and heat from my shower did little to alleviate my discomfort. I went through the routine of putting my makeup on and getting dressed. Somehow, I had to work through the fatigue, having about eighty head of cattle to move and no time for rest. Hopefully, caffeine would work a miracle in me. Woe to the world around me if it didn't. Picking up my boots and jacket, I headed downstairs.

Calvin was seated at the table, two steaming mugs in front of him. He nodded at one, a wry smile on his face. Internally, I blessed him for not saying good morning. My body shuddered in ecstasy as I sipped the warm, liquid comfort. After a moment, I opened my eyes to see Calvin staring at my right hand and felt heat spread across my face.

"Who?" His voice concerned and resigned at the same time.

"Johnny Khyle." I shrugged.

Calvin's eyebrows arched at the name. "Tell me about it," he suggested softly.

"I don't know exactly. We—Asher and I—were having a great time. Johnny was there. He'd been drinking. He made comments and I could tell Asher was getting irate. When we were leaving, Johnny was waiting in the parking lot. He had Bill with him, you remember Bill?" I asked, and when he nodded, continued. "Well, stupid Johnny kept talking smack. I don't think he recognized Asher or anything. I figured if he did, and if he were injured, he'd come after Ash with a lawsuit."

"So, you felt the need to step in and defend your six-foot-five date?" Calvin asked skeptically.

"Enough with the size references. Size didn't matter. I felt responsible. Ash was there as my date. Johnny wouldn't have given him the time of day if it hadn't been for me. I didn't want to be the cause of that kind of stress in his life. Johnny stepped in, trying for a sucker punch and I...I...*reacted.* Look, I didn't plan to do anything, it simply happened, okay?"

Calvin chuckled quietly. "And how did Ash take that?"

"He got angry, if you can believe it!" I said in exasperation.

"KatyBeth, I've gotta tell ya, you may know horses like there's no to-morrow, but you've got a few things to learn about men." Calvin nodded in sympathetic humor. "Yeah, I can see how he'd be angry about that one."

"Well, I can assure you, and him, it won't happen again."

"That's probably good. It's okay, ya know, to allow a guy to be a guy when he's with you."

I snorted. "What's that supposed to mean?"

"It means that no one would think less of you if you took a step back and permitted someone else to be strong in your place."

Switching subjects, I asked, "Is he up yet?"

"He left the house about forty-five minutes ago. I'd tread carefully. He's got a lid on it, but he's simmering pretty hot. Give him some space. Now let me see your hand." Calvin leaned forward. I placed my hand in his where he gently looked it over.

"I don't think you broke it, only bruised the heck out of it. You gonna be okay to ride today?"

"Of course." I stood, pulling my hand away, and taking our cups to the sink. Calvin rose as well and as I turned around, gently pulled me into his arms.

"I like him, Katy. I don't want to, but I do. And it's obvious he thinks the world of you. I'm happy for you, truly...and I hope this works out the way you want." He placed a light kiss on my forehead.

Right at that very moment, of course, Asher entered the kitchen, taking in the embrace. I'd stepped back from Calvin, but he'd seen, nonetheless. *Isn't this about perfect.* I felt my chin rising in sheer stub-bornness. I'd done nothing wrong and wouldn't be made to feel like I had all over again.

Asher gave Calvin a look that would possibly keep him awake at night for the rest of his life. Then, turning, he slammed the door on his way back out. I closed my eyes, gritting my teeth, and heard Calvin's sigh.

"Go after him, KatyBeth. Explain what this was and what this wasn't. I can't get anywhere near him right now or he'll tear me apart."

"You just said to tread carefully and give him space."

"This calls for a different kind of action. Go, Katy. Trust me."

I left the house in a huff, not sure where Asher had gone. Noticing the open barn door, I headed in that direction. Hearing a muffled thud from inside, I quickened my pace, then, as I entered the barn, came to a dead stop. Asher was tossing around an eighty-plus pound bale of hay like it was a rag doll. I can lift them easily, but to throw them around like he was doing? I knew he was strong, but to see the evidence of that strength unleashed? I watched in silent fascination for a couple of minutes, content to let him vent in this way.

When Asher became aware of my presence, he picked the bale up and tossed it back on the stack he'd taken it from. His chest was rising and falling from his exertions. His eyes were still murderous. His mouth was set in an angry line; hands were balled into fists. Looking rather predatory, he began walking towards me. A part of me advised I should run. *Now*.

Another part, the way more sensible part, insisted I stand still. If he *was* stalking, then running would only further inflame him. Besides, I doubted I'd make it far before he caught me. And that would have been galling, to say the least.

When he was right in front of me, I spoke in what I hoped was a soft and soothing voice. "Ash—" He cut me off with one upheld hand, index finger raised. I fell silent and let him work through his issues.

"What the heck was *that*, Kate?" He pronounced each word slowly and deliberately, anger still strongly evident in his voice.

"It wasn't what you thought. It wasn't what it looked like."

"*No*? So, I imagined Calvin standing in your kitchen with his arms around you and his mouth on you?"

"I told you; Calvin is like a brother to me. The hug...was...he was offering comfort."

"And the kiss?" Asher snapped. "Was that comfort, too?"

"He kissed my forehead, Ash. Nothing romantic about it."

"It didn't look... He doesn't feel..." he began, then stopped before continuing, trying to finish his statement. "I didn't like it."

"Trust me, you've made that abundantly clear."

"It should be me." He indicated me. "All of you; I want it all."

"Well, you didn't offer. And, as a friend, Calvin did. And I took it, as a friend." My eyes were flashing up at him, not in the least cowed by his temper.

"I want to be able to touch you that way, without fear of losing control. I just can't...yet."

Remaining silent for a moment, I allowed his words to register. Taking a deep breath, I stepped closer, leaning forward until my forehead rested against his chest. My hands settled on his hips and I wondered where my boldness came from.

Asher froze at my touch, his body trembling lightly. After a moment, he enclosed me in his arms, releasing his breath in a long sigh. Rubbing my head against his chest, I took this moment simply to appreciate him. To appreciate the fact that I was standing here, wrapped in Asher's embrace. His eyes were peaceful when I lifted my gaze to his, offering a small smile. Returning it, he very tenderly touched his lips to mine. Holding still, I simply enjoyed the contact.

After a moment, he pulled back, releasing me. "I need to change." Asher paused in the doorway. "I'm sorry. This is all rather new to me as well—jealousy was an unexpected emotion."

Asher-

Asher entered the kitchen and found Calvin waiting for him. They greeted each other with a nod.

"Everything all right, now?" Calvin's manner was direct with friendly overtones as he leaned against the counter.

"Yes."

Calvin detected a touch of steel in Asher's voice. "Listen, Ash... Katy's a real nice girl. I've known her my whole life, almost. She's like a sister to me."

"A fact you'd like to change." Definitely steel there in his voice.

"I don't deny it. KatyBeth doesn't see me like that, though. She doesn't...look at me, the way she looks at you."

"She admitted as much." Asher replied, folding his arms across his chest. "She does love you, though."

"As a brother only." Calvin nodded.

"Where's this going, Cal?"

"Why do you call her Kate?"

Asher contemplated him carefully before answering. "I see her as a woman, not a little girl."

"Your woman?" Calvin challenged.

"I'm doing my best to assure that outcome, yes."

"Fair enough. I've no problem with that. But, Ash? You be careful. As you pointed out, I do love her. I'd marry her in a heartbeat, if she'd look at me the way she looks at you. And I don't care if you're ten feet tall; you hurt her and I'll break you."

Asher smiled. "I'd expect nothing less."

Calvin nodded. "And don't let her walk all over you, either. She runs a pretty tall bluff. Don't be afraid to call her on it. I'd better get out there and help her."

"See you in bit."

Kate-

"KatyBeth, the little brawler!" Deken teased as he and Derek entered the barn. He lightly punched me in the shoulder as he danced around me, imitating a prizefighter.

"You heard?" I asked with my back to them.

"Yeah, we heard you laid out Johnny Khyle in Buffalo Bill's parking lot," Deken said.

"What happened, Katy?" Derek, who was typically the more serious, sensible twin, asked.

"Johnny was drunk and flapping his yap. He and Bill tried to start a fight with Asher. One thing led to another and Johnny got smacked."

"Uh...we heard you broke his nose." Deken snickered.

"I didn't stand around trying to find out. He went down, Asher told Bill to get him out of there. We went inside to get some ice for my hand. End of story."

"I'd be careful. He's furious right now. And you know Johnny. You might have laid him out, but he's not the kind to take this quietly," Derek warned.

"I'm not worried about Johnny Khyle. We all know he's an idiot," I told them. "Coffee's on in the house. Go on in and get some."

Deken put his arm around my shoulder, a nonchalant action, and squeezed lightly. "You know we're here for you." For once, he was being serious. Hearing a muttered curse, I looked towards the door. Asher and Calvin were standing there and Asher's eyes were on Deken's arm. Calvin whispered something up at Asher.

Not again, I thought. Calvin approached, leaving Asher where he stood, giving Deken a very pointed look that he missed by a mile. Derek saw though, and knocked Deken's arm off my shoulder. "Come on, Deke, let's get some coffee."

Asher made his way to me and I could see, for the most part, he was calm. "Who do you want to ride today?" I asked quietly.

"Duke is fine," he replied. "Is it always like this around you?"

"What do you mean?"

"The male attraction factor and you."

"They're friends. You're going to have to get used to the fact that I have friends, of both genders."

"Do they all have to touch you?"

"Touching is generally a part of friendship, besides we'd look like a bunch of idiots walking around trying not to touch each other all the time."

"I'll get Duke," Asher grumbled as he walked away.

Kate-

Cattle stretched out before us, moving slowly, lowing as they went. The scent of pine, cattle, and dust was thick in the air. We weren't pushing the herd, allowing them to graze as they moved. Looking over my shoulder, I caught Asher and Duke as they expertly discouraged a steer from darting into the brush. Turning, I ambled Jet over to them. "Nice work. Everything good?"

"I had a fantastic teacher." Asher grinned.

"Glad you think so. It's not too much farther, another hour or so. You holding up alright?"

"I'm good. Truly." Asher leaned down and scratched Duke's shoulder. "How's your hand?"

"I don't even notice it." I held up said hand, flexing it, proving I was all right. The look Asher gave me said he wasn't buying it. "It's sore, no denying that, but I'll live."

His blue eyes searched my face. "I didn't want you to get hurt in the first place."

"I know; neither did I. Life happens, though. And when it strikes, you just gotta roll with the punches."

"Hm." Was his noncommittal reply. "Think they'd notice if we strayed away for a couple minutes, or more?"

"What do you have in mind?" Heat bloomed in my middle at his question.

"Many things, but for the moment, I simply need my mouth on yours."

That heat flared to a throbbing coil; my breath shuddered out of me as my eyes darted ahead of us. Deken was on point, Derek and Calvin were to either side of the herd, keeping them loosely bunched. Calvin, I saw to my irritation, had stopped to allow the cows to move on ahead. One leg was wrapped around his saddle horn and he was looking in our direction. "Crap."

Asher followed my gaze. "They'd notice."

"Seems so. Hold that thought, okay?"

"Trust me, it's a constant."

Forty-five minutes or so later, Deken whistled shrilly, indicating he'd reached the pasture these cows were destined for. He pulled his horse aside as the rest of us brought up the rear, moving the others to join the lead cattle. Once they were settled in and grazing contentedly, we turned back toward the ranch. Asher rode at my side, the others grouping around us.

"Not bad, Ash. You did well." Deken said.

"Looked professional." Derek added.

"I had good instruction."

"That you did." Calvin agreed. "Something happen back there? I saw you guys had stopped."

"No. Nothing happened." Calvin gave me a pointed look that I chose to ignore.

"How long will these cows be here?" Asher asked, directing Calvin's attention away from me.

"We'll let them graze this valley for the summer," Calvin replied, turning to him. "Then, come fall, bring them back down to a lower pasture."

"There's plenty of fresh water, lots of green grasses. These babies will fatten up nicely." Deken added.

We fell silent then, enjoying the ride. The trail narrowed, taking a downward, left-handed turn as we entered the shade of a thick stand of trees. Deken once more took the lead, with Calvin and Derek following him. I was behind Derek, Jet moving at an easy gait over the pine needles, when I noticed Asher wasn't behind me. Turning the gelding, I headed back up the trail. Asher had dismounted just inside the tree line, but out of sight from the others. He stood, the animal between us, facing back up the trail. Not even questioning things, I pulled Jet to a stop, and quickly dismounted, moving around Duke. "You alri—" My words cut off as Asher's arms snaked around me. His mouth found mine even as he crowded me against the painted gelding.

That heat from earlier was in full bloom once more. "Sometimes this is all I can think about." Asher breathed against my skin, his mouth warm and firm. His teeth grazed my neck sharply before his lips were once more on mine. Lost. I was lost. Floating somewhere delicious.

The sound of a horse coming fast, broke us apart. With a trembling hand, I wiped my mouth, and stepped back from him.

"I won't apologize. I warned you I needed my mouth on yours."

"I know." I rasped. Before the other rider arrived, I remounted Jet and Asher climbed back aboard Duke. Calvin came around the bend, his eyes sharp. "Everything alright?"

"We're good." Asher said, offering no other explanation. After a moment's hesitation, Calvin turned his horse around and led the way out.

CHAPTER ELEVEN
A Strong Propensity for Violence

Kate-

The film crew began arriving two days later in a long caravan of expensive rigs. In the mix were six large RV's, three stock trailers, and four semi-trucks. Things turned chaotic quickly.

I assisted with the horses, getting them unloaded and settled. One, I noted, was corralled by himself. This one pawed the dirt, alternately laying his ears back, then swiveling them forward again. He'd snort and throw his head around. Drawn to his antics, I vowed to get a closer look later.

We stayed busy well after the sun set. Asher and I barely had a moment to wish the other a goodnight. The following morning had us running as soon as our feet hit the floor. Asher was meeting with the costume department, getting measured and fitted for his wardrobe. I was helping with last-minute placements for the livestock and incredibly more people were arriving. I'd seen Asher only once or twice, and only from a distance. He texted a couple times just letting me know he was thinking of me. I enjoyed the pictures he sent, and laughed at some of his facial expressions.

We'd arranged for a BBQ-mixer to get better acquainted with all the various persons involved in the production. As I stepped from the back-door, my arms laden with paper plates and napkins, I shaded my eyes and looked around, hoping for at least a glimpse of Asher. Soft laughter coming from near the oak tree drew my attention. The voice was feminine with a throaty quality to it. Searching in that direction, I found Asher talking with a brunette.

A petite, sophisticated, attractive brunette. Her hand was on Asher's arm, fingers digging in, looking more like claws the way she was clinging to him.

I was going to break her fingers.

One-by-one.

A rush of fury carried me in their direction. Suddenly Calvin was beside me, gripping my arm with vise-like strength, turning me around. Briefly, we stopped at the tables to relieve me of my burden, then he began walking me in the opposite direction.

"Easy now." He shook his head. "The two of you. He's not even remotely interested in that woman, so hold your horses. That's Jessica Stevenson; she's Asher's co-star. They *have* to get acquainted. It's part of Asher's job."

Suddenly, I found myself seated on one of the matching chairs in the office. I blinked my eyes. Calvin closed the door firmly behind him and sat across from me. "You feeling any better?"

"*Who* is she?"

"I told you. She's Jessica Stevenson. She's an actress. Jessica plays Asher's love interest in this film."

"And what does *that* mean?"

"KatyBeth Reilly! Come on now. You're bigger than this. You *both* are simply going to have to get over this whole jealous, he's mine/she's mine thing you've got going on. Asher is an actor. This is his job. If he must kiss her, then realize he's pretending—he's not enjoying it. And if you can't take it, then you should excuse yourself from being present during those times."

"Why are you telling me this?"

Sighing, he said, "Because I'm your best friend. I know where your affection lies, and I know where his lies. You two need to bring things down a notch. This won't last if everyone has to walk around on eggshells."

"Are you mad, Cal? About Asher?"

"No, I'm not mad, Katy. If he makes you happy, then how can I be mad about that?"

Standing, I gave him a hug. "You're a good friend."

"I know I am." He ruffled my hair.

"How did you know?" Bewilderment was thick in my skull. *What was happening to me?* I might lose my temper occasionally, but I'd literally been intending to do violence to a woman I'd never met before.

"That you intended to hurt her?" He chuckled. "Are you kidding me? You're a pretty easy book for me to read, Katy. You had violence written all over your face. I thought I'd better step in before you did something you'd regret."

"You're the best, Cal. What would I do without you?"

"You'd probably be in jail right now."

During a lull in the afternoon, Deken slid up to me as I cleared away dishes from one of the long tables we'd erected on the patio. "Why the long face?"

"I'm fine, Deke, why?" I swatted at a fly, distracted by the whirlwind in my head.

"Well, you haven't been your normal sunshine self today, first off. This glum mood have anything to do with the brunette?"

"A tad," I admitted dryly.

"You want me to take her out?" He eyed the target, his tone conspiratorial.

"*If* she needs it, then *I'll* be the one doing it."

"Why not go stake your claim? Let her know she's trespassing."

"Don't tempt me, Deken," I grumbled good-naturedly.

"Hey, I didn't say anything about hurting her, let her know the ground rules is all." I looked at him in question. "Look, here you are, *way over here,* being all disgruntled, and she's enjoying your absence *and* his company. Go over and introduce yourself. It's what I'd do." He shrugged.

"You're bad, Deken," I grinned.

He smirked. "Nah, I got you to smile though, didn't I?"

"You did. Thanks. I think I will go over there."

Asher-

Asher kept a blank expression on his face despite the constant chatter of the woman next to him. He missed Kate. He *wanted* Kate. She'd been distant ever since the film crew arrived and he wondered if she wasn't already fed up with him and this circus.

Would she retreat, back away, and decide he wasn't worth the effort? He hoped not. Asher honestly didn't know what he'd do, or how he'd handle it if she did.

Kate-

Asher was seated in one of the folding chairs out on the lawn, a glass of iced tea in his hand. Jessica Stevenson sat next to him. She was speaking, but as I watched their interaction, he seemed distracted. He looked up as I approached and a genuine smile spread across his face, like sunlight breaking through the clouds. I loved that smile, and couldn't help but return it.

Asher stood when I got closer. His hand slipped to my shoulder, lightly squeezing, and placed a soft, quick kiss at my temple.

"Jessica, I'd like to introduce you to Kate Reilly." Asher took my hand. "Kate, this is Jessica Stevenson."

"It's good to meet you, Jessica." I looked her in the eye.

"Oh, hey, you too, Kelly."

"It's Kate, Jessica. Her name is Kate," Asher said.

"Oops. Sorry, Kate. My mix-up." Jessica smiled up at me, her expression coy. "I play Asher's love interest in *Dust Devils*."

Keep it up, sister. I smiled back. "Yes, I heard that already. I guess it's fortunate Ash is such a good actor." Jessica gave me a cool look. I could literally see her taking my measure and hoped she came up with a correct estimate; I could take the gloves off if she needed me to.

"Have you met Rupert or Xavier yet?" Asher no doubt had picked up on my irritation.

"No, I haven't. I'm supposed meet the wrangler, too." Xavier, I knew, was the director; who Rupert was, I couldn't say.

"Let's go find them." Asher quickly steered me away.

Rupert turned out to be a likable, middle-aged man of medium build. He shook my hand enthusiastically. "*Very* pleased to meet you, Miss Reilly." He smiled warmly.

"Rupe, if we can get a copy of the script for the next few days, Kate can make sure I'm properly prepared." Asher told him.

"Of course, I'll get you one shortly. Excuse me." Rupert nodded as he walked away.

"So, what's Rupert's job here? What does he do?" I asked.

"Rupe...is like my liaison with the studio. At times, he acts as my manager. Though he's not, technically, I do occasionally employ him to fill that role when it suits me to do so."

"Oh yeah? How so?"

"I'll tell you sometime." Asher grinned. "Let's go find Scotty."

Scotty Wilcox was a redhead. He was maybe in his late twenties and had a build like a bull rider. Turns out I wasn't too far off the mark; he'd retired a few years back after a rather serious injury. Scotty had decided he could make a safer living doing what he did now, which was handle the livestock for Black Hills Entertainment. I learned all this from Asher as we made our way in the Wrangler's direction.

Scotty was also a flirt, a wolf with red hair. Asher hadn't warned me about that.

"Scotty, I'd like you to meet Kate Reilly. She's the one who's been giving me the equestrian lessons," Asher said as he introduced us.

Scotty carefully looked me over. His expression wasn't lewd, simply appreciative. He then said, "And where do *I* sign up for riding lessons?"

"Excuse me?" I couldn't have heard him correctly.

"Behave yourself, Scotty. This one's taken. Get it?" Asher slipped his arm around my waist, pulling me into his side.

"You might wanna brand this one quick, Ash. Turn your back and I'll be here to gobble her up." He smiled, a roguish light in his green eyes, and I couldn't help but smile back. He was a likable, friendly-wolf.

"Trust me, I know. And you'd have to get in line. She's already got a fan club," Asher stated dryly, causing me to roll my eyes.

"A fan club, you say? Do I get a t-shirt if I join?" Scotty asked.

A large buckskin horse trotted up to the fence, neighing shrilly, bringing our conversation to a halt. He stuck his head over the rails, reaching toward me in an inquisitive, friendly manner. Quietly, I stepped closer, noting Scotty's tension as I did so. The horse turned out to be a stallion; he must have smelled our horses on me. I held still as the buckskin whiffed my clothing, then slowly began to scratch his nose and forehead. He nickered quietly, enjoying the attention, as he rubbed against my chest.

"What kind of training has he had?" I turned my gaze to Scotty.

"The expensive kind. Though he's a stud, Buckdun behaves himself. He's great for the rougher country like this. He's actually a very gentle horse to ride."

"Can't have your movie star injured can we, big fella?" I patted the horse's neck.

"Maybe you'd like to ride him, see how he feels?" Scotty asked.

"Yeah, I'd love to. Is that okay, though? I mean, he's the studio's mount, right? Won't they object?" I asked.

"Nah, they trust me. Besides, I'd like to see how you handle him."

I wasn't sure what to make of that. Maybe he wanted to be certain I was doing a thorough job with Asher. "Where do you keep his tack?" I opened the gate, stepping inside the arena. Scotty and Asher followed close behind me.

"We haven't unloaded it as yet. You have something that might fit him?" Scotty asked.

"I would imagine so. What type of bit does he use?"

"He prefers a snaffle. I used a double twisted-wire for the last couple years, but you can basically ride him in just his halter."

"Ash, want to give me a leg up?" I turned to him.

"Is that safe?" Concern flared in his blue eyes.

"Scotty thinks so. I'll soon find out." Asher leaned down and cupped his hands. Raising my knee, he lifted me easily onto the broad back of the stallion.

"Thanks. Now step away, please. Both of you."

"Careful, Kate," he warned, gently.

Buck had a nice easy gait, even at a trot. Momentarily, I moved him further into a well-collected lope. He was amazingly smooth.

A lot of finesse had gone into this horse's training. Buck wanted to go faster. We had room in the corral, so I allowed him more speed, leaning over his withers and gripping his mane. After a few laps, I leaned back, easing him to a walk. He responded willingly to the lightest touch. Patting Buck's neck, I enjoyed the feel of the big horse under me. Turning back to the gate, I saw quite a few more people had lined up at the fence.

Sliding down from Buck's back, I turned to face Asher and Scotty, who'd been watching me closely.

"You ride beautifully." Scotty said sincerely.

"Thanks." I turned to Asher, nodding at Buck. "You're lucky. He's a fabulous horse. You're going to enjoy him."

"I enjoyed that. Very much," Asher ignored my comment about the horse. "Watching you." Heat bloomed in my middle at his words, at the look in his eyes.

"Miss Reilly?" I blinked, jerking my gaze from Asher's. "I wonder if you'd be willing to assist me with something." Scotty asked.

"KatyBeth," I told him, smiling. "Sure, what do you need?"

"Believe it or not, I'm having some difficulty with one of our horses. As you can see, we have several buckskins here. They're intended to be the 'same' horse in the film. Obviously, we'll have to dust or paint them in some cases, to make sure they all look alike. We'll use our stock for the scenes with Asher, and your stock for the extras in the film. I'd like you to take a look at this horse; he's the one isolated in the corral there." Scotty indicated the animal in question.

Looking where he'd pointed, I saw the horse I'd determined to get a closer look at from the previous day. Intrigued, I headed over when Asher caught my wrist. "Not tonight, Kate. Take a look at him later, huh? Besides, Rupert's on his way with the script. You can help me read lines and make sure I'm ready for whatever needs to be filmed tomorrow. Okay?"

"Will that work for you, Scotty?" I asked the redhead.

"That's fine," Scotty said. "I'm going to finish getting these horses settled, then I'm calling it a night. See you both first thing in the morning."

Later that night, after my shower, I found Calvin, the twins, and Asher playing a hand of cards. "Deal me out, fellas," Asher said as I entered the kitchen. "I've got work to do."

"Lame." Deken coughed under his breath.

"Yeah, likely excuse, Ash," Derek said.

"Whatever, *I* won," Calvin stated, scooting back from the table.

"You really need to study your lines?" I asked quietly as he came to stand beside me.

"I do," he replied. "Is there some place we can go to be private?"

"It depends," I said, then asked in a raised voice, "You guys going to watch a movie?"

"Yeah, that sounds good," Deken said.

I looked at Asher. "The kitchen will be sorta quiet. Will that work?"
"It'll do."

We remained at the table for the next couple of hours, reading through the few lines he had; Ash teased I'd make a great actress. Occasionally, he'd touch my hand or my arm. I think he'd simply been stretching, maybe trying to relieve some tension, then he'd go back to his work. Suddenly, Asher leaned forward, taking a firm, but gentle hold of my chin. "Don't make a liar out of me, Kate—I *am* in control of myself."

When his lips found mine, they hesitated, as if testing himself, or was maybe letting the anticipation build. He hadn't shaved in a couple days, his whiskers a soft caress against my face. His lips parted slightly and I shuddered at the sensation. A moment later, he nibbled at my bottom lip, before pulling back. Those incredible eyes of his searched my face, a slight grin playing around his mouth. "You're tired." He said softly, his breath tickling my skin.

"So are you." I stifled a yawn.

"Tired makes me think of sleep. Sleep makes me think of bed. Bed makes me think of you, and that's a dangerous combination right now." His rumbled words made my pulse spike and my heart race. Silently, I studied him. Blowing out a breath, Asher stood, then pulled me to my feet. "How about you have mercy on me and head to bed before my control snaps, huh? I'll see you in the morning." Leaning down, he pressed his lips to my forehead, his hands holding on to my shoulders. Then he stepped back and let me go. It took me a moment to find my legs. Releasing a soft breath, I turned, walking past the guys in the great room, ignoring their silent knowing looks.

Asher-

Kate was killing him. Asher could not remember a time in his life when he'd felt this torn and inside out. Ever. Not when he'd gone through intensive physical and psychological training and military exercises. Not even that time his recon-team had been pinned down under heavy enemy fire. None of that compared with the feelings, emotions, and needs Kate created in him.

Every touch, every look, every word she spoke brought Asher to a new level of longing. It was through this experience he decided there must be a God. Who else could create such an exquisitely painful and equally pleasurable need? Who else, but God, could, within the same body, bring him the means of his destruction and his salvation? For every instance he felt on the verge of shattering, he felt an even more potent need to do the right thing. It was a dichotomy of burning and instant healing.

CHAPTER TWELVE

Boundaries? What Boundaries? Did You See Any Boundaries?

Asher-

Asher had never been jealous a day in his life. Had never cared about anyone enough to be jealous before. He was jealous now. He'd caught the admiring looks of the film crew, the construction crew, even the other actors when they laid eyes on Kate.

The only thing keeping him together was that she never, ever responded to any of them the way she responded to him. Her blushed skin and shaky breath only occurred when *he* looked at her. She never even seemed to notice their attention.

Asher decided he wanted to speed some things up; have an official title for their relationship. He decided it was time for him to publicly stake his claim. Kate had said she wanted to take things slowly; did that mean keeping their relationship under the radar? Would she be agreeable to bringing it into the open? He wondered what her parents would think, what they'd say. Would they approve? What would he do if they didn't?

Kate-

The first official week of filming *Dust Devils* was hectic and bizarre. My head spun from the crazy schedule of night shoots, afternoon shoots, early morning, and late morning shoots. Constant adjustments were made to the script, to wardrobe, makeup, settings; then there was the fact that making a movie didn't follow the same course watching a movie did. Nothing went in order. Scenes seemed so random, I found it hard to sense of it all.

Amid all this chaos, I finally heard from Candi. Sort of. She didn't call, simply sent a text explaining she needed time and space to work through some issues and when she was ready to talk, she'd be in touch. I guess I'd simply have to be patient with her.

One early morning a couple days after filming had begun, I entered the kitchen in desperate need of coffee and found Samuel, Cory, Calvin, and Asher seated at the table. I stopped in surprise, then continued into the brightly lit room, wincing from the light.

"Hey," I grumbled reaching for a mug. "I didn't know you guys were coming in."

"We arrived around one this morning," Samuel said. "It's good to see you, Katy."

"It's good to see you, too," I lied. Asher winked at me as he was, by now, well-aware of how fond I was of mornings; which is to say, I typically despised them, especially early mornings before I've had coffee. He'd wisely kept his *good morning* to himself.

Asher had to meet with Josey, the costume designer, first thing this morning for yet more fittings; he was such a large man, many modifications had to be made to accommodate his size.

Somewhere on our property a construction crew was erecting a cabin, a barn, and a town. Most of these structures would be used mainly for the outdoor shots. A few small, temporary sound stages would be used for key scenes, I was told.

We spent a lot of time, it seemed to me, moving to various locations on the ranch. The camera crew would set up for a shot, or a series of shots, in which Asher would be tracking some adversary through the wilderness;

or there'd be scenes where he would ride, mostly Buckdunn, or one of the other horses. I found it incredible how many shots were made of the same scene, only from various angles and with differing lighting.

Thankfully, Xavier hadn't scheduled any evening shoots tonight, so Asher and I were able to enjoy dinner at the table. The experience was both comfortable and uncomfortable. Asher seemed relaxed; I was a little tense though. He joked with Dad and Calvin, Samuel, and Cory. He asked more questions about the running of the ranch—how much land sold for around here, what the market was like for cattle and horses. It was comfortable because I could see that Mom and Dad seemed to have genuine affection for him. It was comfortable because I enjoyed their conversations, and easy manner.

It was uncomfortable because my boundaries were smeared, like the distant, indistinct shimmers in a heat wave. It was uncomfortable because I struggled, trying to remember those boundaries and re-establish them. I knew I had, once upon a time, had boundaries. My set-in-steel limits of right and wrong. Of understanding my desire to be closer to Asher, yet remembering the reasons to keep my distance. It was uncomfortable because every so often I would catch Asher looking at me and his eyes spoke volumes.

He was having a hard time remembering boundaries too.

The strain of trying to appear unaffected was growing by leaps and bounds this evening. Of pretending to those around me I wasn't interested in Asher as a man, that I wasn't attracted to him. It was almost unbearable in my current state of exhaustion and I knew I'd have to excuse myself soon; my head had begun to pound. I waited another five minutes or so, then stood, trying not to sway. "I'm going to bed, guys. Good night."

"You've been quiet tonight," Dad observed.

"Just a little tired and I've got a bit of a headache. I'll see you all in the morning." I raised my hand, turned from the table, keeping my gaze down, and quickly left.

Making it to my bedroom, I collapsed, trembling on the bed. My breath came fast, matching my pulse. Moaning quietly to myself, I rolled over, planting my face in the pillow. *Sex.* I can't deny it was on my mind, but I wasn't thinking *only* of sex.

Honestly, I knew what sex *was*, but other than understanding its general conceptual function, I'd had no experience with it.

I'd been raised knowing sex was something for married people. This was a line I'd never come close to crossing before. I didn't *think* I was close to crossing it now, but certainly the subject had been on my mind of late. Properly, on my mind, within the context it was designed for.

Suddenly, I found myself seriously considering the idea of being married to Asher and all that would entail. There would be no lack for passion, I was sure.

That he felt physical attraction for me I did not doubt. I'd seen it in his eyes, could feel it in every touch. But the idea I spent most of my time considering was this: Aside from the physical attraction we felt for each other, was there more? Did Asher and I have more in common than a strong physical desire for one another? Could a relationship between us last? Could *we* endure?

If Asher didn't care, didn't want me for anything other than a flirtation, an easy or convenient distraction, then why waste my time with him? On the other hand, I wasn't sure if I hadn't already traveled too far down this emotional road that I wouldn't feel pain when and if it ended. And that scared me. What would he do? Why was he with me? When this job was over, what would happen to us? Would there even be an *us*? Then again, why did this decision rest solely on what Asher wanted or didn't want?

What did *I* want?

Was I so timid that I'd only move, only commit to this relationship, if he moved first? Somehow that didn't sit well with me—I wasn't a coward. I wasn't about to announce my intentions to the world or anything, but that didn't prevent me from coming to a decision about him on my own.

I tried to step back and look at Asher objectively. As hard as it was to do, I tried to look at him without noticing his physical attributes. Was there more to him that I admired other than his good looks?

I believed so. Asher was sincere and honest. He was not applying any undue pressure on me physically. He was respecting my request that we not have a sexual relationship. He was respectful and careful with Calvin, a very good friend who Asher knew loved me.

So far, so good.

Asher wasn't completely mine. *Yet*. I knew I wanted him to be mine, though. All mine.

And I guess, there was my answer. If I wanted him in that way, with that kind of permanence, then, yes, there was way more to love about him than his looks. If we could respect each other so avidly right now, then I could see us enduring. So, why did this have to seem so complicated, and, *why do I have to over-analyze everything*?

Pushing off my bed, I headed to the bathroom for a shower, the heat helping to ease my tension. The thought of his leaving and me never seeing him again, was... well, it was *frightening*, the intensity of the pain I felt.

In that, too, I had my answer. For better or for worse, I had already committed myself to this, to him. My only choice now was to see this through to completion, whatever that might be. Whether a painful, destructive end, or a fantastically beautiful one, I knew I was in for the long haul.

After my shower, I lay back on my bed, then abruptly leaped up again.

It was too stuffy in here.

Opening the window, I hoped to coax a breeze in to cool my fevered skin. I sat down on the window seat and closed my eyes, concentrating on lowering my heart rate. It didn't help that I took this opportunity to think about how acutely aware of him I'd been this evening. Slowly, deeply, I breathed in the cool mountain air, until I could feel myself calming down. I pulled the towel off my head, letting my hair hang loose, and reached for the brush by my bedside table. Gently, I combed through the tangles, both in my hair and in my head.

Asher was out of my class; I knew this better than anyone. Maybe it was better put that he was outside my world. It really had nothing to do with "class," so to speak. He was from Hollywood; I was from the backwoods country. Our worlds didn't normally collide.

And yet, in this instance, they had. They'd collided. We'd met. And we desired each other.

We hadn't spoken yet about a future together, other than that he wanted me in the foreseeable one. I didn't know what expectations he had. Would he want me to move? Leave my family behind? *Could I do that?* Did he want children? So many thoughts rambled through my exhausted mind and I was having a hard time focusing on any one of them.

A knock sounded gently on my door.

"Come in," I called quietly.

Dad stuck his head around the corner of the door. "How's the head?" he asked gently.

"A little better. Thanks."

"You got a minute?"

"Sure."

Dad came in and closed the door. He sat on my bed, folding his hands in his lap. Taking a careful breath, he looked over at me. "Katy, you're a grown woman now. It's hard for me to accept that fact, but I realized it these last few days. Watching you...and...watching Asher." I flinched at the sound of his name. Dad noticed. "We always thought it'd be Calvin." My eyes glistened as I shook my head. "You like him; Asher. A lot, I'd say," he spoke gently. "And, I think it's fair to say he holds a strong attraction for you as well. I know you're an adult and I can't tell you what to do, but...I simply want to caution you to take things slowly. *Be wise.* You don't know him well yet. Take the time to get to know him. Don't rush into anything. What I've seen of Asher so far—I like him. He seems to be a good man. And more, he seems a gentleman.

"However, *you* are my daughter, and I love you and I don't want to place you in a situation you might be unequipped to handle.

"Passion is a *good* thing, when within the bounds God intended. Outside of that, it can be destructive. And even the strongest person can be overcome. I trust you. And for the most part, I even trust him. But, as your father, I need to do what I can to help you stay safe and strong. The twins will be around to keep an eye on things if Calvin and I are gone. I think having the knowledge Deken and Derek are near will give you and Asher the added strength to withstand any temptation."

While Dad spoke, I'd remained silent; I wouldn't dishonor him now by denying what was the truth. I knew he was being honest with me, was treating me like an adult, and I could only feel gratitude for him, for both my parents. Dad hadn't accused Asher or me of anything. He hadn't laid down the law. He simply and honestly spoke the truth to me. Knowing he saw me as having that kind of integrity, saw Asher as having integrity, too. Well, that right there gave me the courage to do the right thing, to remain strong.

Asher-

Jackson knew. Asher could see it in his eyes. The look wasn't angry or even suspicious, but it *was* thoughtful. Jackson loved his daughter and cared for her and Naomi deeply. Asher wondered what Jackson intended to do with this newfound realization of his daughter's new admirer. They'd have to tell her parents, he decided. It was the right thing to do. The respectful thing to do. Asher intended to bring it up to Kate soon. He'd never had to deal with a girl's parents before, and found the experience new and a little unsettling.

At three-thirty-seven a.m. Asher received a text message. *Check the news.* Immediately deleting it, he opened his favorite news app and instantly found what he was looking for. The headline read: *Allied forces confirm the death of Ali Assaad—top Al-Qaeda Militant Leader.*

Asher lay back against his pillow, a grim smile playing on his lips. Another one down; how many more to go?

Kate-

We cut filming short on the Fourth of July; some of us went to Cody to catch the last of the parade and the fireworks show. Seeing the festivities through Asher's eyes seemed to make it a new experience for both of us. I couldn't help but fall in love with our little town all over again. On the way home—right after midnight—red and blue lights lit up my rearview. Groaning, knowing who was pulling me over, and why, I glanced at Asher to see how he was reacting. He seemed calm, almost expectant. Pulling the truck to the side of the road, I turned the engine off. Andy shined his light in the driver's window a moment or two later.

"Evening, KatyBeth. License and registration, please."

"Sure," I grumbled, reaching for the requested items. Asher silently handed me a shiny, black business card, and nodded in Andy's direction. Taking the card, I passed it along, wondering at it. I finished gathering the requested items, and held those out to Andy, who ignored them as he stared at the card I'd given him. Nervously, he glanced at Asher, then mumbled he'd be right back. Nonplussed, I watched him walk back to his cruiser, where he sat and stared at the card for a moment longer before dialing a number with his cell phone. I looked at Asher. "What's with the card?"

"Officer Andy is about to learn some manners."

"What does *that* mean?"

"It means he won't be bothering you any longer, unless you're actually breaking the law."

"Who's he calling?"

"A higher authority."

I was about to ask what he meant, when Andy turned his red and blue lights off, and sped away. I did a double-take, trying to figure out what, or whom, he could have called that might have caused this reaction. Drawing a blank, I turned to Asher who chuckled darkly. "See? No more harassment from Officer Andy. You're in the clear now."

"Uh, thanks...*I think*."

"My pleasure." He sounded smug and satisfied. *Who could he have called that had that kind of clout,* I wondered.

Kate-

Not being permitted at the site for the next scene Asher was shooting, I hung out at the barn catching up on the horses I had there. It was most likely a good thing, because he'd be filming a love scene—the only love scene—with Jessica. Asher assured me this was strictly a kissing scene; his shirt would not even be unbuttoned.

The idea of that woman, and her mouth and hands on Asher, made violent, unkind thoughts enter my head again—I settled for a third cup of coffee. Asher hadn't left the house yet, promising to see me before he did.

I was at the sink, rinsing out my mug, when I heard Asher behind me. Looking over my shoulder, our eyes locked. He studied me silently for a moment before finally saying, "Your dad is very astute. I've tried to be careful, but he's noticed."

Turning fully around, my back now against the counter, I silently nodded in agreement. Asher moved closer. Though he wasn't touching me, the heat from his body danced enticingly along mine. Slowly, cautiously, he reached out, fingers trailing across my lips, outlining them with his thumb. Tenderly, he cupped my face, his thumbs brushing across my cheeks, his body now aligning with mine. My hands came up to grip his wrists, leaning into him. Against my forehead, he whispered, "I have no desire to disrespect your father, Kate. Or you." Unable to speak, I simply held him close. Turning my head, I placed a kiss against his palm. A rumbling noise sounded from deep in his chest. His lips lingered. "I've gotta go. Hopefully this shoot won't take long." Asher pulled away, releasing me as he stepped back. "It's Friday. Let's take a break tonight, go get pizza or something. Cut loose a bit. We're both wound tight, and it'd do us some good. We'll make a group of it. That sound all right with you?"

"It *really* does. I'll let everyone know. What time do you want to go?"

"Let's say six-ish. I'll see you, hopefully, no later than early this afternoon." Asher leaned close once more, tenderly kissed me, then turned to go.

Asher-

"Cut! Asher, you need more passion! This is an embrace, with the woman you love and wish to marry," Xavier urged. "Take a minute, get a drink. Relax. We'll revisit this scene in ten."

Asher stormed from the room serving as the interior for the doctor's office. He absently noted everyone within the vicinity seemed to find somewhere else to look as he walked past. He heard Jessica griping under her breath about his inability to do a love scene. Asher rolled his eyes and ground his teeth.

He had plenty of *ability* to do a love scene! He'd done many love scenes. Faking passion was not something new to him. He was an actor! His problem was not an inability to fake passion, but rather with the subject he had to fake it with. Also, it felt strangely like he was cheating on Kate. And that idea was intolerable.

Samuel handed him a bottle of water, which he accepted gratefully. Asher opened it and took a swig to rinse his mouth, then spat the water on the ground. Taking a longer drink, he nearly finished the bottle.

"What seems to be the problem?"

"Jessica!" Asher growled. "Me. Kate. I don't know. This has never happened before. I'm your average hot-blooded male. Jessica is, no denying it, a beautiful woman. Kissing her should not be distasteful. And yet, somehow it is. It's Kate. She's not here right now, but then again, she is. Kate's right *here*." Asher tapped his head.

"Perhaps you'll need to use that to your advantage. Imagine it's Katy you're kissing." Samuel suggested.

"I'm not sure that would be a good idea. If my imagination is convincing enough, my body may not wish to stop." Asher chuckled.

"That sounds like an interesting conversation, my friend. Still," Samuel looked at his watch. "You need to solve your problem, in another six minutes."

"I know. Let me think." Asher stretched his big frame, feeling his muscles ripple. He'd told Kate the truth; he was wound tight. He felt coiled, like a snake, ready to strike with the slightest provocation.

In his head, he knew he could do this scene. It wasn't particularly trying. His character, Jon, enters the doctor's office through a back door... Asher replayed the scene silently in his head, going over every sequence, every detail, every line. Somehow it was no longer Jessica as Lillian, Asher pictured kissing. It was Kate. He longed for her, to crush his body against hers. To really have her and feel her response to him. Asher's nostrils flared, his jaw clenched, his shoulders stiffened with strain.

"That's *it*!" Xavier said, from a dozen feet away. He'd intended to speak with Asher, when he'd noted the physical changes taking place on Asher's face. Xavier had watched in silence until he'd seen what he'd been looking for in his actor. "*That's* the look I need, Ash. Whatever you're thinking of right now, don't stop. I don't care what it is, I don't need to know. I simply need to capture it on film. Let's go, everyone! Places!"

Kate-

Breathing in the cool morning air, my head began to clear. Asher'd said we had to be careful and he was right. I was trying, but it wasn't easy when my body was being awakened to such yearnings.

Deciding I needed a quick intervention to get my mind off Asher, I cared for the chickens—a perfectly mundane task, and collected the eggs. Nothing in the least romantic or passion-inducing about that. Then I cleaned the horse stalls and turned them out in the paddock. I caught one of the new geldings and after riding him, because it had been a long while since I'd ridden Red, I saddled him as well. I didn't bother with the arena; Red and I needed a good solid ride.

I set the big red horse to a gallop almost from the moment we left the ranch yard. We passed several members of the film crew who either waved or stood by and quietly watched our passing. Near the Jump Off, I came upon Scotty exercising one of the buckskin geldings that were used as a spare for Asher. I brought Red to a stop; he fought that, dancing around, pawing the ground, determined to continue our ride.

"Where you headin' KatyBeth?" Scotty asked.

"Just giving this big fella some TLC. I'll be back in an hour or so. Ash wants to go into town tonight, take a break and get pizza. Pass it around, will ya?"

"Will do. You think you might have an opportunity to look at that horse when you get back?"

"You know what, Scotty? I will have. Don't saddle him or anything. Have his gear available for me, though. See you in bit."

CHAPTER THIRTEEN

This Time the Fight is Mine

Kate-

I stood in the middle of the large arena, the sun warm on my back, and a little trickle of sweat ran between my shoulder blades. My wild run with Red had loosened me up. I was ready for whatever this horse had to throw at me. I adjusted my baseball cap and tightened the elastic in my hair. Scotty stood next me.

"Tell me about him, Scotty." I looked the golden colt over, admiring his form.

"His name's Brisco. He's four. I had him cut when he was a yearling."

"He's your horse?"

"Was. I sold him to the studio. The final bill of sale is contingent upon his being ready and ride-able. You know my back is bad from that bull-riding injury, right? Just can't take the rough pounding anymore. I can ride him, and for the most part he takes everything well but as you can see, he's wound tighter than a top. He's such a beautiful animal; I didn't have the heart to dump him. I've been waiting until I had some free time to work with him, but never seem to find any. When Asher mentioned you and your skill, well, I thought I'd give it a shot."

I nodded. "Fair enough. Please step out of the arena, and, Scotty, keep everyone else out as well. No one, and I mean *no one*, comes in here. Got it?"

"Sure. I got it." Scotty gave me a quick piercing look, then left the pen.

Scotty had left Brisco's saddle and bridle on the ground beside me. Picking up the halter and lead rope, I walked toward the big dun.

Brisco snorted; his nostrils extended as I opened the gate to the small round pen he was in. He made a rush for the open gate, but I waved the rope at him and he shied away. The big horse trotted to the far side of the corral and stopped with his backside faced in my general direction. He threw his head high and rolled his eyes, snorting loudly.

Big, tough, guy, I thought. *Well, Brisco, you're about to learn some manners. And the first one is, you never, ever show me your backside unless you want me to smack it.* And with that, I hauled off and slapped the rope across his rump. He squealed and jumped, kicking out with his hind legs. I wasn't within reach, but I didn't like the attitude behind *that* action either, so I waved the rope at him again, and soon had him running in a tight circle around the small pen.

I kept Brisco moving for about five minutes; then I lowered the rope and mellowed my voice, "Whoa, big fella. Easy does it. Whoooa."

By this time, Brisco had worked up a bit of a sweat, but he settled down enough to stop, turning to face me. Staying in place, I called to him. After a moment, he lowered his head and stepped lightly in my direction, continuing one step at a time until he was right in front of me. I didn't make any attempt to move, just kept talking to him, soothing him. After a moment Brisco was rubbing his head against me. Carefully, I moved my hand up, rubbing his forehead, scratching all around his ears. I wanted to see how sensitive he was, if he startled easy; I found nothing to indicate he was bothered. Reaching in my pocket, I pulled apple bites out, offering them to him; he took those readily enough, chomping them in quiet satisfaction.

Brisco stood patiently as I haltered him, then led him from the pen to where the saddle and bridle were sitting. Using the rag from my back pocket, I did a quick rub-down on the horse, making sure he had no burs or sores that might be affected by the saddle or my weight once I mounted him. Brisco stood still, giving me no problems, seeming content to receive attention from me. After the gelding was saddled and bridled, I walked him in a wide circle, watching for any sign of lameness, and found nothing.

Adjusting the stirrups, and making sure the girth was tight, I gathered the reins and stepped lightly into the saddle. I sat still for a moment or two, allowing the horse to adjust to me. Once I could feel him settling down, I put him into motion.

We started at a walk and gradually moved into a canter. I stopped him and started him again. I worked him with leg pressure, side-stepping him several paces. I slapped my hand on my thigh, trying to get him to do something. I could tell what Scotty meant, Brisco was doing what I asked, but you could feel the tension inside waiting to erupt.

I wanted the eruption.

We rode this way for another thirty minutes. During this time, I absently noticed Asher and Samuel had returned. They joined a group of people, including Cory, watching silently from the fence line.

I brought Brisco to a stop, spun him in a tight circle, then shot him off at a dead run. I brought him skidding to a stop, then repeated the process.

All hell broke loose when I asked the big horse to back up.

Brisco reared a bit and jumped sideways, angrily shaking his head. I steadied him, then tried again to get him to back up. The golden horse gave a giant leap to the side and reared high, hooves pawing the air. Leaning forward over the cantle, I waited for him to descend. As soon as I felt him touch down, I dug my heels into his sides; he squealed in anger and leaped forward in bucking spurts.

This continued for several feet, then I decided I'd had enough. I pulled his head up and around with his nose facing back at me; in his struggle we almost went over, but he managed to keep his balance.

Spinning him in a tight circle, I kicked him forward again. Like before, Brisco moved well until I asked him to back up. He reared high, once more fighting me. This time, I didn't wait for him to come down, but kicked my boots from the stirrups and jerked him over backwards. Asher gave a frightened yell, but I kept my focus on what I was doing. Distantly, I heard Samuel and Calvin trying to calm him down. *Good, keep him out of here.*

As Brisco lost his balance, keeling over, I rolled to avoid being crushed by his massive frame, and heard the saddle tree crack with the impact. The gelding thrashed, legs in the air, before scrambling upright. I'd been watching for this. As soon as he had his stomach under him, I leaped back into the saddle, one of the split reins still in my grasp.

Lurching to his feet, Brisco snorted, then stood still, his whole frame shaking. Speaking softly, I rubbed his shoulder. Gently, I leaned down and gathered the other rein; and once again, asked the big horse to back up.

This time he did so without a fuss. I backed him clear across that arena, from one side to the other. Then I moved him forward into a figure eight. The saddle was uncomfortable with the broken tree, but I only needed it to last a few more minutes. Once again, I brought Brisco to a sliding stop, then backed him up.

He gave me no further problems—seemed calm and willing to please now—so I brought him to a stop. Scratching his shoulder, I spoke in a soothing voice. Brisco's ears were pricked in my direction; he was listening to me. His head was lowered; there was no pull to the bit. He'd given himself to my will. Knowing this was as much as I'd be able to do today, I went ahead and dismounted.

Though I'd heard his frightened yell, I did not look towards Asher, simply not having the strength to face him yet. Unsaddling the gelding, I rubbed him down, and checked his mouth to make sure he wasn't sore or injured. Satisfied he was sound, I fed him a couple more apple bites, before turning him back into the round pen.

Turning the saddle over, I did a quick inspection. It didn't take long to see Scotty'd need a whole new rig. Kneeling beside me, he gently asked, "Busted that one right up, didn't he? You alright?"

"Sure. Sorry about the saddle. I think we made progress. I'll put some more time on him; I think that's all he really needs."

"I sure appreciate it. Listen, you'd better go talk with Ash. That spill really spooked him. Your buddy Cal and I kept him from coming in here, but I think he needs to see you. I've never seen the big guy lose it like that before." Nodding, I stood, looking for Asher. "He's in the barn. That fella Samuel is keeping everyone out until Ash has himself well in control. Go on, Katy, I'll get this."

"Thanks, Scotty." Pulling my ball cap off, I deftly took the elastic from my hair and ran my fingers through it. That seemed to ease a little of the tension I felt. When I reached the barn, Calvin, Cory, and Samuel were standing guard. Samuel nodded; his eyes concerned. Calvin looked me over, could see I was uninjured, then he too, nodded.

"He's in there. You scared him; be gentle, okay?" Sammy said.

"I'll make sure you guys have a minute. No funny business, though." Calvin smiled when I tossed my ball cap at him as I walked by.

Asher-

When Asher arrived back at the house, he'd immediately noticed the group crowded around the arena. His sharp eyes had quickly spotted Kate on the big horse. He didn't remember moving toward the gate, but somehow, he found himself there, his hand on the latch. Vaguely, he'd heard Scotty trying to reason with him; the short, redhead bravely stood between Asher and the gate. It was Samuel who convinced him to remain where he was—if Asher entered the arena now, Kate might become distracted and in such a situation, could prove fatal to her.

So, Asher stood there outside the fence, feeling more helpless than he'd ever felt in his life. He watched the woman he knew he was in love with clinging to the back of the wild horse, her body twisting and moving with the crazed actions of the animal she rode.

When the dun horse went over backwards, and her name was ripped from his throat, Asher lost all ability to function. Calvin, Scotty, Cory, and Samuel had launched themselves at him; each taking a hold, trying to reason with him and prevent him from entering the corral. It was a useless endeavor. Had Asher been able to move, to control his body at all, he would have killed them. The horse, too.

His heart resumed its thunderous pace when he saw Kate was, once again, in the saddle and in control. His breath came in sharp bursts, and his mouth tasted of copper. He shivered all over. Without a word to anyone, Asher turned and walked away, unsure of where he was even going.

Kate-

It took a minute for my eyes to adjust when I first entered the barn. When they did, I found him standing in the middle of the building, hands on his hips. Even in the dim light, I could see his face was still white. Asher didn't move, though I was sure he'd heard me. His entire frame was rigid with tension, like barely suppressed energy masked in a still, quiet façade.

Calmly, I walked past him to the small fridge near the tack room to get a bottle of water. My mouth felt dry and dusty and somehow, I knew in a moment I was not going to want a dusty mouth. For some insane reason, I suddenly thought of that old Orbit chewing gum commercial: *For a good clean feeling, no matter what!* I could hear the British woman's accent in my head, and chuckled nervously. At the sound, Asher sucked in a sharp breath, so I turned to face him. Holding still so he could see me clearly, I waited. He still hadn't moved, other than to turn his head to follow my progress across the barn.

In fact, the only thing moving on him was his chest. He breathed slowly, deeply. His eyes...they roved all over me, seemingly assuring I was in one piece.

I inhaled, about to speak, when something in his eyes, some look, suddenly made it impossible. Asher's hard stare held for a moment longer, then he lost the battle. I saw the moment his strong will failed and had seconds to brace myself.

He crossed the barn in three long strides; his arms wrapped around me, lifting, and pulling me against him. I lost my grip on the bottle, unsure where it landed. Trembling, Asher buried his face in my hair, and just breathed. He held still for a long moment, almost undecided as to what his next move would be. A low, almost pained sound came from deep inside him and I felt him lift his head. He must have found what he'd been looking for, because suddenly he was moving again—still holding me. My arms were tight around his strong neck; my fingers curled into his thick, dark hair. Asher slid his hands down my back, my sides, to my hips, making me shiver.

His hands slid farther down my thighs, grasping, lifting me still further, warming me through my jeans. Suddenly, my back was against a wall, a bench or something firm was under me. *We must be in the tack room.* Asher held still now, his body pressing, holding mine in place. One arm was around my waist and the other around my thigh; his face was buried in my shoulder. He shuddered violently, seemingly trying to regain control of himself. "Kate," he muttered, his voice low, pleading, and vibrant with need. "Tell me to stop." Before I could consider, much less comply with his request, Asher's hands were moving again. At my hips, he squeezed, then jerked me closer. Upward, his hands glided over my ribs, around to my back, across my shoulders. At my neck he stopped. His body still trembling, still holding mine firmly in place, as he seemingly willed himself to go no further.

His will was still shot, apparently, because with a groan he hooked his thumbs under my jaw and firmly pushed upward.

Asher's mouth barely touched mine. He moved his lips, a light pressure, slowly back and forth. Pent up tension and frustration had me whisper, pleadingly, "*Kiss* me!" He locked in place for all of one breath, then *finally* his mouth slammed against mine.

When Asher had kissed me before he'd been gentle; he wasn't gentle now. He was relentless. His hands weaved themselves into my hair, gripping, holding me. Mine were wound tightly around him, straining to be closer, neither of us even considering stopping or separating.

I honestly have no idea how long we stayed that way, or what might have happened had the interruption not occurred when it did. I'd like to think once the initial burst of heat had burned, we would have come to our senses. Asher and I both heard someone loudly clearing his throat from behind us. Asher's shoulders were so wide, he was so big, I couldn't see who it was. But I distinctly heard Asher's growled warning at whoever it was.

"You two need to pull it together." Samuel ignored the implied threat. "Jackson just pulled up."

Reluctantly, Asher released me; his fingers slowly untangling from my hair, pealing his body from mine. His mouth was red; mine felt swollen. We were both breathing hard. Glancing around his shoulders, I saw Samuel had his back to us, still trying to give us some privacy.

"Are you alright?" Asher rasped, his lips against my forehead.

"I think so." I whispered back. "You?"

"I honestly couldn't say. But your dad is out there, and I'm going to need a moment to cool off before I leave this room." He moved to the side, giving me room to slide off the bench he'd had me braced upon. I waited a moment for the room to stop spinning before gingerly slipping down to my feet. "Go on, Love." He jerked his chin towards the door. "I'll be along in a moment."

I took a steadying breath. "I'm going to get ready...if you still want to go out?"

"I do. I'll see you in a little while."

Kate-

Asher, Calvin, and Samuel went to the counter at Billy Bob's Pizzeria to place our order. The twins headed directly to the old-fashioned juke box in the corner, and Cory slid onto the seat across from mine; his gaze very direct. Inquiringly, I stared back at him. "We haven't had much opportunity to chat, KatyBeth," he stated in introduction.

"So I've noticed, Cory."

"I can't figure you out," he said finally, implied accusation in his tone. I remained silent—*if you can't say anything nice, it's best to say nothing at all*—and figured he'd eventually get to the point. "What's your angle here?" he demanded. "What are you after? Oh, I can see you've got Asher wrapped up nice and tight, but I'm still trying to figure out why. What do you hope to gain?" I took a calming breath, determined to not lose my temper. Cory watched, gauging my reaction. "You're beautiful, don't get me wrong. But Ash knows *a lot* of beautiful women—what's so special about you?"

"There's nothing special about me, Cory." My lips felt stiff. "I'm simply me."

"Well, there's something. I've never seen Ash like this before."

"Maybe you should ask *him*, then. I really can't help you."

Cory studied me, waiting for me to defend myself in some way. I refused to give in to his challenge and after another moment or two he said, "Ash goes to church with you." He said it like he was somehow personally offended by Asher's actions.

I smiled. "Yes, I'm aware."

"You really expect me to believe you're some goody-two-shoes, innocent and all that?"

"I don't really care what you believe, Cory."

"You know you're not innocent; you're no better than I am."

"I never claimed to be."

"You're *Christians*, right? Just a bunch of judgmental bigots looking down on everyone else."

Before I could respond, Asher returned. "Cory, *that* is enough." His voice was low and furious as he sat beside me.

"It's alright, Ash. I'd like to address this." My gaze stayed glued to Cory as I said, "*Real* Christians don't hate anyone. There're a lot of folks who call themselves Christian that pay no attention at all to the teachings of Christ. I can't do anything about those people. I'm only in charge of myself. And I don't *hate* anyone. To do so would be tremendously hypocritical on my part. But, it's not hateful to say something is wrong or to even disagree with it." Cory silently stared at me, so I tried again. "Do you like lies?" Cory shook his head once. "So, does that mean you hate people who tell lies? Because, by your reasoning, not liking lies means you hate anyone who tells a lie." Stubbornly, Cory remained silent; I figured this had more to do with Asher's presence than anything I was saying. "I can dislike lies and still love the person who tells them. Can't you see that? I would have to hate everyone, *myself* included, if I could only love those who are without fault. And, it's not judgmental to say I dislike lies or that telling lies is wrong—I have to remember that in God's eyes—I'm just as guilty as the next person."

Cory stared silently, then nodded and stood, rapping his knuckles on the table, though I thought I detected a slight softening in his gaze. He took his cup, heading towards the soda fountain.

Concerned, Asher leaned over, pressing a kiss to my temple. I smiled and squeezed his hand to show I was fine, and hoped Cory and I had come to an understanding, truly not wanting to be a source of conflict. Asher kissed my temple again, letting his lips linger.

A little while later, I felt him stiffen. Glancing up, I followed Asher's gaze, and groaned inwardly; Johnny Khyle had just arrived. He stood inside the double doors, letting his eyes roam around, no doubt searching for the most action he could find.

The instant his gaze landed on me, Asher flexed, preparing for a fight. I gripped his hand tighter, hoping everyone would stay calm.

Asher glanced down, relaxing when he saw the pleading look on my face. He took a deep breath and settled back in his seat. Samuel, however, was on full alert. I caught the slight nod Asher gave him as they'd exchanged looks. Samuel's gaze focused on Johnny; the look a calculating one. A slight, ill-humored grin slowly spread across his face.

Johnny strolled his way past us to the bar, letting his gaze linger over me. He ordered a drink, then turned to face our table again. I noticed Jessica perk up as she saw him. After a minute or two of checking each other out, she made her way over.

He greeted her with a smile and indicated the seat next to him. As annoying as Jessica was, I worried about her with Johnny. She only saw his handsome face—I knew him for a first-class pig. I hoped for her sake she would wizen up and see through his smile.

Asher asked if I wanted to stay longer, and I shook my head, thinking it would be a good idea to head home before anything happened. As we stood, I glanced over my shoulder and saw Johnny and Jessica were no longer at the bar. A quick look around the room proved they were nowhere in sight.

"What's the matter, Katy?" Calvin asked.

"Did Jessica leave with Johnny?" I hadn't seen them leave, but I'd been focused on Ash.

"Yeah; I tried to warn her. She wouldn't hear anything I had to say; warned him, too, though he probably took that as a challenge."

Our group gathered in the parking lot, chatting for a few minutes, laughing, and reminiscing about the fun we'd had earlier. Suddenly, I heard a loud catcall and cringed. Johnny stood beside his jacked-up truck, one arm resting on the painted, shimmering flames that spread across the hood.

"Come on, KatyBeth," he called over the music coming from his speakers "come let your hair down." Jonny slung an arm around Jessica, pulling her close.

Asher growled, taking a step towards him; I quickly grabbed his arm, holding him back. "Ash, ignore him. *Please*? We've had such a fun night, don't let this turn into a fight again."

"You're staying out of this," he said firmly.

"Hey, ugly, let her go. She's got it comin'," Johnny taunted suggestively.

"Johnny!" I yelled, still firmly holding onto Asher's arm. "Shut your stupid mouth, you idiot!"

"You won't catch me off guard again, Katy. I'm ready, and I'd take you conscious or unconscious—it's all the same to me."

Asher advanced several feet this time before I was able to stop him. Honestly, I wasn't sure I had stopped him. As I was breathing a sigh of relief, he quickly turned, flipping me carefully over his shoulder. Suddenly, I found myself upside down, staring at the asphalt in Billy Bob's parking lot.

Asher-

Asher knew when Johnny began spouting his disgusting innuendos about Kate, he was still not recovered from the shock or acute fear he'd felt earlier this afternoon. And like this afternoon, he'd immediately spotted the danger. Unlike then, however, Asher knew exactly how to handle this—with fist and fury.

In a matter of seconds, he had Kate over his shoulder, ignoring her demands. He gently delivered her into Calvin's care. "Do *not* let her go. For *any* reason." His voice and tone held all the promise of hell to pay if Calvin deviated even a little. Glancing at Samuel and Cory, he said, "Make sure she stays put. And you two stay out—this one's mine."

Scotty said something about watching for cops and Asher turned, bee-lining directly to where Johnny stood smirking.

"You'll be lucky, if I kill you." Unmistakable promise throbbed in his voice. "Right now, I'm just going to make you scream." Asher barely took note of the shocked look on Jessica's face, though he did see the fear and uncertainty flash in Johnny's eyes as he finished with a warning to the actress. "Unless you want blood on your clothes, you'd better walk away." Jessica took a couple steps back, but remained close, as if she wasn't convinced violence was about to be committed here.

"Come and get it you freaking puke," Asher taunted. Growling, Johnny swung a roundhouse that Asher easily sidestepped. They danced that way for several minutes. Johnny trying again, and again to land a punch, Asher easily avoiding every attempt. From the look in Johnny's eye, he was beginning to feel desperate, beginning to feel as if his opponent was only playing with him.

Suddenly, without warning, the tempo changed. Asher struck, going on the offensive, slapping Johnny across the face, snapping his head back and splitting his cheek open. Before Johnny could set himself, Asher backhanded him, this time with his left hand. The force of the blow spun Johnny around, slamming him into the side of his truck. His head bounced off the door, his lips bloody. For a moment, Johnny clung to the handle, seemingly trying to steady himself and catch his breath. Shock was evident in the whiteness of his face. Asher move behind him, and Johnny swung around, his back now against the truck.

"We're not done yet." Asher told him, waiting.

Johnny suddenly lunged forward, whipping a knife from behind his back. He smiled in triumph. "I'm gonna kill you now," his words slurring through his shredded and swollen mouth. "Then I'll have her, good and hard."

Asher let the fury take him. With lightning speed, he spun, kicking Johnny's wrist, breaking it, sending the knife flying. Johnny screamed a high-pitched shriek. Jessica stumbled backwards, falling to her knees, covering her ears with trembling hands; her eyes frozen wide open. Asher picked Johnny up by the shirtfront and threw him into the side of the truck, denting it. Instead of letting him drop, as Johnny was desperately trying to do, Asher held him, bracing him against the truck. Holding him with his left hand, Asher punched Johnny repeatedly with his right.

Finally, Asher let him drop to the pavement. Looking with disgust at the crumpled, broken man, now sobbing and vomiting on himself, he warned, "Next time, I *will* kill you." Then Asher turned to Jessica. "We're leaving. Now." Unable to speak, she turned to our group, her breath rattling out of her.

By the time Asher made his way back to Kate, everyone else had cleared out. It was only the two of them. She didn't speak at all and he wondered what was going on in her head. After a moment, he gently took her by the hand, leading her to the bike. On the ride home she'd wrapped her arms around him, holding him tightly.

CHAPTER FOURTEEN

Boys Will Be Boys... and Men

Kate-

Mom and Dad went to bed shortly after we got home. They'd been concerned when they'd first heard of the trouble, but were quickly relieved to hear I'd come to no harm, and that Asher had so thoroughly defended me. Calvin and the twins were seated at the table along with Samuel and Cory. Everyone else had either gone home or to their own sleeping quarters.

My thoughts were in a whirl and it was difficult to pin any of them down. Leaving them to their conversations, needing fresh air, still somewhat keyed up, I went out the back to the patio, shivering in the chill. After a few moments, Asher joined me. "You okay?" he asked, breaking the silence. If I'd been worried somehow Johnny might have been able to hurt Asher in any way—after watching them—I had to admit the only injury Asher might have received was simply from the extreme hardness of Johnny's skull.

As far as skill went, there was absolutely no comparison.

I'd seen Johnny fight before, knew what he was capable of. Asher made him look like a second-grade kid trying to take on a heavy weight prize-fighter.

Leaning against the railing, I crossed my arms over my chest. "Weren't you scared at all when he pulled that knife?"

"No," he shook his head, his demeanor calm and certain "not even a little bit."

Exasperation rocketed through me at his show of confidence. "How can you even *say* that?" With a growl of frustration, I slapped my hands against my thighs. "You could have been killed."

"As you might have this afternoon."

"That's different. I train horses, it's what I do."

"And I know what I'm doing. I wasn't in any danger, trust me."

"He had a *knife!*" Agitation and remembered panic had my voice rising a couple of octaves.

"Kate. *Love,*" Asher pulled me into his arms, his voice soft and gentle. "It may have looked frightening to you, and I *am* sorry you were worried, but believe me, please, I *do* know what I'm doing—I wasn't in any danger, at all."

Not entirely convinced, I decided to let it drop, especially since he was, in fact, safe, here, and holding me. Asher pulled me closer still, his mouth against my forehead. His body heating and calming mine.

Asher-

As he lay in bed that night, Asher thought back over the day. It had been a lot. A lot to take in and process. His thoughts whirled considering it all, before landing on Kate. Always his thoughts were on her. He could still taste her skin, still feel it on his lips. His hands tingled in remembrance. This afternoon, in the barn. He'd come close, so close to forgetting himself. Forgetting his promise to not take things too far. She hadn't helped. Kate. Her desire had been burning hot. Making him want her even more. Absentmindedly, he rubbed his knuckle and felt the bruise; his thoughts shifting to this evening. To how things could have gone so very, very wrong. He regretted nothing he'd done to Khyle. Only regretted causing Kate any disturbance. She'd been worried about him. Concerned for him. She hadn't been shocked or disgusted. She hadn't feared him, and that was what he'd feared the most. That if she ever saw him like that...he couldn't put voice to those thoughts. Instead, she'd held him tighter, pulled him closer. She still loved him. Asher would be forever grateful for that. His mouth curved as warmth settled in his chest, his emotions running strong.

Kate-

The following morning, as I reached the patio, returning from the morning feeding, Asher stepped outside. My pulse kicked up a notch and I took a moment to appreciate him.

"Good morning." His blue eyes smiled. "You look beautiful."

"I was just thinking the same about you."

"How're you feeling? No residual effects from yesterday?" he asked.

"None. You?"

"Never better." Asher pulled me close, his mouth lingering against mine. "Never better," he repeated, his lips teasing, gently nipping mine. "I've been thinking..."

"About?" I breathed.

"Yesterday."

"What about yesterday?"

"I was thinking...about what happened in the barn." Teeth grazed my jawline, making me shiver.

Heat bloomed. "What about it?"

"If I remember correctly, you didn't tell me to stop, like I'd asked you to."

"Um, no, I guess I...didn't...didn't want you to stop. Right then." Concentration was near impossible as his mouth continued provoking mine.

"That's not being very careful, now is it?"

Trying to pull him in for a real kiss, tired of the teasing, I whispered, "I'm sorry."

"I'm not." Asher pulled away from me, the look in his eyes serious. "Don't ever be sorry for feeling that."

"Okay, I won't be sorry about it," My forehead came to a rest against his chest, his heart thumping fast. "Maybe we should forget about it, for the time being at least, though."

"I can't forget about it, can't forget about you. The way you feel, the way..." Asher stopped. "I know; not helping."

Chuckling, I stepped back and shivered under the heat from his gaze. As I reached for the back door, I said, "The coffee's on, did you have a cup?"

"Not yet. I'm going for a run; save me a cup, will you?"

Nodding, I smiled, then headed inside.

Later that morning as Asher read over the script, I drove to the location the next scenes were to be shot at. I wondered how many extras would be used for today's cattle drive scene and where the director had found them; and if I'd know any.

When we arrived, Xavier quickly pulled me aside, needing to talk. He'd appreciated my riding abilities so much, he'd decided *I* was needed for the cattle drive scene as well. I stammered and blushed my way through a refusal he refused to hear. Before I knew it, I was whisked off to wardrobe and makeup. Having long hair and a substantial chest, I had no idea what they'd be able to do with me.

Turned out making movies really was like magic. My hair was twisted and pinned on my head to keep it in place. I was given a binder bra to give me a flatter figure and a heavy leather vest, two sizes too big, to wear over the large men's western shirt. Standing back, looking at myself in the mirror, if I hadn't known I was a woman, *I'd* even be convinced I was a man.

They found a large brimmed grey hat to help hide my hair. Makeup made me look like a young man in need of a shave. My shirt was a nondescript, faded blue. I was given a dirty brown bandana to hide the graceful curve my neck possessed. At least, that's what the nice lady helping with my costume told me. My pants were brown and I wore a pair of chaps. The other extras and I were told to wait by the horses for further instruction.

As Scotty walked by, I was tickled he didn't recognize me. "Hey, Scotty, pretty good disguise, huh?" I teased.

"Katy? My word—that *is* you. Wow, you look good, but I gotta say, I prefer you with less facial hair." Scotty laughed as he gently tugged the brim of my hat. "I'll see you in a minute. I need to get these horses finished."

"You need a hand?"

"I could use one, yeah, but with you as an extra today, Xavier wouldn't like it. Thanks though, see you in a few."

Asher-

Asher was impatient. Wardrobe and makeup took longer than he wanted. Kate was out there waiting for him, surrounded by men; and she was beautiful. Sarah, his makeup artist, had to ask him to sit still several times. Twice she'd had to reapply his whiskers. Then, wardrobe couldn't locate his vest. That took ten minutes to track down. By the time Asher was finished and outside the trailer, he thought he'd have ground his teeth down to the gums. And of course, when he found her, she was indeed surrounded by a group of interested men.

Kate looked like a man; at least they'd dressed her like one. Asher'd heard she'd been conscripted for today's shoot. He spotted her right off the bat. She was still beautiful. Still desirable. And every man there noticed it, too.

Kate-

A few of my fellow extras introduced themselves; I was the only woman in the group. Scotty walked up then, and began assigning horses. He turned to me. "Katy, I think I've got Red saddled properly. You want to check him?"

"Sure." I was beyond tickled Red would be in the movie.

"The gunsmith is coming. He'll go over a few things with you all, then we'll prepare for the shoot. You all have fun. And be safe."

Rodney Stewart—no relation to the singer by the same name—was the gunsmith. He assigned each of us a weapon. Rodney made sure we understood our firearms. He explained that these were real guns, and could shoot real bullets, though they'd only be loaded with blanks if any shots were needed. Ours were all empty. As I listened to him explain about real bullets and dummy rounds, I couldn't help but think about one of my favorite comedies, *The Three Amigos*, when Lucky gets shot and shows Dusty and Ned the *real bullets*. Silently, I chuckled, trying not to disturb the others. Scotty noticed, though, turning in my direction, an inquiring look in his eyes. I whispered, "Sorry. This made me think of *The Three Amigos*."

Bless him, Scotty knew exactly what I was referring to. We both had to stifle our laughter several times.

As we waited for Xavier to call the scene, Asher made his way over. I'd wondered if he'd be able to pick me out, hoping he'd be able to. Sure enough, he'd spotted me right away.

"I can honestly say, Kate, you're the first man I've ever found myself attracted to." He tweaked the brim of my hat with a grin. *Queue Aerosmith's Dude Looks Like a Lady,* I thought to myself.

Before I could respond, Scotty said in a mock-serious tone, "You son-of-a-motherless-goat." His comment had me doubling over in laughter, tears streaming down my face. Scotty wheezed; he was laughing so hard. Asher'd apparently never seen *The Three Amigos,* so our humor at his expense was lost on him. After I'd caught my breath, I promised we'd watch the movie soon. He tweaked my hat brim again, humor in his eyes. I think he might have done more, but several of the other extras approached us.

"You guys are in for a treat." Asher said. "Kate's a genuine cowboy. She's the real deal; I've learned a lot from her already." Heat touched my face, as I saw the appraising looks from the men around me.

Shortly after, the scene was called and we mounted up. It took close to a couple hours to film and went off without a hitch. I'd been able to give some helpful hints to my fellow riders; and we looked, if I do say so myself, like an experienced trail crew. Asher, of course, was the trail boss, and he filled the role well, having had previous real-life experience. I enjoyed myself immensely; however, I'll admit it was nice to be in my own skin again. Leaving my hair down, I reveled in the feel of its freedom after it had been pinned so tightly to my scalp.

Sitting on the tailgate of the Jeep, I waited for Ash to finish with the wardrobe people. A few of the other extras I'd met earlier came over, chatting with me—flirted really. I was flattered, yet guarded, not being interested in any of them.

After about fifteen minutes of small talk, one of them—Clancy—finally worked up the nerve. "I'll be in the area for the next couple of weeks; you want to catch dinner one night, you and me?"

I inhaled, preparing to answer his kind request—wondering at the same time, how he'd missed the familiarity between Asher and me earlier. Maybe he'd chalked it up to simply working together and nothing more—however, before I could respond, I heard, "Not happening."

Everyone turned to the source. "Sorry," Asher said, "but Kate's spoken for, guys." He didn't look at me as he spoke, but rather the five men standing around me.

"Sorry," Clancy stated affably, hands out to the side. "I didn't know."

"Now you do." Asher's voice was friendly, the look in his eye not so much.

"I didn't mean anything by it, man. If I'd known, I wouldn't have said anything. I'm not trying to stir up trouble."

"It's fine, Clancy. Don't worry about it. As Asher has indicated, I'm not—"

"She's not available." Asher interrupted.

Clancy nodded, an uncomfortable look on his face. "I'll see you around then, I guess." Asher watched him walk away, let his eyes touch over the others, encouraging their departure. After they'd gone, he placed his hands around my waist, lifting me to the ground. I waited for him to speak. He didn't. He simply closed the tailgate and walked to the passenger door, opening it for me. Climbing in, I handed him the keys. Asher closed the door, then made his way to the driver's side and stepped in.

After about five minutes, silence the only thing being exchanged between us, I said, "You want to tell me what that was about?"

"Only being honest with him."

"You were kind of rude. Clancy wasn't being a jerk. He asked me out is all."

"I was letting him know you're not available, *is all*."

"You sound jealous. I was about to let him know I was kind of seeing someone." Exasperation sparked in me.

"I *was* jealous." Asher stared through the windshield. "I *am* jealous."

"Why? I don't understand. Did I do something?"

"No, you didn't *do* anything. I'll need to work on that, I guess—my reactions to all your admirers."

"Ash, I hope you don't think I did anything to cause this; I didn't. I don't flirt. I didn't look for this reaction, from them, or from you. I'm not like that."

"I know that; it's one of the many, many things I admire about you. You're beautiful beyond words and yet, you have no idea the power you wield over us mere mortal men."

"Be serious. I'm sorry you were jealous."

"I *am* serious, very serious." His voice shifted, the tone becoming grave. "I know I told you we'd take things slow. And I'm still willing to do so. However, I find myself in need of more. I need to *know* you belong to me and I belong to you. I need it clear between *us*. I need it understood by those around us. You may not take seriously the attraction the men you associate with have for you, but from the small amount of time I've spent with you, *I* sure have noticed it."

He suddenly stopped the Jeep, putting it into park on the side of the dirt road. Turning to me, he reached out, entwining our hands.

I looked at him. "What are you saying?"

"I think it's time we redefined the nature of our relationship." Asher leaned over suddenly and kissed me. Just a gentle pressure of his lips on mine, but I sighed quietly, my eyes fluttered closed. His breath tickled my face as he pulled back, and I blinked my eyes open. "There is *no* denying I feel a very strong physical attraction to you," he hesitated a moment, seemingly unsure how to proceed. "I'm not innocent like you, Kate. I've been with women—I can't change any of that. What's stupid is I never felt even a *fraction* for them what I feel for you. When I'm with you, I want to be a better man. You inspire me."

Asher gripped my hand, squeezing gently before continuing. "I want you—you know that. It's killing me how much I want you, literally *killing me*. But it's more than that, more than strong desire. There are other needs I'm feeling, and they're as powerful as the physical one. I don't know how to describe it. It's your laughter. Your thoughts. Your needs. Your desires. It's your dreams. Your likes and dislikes. Your smiles and your frowns. It's your fears. It's you, Kate. I need you. I want *you*."

Quickly, I swiped my hand across my eyes, thankful I wasn't wearing any mascara, because I was sure it would have been running. Unfortunately, the tears continued to fall. "Every single word you said is what I've been thinking in my head. I mean, not the whole part about being with other women, but the part about the needs. I have those same needs for you. And, you inspire me, too, Ash."

"So, where do we go from here?" Asher placed a soft kiss on the tip of my nose as he wiped the tears from my face. "May I make a suggestion?"

The smile I gave him was a little wobbly; Ash gently squeezed my hand again, lifting it to place a kiss against my knuckles, his teeth lingering there. "Let's start by telling your parents. Everyone else seems to have figured it out, and I'm sure they've picked up on us, too. But I still think we should tell them first, you know...officially. If they have any concerns about our relationship, I'd like to hear them now."

I nodded. "Have you told your parents yet?"

"I'll call them tonight," He promised. "Now that's settled, I have something in mind." The look in his eyes sent heat spiraling through me. Asher started slow, refusing to rush. Moving in controlled, deliberate actions, he leaned closer. Pulling the collar of my shirt to the side, he placed a kiss on my shoulder. I felt his breath on my skin, felt his slow inhale, heard his throaty growl. Slowly, in agonizing purpose, he rubbed his mouth, his lips up my neck to my ear, then on to my jaw.

His mouth teased along my jawline, kissing up to the corner of my mouth, then held steady for a moment. His arms slid around me, pulling me closer, difficult in the small confines of the Jeep. His mouth left my skin and I knew instant frustration, trying to pull him back. Asher chuckled as he traced my collarbone with his index finger, then up to my mouth. His thumb stroked my lips, then he slowly lowered his head.

Our lips met with gentle intensity, me surging against him, desperate to be closer. My hands came up to his chest, grasping his shirtfront. Asher leaned into my touch, seemingly enjoying the feel of my hands on him. Far too soon, he pulled back, putting some distance between us. With a somewhat impish grin was on his face, he said, "So not helping my self-control." My mouth lifted in answer, our eyes holding for moment or two, then Asher drove us home.

CHAPTER FIFTEEN

Mom, Dad, I Can Explain—Maybe

Kate-

Later that afternoon, as I was peeling a cucumber for the salad, Asher was suddenly behind me. His hands on the counter, one on either side of me, his chest against my back. He nuzzled along my shoulder and neck. His teeth grazed my ear lobe and I shivered, dropping the cucumber and knife in the sink. My breath caught in my throat as my eyes began to close. "Mmm..." he said, his lips against my throat. "I don't know if you can imagine how it makes me feel to be able to do this."

"I know how *I* feel when you do that..." I reached my hands up and ran my fingers through his hair, pulling him closer. He chuckled softly as he nipped the skin on my neck again, before pulling back. His breath ruffled my hair even as his forehead rested against the back of my head. I was about to turn in his arms when we heard boots on the porch, fast approaching. Asher stepped to the side and leaned against the counter, crossing his arms over his chest. I picked up the cucumber and after rinsing it off, began to peel it again. Calvin gave us a sharp look as he came in. I slid over to give him room at the sink to wash up.

"No need to ask how you two are doing." Calvin stated. "I can smell romance in the air."

My mouth curved upward as Asher chuckled. "You're sharp, Cal. If you'd asked, I'd have said we're fantastic. Satisfied?"

"Not hardly. You're stealing my girl." Though his tone was serious, his demeanor was friendly.

"I'll take good care of her, I promise," Asher assured him.

"Yeah, you do that." He grinned to show he was kidding. "So, are you two going public, or is this still a secret?"

"A little of both, really. I mean, I've nothing to hide, however for the sake of Kate's privacy, I think it'd be best for the public at large to be unaware of who she is. My friends and family will know her, of course; and I would imagine after a while, people will find out. But for the time being, I've no plans to broadcast it." Asher placed a soft kiss against my temple.

"Dinner will be ready in about half an hour, Calvin. Would you let Mom and Dad know?" I asked.

After he'd left, Asher said, "We'll tell them after dinner." Nodding, I continued with the dinner preparations, a small smile on my lips.

An hour later Dad pushed away from the table. "That was *out*standing, Katy. I haven't had a decent burger in ages."

"Thanks. Did everyone get enough?" I took my plate to the sink and ran the water to fill the basin. Agreements were heard all around. "It's a nice night out; I was thinking about making some coffee, maybe having a fire?"

"That sounds awesome." Calvin agreed. Everyone stood, helping Mom and me clear the table. Asher and Deken rinsed and stacked the dishes while I washed and Calvin dried.

By the time we were finished, Dad had the fire going and we arranged our chairs around it. We'd been out there for a few minutes when Scotty suddenly joined us. "You all mind some company?"

"Not at all. Pull up a chair," Dad said. Standing, I ascertained who wanted coffee, then headed in to get it. Asher followed, offering to help. Filling a tray with some cookies Mom had made yesterday, I handed those to him and followed him out with the thermos and mugs. Once everyone was served, I settled into my chair beside Asher.

Nighttime in the country is one of my favorite things—watching the stars blinking into existence. Hearing the birds call back and forth. Every so often we'd hear an owl. Once or twice, I caught a brief glimpse of a bat in search of food. A slight breeze blew, relieving any lingering heat from the day. The fire smelled good, and of course the flame was pretty. Add to that the smooth warmth of the coffee and the excellent company, and you had a near-perfect evening. Jack and Jill were curled up on the ground between Asher and me. "This is nice," I said quietly, blinking my eyes sleepily.

"Yes, sweetheart, it is." Mom agreed.

"Thanks, again for dinner." Dad took a sip of his coffee. "You make the best burgers, Katy."

"Dad's right." Calvin patted his stomach. "That was *awesome*."

After a moment of silence, Scotty said, "I love the smell of a good fire."

"Yeah, makes me want to go camping." Deken sounded wistful.

"We should plan a trip, before winter hits," Derek agreed.

"Sounds good to me," I said.

"Count me in." Calvin sipped his coffee.

"I'm in love with, Kate," Asher stated. I know he spoke in a normal voice, but for all the effect it had on the small group, he may as well have shouted it. Everyone around me suddenly got very quiet, except for Calvin who was coughing into his hand, coffee dripping down his chin.

"You gonna make it, Cal?" Deken grinned, his eyes on Asher.

Mom and Dad were looking at me. I was looking at Asher. *He said he was in love with me.* I knew he wanted me, but this was the first time he'd said he loved me. My parents were now looking back and forth between us. If I listened carefully, I was certain I would hear the opening strings of the theme song from *The Good, the Bad, and the Ugly.*

"Yeah," Calvin choked. "I'm fine. Just didn't expect him to say it quite like that."

"I take it you knew about this, Calvin?" I didn't *think* Dad sounded angry.

"Only for a couple of hours," Calvin said. "I had my suspicions about him, though."

"I *knew* it!" Derek said. "Knew something major was going on between you two."

"Well, I think we all knew they were attracted to each other. It doesn't really come as a surprise to anyone, does it?" Mom smiled at me.

"I do," Asher said earnestly, catching my eye. "I *love* you." Dad shifted in his seat, drawing Asher's gaze. "I didn't intend to announce it quite like that, Jackson; sorry if it was out of line. I think it's best that you, Kate's parents, know. I don't want any secrets between us." He took my hand, holding it gently and firmly. He gave me an encouraging smile, and the look on his face was one of extreme satisfaction, like he'd accomplished something he'd long desired to do. I couldn't help my own smile.

"Understandable, but what are your plans once this contract is finished?" Dad asked. Asher didn't pretend to misunderstand what he was asking; I felt he respected my dad more for being unafraid to be direct with his questioning.

"Our plans are to keep seeing each other. Kate's all about taking this slow," he gently squeezed my hand. "We're taking the time to get to know one another."

"And the future?" Dad asked. "What kind of plans have you made for the future?" I shot him a look of exasperation he missed by a mile as he was still staring at Asher.

"Well, I haven't made any special plans with Kate, yet. But ultimately my goal is marriage." My heart squeezed tightly in my chest, my grip on his hand tightening.

"By my calculations," Dad said, "you only have about three weeks or so left under our contract with the studio. How do you plan to maintain a relationship by long distance?"

"I intend to relocate here. Until then, I'm hoping Kate can visit me on location occasionally. It'll be hard if we've got to wait a month or more to see each other."

"And what do you have to say, Katy? Any thoughts you want to share?" Dad asked gently.

"I'd...like to be able to see Asher as often as I can. If that means going to visit him, then I'd like to be able to."

"You couldn't go by yourself, honey. That wouldn't be right," Dad said, "And what about the expense of that kind of travel?"

"I'd take care of any expenses, for Kate and for whoever can come as chaperone," Asher said.

"I think that sounds fair, dear," Mom said to Dad, who nodded in agreement.

"I'd like Kate to meet my parents, Tiernan and Callie Fitzpatrick. Currently, they live in Ireland, near my grandparents. I'll see if they can get away for a visit. I'll try to make things as easy for you all as I can, but there'll be some difficulties that'll pop up—the main one being the press. I'm going to try to keep your identities undisclosed for as long as I'm able. That should help, at least for a little while. Eventually the public will know all about you, and that's fine, it'll simply be easier and smoother if it happens slowly."

"Will Katy be in any danger?" Dad asked.

"She'd better not." Calvin sat forward.

"I'll make sure she has the best protection."

"I trust you." I squeezed Asher's hand.

"I'm glad to hear that, because trust will be essential between us." Asher turned to Samuel and Cory. "What do you think? Is now a good time?"

"If you're really that serious, I could not think of a more appropriate time. Some privacy might be needed, though." Samuel glanced toward the twins and Scotty.

"What's going on?" I asked.

"Patience, love. I'll explain everything," Asher said. "Deken, Derek, Scotty, I'm sorry, but would you all mind excusing us? There are some things I need to discuss privately with the Reillys. Thanks, guys."

"That include me?" Calvin started to rise.

"No, Cal, you should stay. You need to hear this, too," Asher said.

Asher kissed my hand, then stood and walked around the fire to face us. He caught my eye and smiled. "Don't look so worried, Kate. I promise, I'm not about to confess I'm a serial killer or terrorist, or anything like that."

What is going on? "Good to know." I sat forward in my chair, my curiosity getting the better of me.

"First, before I tell you a little more about my history, Kate, I have a slight confession to make." I tamped down my rising apprehension. "You remember, I'm sure, the first time we met? In Casper?"

"I do."

"After you left, I noted the name on the side of your truck. I did some research, but was unable to locate a business by that name, so I called Sammy. Samuel has experience, and resources to locate people.

"Which brings me to another revelation. I told you how I became an actor. What I didn't tell you then, because I wasn't sure I *could*, was that I was at that time and still am, occasionally employed by the government. I've had *extensive* combative training—I told you I knew what I was doing and was in no danger from Johnny.

"The agency I'm employed for contracts with the government and I have many connections with various branches of the military. I'm not enlisted. I'm not an officer. I never have been. I've consulted with them only. Sammy was my handler. That's how we met."

"What do you mean, 'consulted' with the government?" Dad asked. *Good question, Dad!* Silently, I struggled trying to process this.

"I'm not what you might think of as a *spy* or anything like that. I'm no Jason Bourne, James Bond, Jack Reacher, or Jack Bauer. Though I do maintain a cover—acting *is* my cover—I simply *help* various persons within the military to solve problems. It's a little more involved than that, but that's what I can tell you. At any rate, I called Sammy, gave him the name on the truck and your name, Kate. Jeff, your friendly barista, was kind enough to supply that much for me. Sammy pulled a few strings and found you.

"I'd been offered this role about nineteen months ago and had turned it down. The studio knows nothing about my cover—they have no idea.

They were progressing with production, trying to find another lead actor. I happened to know the studio was still trying to find a proper location for filming. Sammy's *very* thorough in his research. Within a few hours or so, I knew...let's say, I knew *a lot*. The most important thing I discovered that day, Kate, was your marital status. My plan had little value if you turned out to be married or even engaged.

"I contacted Rupert—who, as I mentioned before, has acted as my agent on occasion. I informed the studio that I'd reconsidered their offer and would make this film, on one condition and one condition only. You, Kate, had to be my assistant. I chose to forfeit my fee for this film so the studio could offer you a substantial enough amount to tempt you to agree to those terms. The way I saw things, your ranch would benefit and the studio would as well. And *more* importantly, I'd have the opportunity I'd wanted, which was to get to know you. I had Rupert make all the arrangements...and here we are."

My brain was buzzing, thoughts flying about in a whirlwind. I tried piecing things together so that what Asher had told me would make sense. So far, I was floundering.

It was unfathomable that Asher would agree to make this movie for virtually free, so that I might be paid to be in his company. Not to mention, despite what he said, he was some sort of spy who maintained his cover by pretending to be an actor in the Hollywood scene. Not to be overly dramatic, but for lack of a better word, it was preposterous.

I think I may have been waiting for a "gotcha" moment. I listened for the other shoe to drop. All I could hear was the comforting crackle of the fire, the chirp of crickets, and my heart hammering in my chest.

"Say something, love," Asher took his seat next to mine and turned my chair to face him. I'd been staring into the fire, and hadn't been aware everyone else had risen, leaving Asher and me alone. They seemed to know this was an important moment between us. My mouth opened and closed several times, unable to force sound past my lips.

My voice barely above a whisper, I finally croaked, "I'm...thinking."

"Do you have any questions for me?" *Was he kidding?* I had *tons* of questions! If I could just get my head to work straight, I might be able to wrap my mind around one and ask it.

Asher took a breath, intending to speak again, but I forestalled him with a raised finger. Finally, I said, "You, um, you work for a private contractor, who works for the government? And you maintain your cover by pretending to be an actor? And you signed a contract with this studio, agreeing to make this movie for free? So that you could get to know me? Is that what you're saying?"

"More or less."

"You, what? Fight terrorists, or something?"

"I gather intelligence. I'm not in combat, but support those who are."

"The lessons I gave you—were those real or were you only pretending?"

"Those were real; to do this role I did need your help. Truly. I didn't lie or intend to mislead. I was being as honest with you as I could. When I said you'd intrigued me from the start, I was being honest." The look in his eyes was almost pleading. "You didn't appear to recognize me in that coffee shop. The idea of simply being a normal guy, not an agent, not an actor, just a guy getting to meet a girl. The temptation was too great. I wanted that opportunity too much."

My ears were ringing and I shook my head trying to clear it.

These shocking revelations were exactly that. They were shocking. *I* was shocked. I wasn't sure what I should be feeling, much less thinking. A part of me was screaming her head off about being lied to, and how on earth could I ever trust him if the foundation of our relationship had begun with a lie? Another part of me was telling *that* part of me to shut her mouth and simply let me think.

Asher knelt in front of me, the hard plane of his stomach against my knees. With elbows on the arms of my chair, he leaned closer, his voice somber. "Kate, what should I have done differently? You were leaving; you wouldn't talk with me. I truly saw this as my only opportunity to get to know you. Can you honestly fault me for that? I didn't lie about my identity. I only manipulated some events from behind the scenes. I was trying to create a setting where you wouldn't see me as a celebrity, where *you* would be on equal footing with *me*, where you'd be comfortable with me. Was I wrong?"

Blowing out a breath, I leaned back in my seat, needing distance to think. Closing my eyes, I contemplated all he'd said, all Asher's reasons. When I considered what he'd sacrificed financially, the efforts he'd made to track me down, to place himself in a position of close proximity, simply to get to know me. To allow me to get to know him, all the while knowing he had no guarantees, that he was by far taking the bigger risk. When I considered all of that, I found I was unable to find fault with what he'd done. I was entirely blown away.

Opening my eyes, I mutely studied him, his thick brows were drawn in concern. Those blue eyes focused unflinchingly on mine, waiting for my decision. I tried to find the words to offer him, to tell him I wasn't angry. I was *flattered* even. But they stuck in my throat, emotion near to choking me.

"Was I wrong, Kate?" he asked. Words were still impossible, my throat still tight, even as my lips trembled. "Do you forgive me?" he asked now, a pleading, almost hopeful look in his eyes. Before my mind could catch up to my actions, I'd launched myself forward, my arms around his neck, holding him, squeezing him tight. "I'm so sorry, love," he whispered in my hair.

"Don't be sorry." I rasped, finding my voice again. "I'm not mad. Not at all. It was *a lot* to process. I can't believe you did that. Especially after the way I treated you." My heart felt as though it would burst from all the emotion it currently contained. Kissing his neck, I felt him shudder. Enjoying this reaction, I placed another kiss on his neck, and heard the low rumble from his chest. Feeling bolder, I gently nipped at his ear, allowing my teeth to linger. Asher actually growled, *that* sound doing all sorts of things to me. His arms wrapped around me and I was lifted from the chair as he stood. His mouth found mine, warm and inviting. "I *love* you, Kate," he whispered against my lips, his hands firm on my thighs, holding me up.

"I love you, too, Ash," I whispered back.

He let me slide to my feet, his gaze one of happy, hopeful surprise. "That's...*you*..." Asher took a deep and shuddering breath. "Say it again." Gone was the restrained manner he'd been holding himself to. Asher was suddenly intense. Demanding.

"I love you, Asher."

"*Again.*"

"I *love* you."

"I've been waiting, *I swear*, an eternity to hear you say that to me. Thank you, Kate."

Asher-

You need to leave Cody in 3 weeks. Pick your ticket up at the United departure counter within 24 hours. Asher glared at the screen of his cell phone. Finally, he hit the delete button. He'd been hoping for more time, especially after the last job he'd completed. Asher knew this must be serious for them to contact him again so soon.

He didn't want to leave Kate. He'd never really considered he might not return from an assignment before. The thought of never seeing her again, of putting her through that, left him cold and unsettled. Anxious. Samuel advised it was time to get out; time for him to walk away. His feelings for Kate now posed a distraction, one that could prove deadly in the wrong circumstances. Asher was seriously considering the idea. He'd need to make a final decision soon.

CHAPTER SIXTEEN

Storm Clouds

Kate-

Yesterday had been overcast, the air heavy and damp, hinting at a coming rain. Today we had thunderstorms. I stood just inside the barn door, looking into the yard. My shoulders hunched as I dug my hands deep in my pockets. It wasn't cold; I was simply feeling dismal. The rain came and went, from a heavy downpour to a soft, steady drizzle and back again. Occasionally, thunder rumbled across the mountains and lightning brightened the sky. It wasn't the weather that had me feeling glum.

In two days, *Dust Devils* would be finished, as far as the ranch was concerned, as far as *I* was concerned. Of course, there would still be the cutting and editing, but filming at the ranch was complete. Asher had intended to remain for a while, but yesterday he'd received a phone call. He'd said it was government stuff, and he'd explain more later. I was curious to know more about this side of his life and was hopeful he'd soon be able to share more with me.

These last two and half weeks with Asher had been wonderful. And I'd been happy. Extremely happy. I *still* was happy, though today it was a *depressed* happy. Asher thought he'd be gone for a couple weeks on whatever errand the government had in store for him. Two weeks is not that long; but after spending the last three months in his company, day in and day out—evenings too—well, two weeks without him was going to seem like a *very* long time. And, to make matters worse, when I'd asked Asher if he was ever in any danger doing whatever it was he did for the government, he'd quietly assured me he was not. Still, part of my mind wondered if we agreed on the same definition of "danger."

Glaring at nothing, I kicked at a tiny rock, then jumped nearly a foot in the air when Red gave a shrill neigh from behind me, striking a foreleg against the stall. Glancing over my shoulder, I found my big gelding with his head hanging over the half-door, looking in my direction. Chuckling, I turned to him. Bobbing his head up and down, Red encouraged my attention. Smiling despite my mood, I headed over. The gelding affectionately pressed his nose into my chest and suddenly, I wanted very much to go for a ride.

Riding in a good rain was something Red and I had always enjoyed and it had been close to a year since the last decent rain, so we were due. Patting his neck, I said, "Be right back." Turning quickly, I ran to the house. Today, Asher was busy with Xavier, doing some re-shoots. My presence hadn't been needed.

When I poked my head into the office to let Mom know my plans, she said, "You may want to check with Calvin, dear. I think there was something he wanted to talk with you about." She smiled at me over her readers.

"Do you know what about?"

"No, he didn't say, only that he wanted you to check with him if you went off alone."

Interesting. "I'll find him before I go," I assured her.

Running up to my room, I grabbed an older straw cowboy hat and a light duster jacket. While upstairs, I knocked on Calvin's door, but there was no answer. Shrugging, I headed back down. On a whim, I decided to take a firearm with me. It had been a while since I'd been out in the back country and you never knew what you might run into up there.

Mom watched me in silence for a moment, as I pulled both my rifle and sidearm from the safe. "Are you expecting trouble?"

"No, only being careful."

"Smart," she nodded.

"Yeah. Hey, do you know where Cal is today?"

"I think he was going to be around here; he didn't say he was going anywhere."

"Okay, I'll keep looking for him. I'll see you in a few hours," I told her as I left.

By the time I'd finished saddling Red, I still hadn't seen Calvin, so tried his cellphone. It went to voicemail. I sent him a text, letting him know where I was going.

Red waited impatiently, so I stepped into leather and we headed out. By noon we were well north of the Jump Off, rain coming off and on from a torrent to a sprinkle. The wind shifted, and suddenly I smelled a very faint amount of wood smoke. Gazing around, I pondered the horizon. We didn't have a fire lit at home; it wasn't cool enough for that. Deciding I'd better follow the scent, wanting to make sure there weren't any unmanned fires left burning, I put Red back into motion.

I rode for another hour or so, covering roughly two miles, making a wide loop around the area where I'd first smelled the smoke. Several times I'd caught it again, but only faintly. I wondered if someone was camping on our land. It wasn't hunting season yet; and even so, we had the perimeter well-marked with signs indicating this was private property.

During a brief break in the weather, I stepped down from the saddle to stretch my legs and give Red a break. Mentally, I pictured the lay of the land, considering each possibility. If someone were to be camping out here, they'd most likely be close to a water source. North of here, a small waterfall cascaded down, forming a pool. About twenty yards east of that pool was a clearing offering good protection from the wind.

So much for a relaxing ride in the rain. We'd continued on, going a couple hundred yards or so, when Red suddenly gave a loud snort. His head was raised, his ears pricked forward. He trembled beneath me and I searched the trees around us, but saw nothing to indicate concern in the gloom of the day. Unbuttoning the front of my duster, I slid it back behind the holster of my gun, and loosened the retention strap. After a minute or two of tense scrutiny, Red settled down. Quietly, I urged him forward, continuing towards the clearing.

I'd gone maybe another hundred yards when I heard horses thundering from behind me. Turning Red, I waited to see who approached. My hand automatically slipped to my sidearm; I eased it from the holster, holding it at my side. The trees and gloaming were so thick it prevented me seeing too far down my back trail, no more than ten yards or so. Suddenly Calvin, Asher, and Samuel were coming toward me at a fast clip. They slid to a stop when they saw me, looks of relief on their faces. Their horses were well lathered, indicating they'd come far and fast in a short time.

"What's going on?" I asked, holstering the gun.

"Kate, thank God." Asher quickly stepped down, moving toward me. Unsettled by their sudden appearance, Red quickly laid his ears flat, striking out with his foreleg, indicating Ash needed to keep his distance. Asher skidded to a halt, his eyes now on the big red horse rather than me.

"Easy, Red." I patting his neck. "Stay back a moment," I instructed. "You all want to tell me what this is about?"

"Why don't you step down for a moment so we can talk, huh?" Calvin suggested.

I slipped from the saddle, keeping between Red and Asher, wanting to be sure the big gelding wouldn't see him as a threat and decide to attack again.

"Did I spook him?" Asher kept his distance; though I could see he wanted to reach for me.

"A bit. You all came on so quickly, he went into protection mode. He'll calm down in a minute." I replied.

"Sorry about that," said Calvin. "Listen, I meant to tell you last week, while I was riding, gathering up those yearlings, I found tracks. They don't belong to any of the ranch or the film crew—I know all those horses. This is someone else. And...I found a butchered calf, carcass mostly buried, way back up the hill. I lost the trail, but I've been trying to keep an eye out for the poacher. I'm pretty sure it's not someone on the film crew—I should be able to track them to and from the staging area. I let Asher know about it and we've been keeping an eye out, but hadn't gotten around to telling you yet. I worried when I got your text, so called him, and they came running."

"Why didn't you just tell *me*?" Irritation bloomed hot and fast.

"You've been so happy lately; I didn't have the heart to tell you. I knew you'd worry about it, and I was hoping to have it solved by now. Sorry, I should have told you."

"Yeah, you should have, but I still love you." I smiled at him. "*You*, on the other hand." Dropping Red's reins, I poked Asher in the chest. "What's up with *that*? You need to tell me these kinds of things. I'm a big girl. I can take care of myself. And this is my ranch. *My* responsibility. Okay?"

"Kate...you're right. I should have told you. I should have insisted Calvin tell you." Asher nodded. "I'm just... It's not easy to turn off the desire to protect you."

"Yeah, yeah...likely excuse." I grumbled good-naturedly.

"What brought you out this far, Katy?" Calvin asked.

"Seemed like a good day for a ride and I'd nothing better to do." Catching the look exchanged between Calvin and Asher, I asked, "*What?*"

"Nothing; I guess I didn't believe Cal, when he mentioned that. You really like to ride in the rain?" Asher asked.

"I do—it's relaxing," I shrugged, then went on to explain about the smoke I'd smelled and my speculations.

By now Red was calmly nipping at blades of grass, several paces away. Asher took the opportunity to pull me tightly to him. His hand brushed the holster and he looked down at it.

"It's been a while since I've been this far north; figured it was better to be safe than sorry."

"Smart." Samuel said. He'd been quietly observing us during our conversation, his eyes flickering carefully around us as we spoke.

"Since we're this far," I told them, "I want to go ahead and check that clearing out."

"May as well." Calvin agreed. Asher hesitated, then nodded his assent, before turning to his horse. Mounting, we continued onward.

We rode maybe another half mile before stopping again. I was trying to come in from the south, staying downwind from where I expected them to be—if anyone was there in the first place—when we caught a strong flow of wood smoke. Red could smell it too; his nostrils were distended. When I figured we were around a hundred and fifty yards south of the clearing, I brought him to a stop, not wanting to alert anyone to our presence.

After dismounting, Asher stepped close to me. "I don't suppose there's anything I can say to get you to agree to stay behind with the horses?" He rested one hand lightly around the back of my neck, fingers softly caressing.

"You suppose correctly."

"That's what I figured," he sighed, pulling me closer, his arm wrapping around me. He tilted my head back, so my mouth was right where he wanted it. Then he was kissing me. And then—

Asher-

Asher held Kate close, her body nearly flush with his. He kept one hand at her neck, near the juncture of her shoulder. He used his thumb to gently push her chin up. Then his lips were on hers. While she was otherwise distracted, he gently, yet *firmly* applied pressure to the muscle at the back of her skull, sending her into unconsciousness.

Asher heard Calvin's concerned start when Kate suddenly slumped in his embrace. He easily swung her up in his arms, and carried her to a tall, thick fir tree where he laid her under its protective branches. Kissing her softly on the forehead, he said, "Sorry, love. I'll apologize when you wake."

"What'd you do to her?" Calvin demanded.

"Relax, Cal. She's fine; you know I'd never hurt her. She's only sleeping; I didn't want her coming with us, and she was determined to go. Tying her up simply wasn't an option I was willing to take. You'd better stay here and let Sammy and me handle this. Keep an eye on her. Take her sidearm in case anyone gets past us. Calvin, do *not* be afraid to use that. You hear?"

"You know she's gonna be furious when she wakes up. Katy comes across as sweet-tempered mostly but, if you *cross* her, she'll come undone on you. Just a word of caution." Calvin stiffly moved to her side and sat down.

"Yeah, I figured as much." Asher responded, his voice low and determined, before turning to Samuel. "You ready?"

Samuel started off on foot, Asher following, heading in the direction of the clearing. On the ride to their stopping point, Calvin had filled them in on the description of the area they were now looking for.

Once they were in the tree line, out of sight of Calvin, Samuel slunk off to the right of Asher. The two men moved through the trees in near silence. About fifteen lengthy minutes later, Samuel and Asher came upon the small campsite and spotted three men.

One of them was Johnny Khyle.

Asher felt a sick fury rock through him. It took a moment before he was able to comprehend what they were saying. Johnny sat on a broken stump, a beer in hand. To his right sat another man, maybe in his early thirties. And Bill was there also. By the number of empty cans lying around, they'd been here a while. Johnny's face still had some slight bruising from the last time he and Asher had met; his right hand was still bandaged.

"What's the plan, Johnny? We been out here nine days. You promised me a woman—I ain't seen any. If Bill hadn't confirmed your word she was a looker, I'd've told you to shove it."

"You'll have your woman, Larson. What's left of her anyway. I told you, *I* get her first. You two can watch and help me hold her down—she's a fighter."

"And what happens if her big fella or Calvin shows up?"

"Well, we kill them, Larson. And her too, after I've had my fill."

Asher never put thought to his actions. From one moment to the next he was in motion. Samuel, though expecting it, still had to scramble to catch up. Bill was closest to Asher; he was taken down with a short jab to the head. Before Bill hit the dirt, Asher had moved on to Larson, driving a solid fist directly in the man's solar plexus, then shoving him out of the way, continuing toward his target.

Johnny had fallen backward off the stump when the huge, shadowy bulk of Asher suddenly appeared in their campsite. He scrambled, reaching for the shotgun lying in the dirt near his log.

With his good hand, Johnny gripped the stock, was just lifting it when Asher reached him.

Asher sent the shotgun into the dirt, and a screaming Johnny to his knees. His well-placed kick had shattered the man's arm. Furious, and not finished, Asher reached for him. Johnny kicked out, no doubt trying to keep him away. Asher blocked the attempt, stomping on Johnny's leg, feeling it snap as Johnny's shrieks of agony pierced the night.

Kicking the broken leg aside, hearing another snap as he did so, Asher reached for the other man, lifting him bodily. Holding him up, he punched three sharp jabs into Johnny's stomach. Then slammed his fist twice into Johnny's mouth, pulverizing his lips. He was pulling back to finish the job, when Samuel grabbed him from behind, jerking Asher backward. "*Enough*! You'll kill him!"

Enraged, Asher turned to face this new assailant. It was a moment before he recognized Samuel. Breathing hard, he looked around, a little shocked and disgusted. Johnny was a crumpled, broken heap on the ground at Asher's feet. Bill and Larson were both out cold.

Kate-

I woke with a start, my head slightly thick and throbbing mildly. Blinking my eyes slowly, I tried to comprehend what had happened.

I was sitting on a horse; it was walking steadily. The rocking motion was soothing and I nearly went back to sleep. Well, with the rocking motion and the warm, comforting chest I was snuggled against, who could blame me? I began to think about that warm, comforting chest. It really was nice and smelled good. Nuzzling my face closer into its embrace, I enjoyed the deep murmur of pleasure that rumbled softly from within.

Strong arms tightened around me, pulling me closer still.

Asher was holding me. I was seated across his lap.

He was sitting astride a horse. And it was dark.

Wait.

What were we doing riding a horse together in the dark?

Sitting up, a part of me suddenly became alert to the idea that not all was right.

Asher brought his horse to a stop.

We were a little way south of the Jump Off. The sky was clear now and the moon full; I could see our location quite clearly. I sat still for a moment, then, as my memory replayed all that I last remembered, I launched myself off his horse. The gelding shied violently, snorting and bucking, bringing a twisted sort of pleasure.

When Asher hit the ground a minute later, that pleasure increased. Not waiting for him to speak, I roared, "You *JERK*! How *dare* you! Who do you think you are?"

Asher rolled into a sitting position, allowing me to see he was uninjured by the fall. A tiny part of me breathed a sigh of relief. He didn't move, and kept silent, his eyes glued to me. His staying down had probably been a wise and calculated move on his part. If he'd stood up, I was sure I would have hit him. I wasn't sure I wouldn't hit him anyway, even if he was down.

"Answer me!" I hurled at him. Asher continued to watch me, offering no apology or explanation. *"Dang it!"* I shrieked. "This is *serious!* What you did...You...you had *no* right to treat me like that."

Still, he remained silent.

"*Fine,*" Fury roiled so hot inside me I felt physically ill. Turning away, I began walking, well stomping, home. I didn't hear him rise, didn't hear him move. Suddenly, I was seized from behind, spun around, then found myself flat on my back in the damp grass. *How was he able to move like that?*

Asher strategically lowered himself on top of me, effectively pinning me beneath him. He was simply too heavy to budge, my legs rendered useless. Though I knew my efforts were sure to be wasted, I tried punching him, my fist grazing his cheek as he partially blocked me. He easily, *curse him*, caught both my arms, forcing them back, entrapping them against the earth.

With mouth tight, I simply glared at him with every last ounce of the fire inside me. To his credit, he didn't look amused. Rather, his face was calm, his eyes somber, maybe a little anxious. Still, he'd made no sound, had not uttered a single word, only continued that silent study.

"Get off me. *Now.*" My jaw hurt from how hard I was clenching it.

"Not yet." Asher finally spoke.

"You...there aren't enough bad words for what you are." Knowing it was in vain, I struggled against his grip. "Get off me and leave me alone. I don't want to *see* you right now. Maybe not ever again."

"Kate." He breathed, my name a prayer on his lips. "Sweet, stubborn, beautiful Kate. I can see you're furious—I expected no less. I'm not moving until we work this out. You mean too much to me."

"Bully for you," I said acidly, turning my head away from him. My entire body ached from the tension, the fury. I tried loosening those muscles, seeking relief from the discomfort.

"*Please*, understand. I had to make sure you were safe. You were being stubborn. You wouldn't stay behind. I didn't know what I was going to find in that clearing. If there was any chance you might have been harmed...please, don't fault me for wanting to keep you safe. Kate, *love*, I love you." Asher's voice was soft and pleading.

Frustrated tears formed in my eyes as I considered what he'd said, knowing there was wisdom in his reasoning. Unable to process the emotions raging inside me, trying to calm myself, I took a deep breath. At least, I tried too. It's kind of hard to breathe deeply with a massive weight sitting on your chest. Squirming, I once again tried to move, succeeding in getting a leg to the side. In doing so, Asher inadvertently settled more fully between my legs, his breath catching in a ragged sound. His eyes were half closed, unfocused, his head thrown back, teeth clenched, jaw tight. The muscles in his neck bulging in acute strain, even as a low moan slipped past his lips.

I froze my movements, holding still, not even breathing, watching him, his facial expressions, in fascination.

Pleasure, that's what was on his face. Pure *pleasure*. A hot ripple echoed in my stomach, stealing my breath.

Asher's blue eyes suddenly flashed open, burning with such intensity. His gaze snapped to my mouth. With his right hand, he quickly, *gently*, took both my wrists, holding them. As he relinquished his hold, his left hand slid slowly, firmly down my arm, just grazing my armpit, over my ribs, my hip, continuing down to my thigh. There he reversed course, taking the same path he'd burned before. His hand now moved to my face, brushing my hair back, his thumb firmly smearing my lower lip, parting it.

His mouth lowered to meet mine. Hesitating, he breathed against me, thumb still in place, palm holding my jaw. Slowly Asher rubbed his lips against mine, his nose caressed, dragging out the anticipation. Then slowly, *finally*, he touched his lips to mine. With infinite care he deepened it, took me deeper, stealing my will.

I forgot my anger. Forgot what we'd been fighting over. The only thing I knew right now was *him*. Asher. With his mouth, his hands, he claimed every part of my awareness. I met him with as much desire, as much need, as he had for me. Tugging against the grip he had on my wrists, I struggled against my bonds, wanting to hold him now, not fight him. Asher released me and my arms wrapped around him, were in his hair, on his back, his shoulders, his neck, his face. Straining against him, I tried bringing myself closer. Asher's arms were under me now, lifting me up to him. Then we were rolling and somehow, I was on top.

Asher's hands were firm against my thighs, kneading, holding me tightly to him. He leaned up, growling softly against my skin. When his mouth left mine, moving along my neck, across my collarbone, I gasped, my head spinning.

"*Kate*...." He growled against my fevered skin. "Please...."

The sound of his voice brought some clarity to mind. Barely able to discern what we were doing, a small warning bell began clanging in my head. I almost, *almost*, ignored it. Oxygen hit my brain as I took a shuddering breath, and with it I could think a little clearer. "Stop." I somehow managed.

Asher growled in response, his arms pulling me closer, as he once more rolled us, pinning me beneath him. I felt a moment of sheer panic, because I wanted, desperately *wanted* to surrender to him. Right here. Right now.

"Asher! *Stop.* Please!" I tried to reason with him. His mouth moved back to mine, forestalling any further words. I did the only thing I could think to do at that point; I wasn't strong enough to fight him. I was barely strong enough to fight myself, and I knew he was going to have to win this battle on his own. I stopped fighting; I shut down, forcing myself to relax. My arms went limp. My mouth became slack. My eyes opened, staring unfocused at nothing, taking small, calming breaths.

Growling in frustration against my swollen lips, his hands wrapped themselves in my hair, shaking with strain. His mouth moved forcefully against mine, trying to gain a response. When I continued to remain motionless, lifeless, he stopped. His breath was ragged as he laid his face against my neck. Softly, he kissed there, once, twice. After a moment or two of silence, he rolled off me and lay on his back, eyes closed, breathing deeply.

Holding still, I tried to wrap my mind around what had just occurred. How we'd gone from the point of my rage and fury exploding, to the passion we'd just displayed. My head pounded with the effort, so I stopped, forcing my mind in another direction. Back to what had taken place earlier this afternoon. There were parts about today that I didn't know, and suddenly, I found myself wanting to know.

Rolling, I sat up a safe distance from him and crossed my legs, my hands resting in my lap. "Ash?" I whispered. "Where are the others? Cal and Sammy?"

Asher took a deep breath, held it for a moment, then sat up to face me. His face was still flushed, his desire barely under control. "They took the trespassers back to the ranch, where the police will surely be taking them into custody." His voice low, steady. "I stayed behind with you."

"Who were they? What did they want? And *please,* tell me the truth."

He rubbed his hands over his face. With growing anxiety, I noted the bruised and scraped skin of his knuckles and waited for him to continue. "It was...Johnny Khyle and two companions. One, I believe, was the guy with him that night you punched Johnny. I didn't know the other one; Calvin didn't seem to know him either." Asher halted, clenching, and unclenching his jaw before continuing. "Johnny intended to...rape you." He struggled to speak, needing to swallow, breathing hard. "They were all going to...join in, and...when they were done...kill you." Rage burned in his voice.

As I listened, the blood drained from my face and I swallowed back bile. Tears pricked my eyes, and I couldn't seem to make my lungs work. I knew I was probably in shock, feeling as if I was going to vomit, or pass out, or both.

"Once you were...out of it, I had Calvin stay behind, to keep you both safe; I know what he means to you. Samuel and I went after them. I won't deny they were roughed up and I don't regret what I did. I'd like to have them here right now." Asher had to stop, visually calming himself before continuing. "Sammy, Sammy had to stop me...before I got too carried away.

"I...I broke Johnny's jaw this time. And one of his legs. Twice. Maybe a couple of ribs, too. And his arm. Bill and the other guy, the one I didn't know, went down easy. Sammy was able to keep a clearer head than I. We'd observed them first, did some surveillance, making certain they intended harm, before we acted. If they were nothing more than a couple of drunks out poaching, we'd have informed the authorities of their position and allowed them to handle it. After we heard, after I heard in *graphic* detail what they intended for you... They're fortunate Sammy was there. Maybe that's why I lost it a moment ago."

It took me a couple lengthy moments to gather my thoughts, to have words. "I don't...even know what to say."

"You can say you still love me. That you're not angry with me any longer. That you understand."

"I understand." I nodded. "I may not have liked it. I don't want you to *ever* do that again, but I understand. I won't make you promise. Somehow, I know if you ever felt the need to again, you'd break that promise, and I'd be hurt. And angry."

"Smart." Asher winked at me.

"Ash, I still love you. I *love* you. I'm not angry, *that* much, any longer."

Asher was kneeling beside me faster than I would have thought possible. He took my face gently in his hands, the cuts and bruises on his knuckles standing out starkly, and touched his mouth to mine. It was a tender kiss, not passionate. There was heat, but no flame. It said many things. He loved me, too. He was sorry. He was profoundly relieved.

"That horse is back at the barn by now, I'm sure. We'd better get moving. Can you walk, or would you like me to carry you?"

"I'll walk." He pulled me to my feet, and placed a gentle kiss against my forehead. Then, taking my hand, we made our way home in the moonlight.

CHAPTER SEVENTEEN

Shades of Depression

Kate-

Three days after Asher left, a little after nine in the morning, I stood in Cabin number one. I was supposed to be readying it for guests arriving later today.

"I'm *not* depressed." I grumbled aloud, before amending, "I'm not *that* depressed." *Oh, who am I kidding?* I was disgustingly depressed. And I had been ever since I'd dropped Asher off at the airport. I wasn't eating right, wasn't sleeping, couldn't concentrate. Not even the dramatic events with Johnny Khyle, Billy Simmons, and Randy Larson had postponed Asher's departure. Their trial date had not yet been set. Asher, Samuel, and Calvin would need to testify when the time came. Sheriff Joe had informed me that I'd most likely have to, as well. We were simply waiting for the subpoena. "Fine." I threw my hands up. "I'm a mess. A big *pathetic* mess. Happy?"

"Talking to yourself is a bad sign, you know," a voice spoke from behind me. Gasping, I spun to find Cory standing in the doorway, trying to hide a chuckle.

"*Yeesh,* Cory!" My hand pushed on my heart. "You scared the snot out of me."

"Sorry." He grinned. "Sammy thought you could use a hand in here."

"Oh. Yeah, thanks. I appreciate it."

I had Cory open all the windows in the cabin to air it out and make sure all the garbage cans had liners. While he did that, I went upstairs to prepare the beds. I finished the first room and had moved to the second when Cory came to find me. "That's done. What else?"

"Those towels can go in that hall closet there." I indicated the laundry basket right inside the doorway. Finishing the second bed, I was placing the quilted throw pillows when Cory cleared his throat. Glancing over my shoulder, I paused. He looked a bit...uncomfortable, almost nervous, and I wondered if something was wrong.

"I just wanted to say...I'm sorry...for the way I treated you. I know I was a jerk. I've known Asher most of my life; I sort of idol-worshipped him as a kid. He always seemed so strong and for the longest time it was only him, me, and Sammy. No one else. Then you came along. I've never seen him like that. It scared me. I can see you really do love Ash and I'm glad he has you. I hope...I hope we can put all that behind us."

I hid the grin that tried to break out; I wasn't gloating, was simply pleased by his attempt to fix things. "Of course, Cory. As far as I'm concerned it's in the past and I've already forgotten it."

Cory caught me off guard, pulling me in for a quick hug before releasing me and stepping back. "Good, glad that's settled. When's this family supposed to arrive? Will they need to be picked up from the airport?"

"They should be here around two, I believe. And they're driving from Seattle, so no, they won't, but Tiffy, our other guest, will. Her flight gets in around four."

"Maybe I'll go pick her up for you." Cory offered.

"That's already taken care of, Cory." Samuel stated as he joined us. "I'll pick her up for you, Katy."

I thanked Cory for his help as I finished up. Waving off my gratitude, he headed towards the stairs. Samuel tracked his progress, then returned his gaze to me.

"I know you haven't heard from Ash since he left and wouldn't want you to miss his call."

"Am I that obvious?"

"We're all like this when the one we love is absent from our lives."

"Sounds as though you're speaking from experience."

Samuel hesitated, seemingly weighing his words with care. "Sarah. My wife. She died nearly seven years ago. I hated being parted from her. I know Asher feels the same about you."

"Sammy, I'm so sorry." Guilt settled like a stone in my middle. "If I'd know—"

"It was mine to share." He quickly interrupted. "Not Asher's."

"Still." I shrugged. "I feel terrible for even asking."

"I know; it was my choice to tell you. You're one of us now; it was time."

My eyes pricked at his words and I blinked them to clear my vision. "Thank you, Sammy."

"No, Katy. Thank *you.*"

Asher-

Irritated, Asher stared into the distance. *Every* lead, *every* trail had gone cold. It seemed as if every *conceivably* open door had slammed shut in his face. And to ice the cake, he couldn't stop thinking about Kate. It wasn't simply mental. Physically, he felt her absence. She was like a phantom limb. Absent, yet felt, missed. Craved. Unreachable.

The airport was crowded; passengers, parents with crying children, everyone scrambling to make their flights, scrambling to make it home to *someone*. Asher was desperate for this assignment to be finished. The noise and chaos of the world were getting to him. He needed the silence of the mountains. He needed Kate.

Chasing yet another lead, Asher boarded the plane. Finding his seat, he sat back, closing his eyes, trying to drown out the concussion of noises around him, and thought of her. Thought about the moment he'd see her again, pictured the scene in his head, imagined the way it would feel when he held her.

Then maybe he could wrap his mind around this latest puzzle; harness and solve it. The information was out there. Someone *knew* something. If he could only find the link. When he was with Kate, things made better sense. Just a few more days...

Kate-

The Hunter family arrived a little after two-thirty while I was in the barn unsaddling the mare I'd been working. Hearing the crunch of gravel, I glanced at the clock, noting the time.

Mr. and Mrs. Hunter were in their forties, I guessed. They had two children, ten-year-old Danny, and thirteen-year-old Karen. They were already in the office, filling out paperwork, when I stepped inside. I smiled at the kids, noting the young man's excited interest in my boots and spurs.

"Dan, Sarah, this is my daughter, KatyBeth. Katy, these are the Hunters. This is Danny and this is Karen. They've come all the way from Seattle, Washington to visit us." Mom said, by way of introduction. I shook Dan's and Sarah's hands, then turned to the kids.

"Pleased to meet you, Danny. And you as well, Karen." Danny grinned, shaking my hand enthusiastically. Karen, on the other hand, seemed far more reserved, barely offering a nod in my directions; I guessed the country didn't seem very exciting to her.

"Are you a *real* cowboy?" Danny's grin was infectious, my own grin answering.

Before I could respond, Karen replied, "She's a *girl*, Danny. It's cow*girl* not cow*boy*!"

"Ah, you can call me cowboy if you want. I knew what you meant. And, yes, I'm a *real* cowboy." I smiled, then turned to Dan and Sarah, asking if they were ready to see their cabin.

After showing the Hunters where they'd be staying and getting them settled in, I explained the meal schedule. "We've a couple of hours yet until it's time for dinner. You all have driven a ways; would you prefer to rest before dinner, or do you want to come view part of the ranch with me?"

Dan and Sarah indicated they'd be resting after the long drive, but Danny and Karen wanted to get out and do something. After getting permission from their parents, I told Danny and Karen to change if they needed to then meet me at the barn. Danny was ready now; Karen said she'd meet us there.

"Are we going to ride horses now?" Danny asked.

"Not today, maybe tomorrow. I'll need to gauge your experience level first. Have you ridden before?"

"A couple times. Karen has too."

"Did you own horses, or were they friends' horses?"

"I *wish* we owned horses. Mom took us to some riding stables when we were younger and we had a couple months of lessons before Daddy lost his job, and we had to stop. He's working now and this is the first real vacation we've taken. I was so happy when they picked this place. Daddy said he needed some peace and quiet. I thought Karen was going to go through the roof." Danny grinned, rolling his eyes. "She's mad 'cuz all her friends went and did something fun, like went to the beach, or on a cruise, or to Disneyland for their summer break. She said, 'And here I get to go to a petting zoo for grownups!' I love it, though."

"Well, let's hope we can show her a good time, and maybe she'll change her mind about this 'petting zoo' for grownups, huh?" When Karen finally arrived at the barn, I explained to them what I had in mind—to see if Dad needed any help where he was cutting wood. Again, Danny was willing and ready, Karen simply rolled her eyes.

We reached the area Dad was working in quickly; I made the introductions in our little group.

Danny and I worked alongside Cory and Calvin for over an hour, dragging and stacking wood while Dad ran the chainsaw. Karen sat in the Jeep the entire time with her earbuds in. When my watch read four p.m., I decided to call it a day. Samuel would be arriving with Tiffy soon.

Other than one small skirmish I'd had with Karen, the afternoon went well. She'd expressed a strong disdain for the us and the ranch. I'd gathered she hadn't wanted to come, and didn't begrudge her, her disappointment. Though, I did have to explain this was a real working ranch and she would treat us with respect and courtesy.

Samuel wasn't back from the airport quite yet—the flight might have been delayed. I figured if there'd been a problem, he'd have called. The horses were all hanging around the barn, waiting to be fed. We walked among them while they were eating and I pointed out the different ones, telling a little about them: their genders, names, and personalities.

Karen picked Duke and Danny picked Dollar as their favorites. I told them they'd made good choices. Then I let them meet Red and Jet, and showed them our guest board, located in the entrance hall of the main house. We hung pictures and postcards there from various guests who've stayed with us.

I think I earned some serious points when they saw a picture Mom must have recently posted of me and Asher. We were standing together with Buck in the background. Asher had an arm draped casually over my shoulders.

"Oh. My. *Gawsh*. Is that...is that...is that freaking *Asher Fitzpatrick?*" Karen asked breathlessly.

As I stared at the picture, longing built and my face began to heat. "That's him."

"Was he a guest here?" Karen asked, her voice taking on the qualities of a pubescent young man.

"He was, yes. Actually, Asher left about four days ago; can you two keep a secret?"

"Yes!"

"Okay then, but I'm trusting you." I gave them the serious eye. "So, Asher was filming a movie, right here on the ranch—I gave him riding lessons."

"No way." Karen breathed, her eyes looking glossy.

"Sweet!" Danny said.

"Did he stay in one of the cabins? Was it our cabin?" Karen asked.

"No, he stayed in one of the rooms here in the main house."

"Can I see the room?" Karen asked.

"Uhhh, no, because it's occupied right now." I thought it was good Cory and Samuel were still here. What excuse could I have given for not showing the room if it was technically empty? Asher still had things stored there; I'd been tempted to go in and smell his clothing. The thought sounded desperate, even to myself. I missed him so much.

Just then, I heard the ranch truck and knew Samuel was back. Tiffy Fraser was a petite young woman. She had red hair; it wasn't orange red and it wasn't auburn, but a strange combination of both. It fell in soft waves to her shoulders, framing her heart-shaped face. Her skin was a beautiful, creamy ivory with a light sprinkling of freckles across her nose. Her eyes, however, were easily her most striking feature.

They were beautiful—a smoky, misty gray. It was the *look* in them that caught me. Vulnerable. Haunted. And old. Not aged, like she was an older woman; she looked to be around my age. It was her life experience that had aged her. She'd been through something big and traumatizing. My heart went out to the young woman. I wanted to wrap my arms around her, give her a big hug, and tell her she would be okay.

Instead, I settled for a warm smile as Samuel introduced us. I detected something different in his demeanor towards her, but couldn't pin down exactly what the difference was.

"Your ranch is very beautiful, Miss Reilly." Her voice had a pleasing quality about it.

"Thank you, Tiffy. Please, call me KatyBeth or Katy. We're so glad to have you. How was your flight?" I gave her hand a gentle squeeze when she'd offered it in greeting.

"Fine. Thanks for asking."

After making the introductions, I showed her to her room and helped her get settled. Later that evening, we gathered around the fire pit. Dad and Calvin had carried several logs over and soon had a roaring blaze going. Mom brought out a bag of marshmallows and some long sticks for roasting. We'd been sitting outside for about fifteen minutes; I know, because I'd checked the time on my cell it seemed every minute on the minute, when my phone rang. It was a little after seven. "Hello?" My voice came out all sorts of breathless as I stood and made my way inside, needing this time alone with Asher.

"Hello, beautiful," said the most amazing voice on the other line.

A surge of emotion made it almost impossible for me to respond, but somehow, I managed. "It's *so* good to hear your voice."

"It's good to hear yours as well. I miss you."

"When are you coming home?" I pulled out a chair at the kitchen table and sunk onto it.

"In eleven days."

"That's *so* long."

"I wish I were there, right now. Tell me what you're wearing. I want to picture you in my head."

"Um...I'm wearing my favorite pair of jeans. You know the ones, with the tag missing on the back pocket?"

"I do. I like those on you; they're soft." Asher inhaled slowly. "Go on."

"I have my wooly house slippers on, and my faded red sweatshirt. My hair's not done."

"Mmm, I *love* you."

"I love you, too, Ash. So much."

"Are you wearing any perfume?"

"Yes, the amber one you like."

Asher growled softly in my ear. "You're killing me now. Wear that when you come to the airport."

"Okay. I will." I whispered. "I almost went into your room today; I just wanted to smell you, your clothes..."

"Why didn't you?"

"I didn't want to see how empty the room was, see that you're gone. I swear I see you everywhere. When I go to the barn, in the tack room. I'm pathetic, Ash, absolutely pathetic." I laughed quietly at myself.

"No, you're not. You're amazing. And beautiful. And lovely. And *mine*. All mine. And you're desired. And desirable."

Emotion clogged my throat, making it near impossible to say, "Thanks, you're pretty awesome yourself." Then to distract myself from my acute longing, I asked, "So, where are you? Can you tell me?"

"I can't. I'm okay, though. I'm safe."

"What have you been doing? What were you doing before you called?"

"I took a shower before calling; I thought it would help. I'll have to take another." He laughed at himself now. "I've been reading, and after my second shower this evening, I'll read some more."

"Can you tell me what you're reading?" I tried distracting myself from the thought of him in the shower.

"I can. You'll like this; I'm reading *Twilight*."

"You're *kidding*." I chuckled. "What made you decide to read that?"

"You said it was your favorite. I wanted to see what you liked about it. See if I needed any pointers."

"Trust me, you *don't* need any pointers." I assured him. "What chapter are you on?"

"Just finished chapter eight."

"*And*? What do you think so far?'

"I was prepared for the worst but honestly, it's good. I can see why it's popular."

"Are you kissing up? Or do you really feel that way?"

"I want to kiss *you* and I really do feel this way."

"*Wow*. Thanks." A small giggle escaped. "What time is it where you are?"

"I can't say, love. This is supposed to be a secure line, it's being bounced through several signals, but still..."

"Oh." I tried not to ponder that too much.

"Tell me what you've been doing since I left."

"Some new clients arrived today. I scored big with two tweens. Mom posted a picture of you and me on the guest board and the girl, Karen, about died when she saw it. She's got a *major* crush on you."

"Hmm, maybe I can send her an autographed picture. Do you think she'd like that?"

"Would you? She'd *love* it. She has a brother; his name is Danny. He's ten and Karen's thirteen. Thank you, Ash."

"You're welcome. Any other clients?"

"Well, Danny and Karen are the children of Dan and Sarah Hunter, who drove over from Seattle. They're here for a week. Then we have Tiffy Fraser, who's from Utah, and I'm not sure about her yet. She's my age physically, but she seems so much older, like she's lived a long life already. I don't know how to describe it."

"You're very observant; you'll have her figured out in no time, I'm sure. And I meant that as a compliment."

"You're full of compliments tonight."

"Sammy said you're down, I want to cheer you up. I don't like that I made you sad." His voice was soft and serious now.

"*You* didn't. I'm sad because you're not here, not because you did anything," I quickly explained.

"I know. But you're still sad on my account. I want to make you happy. I love your smile. I miss it."

"I miss you, too. I miss your arms. I miss hearing your heartbeat. I miss your laughter." Feeling bold, I added, "I miss your *mouth*."

"You miss my mouth?" he asked quietly, his voice smooth and even.

"Yes. Your mouth. The way it feels on mine. On me. I miss it. A lot."

"You *really* are killing me. I won't be sleeping tonight...I may need to slip out for a run."

"Sorry. I only wanted you to know that I miss you, too."

"I know, I know," he said, his voice gentle now. I braced myself for words I could feel were coming. "I have to go."

"Okay," I whispered, trying to hold the tears back.

"Don't cry, Kate. I love you and miss you and I'll see you in less than two weeks. Are you near a calendar?"

"Yes," I said, still whispering, tears streaming down my face.

"Look at today's date. I'll call you again, same time, in three days. Okay? Mark the calendar. It's not that long. We can do this. Did you mark it down?"

"Yes."

"I love you. Sweet dreams. I'll call you in three days, I promise. Good night."

"Good night; I love you, too. Be...be careful."

"You be careful, too."

"I will," I choked out, my voice breaking. When the line went dead, I held the phone to my chest, wiping tears from my eyes.

Asher-

Talking to Kate was both better and worse. Better, because he got to hear her voice and found it as soothing as he'd anticipated. Worse, because as soothing as Kate's voice was, it was also equally stirring. He felt the need to see, to hold, to feel her, growing within him. He laughed at himself and groaned in frustration. It was also worse because hearing her anguish gutted him.

Asher stared unseeingly down at the newest packet of papers he'd received. Knowing he'd have to come up with an answer to this puzzle soon, he still couldn't stop thinking about her. Standing in swift, jerky movements, he rubbed his eyes and ran his fingers through his hair in irritation. He'd showered twice today already. Neither hot, nor cold water had helped. Running made him physically tired, but it didn't help him focus. Talking with Kate had been the only thing that sharpened his senses enough to make a difference. Problem was, he couldn't stay on the phone with her, or communicate the problem *to* her—she had to be kept out of it.

After dropping down to do a hundred pushups, Asher sat in the leather chair in his hotel room, trying to harness his thoughts. When that failed, his mind still refusing to cooperate, he blew out a breath and let his eyes wander. His gaze landed on his bed and immediately jumped beyond that, not needing any more distractions brought on by fantasies about Kate. From the bed, they moved to the nightstand and saw the book. *Twilight.* He grinned. Maybe reading would help. He fervently hoped Cory never found out about this. He'd never hear the end of it. *Ever.* Chuckling, Asher opened the book.

Kate-

In the distance, one of the horses neighed, reminding me to get my butt in gear. After showering and dressing, not feeling very enthusiastic about the day, I opened my door and paused. On the floor, folded neatly right in my doorway, was a piece of clothing. I looked up and down the hallway but didn't see anyone. Picking it up, I stepped back into my room and closed the door. A moment later, I was glad I had.

The scrap of clothing belonged to Asher, one of his sweatshirts, his cologne lingering on the fabric. Bringing it to my face, inhaling deep, the tears streaked unchecked down my face. A part of me wondered how it had gotten there. When I'd calmed down and was able to think more clearly, I figured it must have been Samuel. Asher must have been in touch with him after we spoke last night. I inhaled his scent one last time, then refolded the shirt, putting it under my pillow.

After breakfast, the Hunters met me at the barn for their scheduled riding lesson. I ascertained their experience, and after catching the horses, had Dan and Sarah groom their mounts, while I assisted Danny and Karen with theirs.

As I was helping them with the fit and straps on their riding helmets, Samuel appeared at my side. "You got a minute?" he asked quietly.

"Sure. Just a moment, folks, I'll be right back." I followed him outside away from prying eyes, and waited.

"Tiffy asked me to request private lessons from you. She's very nervous around horses and strangers and doesn't want to embarrass herself in front of everyone." He paused briefly before continuing. "I told her I didn't think it was a problem, but she insisted I speak with you."

"Yeah, of course. Thanks for letting me know. And thanks, for the shirt." Samuel nodded in understanding. Returning to the Hunters, I saddled Jet and led everyone to the large arena. I thoroughly went over the basics of riding safety, then had them mount up. After I checked everyone's stirrup lengths, I had them start off walking in a large circle around me. After ten minutes or so, I mounted Jet, who of course, had to show off a bit by jumping around, then we got down to business.

I thought we had a good ride; they listened well and were able to follow instructions and control their mounts. Karen showed true ability, and I praised her poise in the saddle. She seemed to sit up straighter after that, a small, pleased smile playing on her lips.

Two hours later, when the lesson was over, Dan and Sarah excused themselves to walk and stretch their legs; the kids stayed behind to give me a hand. As the youngsters moved around me, helping with the horses, brushing, carrying tack, I noticed a real change in Karen's demeanor, and only occasionally caught a worried or frustrated look in her eyes. We'd just finished grooming the horses when a special delivery van arrived. Jack and Jill ran out to see who it was, sniffing all around the vehicle. I walked out to the driver. "May I help you?"

"Looking for a Miss Kate Reilly, a Miss Karen Hunter, and a Mr. Danny Hunter," the uniformed woman replied.

"I'm Kate Reilly, and these are Karen and Danny," I said.

"Then, these are for you," she replied, handing the kids each a large padded manila envelope. She handed one to me as well, then said, "And I have something in the back for you, Miss Reilly."

Karen and Danny eagerly tore into their envelopes, wanting to know what had been sent and from whom. I was curious to know as well, though I had a sneaking suspicion. When the driver appeared from the back of the van holding a vase of two-dozen beautiful, long-stemmed red roses, my face warmed pleasantly. Hearing Karen's ecstatic shriek, I turned, hoping nothing showed on my face.

"*KatyBeth*! However, did you *do* this? It's a *signed* photograph from Asher Fitzpatrick! I can't believe this!"

"He even wrote my name, KatyBeth!" Danny said in awe. "Look, he wrote, "Hello Danny, I hope you enjoy your stay at Blues Avenue Ranch. I enjoyed my time there and miss it very much." Then he signed it. This is *so* cool!"

"You must still be in touch with him! When did you talk with him?" Karen asked.

I signed the delivery form and accepted the flowers, their fragrance swirling around me. Blinking back a tear or two, I turned to face the kids' questions.

"Asher and I have remained friends. I mentioned to him that you were both fans and he must have sent these. I think that was very, very nice of him," I replied.

"Did he send you the flowers? Did you get a picture?" Karen asked.

"Let me take these up to the house, then I can open my envelope. You haven't told me what your picture says, Karen."

"It's similar to Danny's, though he says that Duke was his favorite horse. That's cool, because he's my favorite, too! My friends are going to *flip* when they hear this!" she gushed.

Setting the bouquet on one of the shaded tables on the patio, I opened my envelope. My eyes devoured him, noting every little detail. Asher was smiling my favorite smile; his eyes held mischievous allure. He'd signed it simply, "Love, Asher." I let the kids hold the picture and discuss their favorite things about it while I opened the card that came with the flowers.

"Hello Beautiful. You mean the world to me; I hope you know that. Hearing your voice last night was like cool water to a thirsty man. Thank you for being mine. For being you. I love you, Ash."

I read it through several times, my fingertips lightly tracing the shape of his words. It must have cost him a small fortune to get these here so fast, my mind couldn't wrap around it. Samuel and Tiffy joined us a moment later.

I nodded at them, then turned back to the kids. "I see your parents coming. You want to show those to them?"

"Yeah! Come on, Danny!" Karen cried as she leaped off the patio, running toward her parents.

"I'm going to take these inside; be back in a moment." I told Tiffy and Samuel. After placing the roses on the kitchen table, I took the picture up to my room and set it on my pillow. The small card I folded and stuck in my pocket. When I came back downstairs, Tiffy was sitting at the table, looking at the flowers. She glanced up at me as I came in the room.

"They're beautiful." She murmured, her gaze returning to the roses.

"Thanks. I think so, too."

"My husband used to send me flowers all the time." She tenderly fingered a crimson petal.

"That's nice," I said gently. "What's his name?"

"Casey. His name was Casey."

"*Was*? Has he...? Is he...?" I didn't know how to frame the question.

"He died in Afghanistan. He was a Marine."

"I'm *so* sorry. When did this happen?" I sat beside her. *Why, oh why, does saying "sorry" sound so insignificant in situations like this? Lord, give me the words.*

"Last year. That's why I'm here, you know? Casey *loved* horses. He always wanted to take me riding, but I was too afraid to try. And now he's gone and I'll never have that opportunity. I know it's too little, too late, but

I wanted to do this for him." Tears streamed down her face. Handing her a napkin, I gently squeezed her hand. "You must think I'm terribly weak and cowardly, to be afraid of horses," she said in a shuddering breath.

"*No*. On the contrary," I said with absolute sincerity. "I think you're exceptionally brave. You'd have to be—you married a Marine. Thank you for confiding in me; I'm honored. And if you truly want to learn to ride, I'll be *more* than happy to assist you. But I'm sure Casey would want you to be happy and at peace. Don't beat yourself up over choices you made in the past. We can't change the past. We can only move forward."

"I *know*." She nodded at me, trying to smile. "I know. But I really want to do this for him. For me. I *want* to conquer my fear of horses. You see, I don't want to miss out on any more opportunities if they should arise, because I'm afraid. I want to be ready. Samuel says you're a great teacher, that you'd understand."

"I'm pleased Samuel feels that way about me and my abilities. You let me know when you're ready to begin, okay?"

"Maybe tonight, if you have time? You'll have to be patient, though."

Tiffy's request for patience reminded me keenly of my request that Asher be patient with me and I smiled at her. "I promise to be very patient. If you're willing to try, I'm willing to help. You'll become an excellent horseman. I promise." Tiffy stood up and I did as well; then after a moment's hesitation, I gently wrapped my arms around her. "You'll be okay. You're a strong woman. We'll get through this."

Tiffy went to wash her face and I headed back outside. Her situation had me thinking carefully about which horse I'd use for her. Misty, one of the horses I'd purchased that fateful day in Casper, was a gentle, sixteen-year-old gray mare; she'd be perfect. Catching the horse easily, I took her to the barn, and brushed her until her coat was shining. Karen joined me after a while, though she seemed rather subdued after her earlier excitement, making me wonder if something was amiss.

"Everything alright?" I asked after a few minutes. Several times, I'd caught her speculative glances, before she looked away.

"Yeah," she said, brushing Misty's mane, still not meeting my eyes.

"Thanks for helping."

"You're welcome."

"Are you happy with your picture?" I asked.

"Very much. Thanks again, for getting him to do that."

"You're welcome, though I only mentioned you and your brother were fans. He did that all on his own."

"He must really like you." She glanced up at me, then back down. "Is he your boyfriend?"

Taking a deep breath, I said, "Yes, he is."

"*Wow*. That is like, *really* cool. Did you know him before he made that movie here?"

"No, I got to know him while he was here."

"How did you know?" She paused then continued. "That you liked him...and that...*he*...liked you?"

"Well, I guess it's just something you know. And we talked about it. We tried to be honest with each other. It's important in every relationship that there be honesty and respect."

"And...you feel he respects you?"

"I know he does." A secret smile stole across my mouth.

"How? What does he do? That shows you that?"

Taking another deep breath, I held it for a moment, then let it out slowly. "Well, I guess, I can say that...*I*...didn't want to rush into anything. I told Asher we had to take our relationship slowly, and that he couldn't rush me. He's done that. It's been hard for him, but he's done that, for me."

Karen was quiet for a minute, though I could see plenty going on in her head. When she finally spoke again, she was agitated. "I have a boyfriend, too. His name's Max. He's fifteen. And I...*he*...wants to have...he wants to take...the *next* step. You know? He says if I really loved him, then we'd do it. But I'm not sure I want to do that. Yet. What do *you* think?"

Oh. Wow. I think I'd like to smack Max upside the head, that's what I think. "Have you asked your mom about this? What does she say?"

"Oh, my gawsh, no! She'd flip! You *can't* tell her! They'll say I'm only a child and he's just using me and doesn't really love me."

"It sounds like maybe you already have some doubts about it."

"No, I don't!" she insisted.

"Well, you've at least discussed those negative reactions. Who else have you talked with about it?"

"With Max. We talked about it. He told me what other adults would say to me, or even my friends, and they just didn't want me to be happy."

"And do you think that's true?" Bending, I picked up Misty's hoof to clean it out. "That your friends and family want you to be unhappy?"

"No...not really. I guess...I just really like him. He's the first boy in school that paid attention to me. I'm sorta popular now."

"Hmmm..." I said brilliantly as I started on the next hoof.

"How old were *you* when you first...? You know...?" At that question, I dropped Misty's hoof and stood up. Karen shrugged her shoulders, an almost sheepish look on her face.

Bending back down, I picked up Misty's hoof again and said, "I haven't."

"You haven't? You've *never* had sex? But, *why*? I mean...you're *so* pretty, I can't believe men don't want you. You're dating *Asher Fitzpatrick*! I mean, how can you be doing *that* and not sleeping with him?"

Finishing up with Misty's feet, I turned to Karen. "I'm a little concerned about this conversation of ours. Typically, it should be your mother or father having this discussion with you. Do you even know what your parents' opinion is about sex? Where they stand on it?"

"Well, obviously they've *had* it, because here I am. But that's *really* gross and honestly, I try not to think about it." A small grin played on her lips. "Mom mentioned awhile back that it was for marriage, but that is *so* old-fashioned, you know? I mean, really, Mom?" Her warm brown eyes rolled dramatically.

"Karen, I'm going to be honest with you because you're asking me very pointed and serious questions. Regardless of what I'm about to tell you, I still think you should do your mom the courtesy of talking with her about this. You might be surprised at her response. However, regarding me...*no*, I've never had sex. I'm twenty-two years old and am still a virgin."

I took a slow breath before continuing, "I'm waiting until I'm married. You see, I intend to be married one time, to one man, for my entire lifetime. When two people give themselves to each other, there's an act of trust taking place. You're opening yourself up *completely* to this person. Rationally, I can't see doing that, unless it's with someone who I love beyond even my own life, someone who I *know* loves me the same way.

"I have another reason, though my first reason ties in with it. You see, Karen, I believe in God and what He says in the Bible. I know that God created man and He created woman. He *designed* them to fit together. He designed them to *enjoy* sex. He designed the whole shebang, and as its Creator, He calls the shots. *He* gave the instruction to wait until you're married before engaging in and enjoying sex. He knows children can be created—He designed us that way. He wants to guard against illness and disease, against pain and mistrust and misuse. I trust *Him* to know what He's talking about. Therefore, I'm waiting until I'm married before I have sex. It might sound old-fashioned to you, but God is timeless. He's never old. He's always brand new."

Karen was quiet for a couple minutes. I let her have her solitude as I worked on Misty in silence. A few times I caught her looking closely at me, speculation once more in her eyes. Then she'd look away again. Finally, after about ten minutes, she turned to me and asked, "Is this what you meant when you said you told Asher you didn't want to rush things?"

"In part, yes. It's not only the sex, though. It's me. I'm more than my body parts. I have a mind and a soul. I have thoughts and ideas, dreams and fears, likes and dislikes; I have beliefs and disbeliefs. Before I shared any of these things, I wanted to make sure he was worthy of them. And that I was worthy of him. I wanted to take everything slowly. I wanted to get to know him. I wanted him to get to know me."

"And you did? You got to know him?"

"I'm getting to know him. I would imagine it will take a long time to really know all there is to him, but I want a long time with him, simply learning him.

"Here's an illustration that just occurred to me: Imagine if you will, that you've been invited to *the* social event of the year, and you need a dress. Now let's say that cost wasn't a factor; the person who invited you has indicated he'll cover all expenses. You have two options: One, you can go to a nice department store and find a dress that fits and looks good on you. But you know this dress will have been tried on already by any number of women, maybe even worn and returned. Option number two, the person who invited you requests to have a top dress designer create a dress only for you. Your exact measurements are taken. Your preferences in color, texture, fabric, and style are considered. This designer then creates for you the perfect dress. No one has ever even tried it on. You are the first body it has touched. Which dress would you want? The possibly used, at least tried on for size, department-store model, or the one created uniquely for you?"

"Obviously the one made just for me," she shrugged.

"Okay. Now let's say this designer made this dress for you, followed all your preferences, but before giving it to you, he loaned it out to several people first. Would that same dress still hold as much meaning? Would it still be as special? Or would it now be more at the level of the tried-on-for-size department store version?"

"I guess it really wouldn't be as special to me anymore."

"Now consider your body, your virginity, in the same manner. It sort of loses its precious appeal if you've allowed others to try you on before giving yourself to your spouse through love and commitment, doesn't it? I *love* Asher, but I won't let him try me on, and I won't try him on, before the final agreement is made. I want it to be special. I want to be purely and solely for him and him alone."

After a minute or two, she asked, "Do you guys even kiss?"

That made me smile. "Yes, we kiss. We embrace."

"Is it ever hard to stop at only a kiss? Are you ever *tempted* to do more?"

"Yeah...it can...it can get *difficult*. But this is where trust and respect come in. There have been many times that I've been lost in the grip of passion, and it's been Asher who's had to pull the reins back and stop. If he didn't love me, if he didn't *respect* me, he would have pushed and pressured me. He'd have taken advantage of my weakness and done what he wanted rather than respecting my wishes."

Karen's brown eyes searched mine. "Are you ever afraid if you make him wait, he might not want you anymore?"

"No, I'm not." I shook my head gently. "Karen, I won't deny that if he walked away from me and we broke up, I'd be hurt. It would *crush* me. But logically, I know in the long run, that temporary pain would be much better than to have given myself, to have tied myself to someone who really loved himself more than he loved me. To someone who really didn't care about me in the first place."

Karen chewed her lip thoughtfully for several minutes, then said, "Katy-Beth? Thanks for talking with me. For not flipping out."

"Of course; I hope...I hope I, at the very least, gave you some food for thought, maybe even changed your mind about the whole subject. You're way too precious to waste on someone who doesn't deserve the beautiful gift you are. You have *high* value. You *are* that beautiful, custom-created dress. Don't *ever* forget that."

"Thank you." She hugged me fiercely. "You've given me a lot to think about."

Hugging her back, I said, "You'd better get up to the house, it's near dinner time. I'll be along in a moment."

CHAPTER EIGHTEEN

Whispers of the Heart

Asher-

Marriage. Asher considered the word. Rolled it around in his mouth for a while. Tasted it on his tongue. He was on the last leg of his journey. The plane lifted off and he settled into his seat, closed his eyes, and tried to relax.

He wanted Kate. He *needed* Kate. Marriage would accomplish his goal. Would she accept him? When Asher had first met her, when he'd first arrived at the ranch, all he'd wanted was to get closer to her, to get to know her. As she softened towards him, he'd rashly thought of marriage. He knew that was something a woman like Kate would want. *Then* it had sounded like a good idea; *no big deal*, people did it all the time—they could do it, too. Now, as the word and all its implications became clearer, as he came to realize exactly how permanent and unchanging his feelings for her had become, marriage took on a whole new meaning, becoming crucial, no longer simply an option.

Asher knew he'd have to make some changes. He'd have to permanently leave the Agency. Walk away from the intelligence field. No more missions, no more puzzles. Kate deserved better; she deserved better than a man who was often gone and whose life was frequently in danger. He wouldn't put her through that, not if he could help it.

Leaving the Agency would take a well-planned exit. So many things were going on right now. So many irons in the fire. He wanted Kate, and marriage sounded more and more like the answer to his dilemma. Asher envisioned being married to her. What that would be like. What that would *feel* like. Suddenly, he knew he wanted that more than anything. He'd give up anything, everything; he simply *had* to have her. Somehow, she'd become essential, like air in his lungs. Emotion, longing shot through him, leaving him breathless. He prayed for the right time, for the right words, the *right* answer.

Kate-

Glancing at my watch, I looked up at the arrival board in excitement, noting Asher's plane should be landing *right* now. Jumping up, I left Cory seated where I'd been impatiently waiting. Ignoring his request that I *just chill,* as my rushing wouldn't bring Asher any faster, I quickly made my way to the security gate.

My eyes eagerly scanned the doorway, searching for him in the sea of faces. I was wearing the outfit he'd asked me to wear, the same outfit I'd worn on our first date. I'd dabbed his favorite perfume onto my neck and wrists. I tried calming my pounding pulse, but it was useless—there was no denying my excitement. Eager for my first glimpse of him, I craned my head, standing on tiptoe. Several people filed past me, momentarily blocking my line of sight; I shook my head in frustration. Then they cleared and he was there.

Asher's brilliant blue eyes were trained on me; there was something new, exciting, and purposeful in his gaze. He walked toward me; his mouth lifted in a grin. I don't remember moving, but suddenly, I was running. Asher dropped his carry-on and held his arms out. Launching myself, his arms snaked around me, bringing me closer still, and I knew I was home. A smaller man would have been knocked over. Not him. He caught me easily, lifting me.

At first, he simply held me tightly against him, his face buried in the side of my neck, breathing deeply. I *honestly* tried to remember people were standing around, probably watching; that we were making a spectacle of ourselves. But somehow, I couldn't force myself to care. All I cared was that he was here. I was in his arms. He was holding me.

"I love you." Asher whispered against my mouth. "I missed you."

"I missed you, too. I'm *so* glad you're back."

Somehow, we managed to untangle ourselves and retrieve Asher's luggage. Within a short half hour, we were on our way back to the ranch.

"Tell me how everything is. Have the Hunters left? Has Tiffy been able to sit on a horse yet?" Asher asked after we were on the road, his large hand gently squeezing my shoulder, lingering there.

"The Hunters left a week ago, but they plan to return again very soon." My breath shuddered as his fingers lightly brushed over my collarbone. "We're all doing fine. Samuel's been helping me with Tiffy. She seems to trust him quite a bit; I think she's making great progress. They seem to have a real connection."

"I gathered as much."

"I imagine it has to do with the loss both of them have had in their lives. Sammy's wife and Tiffy's husband...I think they're both finding healing in this."

"I agree and am glad, for both their sakes." Fingers grazed up the column of my neck, causing me to shiver again. "How are *you*?"

"I'm good. Much, much better now you're back. And you?"

"The same."

"Are you tired?" I asked, glancing from the road, to him, and back again.

"A little, but not nearly enough to want to lie down. Unless, of course, you were with me." His finger lightly flicking my nose, a playful grin on his face.

"Hey now, virgin ears back here, let's not forget." Cory grumbled, all but forgotten in the back seat.

"You could always ride in the bed, Cory." Asher smirked over his shoulder.

"Gee, thanks. I think I'll pass. Besides, Ash, you'd be corrupting Katy. And we can't have that."

"I doubt that," he replied. "Kate's incorruptible."

"Not hardly," I grinned. "You tempt me plenty, as you well know."

"You're the one who said you wanted to go slow. I'm only complying with your request. I figure your frustration works to my benefit." His voice took on a smoldering quality.

"How do you figure that?" I hoped my voice sounded calmer to them than it did to me.

"Easy. The more...*tension* there is between us, the more *frustrated* you become *physically*, the sooner you'll want to speed things up." His eyes bore into mine, a look in them I couldn't quite identify. Firmly, I looked back to the road, trying to think through the haze of longing that rose inside me.

"You know the rules, Ash." I quietly said as I swallowed. *You know the rules, too, Katy!* I reminded myself sternly.

"I do. Not until we're married. And I'm not trying to break them."

"La, la, la, la, la, la..." Cory sang loudly, covering his ears with his hands.

"What are you saying?" I ignored Cory's antics.

"You could marry me. You could be my wife. We could speed that up, thereby speeding up the rest of it as well."

What? Is he...what is he saying?

"This is...awkward," Cory stated.

"*What* are you saying, Ash? I'm...I'm not..." I shook my head, completely lost as to his meaning. Turning my signal on, I slowed down for the turn into the ranch driveway.

"We'll talk later." Asher promised.

"Good idea." Cory muttered under his breath. He was out of the truck as soon as I stopped it, slamming the door behind himself, and began loping towards the patio where everyone was gathered.

I sat for a moment in stunned silence, trying to figure out Asher's intent. Looking over, I found him quietly studying me. "Don't worry about it now. We'll talk about it soon, though. I promise. Okay?"

"I'm...I'm not sure I understand."

"It's pretty simple really. But now's not the time. You know how I feel about you. You know that I desire you. We simply need to hammer out some more details. I promise...we'll talk later." After a moment or two, I nodded and allowed him to help me from the truck. Asher closed the door, then pulled me against him, his mouth finding mine, lingering there, stealing my breath. Leaning back, he gazed at me, then led me to the house.

We'd planned a barbeque for Asher's return to the ranch. Because the twins came, along with Gina, we had a decent-sized group. After eating we divided up for an impromptu football game, playing until it was too dark to see. Dad had a large blaze roaring by the time we arrived to gather around the fire pit. I went inside to see if Mom needed a hand. She had the water warming for hot chocolate, and was gathering the necessary items for making S'mores. Leaving her to tend the water, I scooped up two large bags of marshmallows, a pack of Hershey's chocolate bars, and a box of graham crackers and carried them outside.

Asher had a seat saved for me and as we sat down to begin the wondrous process of making S'mores, Cory said, "I still say we won."

"Yeah, we did." I leaned forward to touch knuckles with him. Asher threw a marshmallow at me, bouncing it off my forehead, before it landed on the ground. Jack quickly nabbed that one. Jill sat by, waiting for the next missile. Blinking my eyes in surprise, I stared at him. He cocked an eyebrow at me, challenging me to respond.

"Don't start something you can't finish, mister." I smirked, full of bravado.

"Oh, bring it *on*, sweetheart." His cocky grin flashed as he crooked his index finger, inviting my attack. "If you think you can take me, you're welcome to try."

"Calvin," I looked directly into Asher's beautiful blue eyes and smiled. "Do we still have those squirt guns around?"

"You know what? I think we do. Let me check, I'll be right back." Quickly, he went inside to look, and Deken and Derek gave a couple of light-hearted cheers.

"So...what's going to happen? You and Ash going to square off in a duel or something?" Cory asked, feeding a marshmallow to Jill.

"It's a little more fun than a standard duel, Cory. It'll be like a night-ops mission, only without all the high-tech gear. No flashlights. Only you and your gun. It's hide-and-go-seek, in the dark, with squirt guns. We played this all the time in high school. We'll see how tough Ash really is, now."

"Oh, this ought to be good." Samuel pulled up a chair to sit beside Tiffy.

"What, Sammy? You don't think I could take him?" I asked in mock incredulity.

"Oh, no, it's not that," he assured me, filling his stick with marshmallows. "I can't wait to see Asher floundering around out there. He won't know which way to move. On the one hand, he's a natural-born warrior with a strong desire to win, on the other, he's highly protective of you and will guard you at all cost. Like I said, this ought to be good."

"You may be my first target, Sammy." Asher stated dryly, flinging a marshmallow at him.

"No, no, no; I've no intention of entering this game." Samuel caught the marshmallow and quickly slung it back. "I'll just sit and watch all the action. You'll have to fend for yourself."

Calvin returned with a medium-sized cardboard box in his arms. He set it on the side table and opened it. "All right, who's in?"

We crowded around to inspect the contents. Inside were several styles of squirt guns: hand gun types, some that looked like machine guns, then the bigger bazooka-type ones.

"What are the rules?" Asher asked, looking at me.

"The patio is a safe zone. The house is off limits. Be honest—if you're hit, then you're out—no cheating." I told them all.

"And where do we load up?" Cory asked, selecting a dark green machine gun model.

"Any hose location. There are several around the house and the barn. The water troughs are another source, and there's a stream not far from the main road," Calvin explained.

"How do we divide into teams?" Asher asked.

"No teams," I said. "You're your own team. Everyone can fill up at the hose bib right here. Then Sammy, as you're not playing, you can indicate when it's time to start. We'll give the game two hours."

"Well, as you kids are going to be busy, we're off to bed. Night y'all." Dad said as he and Mom stood. "Katy, make sure the fire's out before you call it a night. You can tell us who won in the morning."

After we were ready, loaded to the max, Samuel sent us out into the night with the strict command to wait for his call before we began. Tiffy sat out, opting to stay with Sammy.

From experience, I knew one of the best places to hide was near the horse corral. The horses knew me well and would alert me to any "enemy" activity. When Samuel sent us off, I raced for the barn, then circled around back, silently making my way toward the corral. If I played this right, I could nail every single one of them without having to refill my weapon.

Samuel whistled and I settled myself, preparing for the battle. I didn't care if someone else got me, but I was determined to get Asher first. Fading into the dark corner of the back corral, the horses gathered about thirty feet from me. I kept one eye on them and one eye roving around. One of the water troughs was within my line of sight, and I knew I could use it as a trap for any unsuspecting players.

I'd been there about ten minutes when one of the horses suddenly shied away from the fence. Staring into the dark, I watched for movement. Confident in my position, I was unconcerned about being seen. After a moment or two, Deken came into view.

Silently he duck-walked along the fence, looking all around himself. At one point he looked right at me, but never saw me. Knowing I was basically invisible, I scanned the area making sure no one else was around, and waited until he was closer. Then, I squirted him square in the chest.

"Dang it!" he muttered, rocking back on his butt, glaring around. Not wanting to give my position away to anyone who might be watching or listening, I remained silent. After a moment he stood and walked towards the house, grumbling to himself the entire way; I couldn't help but grin.

Within another forty-five minutes I'd nailed Derek and Gina as well. I still hadn't seen Calvin, Cory, or Asher, though. Deciding to give up my position and go on the hunt, I waited to make sure no one was sneaking up on me, then silently eased back around the barn. Pausing near the door, I surveyed the area. I knew at least one of them was still in the game—Samuel would whistle when we were down to the last player.

I tried to picture all the spots a man of Asher's size could hide. The first place I thought of was inside the barn itself. Not caring to enter from the main door, as it would surely squeak and give me away, I considered all my options. I decided to make my way back to the corral and enter through one of the unused stalls. Just as I was turning, I sensed movement off to my right. Holding my breath, I tried to locate the source of the noise.

Suddenly, a hand shot out of the dark, effectively covering my mouth, preventing me from screaming as I was pulled upward and backward into the dark interior of the barn. My captor wrapped his arms around me, lifting me against his broad chest, turning me slightly as we tumbled to the ground. He took the brunt of our fall, rolling us over, coming to rest on top of me, even as his mouth urgently replaced his hand on my lips. From one breath to the next, Asher was thoroughly and intently kissing me.

I'd known it was him almost as soon as he'd touched me. Knew his touch, his mouth, his scent that well. I'd missed this, missed him. His silent assault left me needy and breathless as we kissed for several wonderful, uninterrupted minutes.

"*Kate.*" He breathed against my skin, making me shiver. Asher pulled back some, his eyes seeking mine. I could barely discern his features in the darkness. Raising my hand, I lightly trailed my fingertips over his eyes, his cheeks, his lips. Leaning to one side, he captured my hand, turning my wrist to his mouth, inhaling my scent, kissing me there. Asher made a low sound in his throat and I felt him shudder lightly. Pushing, I rolled on top of him, pressing him into the straw, and sat for a moment taking him in. Tenderly, he reached up, cupping my face, drawing me down to him. His thumbs caressed my cheeks, then my lips, softly at first, then with more pressure. "I love you," he whispered, his lips against mine.

"I love you, too."

Suddenly, Asher tensed. "Kate, I'm sorry...."

"For what?" I asked, momentarily bewildered, even as I felt him freeze under me. Then, hearing a sound behind me, without even thinking, I flung myself to the side, my hand inadvertently landing on a water gun in the dark. Grasping it—I couldn't see if it was mine or his—in one continuous motion, I rolled over, firing at our assailant and Asher as well.

"Gotcha," I smiled sweetly at both Calvin and Asher.

"Calvin got me first." Ash replied, looking down at his wet shirt.

"Doesn't matter; I still got *you* before you could get *me*."

"I see; I'll have to remember that next time."

"For what it's worth, I was trying to nail the both of you." Calvin grumbled, equally disgusted by the outcome.

"I guess that's an 'A' for effort." I grinned. "Too bad. How'd you know we were in here anyway?"

"I heard you, uh, when, you know..." He waved his hand in our general direction.

I chuckled. "Do either of you know if Cory is still in play?"

"I got him," Asher said.

"So, I won then?" I stood and dusted myself off. *Yay me!*

"You're a worthy opponent." Asher nodded as he too, stood and dusted off.

"Quit bragging, Katy." Calvin stepped outside the barn. "Let's get back to the house, see what everyone's doing."

The fire had burned low by the time we arrived back. It seemed everyone was tired and our little party dispersed quickly. Soon it was only Asher and me.

"How long are you here for?" I sat down, stretching my legs in front of me, folding my hands across my stomach. I'd put off asking this question for as long as I could. Before Asher left the first time, he'd arranged with my parents to continue renting a room from us, kind of like a boarding house. This way he'd have a place to stay when he was not working, so he could be close to me. Mom and Dad had said there was no sense in him renting an apartment in town, when he'd be here with us anyway; Asher had readily agreed. I'd wondered what he intended to do with his other home in L.A., but didn't have the nerve to ask, not wanting him to think I was pressuring him or anything.

"You're that eager to get rid of me?" he softly teased. Asher pulled his chair close to mine, angling it so that we were nearly facing each other.

"You know what I mean." I mentally braced for his answer.

"I do." He gently nudged my leg with his, waited a heartbeat or two, then said, "I have to leave in ten days." He paused, giving me a moment to collect myself. Only ten days. It was not enough time. "I'll be gone for eighteen days." He waited again, his eyes never leaving my face. Swallowing, I nodded as that was all I could manage right then. After a moment Asher continued, "In four and a half weeks I'm hoping you'll agree to accompany me on a trip."

I tried to smile and asked, "Where to?"

"I'd like you to meet my sister and her family, then after that I begin promotions for *Dust Devils*. You'll need to mark your calendar for the 19th of March; you and I have a date."

"You want me to meet your family?"

"Yes." He flashed his amazing smile. "I've already told Jaime all about you, and she's very excited to meet you. I thought maybe your mom could come with us, you know, as a chaperone."

I'll be honest and admit I was feeling a tad bit overwhelmed at the idea of meeting his family. What if they didn't like me? What if they didn't approve? What if *I* didn't like them? How many of Asher's girlfriends had he brought home before? How would I compare in their eyes?

Asher watched me silently, letting me process our discussion. After a couple minutes, he said, "I've never introduced anyone to my family before. They know this—*you*—are important and they're anxious to make a good impression."

"They've never met *any* of your girlfriends before?" That had me skeptical.

"Never. You're the first. I sincerely hope you'll be the last."

"*Really?*"

"Really."

I inhaled slowly. "I'm not sure if that knowledge helps me or not. I think you just upped the ante in the pressure pot."

"Sorry, love." He chuckled. "I simply wanted you to know you're important. Besides, I've already met your family, it's only fair you meet mine as well."

Suddenly, I remembered what he'd said before about the date he mentioned. "What's happening on March 19th?"

"We leave for L.A. That's the week of the premier for *Dust Devils*. I need a hot date, and you're it."

"Oh, I see," I grinned, blushing under his warm gaze.

"Will you be nervous? Walking the Red Carpet with me?"

"I'll have to...?" My grin faded quickly.

"Mmm-hmm." Now he was grinning.

"I...I won't have anything appropriate to wear for something like that. Can't I simply meet you inside or something?"

"Ah, no. I need you at my side."

"But... I'll need some sort of dress for the occasion, won't I?"

"So, you'll go shopping while we're visiting Jaime."

"Aye-yai-yai."

"It's just a dress, Kate. I know you'll look amazing. If you can make simple denim look hot, I'm almost afraid to see what you'll look like in a gown. I'll have to go armed to fight all the men off."

"Don't be ridiculous." I rolled my eyes. "And, it's not the dress I'm worried about."

"What is it then?"

"All those people! All the lights, the cameras, the noise."

"Don't worry. I'll protect you. Like I said, I'll be armed, you'll be safe with me."

"I'm not worried about my safety, Ash. It's a lot of attention...you know I can take care of myself."

"I do. However, I'd rather like to avoid that necessity if I can help it. And honey, you get attention everywhere you go. I'm the one who's going to be anxious, what with all the slathering men following us around and falling at your feet. It's going to be a zoo."

"I should stay home, then. I wouldn't want you to be anxious or anything."

"Well...I guess, if that's what you want...I can see if Jessica would be my date. She has to go anyway, that might work fine." Asher nodded, looking deep in thought.

"Over my dead body. Or yours. Or hers."

He grinned at me, his blue eyes sparkling in the firelight. "I kinda figured you'd see it that way."

"Paybacks, baby. Paybacks."

"I look forward to it." His smile broadened.

"Wait till you see my dress. You won't be smiling then, I guarantee it." I steadily met his gaze. His smile vanished, but mine returned.

The next morning over breakfast, Asher told Mom and Dad about the trip to Phoenix to meet Jaime. Mom quickly agreed to be my chaperone. She didn't want to go in March though—too close to opening season on the ranch, she felt. "Calvin," she said over her coffee mug, "I think *you* should go."

"What? Why me?"

"The city and the lights will be good for you." Mom said confidently.

"I think the country is good for me."

"Oh, you'll have fun. That kind of stuff is for the young at heart."

Calvin grumbled a bit, but eventually agreed to go. "Will I need a tux?" he suddenly asked Asher.

"Only if you want to wear one. I have to, but as my guest, you're not required to."

"That's a relief."

CHAPTER NINETEEN

Bittersweet

Asher-

Leaving Kate was much harder the second time around. Asher knew he'd have to come to terms with this and get his head back in the game. People depended on him; lives were at stake. The day before he'd left, he'd made some special arrangements. Something to lessen the impact he knew his leaving would make. He hoped she found a measure of comfort in his efforts.

It was only through years of training and experience that Asher'd been able to compartmentalize his thoughts and emotions. He'd been able to confine Kate to the back of his mind, just a small portion of his consciousness, and thereby focus on the problem at hand. Saeed Ishar—Asher's current target—was missing again. This wasn't the first time he'd gone to ground. Asher knew he'd find him; it was only a matter of time. He would continue sifting through everything, examining every detail until something came up. The clues were there; he simply had to find them.

Once the plane landed at Cairo International, Asher began his hunt. Swiftly, effortlessly, he assumed another persona, Benjamin Ahmed, a private businessman. His simple, yet effective disguise in place, he moved quickly, his keen mind working in an ordered frenzy, ferreting out each detail, ruling out all dead ends until a solid trail began to form. The understanding that the sooner he found his target, the faster he'd be home to Kate, drove him faster, spurring him on.

He was close; he knew it.

Closer to finding Saeed, closer to seeing Kate.

Kate-

I'd finished warming up my first horse that morning, when I heard the dogs barking. Asher had already left; he'd be gone eighteen days this time. Far longer than last time and I hated every second of it. We didn't have any guests this week, yet the dogs were still barking. Well, Tiffy was back again. Having fallen in love with the ranch, she'd gone back to Utah long enough to hire a realtor and put her house up for sale. She'd packed what she could into a U-Haul and moved to Cody. Until she found a place—once her other one sold that is—she'd decided to rent a room from us, not anticipating it would take long. Samuel and Cory were still here as well, though Cory mentioned he would be leaving soon, besides, they weren't guests any longer. They were family now.

With the continued racket from the dogs, I rode around to the front of the house to see what the problem was. A flower delivery van was parked in the driveway. Dismounting, I left the big gelding ground tied. The driver was stepping out of the van when I walked up. "Good morning. May I help you?"

"Morning. Yes, I have a delivery for Kate Reilly."

"I'm Katy."

"Right this way." Pete—I saw his nametag—waved with his clipboard. I followed him to the back of the van, where he handed me a vase filled with yellow roses. The arrangement was stunning. Instead of the typical baby's breath, the florist had added bunches of evergreens. The scent of the roses combined with the crisp smell of pine was intoxicating. I signed for the delivery, then waved Pete off. I carefully made my way to the porch, setting the bouquet on one of the tables. Pulling a chair out, I sat down before tearing open the card.

Hello Beautiful. You said yellow was your favorite. I've sent you eighteen roses—I hope they're the right color—the same number of days I'll be gone. Tomorrow you'll get seventeen more. I'll continue to send them until I'm home. Each day, your delivery will contain one less rose, to represent one less day until I see you. I love you; I miss you. Be happy, love. Imagining your smile will get me through. I'll call as soon as I can. Love, Ash.

Reading through his message once more, I counted the roses; there were eighteen. Was he really going to send me seventeen more tomorrow? Though, he'd asked me to be happy, I couldn't help but shed a tear or two. His loving gesture was so *romantic*. Probably the most romantic thing I'd witnessed to date. Every day I'd look forward to getting his roses, knowing it was one day closer to his return. Smiling, I wiped the tears away and carried the bouquet into the house.

As I carried the vase upstairs, I suddenly wondered what I was going to *do* with all those roses.

On the evening of the sixth day after Asher'd left, he called. He couldn't talk long and I could barely hear him, there was so much noise in the background.

The gist of the short conversation was that he loved and missed me and dreamed about me—these were good things. Of course, there had to be dour news as well. Asher would be delayed on his return. He couldn't go into detail, but something was going on and he was needed; and whatever it was, was very important. He'd have a travel agent be in touch to arrange our trip to Arizona, and would meet us there.

Of course, this wasn't the news I'd been hoping for. I knew he couldn't help it, and there was no fault, but I was devastated all the same. Assuring him I would be okay, I reminded him to be safe and that I loved and missed him terribly, holding back the tears until after we'd hung up.

The next morning when Pete arrived with my delivery, instead of twelve roses, there were sixteen; the countdown had been restarted.

Summer was almost over; the days were getting shorter and shorter. Now when I went outside in the morning, I could see my breath in the air. This was my favorite time of year. The trees were beginning to change colors, turning varying shades of orange and red. The horses' coats grew in thick, preparing for winter. For several weeks now, we'd seen geese fly overhead as they made their way south. I loved hearing them call back and forth.

Mom and I did lots of baking and freezing before we left. We'd be gone for two weeks, and wanted to have plenty of food for Dad, Calvin, Samuel, and Tiffy. Being an absolute blessing, Tiffy had volunteered to cook while we were gone. Though, by no means, did the guys need her to, they appreciated her generous offer all the same.

Tiffy's fear of horses was virtually conquered. I continued giving her lessons, simply to improve her horsemanship, but she was completely at ease around them now. As I saw the joy and peace on her face every time she saddled up, I couldn't help but send up a prayer of thanksgiving.

Asher called the night before we left. He was getting ready to board his flight for Phoenix. "I'll see you in a few short hours," he promised. His voice smoldered and my pulse responded accordingly. After we hung up, I did some last-minute packing, then decided to turn in. Tomorrow would be a long day.

Three-thirty came way too soon. I pried my eyes open, trying not to blink in fear they'd close again. Foreigner's *Hot Blooded* was appropriately playing. As my mind began to wake up, it suddenly dawned that I would see Asher *today*. Adrenaline surged through me and I was instantly awake. In no time, I was showered and dressed, my bed made, and I was applying my makeup.

Samuel and Tiffy had volunteered to feed that morning so Calvin could accompany us; that way Dad wasn't driving home by himself. We loaded our luggage and were soon on the road.

Kate-

Impatiently, I waited for the captain to permit the seatbelt light to go off, drumming my fingertips lightly on the armrest. Mom gave me a quick smile. Soon, the flight attendant was making her way down the aisle, thanking us for flying her airline. I appreciated the courtesy; I just really wanted her to hurry up.

My eyes scanned the crowds as we exited through the security checkpoint. Asher stood about twenty feet away, surrounded by a small group of fans. He was signing autographs, but his eyes were on the exit; and once his gaze met mine, he never looked away. I watched as he handed a pen and paper back to a young girl; I saw his lips move, then he was striding toward me.

My eyes were glued to him, thoroughly enjoying the sight of him. In my peripheral vision, I noted cameras were flashing sporadically, and several people were pointing at me. And then, the only thing I was aware of was Asher himself. His arms wrapped tightly around me, lifting me up as he buried his face in the crook of my neck. He held me like that for several lengthy moments, then gently set me down. Turning, Asher gave Mom a light hug as well. "Naomi, it's good to see you. Let's get your luggage, then we can get out of this zoo, huh?" Asher took my bag and offered to carry Mom's as well, holding my hand as we walked. "How was the flight? Any trouble?"

"None. It just seemed to take forever." I gave his hand a squeeze.

"I know what you mean. Are you guys hungry? Jaime's cooking tonight, but it'll take about an hour to get there with all the traffic. We can stop and grab you something if you want? It's not a problem."

"I'm fine, thanks. Mom?"

"I might want a quick snack or at least a bottled water," Mom replied.

"Sure thing. After we get out of the airport traffic, we'll stop and I can run in for you." Asher said.

The car Asher led us to was a black Ford Excursion with dark tinted windows. It was the nicest vehicle I'd ever been in. "Is this yours?" I asked as he unlocked the door and opened it for me.

"It is; I keep it at Jaime's for when I visit."

I ran another appreciative eye over it, then asked if Mom wanted the front seat. She assured me the back was fine, and once we were situated, we got on the road, making one quick stop for her water.

Jaime's house had two stories, and sat a bit farther off the road than its neighbors. It was painted a beautiful pale gold color and had dark wood shutters. The sun was what was amazing here, huge, and bright in the sky. I shaded my eyes against the glare as I looked around. If Wyoming was beginning to feel more like fall, then Arizona still felt very much like summer. Not tropical; there was no balmy breeze. No, the air here was warm and dry. Sweat beaded on my upper lip. Asher took the heavier bags for Mom and me, and we carried our smaller carry-ons. Before we reached the wide front doors, they opened and a woman I guessed to be in her mid to late twenties stood there.

This had to be Jaime. Her eyes were a striking shade of blue, not exactly like Asher's, though beautiful all the same. Their hair was the same color, though. She was a little shorter than I was which surprised me. I guess, I'd figured Asher's family would all be taller, like him.

"Hello! Welcome!" Her smile was warm and inviting. Asher reached back for my hand, bringing me forward to his side; his thumb gently rubbing my palm in comfort.

"Sis, this is Kate. Kate this is Jaime." Asher's voice was warm with affection.

Jaime stepped forward, wrapping me, then Mom in a friendly hug, before leading us inside. "I hope you're hungry. Dinner's about ready."

"Starving," I assured her. The foyer was tiled in large squares of dark brown; I estimated each square to be about twenty inches across. A wide staircase rose majestically off to the right of the foyer, where it wrapped around gracefully to the second story.

"I'll show you your rooms. Take a few minutes to freshen up, if you want. I'll get dinner on the table, then we can eat."

I was showed into a spacious room overlooking the backyard. A beautiful pool with a rock fountain was the yard's focal point. Mom's room was directly across from mine, and the bathroom was to the right of hers. Asher's room was next to mine. I did my best not to dwell on that.

After I'd used the bathroom and changed into something more appropriate for the Arizona climate—shorts and a tank top—I made my way back downstairs. Mom and Asher were already in the kitchen. Mom was standing by a set of French doors that led out onto a brick patio. Asher sat near her at the large kitchen bar, a tall glass of iced tea in his hand. The aroma of dinner was simply delicious, my stomach rumbling in response. "Whatever you're cooking smells amazing, Jaime. If I wasn't hungry before, I can assure you I'm seriously starving now." I said as I entered the spacious room.

Jaime was near the stove stirring a large pot. "Well, Asher said you liked Mexican food, Kate, so I hope you enjoy it."

A door off the kitchen area opened and a redheaded, stoutly built man stepped in. Holding his hand was a younger, smaller version of himself. Asher stood and shook the man's hand. He then picked the little guy up, cuddling him affectionately, before turning to Mom and me. "Kate, Naomi, this is Sean, Jaime's husband, and this little tiger is Michael. Sean, this is Kate," Asher wrapped his arm gently around my waist. "And this is her mother, Naomi. You've got to watch Michael, he likes blonds."

Sean held his hand out to me. "Kate, we're glad you're here."

While Mom and Sean were shaking hands, my attention shifted to the little guy still clinging to his uncle. I caught his eye and smiled. "Hello, Michael." Vaguely, I heard Sean ask how the flight was. Michael stared at me for a moment or two. My face shifted to a grin and slowly, he grinned back. I offered my hand in greeting. After a moment's hesitation, Michael reached out and shook it.

Asher tenderly squeezed his nephew. "Michael, this is Kate. She's Uncle Ash's girlfriend. Do you know what that means?"

"It means you kiss her," Michael said in a clear voice. Everyone was silent a moment, then we were all laughing.

"That's *exactly* what it means." Asher chuckled, leaning in to kiss my forehead.

CHAPTER TWENTY

Beautiful

Kate-

If I'd had any lingering worries about Asher's family, they dissipated that first evening. We ate dinner out on the veranda, talking, and watching the sun as it set in a slow beautiful display. Jaime and Sean let Michael stay up a little longer than normal, because Uncle Asher was there. Michael settled on Asher's lap and snuggled into his shoulder; I couldn't blame him; those shoulders were made for snuggling.

We talked until well into the late hours of the night, laughing at childhood escapades that Jaime and Asher shared about each other. Of course, Mom had to toss in a few of mine as well. Finally, somewhere near midnight, Asher caught me yawning and said, "Bedtime, love."

"I'm fine, really," I choked out over another long yawn.

Asher grinned. "*Bedtime.* You're exhausted; I'll be here in the morning."

Yawning again, I allowed him to bring me to my feet. Mom had gone up a couple of hours earlier. We said goodnight to Jaime and Sean, then made our way upstairs. Right outside my bedroom door, he stopped, turning so we faced each other. His arms slid around me, lifting me higher as he gently pushed me against the wall. His lips were firm, yet gentle. He kissed me unhurried, slow, and deliberate.

After a little while he lifted his head, looking down at me. "I've waited weeks to do that. I've dreamed about it." Tenderly, he nuzzled my face and inhaled deeply. "Your mom is right there in that room, so I'm going to have to be on my best behavior."

"And your sister is downstairs." I acknowledged.

"I don't want to behave." Asher pressed against me, his teeth finding the skin of my neck. "I'd like to misbehave. *A lot.*"

"That's...not...." I breathed, unable to finish my thoughts.

"*I know.* I don't even know why I said that—it doesn't help me either." He released me, stepping back. "Goodnight; I'm thrilled you're here." Then, as if he couldn't help himself, he leaned forward and kissed me again. "Go to bed, Kate, before I do something we'll both regret."

My hands shook as I felt for the doorknob. Somehow, I managed to open it, which was a feat in and of itself considering Asher was still kissing me. Stopping, he pulled back, gripping the jamb tightly. When he paused, I put more distance between us.

"Text me when you're done in the bathroom. I'll wait in my room; I shouldn't see you in your pajamas, not if I'm going to survive tonight." Asher reached for my door, closing it gently, but firmly, between us. I stared at it for a moment or two, then blinked and turned to locate my bags. Gathering the necessary items, I quickly made my way to the bathroom, Asher nowhere in sight. I was back in my room, my cell phone in hand, the lights turned out in less than fifteen minutes.

I'm done. The bathroom's yours. Sweet dreams, mister. I love you; I texted before lying down. I hated to admit he'd been right, but exhaustion slammed into me, and I was asleep before I heard him leave his room.

Asher-

Asher stared at the wall. Desire pounded through him; his hands tightly fisted in the comforter. His body was rigid in agitation where he lay motionless on the bed. *Kate is here.* Right on the other side of that tan wall. He held his breath.

He felt calmer, more in control when she was next to him, but as soon as she was out of reach, out of sight, he began to feel this all-consuming need to see her again.

Samuel had suggested turning in his resignation as soon as possible and making his attachment to Kate permanent. Asher knew the risks being this distracted posed for him and his team. He'd already drafted his letter; it only needed to be sent.

Asher's phone buzzed. He unclenched his fist and looked at the screen. She was in bed. Just on the other side of that wall. Right now, Asher hated tan walls. He rolled over and buried his face in his pillow, swallowing a groan. It was going to be a long night.

Kate-

Bright sunshine woke me in the morning, nothing but blue skies through the large window. Stretching leisurely, I enjoyed the soft sheets. After a couple of minutes, I got up and made the bed, eager to see Asher again.

After dressing, I made my way down to the kitchen. The coffee was on and Asher was pouring my cup when I entered the spacious room. "Good morning," he whispered in my ear as he kissed my cheek and handed me the mug.

"Good morning." I smiled.

Over my second cup of coffee, Jaime asked, "So Kate, what would you like to do today?"

"I'm totally content to simply hang out around the house here with you guys. We don't have to do anything; we can simply visit."

"Okay. Well, the pool is open, feel free to use it whenever, day or night. Ash can show you some of the hiking trails around here. And maybe one day we can go to town and do some shopping?"

"That sounds good. Now that you mention it, I do need to go to town. Asher invited me to the premier for his movie and I need a dress. I went online and made a list of some stores I'd like to check out if that's okay?"

"Just name the time; I'm always game for shopping."

On our third day in Phoenix, Jaime and Mom and I went to town. Sean, Michael, and Asher were going to a local park to fly a kite Asher had purchased for his nephew. Before we left, Asher handed Jaime a piece of paper, saying we needed to stop at the address indicated before shopping. When I asked why, Asher smiled. "Wait and see, love." Then he kissed me soundly before closing my car door.

After giving Jaime my list of stores, I asked if she recognized the address Asher was sending us to. She said she did, but declined to go into further detail.

We'd been driving about thirty minutes when Jaime pulled to the curb in front of a large, ornate, brick-and-glass building. The jazzy gold lettering on the wall above the double doors read, *Solis Fine Jewelry*.

"Oh, you've *got* to be kidding me." I exclaimed to no one in particular.

"He had this commissioned long before you arrived." Jaime responded.

"You know what this is?"

"I do. I helped him with the order. I won't say anything more. Just know that he really, *really* loves you."

Stepping from the car, we approached the doors. I felt underdressed simply walking into this place. An actual doorman, in full uniform, opened the glass door for us. Three people were behind the counter; one woman gave us her attention as we approached. Her suit was tailored to fit; it had to be—there was no way she got that lucky off the rack. Her hair and makeup were perfect. "May I help you?" she asked, her voice cultured and refined. Her hand with her perfectly manicured nails, rested on the glass.

"I'm KatyBeth Reilly. I think you have something on hold for me?"

"May I see a photo ID, please?" After handing her my driver's license, which she thoroughly checked against my likeness, she returned it and said, "My name is Carolyn. I'll be happy to assist you. Please follow me."

She led us into a private room with a velvet-lined table in the center. Four black leather chairs were arranged around it; against the back wall stood a large safe. Beside the safe was an armed guard. Carolyn indicated we take a seat, as she made her way to the safe. When she returned, she carried a large wooden case that she opened and laid before us.

My eyes stared in disbelief. Nestled inside, on a bed of crushed black velvet, were the most beautiful pieces of jewelry I'd ever seen. I heard Mom's quick intake of breath, as I looked up at Carolyn. She must have read the question in my eyes, because she said, "The stones are champagne diamonds, their clarity flawless. Their total weight is four and three-quarter karats. Would you like to try them on?" Words failed me. "Is there something wrong with the set?" she prompted. I'm sure I seemed to her exactly what I was, an unsophisticated young woman, unworthy to view this jewelry, much less wear it. For a moment I felt cowed, but then mentally squared my shoulders and reminded myself that I was KatyBeth Reilly. And Asher loved me, and he'd had this made because he loved me.

"Nothing's wrong with it." I met her eyes. "It's beautiful. Yes, I'd like to try it on."

Carolyn nodded, picking up the bracelet, indicating my right wrist. Next, she picked up the necklace and fastened that around my neck. She let me put the earrings on myself. Carolyn then handed me a large mirror. I could only stare, the set was simply stunning. The necklace was crafted from gold, the chain slender and smooth. Its focal point was a large, princess-cut stone. The earrings matched the pendant, though they had two stones, one above the other, creating an off-balanced sort of figure eight; the largest stone at the bottom, the smaller on top. The bracelet had smaller stones surrounded by tiny, clear diamonds on slender solid-gold links.

As I admired the pieces—turning one way, then another, getting the best view—Carolyn explained what a champagne diamond was. Apparently, they came in several different shades, from a light champagne color to a darker, almost chocolate color. All the stones in my set were of the light champagne color, all in the same princess-cut. Each diamond was certified and insured, she informed me. Carolyn advised that if I wanted, I could leave the set with her until our errands in town were completed, then pick them up on our way home.

This sounded like an excellent idea to me. The thought of running around town with however many thousands of dollars' worth of diamonds just sitting in the car made me faintly nauseous. When we were back in the car, Jaime handed me an envelope. It was a brief, hand-written note from Asher. Each time he called me "Beautiful", I felt as though I was, and that was how it was addressed: *"Hey Beautiful, I'd planned to give you these later, but couldn't wait any longer. I hope you like them. Love, Ash."*

Mom wordlessly handed me tissues and I could only be thankful I'd waited to cry until I was safely in the car. I was now more determined than ever to do Asher proud with this dress.

At Mom's insistence, we checked out several of the nicer department stores; but I wasn't seeing anything I liked. I didn't have an exact image in my head, but somehow, knew I'd know it when I saw it. After two hours of searching, Jaime asked if I'd like to visit the stores I'd listed. They were all consignment-type shops. On the way to the first place, I asked Jaime if she had a sewing machine.

"I do. Are you intending to make your own gown?"

"No, not if I can help it. However, I may be able to piece a couple dresses together if I need to—just making sure I have my options open."

The first shop didn't have anything, but in the second, we hit the jack-pot. At least, I felt so. I'd gathered about ten dresses to try on, varying in color. From those I narrowed the selection down to two. The gold one had a bodice I simply loved. It was fitted and showed my figure well. I had a little cleavage—not obscene cleavage, but, moderate cleavage, leave them wondering cleavage. The golden color was warm and made my skin glow. What I didn't like about it was the skirt; it was way too short for me to be comfortable. The second dress, the brown one, had a beautiful skirt that I adored. To me, it looked like an inverted calla lily. It was chiffon, layered in tiers, and had a slit up the right leg to about mid-thigh. Sexy, but not sleazy. The colors in the skirt were the real knockout. It started off in a deep, warm brown, like melted milk chocolate, and with each layer and tier the shade lightened, until the top was a beautiful pale gold. Unfortunately, the bodice on this dress wasn't very appealing to me; it was also chiffon, but it went high on the neck. I constantly wanted to pull it away from my throat, feeling as if I was choking. I went back and forth between the two, before deciding to get both.

My plan was to detach the bodice from the gold one and reattach it to the brown one. Simple enough. We made a stop at a fabric store to purchase a few supplies, then went to a trendy shoe boutique Jaime thought would be appropriate. She'd been right; I found the perfect pair, pale gold, very similar to the gold on the dress. They had a nice four-inch heel, nothing too drastic; I could walk in them easily. After swinging back by the jewelers, we were finally on our way home.

It was hot, far hotter than Wyoming, and I kept thinking about that huge pool in the backyard. A nice, cool swim sounded amazing right about now. I didn't see Asher anywhere when I went inside, so took my packages up to my room, and decided to change into my swimsuit while there.

Asher was seated at the kitchen table when I came down; he'd risen from his chair as I entered, and I didn't hesitate. I wrapped my arms around him, burying my face in his chest. "Thank you. They're beautiful. You didn't have to do that, Ash."

"I know that; I *wanted* to—I'm glad you like them." His lips pressed against my temple, my ear; his breath gently tickling.

We were all so hot, we decided to swim first, and eat later. Asher ran upstairs to change, but as I was already in my suit, I headed outside. The water looked so enticing, I decided to dive right in. Swimming under water,

I made my way all the way to the shallow end of the pool. As I rose in the water, which came to my thighs, I noticed several things simultaneously. Mom sat to my right, dangling her feet in the water, with Michael perched beside her wearing his life vest. Jaime and Sean were carrying a stack of towels from the house, and Asher was standing about ten feet in front of me. He'd just removed his shirt. He was standing there *shirtless*.

I remembered this view, clearly remembered it. Like it was yesterday, Asher standing in our guest bedroom as I made up the bed. Every ripple of muscle, every firm, tight angle and indention, I remembered them all. I knew I was staring. It was his hands tightly fisted around his shirt that drew my attention, shifting my eyes to his face.

Asher stared back. His bright blue eyes slowly mapped me, his gaze traveled, touching here and there. By the time his eyes did finally reach mine, I'd stopped breathing altogether. Somewhere in the back of my mind, I was aware that around us was nothing but awkward silence. I didn't know what to do, didn't know how to move, how to think. Suddenly, *thankfully*, Michael cried out, "Catch me, Uncle Ash!"

Coming back to my senses, heat flooded my face. I sucked in a ragged breath, quickly turned, and dove beneath the water, swimming away. When I broke the surface again, I was clear at the other end of the pool. In the right corner was a small underwater bench, so I perched myself safely there. From here, I watched as Asher caught Michael in his arms time and time again. Michael's laughs and giggles were delightful; that he and his uncle loved and adored each other was obvious.

Suddenly an image flashed across my mind, a beautiful one: Asher holding another child, *our* child. Tears sprung to my eyes and I carefully wiped them away.

After about ten minutes or so, Asher simply held Michael in the water, helping him swim, telling him how to kick his legs, to use his arms. Jaime walked around the pool and sat beside me. "You okay?" she asked quietly.

"Yeah, I'm all right," I replied, trying not to blush. I'd been hoping, in vain apparently, that maybe nobody noticed the tension between he and I.

"When Asher first mentioned you to me, Kate, I was a little surprised. I knew he dated women. I've seen pictures of him, so I'm able to at least stay informed about his social life. But he's never, *ever* mentioned anyone to me before, not by name, not in any way. Then he called me about four months ago, and told me about his latest movie...and about a girl he'd met. That was it; just that he'd met a girl.

"He's continued to mention you when we talk, telling me more and more about you each time. Then, about five weeks ago, he said he wanted us to meet. Excited is putting my reaction mildly. Kate, I've never seen my brother so happy, or calm; I'm *so* glad he met you." She gave me a quick hug, before slipping into the water, swimming over to where Asher and Michael were still splashing around. My eyes teared again from her touching words.

Michael made a brave attempt to swim to Jaime, who was three feet away, her arms outstretched to receive him. After seeing his nephew safely into his mother's arms, Asher looked in my direction, making a beeline for me. He dove below the surface, coming up at my feet. "I love you." I smiled down at him.

Asher smiled back. "I love you, too."

CHAPTER TWENTY-ONE

Boy Howdy, Now That's a Dress

Kate-

"So, what do you think? Is it alright?" Jaime and Mom were in my room; Jaime had kindly set up her sewing machine under the window for better lighting, and I'd spent several hours a day working on the dress. I turned slowly in front of them, my arms spread to give them the full view.

"Katy, *baby*, you're beautiful. You did an amazing job." Mom stepped closer, gently fingering the filmy material on the skirt.

"Wow, you weren't kidding when you said you could sew, Kate. This is beautiful work," Jaime said. "I've thought it before, I know it now—my brother is a lucky man."

"So, it's not too much? I wanted to look sexy, but not, you know, sleazy."

"Well, I think you nailed it," Mom said. Jaime nodded in fervent agreement.

Glowing under their praise, I studied myself in the mirror. The dress did look amazing. It hugged my figure in all the right places, the color making my skin glow. My waist was well defined and when I moved, sitting or walking, a nice healthy slice of leg, all the way up my thigh, would be enticingly glimpsed. I was sure this dress would stop Asher in his tracks; it would make his jaw drop. I couldn't help the surge of anticipation that flashed through me at the thought.

The premier was a little over five months away, and I felt I was ready. I quickly changed out of the dress and hung it in a white garment bag in the back of the closet.

After dinner, Sean and Jaime asked if we wanted to go for a night swim; their pool was solar-heated, so the water was always warm. Mom announced she was going to bed; I think the heat was getting to her. We didn't get temperatures this warm in Wyoming.

A swim sounded wonderful, so I went up to change. By the time I made it outside, Sean, Jaime, and Asher were already in the pool. Sean and Jaime were floating on a couple of foam chaise lounges; Asher sat on the side of the pool with his back to me, his feet in the water.

Making my way over, I sat beside him. "Hey." I said quietly, by way of greeting, as I placed a kiss on his shoulder.

"Hey yourself," Asher grinned. He slid his hand over, taking mine in his, holding it gently. I looked at him, but his eyes were on the skyline, seemingly deep in thought. After a couple minutes, he slid off the side of the pool and came to stand in front of me; the water rippled gently around him as he placed his hands on my thighs. Warmth enveloped me at his touch. My knees were pressed against his stomach, my feet rubbed along his legs. Asher looked into my eyes; his gaze searching.

His grin flashed again and was gone. "Kate," my name sounded rough; he paused, cleared his throat, then continued, his tone low and full of sincerity. "Kate, I want you for my wife. Will you marry me?" My ears seemed to have stopped working, and my heart seemed intent on leaping from my chest, it pounded so furiously there. Asher turned his hand over, palm-side up, and there in the center sat a ring. It was a golden band; with a large princess-cut stone; surrounding it were smaller diamonds in a shade similar to the set he'd given me days ago. Blankly, I stared at it before looking up at him.

The look on his face struck me as odd. For the first time, Asher looked uncertain, maybe even fearful, his breathing turned shallow. I'd seen him face down a man with a knife and not even flick an eyelash. Now, as he stood before me, he seemed anxious, swallowing noisily. His eyes were on mine as he waited. Suddenly, my mind replayed his words, and it occurred to me what he'd just said. My eyes flew wide. "Yes! *Yes*, yes!"

Asher slipped the ring on my finger, then slid his arms around me, pulling me closer, holding me tight. His mouth was hot and claiming as it found mine. There was a hunger, a fierce gladness, in his kiss.

Before, whenever we'd embraced, there'd always been clothing completely between us. But now, as my palms pressed against the skin of his back, feeling the firmness there, the heat, relishing the play of muscles under my palms, I relished in the connection. His hands discovered the open back of my suit, making me shiver, and I didn't know if this was too much or not enough. I only knew that I never wanted us to be apart.

"Hey now!" Sean called. "I think the pool water's boiling."

Asher's low rumbling growl sounded in my ear, causing me to shudder. He took a deep breath; his hands coming slowly up to gently cup my face. Against my lips, he said, "I spoke with your dad. Both he and your mom gave their consent."

"When?" I whispered.

"A few days ago, when you went to town with Jaime. I needed to ask his permission and discuss with him some plans I'd been making. Of course, these plans were all contingent upon your answer."

"What plans?"

"Now that I have your answer—and I won't let you take it back—I intend to sell my house in L.A. and buy land near the ranch. And I'm resigning from my government work. I've already written the letter. I only need to send it to the powers-that-be. I plan to continue making movies from time to time. But for the most part, I simply want to be with you. I can't live without you, Kate."

"I'd hoped...hoped, and prayed; you have no idea. Yes, a hundred, million yesses." His arms tightened around me, his hands lightly skimmed over my back, his cheek against my ear.

Asher shifted, lightly trailing his lips down my shoulder, causing me to shiver. "Do you have any idea as to when you want this wedding to take place?" Grazing teeth, sent a jolt of heat through me.

"I haven't even thought about it," I gasped. "Do you have a time in mind?"

"The sooner the better, before I spontaneously combust. You're killing me, woman."

I grinned. "Is that so?"

"It is. Once we're wed, we may not leave our room for a week. Or more."

"I see." It was hard to breathe as Asher's fingers were now gently massaging me, reminding me of the time he'd massaged my shoulders so many months ago. Something in the way I appeared must have alerted him, because Asher stopped his hands and gently loosened his arms. Once more he leaned down to kiss me.

"Are we going to see that ring tonight, or what?" Jaime asked from a few feet behind her brother. Asher chuckled under his breath then took my hand in his, turning around. I held my hand out so Sean and Jaime could get a better view as they came closer.

"Congratulations, you two. We're very happy for you." Sean shook Asher's hand.

"I'm *so* happy!" Jaime said, giving me a hug then giving Asher one as well. "This is awesome news. I didn't know you were going to do this *now*. You could have warned me. When did you decide?"

"Thanks, guys; I'm not sure when I made my mind up. I think I just got tired of waiting. I had to know." Asher raised my hand to kiss its back.

"Well, we're absolutely thrilled. I guess it's early, but have you set a date yet?"

"No, not yet," I said. "We'll have to talk about it soon, though."

"I still say the sooner the better. That's if you care to take my sanity into consideration," Asher reminded me, a warm look in his eyes. We lingered a bit longer before everyone decided to head in.

Mom's door was still open when we made our way upstairs. Asher kissed me again before continuing to his room. Mom's bedside light was on so I gently knocked before entering. She patted the side of her bed, indicating I join her, then hugged me tightly. "Ah, baby, you're beaming. Let me see it." I held my hand out. "Dad called me late, four days ago, to discuss it with me."

"And you're okay with it? Dad is, too?"

"Katy, we love you." Mom still held my hand, giving it a gentle squeeze. "And we both, your dad and I, think the world of Asher. If you love him and this is what is right for you, of course we're okay with it."

Leaning over, I gave her a hug, emotion tightening my throat. "Thanks, Mom. I'll call Dad tomorrow."

"You'll need to call Calvin, too."

"I know." I stood, and sighed. "I may call him now."

Asher-

She said *yes!* Asher hummed with energy, and yet felt strangely calm at the same time. Like every missing piece in his life had suddenly clicked into place. Kate had agreed to marry him. Soon she would be his wife; Mrs. Asher Fitzpatrick.

Asher had already called Samuel and Cory; they'd both congratulated him. He'd called his parents. His mother was overjoyed and demanded to know all about Kate. Both his parents were excited for him and couldn't wait to meet her.

Asher sat on his bed with his laptop open, and re-read the document. There were no second-guesses, no wondering if this was the right decision. He was sure. He was absolutely sure. Asher hit send. Because she said *yes*.

Kate-

Calvin was still awake when I called; I could tell by the sound of his voice. "What are you doing?" I asked when he answered.

"Nothing much, just lying here, watching the TV. You?"

"I have something important to tell you."

Calvin inhaled deeply, held it for a moment, then gently exhaled. "Yeah?" he said finally. "What's up?"

It was my turn to take a deep breath. I racked my brain trying to find the right words, to find an appropriate way to phrase what I needed to tell him. "Asher and I are engaged." *What?* That wasn't what I meant to say! The silence on the other end of the line was deafening. "I...I wanted to be the one to tell you."

"Congratulations." His voice sounded steady. "When's the happy day?"

"We haven't set a date yet. Ash says as soon as possible, but I don't know... The holidays are coming. It's already October. I'm thinking after the first of the year."

"I see. Well, that sounds...okay."

"Are you mad, Calvin?" Mentally, I flinched away from his answer.

"*No*, I'm not mad, Katy. Of course not. I won't lie and say it doesn't hurt, because it does, but I'm not mad." He drew in a shaky breath, my heart squeezing painfully as he continued, "I'm not even surprised, really. I knew how he felt about you and how you felt about him. Honestly, I'm happy for you; for both of you. How could I be mad at you?" He paused again. "I just wish you could have loved me like you love him."

"I tried, Cal." I whispered, my voice shaky, hating the idea of causing him pain.

"I know you did. I guess I kept hoping eventually it'd work out between us." We were quiet for a minute, then he said, "Katy, I love you. And I want the best for you. Truly, I'm happy for you."

"That means a lot, Cal. Thank you."

"Thanks for calling and telling me. I'm glad I got to hear it from you."

"You're my dearest friend, my brother. I love you."

"I love you, too."

"I do. I'll see you in few days."

"Goodnight, Katy."

"Night," Ending the call, I took a deep breath, then exhaled in a rush as I fell backward onto the bed. That had been tough, but not as tough as I'd thought it was going to be. Sleep seemed elusive, my mind replaying the events of this evening. As I finally drifted off, staring at my ring, my one thought was that soon I'd be Mrs. Asher Fitzpatrick.

The days seemed to fly by after that; like time had slowed enough to lend some suspense to the activities leading up to Ash's proposal. And, once that was done, perversely speeding up so I felt as if I was always mentally a few days behind, striving to catch up. I was shocked to learn on the last night in Phoenix that we were leaving the next day. Had we really been here for two weeks already?

We arrived back in Cody on a Saturday afternoon; Dad came to pick us up. Saying goodbye to Jaime, Sean, and little Michael had been hard; I made them promise to come visit soon. Tentatively, we were thinking Christmas.

We'd been home for about two weeks when Asher received another phone call—government related. He spent a few hours in his room on the phone. I waited, trying not to feel anxious, knowing news I didn't want to hear was coming.

Asher would leave again on Monday. To cheer me up, before he left, he took me to a local pumpkin patch Sunday after church. We picked out several pumpkins, and spent the afternoon carving them. I guess I was getting better at dealing with his absences. At least I wasn't feeling miserable the whole time.

Asher-

Asher listened calmly to Goldstein on the phone. He regulated his breathing, kept his pulse slow. Asher was *furious*. General Goldstein informed him that his resignation would not be accepted at this time. The assignment Asher was working on was simply too sensitive, too important to hand off to someone else. The agency was strongly requesting he complete this assignment to avoid any red tape or delays to his request. In other words, *we have you over a barrel and you'll comply with our demands or we'll make your life miserable.*

Asher dreaded telling Kate, dreaded leaving her again. He hated what his leaving always did to her. He found a new drive to seek out information and find Saeed Ishar once more. He needed this mission over; he *needed* Kate.

Kate-

December blew in ice cold and white with snow. We'd planned on Jaime, Sean, and Michael coming for Christmas, then received a very disappointing phone call—this time *not* from the government. Michael had come down with chickenpox. So, instead of a house full of guests we were a small group. December was still magical though, as we celebrated Christmas and each other. Asher and I spent endless hours together, talking and making plans. While we wouldn't begin breaking ground until spring, we still met with an architect to begin design on our new home. I found myself looking at room layouts and floor plans, tile and paint, and amid all this I was still trying to come up with an actual wedding date.

We spoke about children. Did we want any? How many to have, how soon to begin having them. I cherished those times together, curled in front of the fire, just...talking.

New Year's came with a bang and with it came the subpoenas to testify against Johnny Khyle. My heart had clenched in chest as I read the summons. We were due in court on the seventeenth.

Facing them had been one of the most difficult things I'd ever done. I'm ashamed to say I trembled through my testimony. But I did it. Johnny Khyle, Billy Simmons, and Randy Larson were found guilty on all charges and sentenced to fifteen years in prison. They'd be available for parole in ten. It wasn't long enough.

Calvin-

Calvin stood in line, waiting to place his order. Gina grinned, offering a little wave from behind the counter. He'd always thought she had an adorable grin. Especially when that dimple to the left of her mouth peeked out. Now that he thought about it, she had a great mouth as well. Well-formed, shapely. He'd never noticed before, that heated feeling circling in his chest. He had to acknowledge it now as he studied the way her teeth worried at that lip. His thumb tingled as he imagined rubbing it across those lips. New, unsettling, though not unpleasant, were these urges being born inside him. Calvin stepped forward, a smile forming, even as he fought not to stare at the familiar, and yet somehow unknown, beauty before him.

Kate-

February seemed to run out and soon March was strolling in. Asher had arrived back just after the first of March, to my immense relief, and though it was early spring, we didn't have time for relaxing. We had new calves to catch and tag, fences to repair, and the trip to L.A. to plan for. I couldn't believe how fast time was flying! About three weeks before we were to leave, Calvin found me in the barn with an important question to ask.

"What's up?" I smiled as he stepped into Red's stall.

"Seeing as how I'm your chaperone in a couple of weeks...I wondered if I could ask you a favor."

"Sure, what can I do for you?"

"I really don't want to be a third wheel when we go...so...I'd like to bring a...date," he stammered.

"Uh, yeah, sure, Cal. That's fine, of course it's fine."

"I'd like to ask Gina. What do you think?"

I stared at him a moment, trying to maintain my composure and not begin screaming in happiness and thereby freaking him out, then calmly replied, "I think that's an *excellent* idea. I'm sure Gina would be tickled pink." *And every other color of the rainbow, too.* "I'd ask her quick, to make sure she can get time off and find a dress."

"I'll call her right now; Asher won't mind, will he?"

"No, not at all," I assured him.

Before I knew it the four of us, Asher, myself, Calvin, and Gina, were loading up the truck early in the morning. Due to our red-eye flight, Samuel drove us to the airport. We arrived in L.A. a little before five in the morning; Asher had a car waiting to take us to the hotel. We had rooms on the fourth floor—a full suite, complete with kitchen, dining room, living room and three bedrooms.

Gina and I were given the largest bedroom, as it had a king bed and its own bathroom. After crashing for a few hours, we freshened up and decided to eat out rather than call down for room service.

Asher showed us around town a bit after dinner. If I'd thought Phoenix was crowded, it was *nothing* compared to the activity in L.A. The noise and lights and *people*, so many people, overwhelmed us. It was quite literally breathtaking. Gina and I did our best to take it all in, feeling very much out of place.

After returning to our suite, Gina and Calvin decided they wanted to go for a swim before bed. "Behave yourself." Calvin admonished. "Don't make me regret this."

I narrowed my gaze as I grinned and waved him along. Asher and I retreated to our rooms to freshen up after dinner. Mainly, I wanted to brush my teeth.

He was seated on the sofa when I came out. In the distance came the sounds of the L.A. traffic, but the room itself was silent, reminding me we were alone. With pounding pulse, I walked past him to the small kitchenette, for a bottle of water. Drinking about half of it before turning around, I tried to calm myself. Asher's gaze was on me, an intense, knowing look in his eyes. I wanted to join him on the couch, but in the same breath, was leery of it.

"What's wrong?" Of course, he'd accurately read my delay tactics.

"Nothing," I whispered, dropping my gaze from his, taking in the coffee table in front of him.

"Come here," Asher said quietly. Holding still, I breathed deeply. Unable to keep my eyes down, I glanced back up and my eyes locked with his. "I *promise* you nothing will happen." His voice held warmth, his tone sincere. "I will *not* cross the line."

I waited a moment longer, wanting to make sure I was in full control of myself. Then, mentally nodding, moved slowly over and sat beside him. At first, he held still, not moving at all. Then, after a couple of moments of silence, he shifted, slowly threading his fingers through mine. My eyes rose to meet his. The look in his told me I was safe, loved, and cherished.

Asher tenderly fit me against his side, his arm wrapping around, pulling me closer. His mouth lingered on my forehead, one hand slowly played in my hair, relaxing me. The other softly rubbed my back in soothing circular motions. "I've missed this."

"Mmm hmm," I nodded against his shoulder. I loved the way we fit together. It was like he had been designed and engineered perfectly for me and me for him. Squirming, I inched a little closer, my hand coming to rest on his chest, enjoying the feel of him under the soft knit shirt he was wearing.

"Careful, love." He chuckled, his lips now against my temple. "I'm resolved not to overstep, but don't tempt me. I'm not *Edward*, you know."

That made me laugh. "Yeah, I've noticed a certain lack of sparkle in the sunlight."

"I also lack his super-human strength—so don't push it." Pulling back, I tried giving us space. "No, no, don't go." Asher fitted me back to his side. Sighing contentedly, I settled back against him. Under my ear, his heartbeat sounded neither calm nor relaxed. Grinning, I kissed under his jaw. "Have you thought any more about a date yet?" Asher asked, probably trying to distract me.

"Not really." I sighed. "I mean I'm still thinking the end of July."

"Have you thought about what kind of wedding you want? Small and simple or large and elaborate?"

"I don't know... What do you want?"

"I'm okay with whatever *you* want. My only prerequisite is that it happens *soon*."

"I see." Smiling, I leaned up to kiss his mouth. After a few moments he pulled back.

"That is precisely *why* I need it to be sooner rather than later," he breathed, rubbing the pad of his thumb across my lower lip. "I'm *tired* of being in control. I want to give in and lose it with you. *Really bad*."

"I know." I snuggled closer, trying to convey I felt the same.

"We *could* get married by a justice of the peace, then have a formal ceremony later with family."

"That's an idea." I couldn't deny the thought had merit and may have crossed my mind a time or two, but I knew if I did that, my parents and others would be hurt.

"Or not," he said, reading the look on my face. "Are you having second thoughts?"

"No!" I assured him. "Not at *all*. I swear. I think I'm just a little over-whelmed thinking about it. I've been so preoccupied with this premier that I haven't had time to really think about planning a wedding. I *will* think about it as soon as this is over. I promise. Besides, I've been pretty busy with house plans, too."

"Fair enough." He held my gaze for a moment, then groaned, rubbing an agitated hand over his face. "Sorry, love." He lifted my hand, kissing my knuckles. "I'm not trying to pressure you. I feel like I'm on the verge of...exploding; I just want it one you'll find honoring."

For a little while, I simply basked in the warmth of his gaze and the heat in his caress. Feeling cherished, I wondered what I'd ever done to have earned the right to be here with him, what I'd ever done to have gained his attention. Whatever it was I was grateful for it. "I meant to ask; how did your letter of resignation go? Did they accept it?"

Asher lowered his gaze, focusing on my hand. I watched as the light in his eye became guarded. "It went as well as could be expected."

"What does that—" Asher moved and I suddenly found myself strad-dling him, my question abruptly cut off as his mouth met mine. Firm, warm hands moved determinedly across my back, dragging me even closer. They travelled south to my hips, gripping, holding me tightly to him. I gasped as Asher's mouth began a southward trek, across my jawline, over my chin, down the column of my throat.

His teeth gently grazed my skin, and I pulled his head closer. He groaned, the sound rumbling against my collarbone where his mouth was driving me insane. One of his hands shifted, rubbing firmly, *demandingly*, up and down my thigh, leaving a trail of fire, the other rose tangling in my hair, lifting it out of the way as his mouth danced along my neck and shoulder.

As quickly as Asher had begun, he stopped. One moment I was clinging to him, our bodies melded together, the next I found myself alone on the couch. He faced away; his arms were lifted, hands clamped tightly behind his head. His entire frame trembled; his back rigid and strained. He stood that way for several long moments. Neither of us spoke as we tried to get our breathing under control.

"I'm sorry." Asher's voice was low and rough. "I didn't mean for that to happen. I lost myself there for a moment. Do you forgive me?" His back was still to me, still tight with tension.

"Yes." I breathed, my mind replaying what had just happened. Heat flared in my cheeks as I considered our actions. Then I recalled what we'd been talking about before. "Of course, I forgive you...but I have to say...it didn't work you know."

He chuckled, sounding amused and worried at the same time. "I admit, I knew it was a long shot."

"They don't want you to stop, do they?"

"No." He turned around. "Not right now." My gaze locked with his, holding steady. I didn't voice the questions I knew were in my eyes. "There's something I've been working on...a *specific* project that I'm intimately involved in, and they're requesting I see it through to completion before they're willing to accept my resignation."

"What does that mean? How long are we talking?"

He must have seen the worry flare in my eyes because suddenly he was kneeling on the floor in front of me. He took my hands in his. I saw honesty in his gaze and felt a little of the tension ease inside me. "I'm waiting for a few things to fall into place and when that happens, I can make the final preparations and get this particular job finished. I'd say sometime in the next six months this should all be over."

"*So long*?" I breathed.

"Pray things go smoothly and everything works out the way I need it to."

"This is really important? This thing you're doing?"

"Very."

My lungs expanded, then slowly I let my breath out again, striving for calm. "I've asked you before if you were ever in danger on these jobs and you said no, but I have to ask again. *Are* you in *any* danger?"

Asher steadily held my gaze for several long moments, then said, his voice smooth, sincere, "I'm *very* good at what I do, Kate. You have to trust me on this." The blood left my face and tears welled up in my eyes. My throat tightened, painfully. I shook my head at him; that was not the question I'd asked. My breath came in short gasps. "*Kate.* It's alright, love. Look at me." Asher took my face in his hands, staring deep into my eyes. He waited until the trembling stopped. "I'll be alright. I will finish this job and I'll come back to you and we'll be together. I *promise.*"

"I love you." I whispered.

"I know." He leaned his head down; his mouth against mine. "I know you do. I love you, too. I won't jeopardize this—*I won't.* You mean too much to me."

"It would *kill* me if anything happened to you, Ash."

"I know. I *know.* Nothing will happen to me."

"Promise me."

"I do; I promise."

CHAPTER TWENTY-TWO

Red Carpet

Kate-

When I awoke the next morning, I lay still, my mind instantly returning to our conversation the night before. Blinking moisture from my eyes, I breathed slowly, deeply, needing to pull myself together; I couldn't afford to fall apart now. Taking another deep breath, I got up, faith assuring me God would see Asher safe.

After spending the day poolside, soaking up the sun, trying to focus on the premier preparations, I headed inside. Gina wore a beautiful, sleeveless dress of twilight blue velvet in classic lines that framed her stunningly. The dress was fitted and floor length with a long slit up the back. She'd paired it with a pair of silver heels. Her red hair was pulled back in a classic look.

"Gina." I breathed. "You look *amazing*. Cal's going to flip."

"You really think so?" Nervously, she brushed her hands down her sides.

"Absolutely." I assured her. "You're a knockout."

I sprayed some of Asher's favorite perfume at my neckline and wrists, then pulled the dress from the closet. I slid the gown on, the fabric caressing my skin. Gina zipped up the back. Next were the shoes and finally, the jewelry he'd purchased. Stepping back, I stared at myself in the floor-length mirror, criticizing every angle, hoping he liked what he was about to see.

"Well, here goes." I breathed nervously.

"Are you *kidding?*" Gina chuckled. "Asher will be picking himself up off the floor. He'll forget everyone's names...*heck*, he'll forget his *own* name."

"That's what I'm shooting for. I wanted a jaw-dropper...I think I managed it."

"Trust me; you did." Gina opened the door to our room and stepped into the living area. I was gratified to hear Calvin's appreciative murmur when he saw her. I waited a moment to let her enjoy his reaction before following.

Asher-

Asher stood at the sink, a bottle of water in hand. He gripped the cap, intending to twist it, when he heard the door to the girls' room open. Pausing, he turned; Gina made her way out, and Calvin made some comment on her beauty. As he grasped the cap again, Kate stepped out. He barely registered the plastic bottle bouncing off the floor, rolling away. Was only vaguely grateful he hadn't yet removed the cap. His bright blue eyes were fully trained on the woman before him.

For several moments he silently stood there, staring, absorbing the shock to his system. Slowly, his gaze moved over her, starting at her feet. He took in her perfectly pedicured toes, with their French white tips. Followed the smoothly curved line of her ankles, noting the sparkle of rhinestones on the buckle there. Most of her right leg was visible, by way of the slit in her dress. He took his time admiring each feature. Her calf was smooth and shapely, her knee slender. Soft folds of golden brown, silky chiffon caressed her thigh, causing his breath to catch.

He took in the way the material hugged the curve of her hips and the smooth plane of her stomach. His blue eyes followed the lines of the dress upward, appreciating the way the fabric cupped and molded to her body. His hands shook; his fingers tingling, longing to touch her. The rhinestone straps of the dress looked as though they were about to slip off her shoulders. Stepping forward, intent on adjusting them, he was suddenly assailed with the warm, musky fragrance coming off her skin. Asher inhaled slowly, deeply. His mouth watered even as his throat became tight and dry. Dimly, he heard Calvin say something, but had no idea what. He couldn't think; he was barely breathing.

Kate-

If a jaw-dropping moment was what I'd been hoping for, I'd achieved it and then some. Asher dropped the bottle of water he'd been holding, completely oblivious as it hit the floor and rolled out of reach. I had the satisfaction of watching his eyes burn through me as they slowly moved upward taking in every detail. What I hadn't anticipated was what his reaction would do to *me*. My lungs refused to work, my knees became shaky, and I was sorely afraid I was going to fall.

Asher moved closer. Calvin and Gina said they were going to wait in the lobby, to give us time. I'm sure they meant time to cool off...because it didn't take a physician to see the fever burning between us. He leaned, dipping his head; his nose skimmed along my neck as he inhaled slow. Deep. His voice was hoarse and low. "Are you *trying* to kill me? Is it not enough that I *dream* about you? That I'm tormented constantly?" He stepped closer still, heat radiating from him. "And now...you do *this?*"

Shakily, I whispered, "I wanted to please you."

"*Please* me?" He shook his head slowly, his mouth against my skin. "You have thirty days, Kate, then we're getting married. I've been holding on by a thread. You just snapped it—I can't wait any longer. Thirty days, do you hear me?" I could only nod. "Let's go then," he kissed my throat, his voice still rough. "Before I do something we'll both regret."

When the limo pulled to the curb where the celebrities were being dropped off, I heard the roar from the crowds, and told myself not to be a coward. The driver opened the door and Asher stepped out. A chorus of squeals and screams rose, followed by the click of cameras. The driver stepped forward, intending to assist me from the car as well, but Asher stopped him. He leaned down, purposefully helping me to the sidewalk.

Asher kept his hand firmly around my waist, his fingertips gently pressed into my side. He didn't let go once, not even for pictures. He held me close, almost possessively, seeming in need of constant contact. I needed it just as much and didn't mind.

Several news correspondents stopped him along our long, slow walk to the doors of the theater—curiosity evident on their faces as they tried to place me. Surely, I had to be *somebody*. He'd been holding my left hand for a picture, and lifted it to kiss the back of my knuckles, that big shiny ring on display. The cameras continued their frenzied flashes.

Though it seemed to take hours to walk the thirty yards or so on that red carpet, it really only took about thirty minutes. Then maybe another fifteen minutes to make our way to our seats and another twenty minutes before the film began. I was happily surprised to see Scotty and completely shocked by his date; Jessica Stevenson looked radiant tonight. She wore a long sheath dress that flared at the bottom in a brilliant shade of fire engine red. I couldn't help it; I did a double take when I saw them holding hands. And for once, as I studied her, I noticed no affectation in her demeanor at all. She seemed happy, content, and sincerely pleased to be with him.

I grinned when Scotty caught my eye and winked. Gina and Calvin sat beside Asher and me. *Dust Devils* was a little under two and a half hours in length and worth every minute of it. I remembered watching each of the scenes being filmed, and was amazed at how well the film flowed seamlessly together, completely and effortlessly captivating its audience.

My jaw ached with tension during the one and only kissing scene. Watching Asher passionately kiss Jessica was extremely difficult. I couldn't look at him and I wouldn't look at her. I felt Gina and Calvin as they silently assessed me, but didn't look at them either.

Suddenly Asher leaned close. "The *only* way I was able to get through that was to imagine I was kissing *you*. Trust me when I say, that took a *lot* of acting on my part." Glancing up, I found his gaze steady and sincere. Chuckling under his breath he continued, "You can unclench your fist now."

"It's *not* funny." I grumbled.

"It is actually. Usually, *I'm* the jealous one."

"Shut up and watch the movie," I whispered, trying not to smile at him.

Apparently, our engagement was huge news, Asher being what most had believed to be a confirmed bachelor and all. I told him the following night after dinner I felt as if I should be carrying his scalp on my belt. "Or, at least I should have notched my lipstick case or something."

He chuckled. "If it makes you happy, love."

I flexed my foot where it rested in his lap so he could massage it. "Should I expect to receive hate mail from your legions of female fans?"

Asher chuckled again as he lifted my foot. His hand slid upward to cup my calf. Dragging me closer, careful inch by careful inch, he placed a kiss on the top of my foot, then my ankle, on my knee, still pulling until I was flat on my back, legs bent over his. "No more than I'll receive from your hordes of male fans."

Trying for bravado, I said, "I don't have fans, male or female."

"I think we've already established that statement isn't true." He leaned over me, his lips dancing on mine, light, teasing touches. Shifting, he nuzzled my cheek with his nose. "Everywhere we go together, I have to tell some poor fool to back off or face the consequences."

I tried to giggle light-heartedly, but it came out more breathless than anything else, "Not true."

Asher snaked his arms under me, lifting, pulling me up and against his chest. His arms tightened possessively, contracting, holding me until I was immobile. His face was against my neck, his lips caressing; softly he nibbled, sending waves of heat coursing through me. "Very true. *Extremely* true." Against my throat, he rumbled, "We need a date."

I grinned, breathless. "Ash, what kind of a wedding do you envision? Do you have anything in mind?"

Asher released me, allowing me to sit beside him on the couch. "Yes, Kate, I have *something* in mind."

I elbowed him in the ribs, "You know what I mean."

"I do."

"You have to wait for the pastor before you can say that."

Asher raised his eyebrow and narrowed his gaze. "You're avoiding my question."

"Well, you haven't answered *my* question yet," I reminded him.

"What I envision?" he asked, a grin on his handsome face. "You want to know what I have in mind?" I nodded and watched as the grin on Ash's face turned momentarily wolfish before vanishing entirely, and he became serious. "All right. What I have in mind is this: First, vows. Second, a long, extended, *uninterrupted* length of time, which you and I will spend in pure enjoyment behind locked doors. Where I will become intimately knowledgeable about every inch of you." I swallowed noisily. "That's what *I* have in mind. Which is why we need a *new* date."

My mind was stuck on that intimate knowledge he planned to have and all that uninterrupted time. I blinked. "I can plan the wedding however I see fit? You don't care about colors or songs, vows, or length?"

"Of course, I *care*." He nipped at my knuckles, kissing the ring and the finger it sat upon. "It's *the* most important thing to me, being married to you. I'll share in all the planning if that's what you want. We'll look at flowers, cakes, dresses, tuxes, we'll look at everything. I just want to marry you. Quickly and permanently."

CHAPTER TWENTY-THREE
Of Friend and Foe

Kate-

While in L.A., in anticipation of Asher's impending departure, he insisted on celebrating my birthday a little early. I tried talking him out of it, but he'd insisted. So, on our last day in town, Asher drove us all to Malibu and we had dinner at *Duke's.* Afterwards, we walked the beach, enjoying the setting sun. It was a stunningly beautiful experience, and I loved him even more for wanting to make it so special for me.

We arrived back at the ranch before the first late snow hit, but only by three days. It snowed for four days, only lightly but enough that we had several inches by the end of those four days. Normally I enjoy our snowfall, but this time it was bittersweet. Asher left again before the last snowflake fell. "Pray this is ends quickly, love."

"I will," I sniffled. "I *am*." He lifted me up for a quick, yet intense kiss, then he was gone, and I was driving back to the ranch in tears. Thankfully, I had tons of things to do regarding the wedding. As depressed as I was, I was equally thankful for the message I'd found waiting for me when I got home from L.A.

Candi had called and wanted to talk. *Thank You, Lord!*

The day after Asher left, I went to see her. Before I made it out of the truck, she was running down the steps. Candi launched herself at me and our arms were around each other. "I'm so, so sorry, Katy," she sobbed. "I was a jerk. A stupid jerk. *So* stupid. Forgive me?"

"Of course, I forgive you," I sobbed equally as hard. "I *love* you."

"I know you do and I love you, too. I've been so miserable."

"I've missed you."

We talked for over three hours. Candi revealed some painful things. Last year she'd begun seeing a guy. I'd only met him a couple times, though he hadn't been very friendly. I'd assumed at the time he was simply shy. Now, I knew better. He'd told her that he loved her, that he wanted to marry her and take her away from our small town. Take her to some big city. I knew Candi had dreams of becoming a fashion designer, but I hadn't known she'd felt a desire to leave Cody. This guy pressured her, pressed his physical advance almost to the point of no return. When Candi had pulled back, he'd called her a whore and trash, stating that was all she'd ever be good for.

Out of shame, Candi had never shared any of this with anyone. She'd harbored those hurt feelings, letting them fester. My involvement with Asher had brought them to the fore and she hadn't known how to deal with them.

We cried a lot as we talked, but it felt amazing to have my friend back. Candi showed me pictures she'd printed from her favorite Internet celebrity sites of me and Asher at the premier; we laughed a lot over that. She also gave me a stack of letters she'd written, but never sent, telling me how sorry she was and how much she'd missed me.

Candi made me promise to let her help with the wedding. She even said she'd be making my dress. We made plans for a girls' night. She would bring magazines and books about wedding planning and she promised we'd get the ball rolling.

Asher and I had agreed *again,* after he'd calmed down and was thinking more clearly, on the date of July twenty-eighth, a little over sixteen weeks away. I called our pastor to verify the date would work, and he agreed to marry us after we'd completed the recommended counseling with him. I hoped it would take Asher no longer than the three weeks he'd estimated to complete his assignment. He didn't know when he'd be able to call me, but promised to stay in touch when and as he could.

Thankfully, my life seemed like a whirlwind of activity, keeping me from dwelling on his absence. Bridal books, fabric swatches, flower samples, and various sketches Candi had drawn up were scattered around my room. She'd taken my measurements and I'd been poked, pinned, and prodded enough to last a lifetime.

I had other things to focus my attention on as well; Gina and Calvin were growing closer. I asked him about their relationship one day when we were out looking for strays. "We're *great*," Calvin said. "*She's* great." He was silent for a few minutes, then asked, "How long have you known about her feelings for me?"

"Oh...not long really...only since like *third grade*." I smirked at him.

"And you never said anything?"

"It wasn't up to me to tell you—it was up to her."

"Was *that* why you never were attracted to me? Because you knew she had feelings for me?"

"No, not at all," I assured him. Then, to be certain there was no confusion I went on to explain, "I *always* felt you were more like a brother to me. I think you're good-looking, but in a detached, sisterly way."

Calvin nodded, then said, "Have you heard from Ash lately?"

"It's been a few days, hopefully he'll call soon."

"What does he *do* exactly?"

Inwardly, I cringed even as I concentrated on the trail, which had become deep in a couple places from the drifts. Before answering him, I made sure my voice was steady. "I don't really know, Cal; he's not able to tell me much."

"Are you ever worried about him?" Concerned curiosity was in his voice.

"I try not to think about it."

"I'm sorry; it's gotta be hard."

"It is, but I'm getting through it by the grace of God and the love of good friends and family. And once this last job is done, he's tendered his resignation and this will all be over." I smiled. "Enough about me. Are you happy with Gina?"

"I really am. Katy, I don't know how I was so blind before. How I missed seeing her. Gina's amazing. She looks at *me* the way you look at Ash. I never thought I'd be this fortunate."

Gina and Calvin were not the only two new lovers. Samuel and Tiffy had become an item, and I anticipated a wedding between the two of them soon. A few days after our snowy ride, I decided to run to town and pick up a couple of items, mainly a coffee, and maybe grab a new book.

In short, I was looking for a diversion. It had now been thirteen days since I'd last heard from Asher, and it was four days past the three weeks he'd estimated to complete this mission. Anxiety crawled under my skin, making me antsy and I couldn't shake the feeling that something was wrong. Thinking maybe a change of scenery might calm my concerns, thinking perhaps I was simply feeling housebound, I took my little excursion.

At Legend's Bookstore, I found a diverting book about fallen angels and human love affairs; it sounded perfect. It was barely two when I returned. As I didn't need to feed for another few hours, I decided to get some reading in.

They were waiting for me in the kitchen. Dad had an arm around Mom. Gina was holding onto Calvin. Tiffy and Samuel were holding hands.

"What's up?" I asked as I set my purse down. When no one answered, I glanced up. It was Gina's face I noticed first, her eyes glistening, her lips trembling.

My heart skipped a beat, stuttered; my breath stuck painfully in my throat.

My eyes went beyond Gina to Calvin. His eyes held fear and pain; the fear was for *me*.

"Cal?" I whispered. He stepped forward, his arms reaching for me, steadying me as I swayed.

"Katy, it's...it's *Ash*...he's...."

Shaking my head in silent denial, I tried to speak, to breathe. The room spun, my lungs refusing to work, as a rushing, roaring sound filled my ears. The next thing I was aware of, I was reclined on the couch; Calvin and Gina were seated, one on either side of me.

Glancing around the room, my eyes searched until I found Samuel. "*Sammy...?*"

"Katy, *listen* to me." He sat in front of me on the coffee table. "Asher is *missing;* that's all I know right now. I'm leaving on the first flight out. We've had no confirmation other than that he's missing."

"What happened?" Fear constricted my throat; my eyes were glued to his. I saw his gaze shift to Tiffy and back. Somewhere in the back of my mind, I wondered what Sammy's leaving would do to her.

"I was told he missed his last check-in."

"When should he have checked in?"

"Three days ago."

"*Three days?* How long have you known?"

"I received a phone call late this morning."

"From who?"

Samuel deliberated silently, his gaze never leaving my face. "You know Ash isn't technically in the military, right?" I nodded. Samuel continued, "He's employed for a private contractor, working alongside a team of specially trained Seals. He's been helping them track down arms dealers working with terrorists. I don't know any more about his assignment right now. The contractor was trying not to make waves and give any indication something was wrong. I have a contact in the Seal unit he was with. They let me know as soon as they were safely able to."

"Where are you going?"

"I can't tell you that. But I *will* find him," Samuel stated, his voice was firm, and it sounded deadly. I was glad.

"Will they let you get involved?" I asked.

"They don't have a *choice*," he growled. "They shouldn't have lost him in the first place."

"He promised, Samuel." I whispered. "He *promised* he'd be safe."

"I know he did, and he'll do everything within his power to keep that promise. He's fighting right now not to break it. Don't lose hope."

Closing my eyes, squeezing them tightly, I tried to stem the tears. It took me several moments to master my voice. "Samuel?" I looked directly at him, making my voice firm. "Please, find him."

"I will," he promised. "I'll bring him safely home, or heads will roll. I'll call you as often as I can to keep you informed." I nodded in understanding. "Cory will arrive sometime tomorrow. He knows the drill and what needs to be done." I didn't know what that meant, but was glad he was coming at any rate; Cory was a clear and touchable tie to Asher.

It was four days after Samuel left before I heard anything. I knew he'd checked in with Cory and Tiffy, to let us know he'd made it safely to his destination.

Trying to stave off the panic and the fear, I withdrew inside myself. Mom and Dad were worried; everyone was. They walked on eggshells, darting glances in my direction when they thought I wouldn't see. I heard the whispered conversations. Each time the phone rang, I jumped, cringing, and they cringed with me.

I prayed and *prayed*. Prayed more than I ever had in my life. When I finally heard from Samuel, it was a short text; the message simply said,

Picked up lead, will know more in a few days.

I tried to find hope in that. I prayed for this lead Samuel had found. I prayed for his ability to follow it and that it would lead him to Asher. I prayed Asher was still alive and safe and that he'd come home to me. Time seemed to drag by. I wondered what Samuel was doing; we hadn't heard from him in a couple days now. *How* would he follow the lead? What kind of lead was it? Was *he* safe?

Now, I worried about Tiffy as well. She'd already lost her husband and now Samuel seemed to be missing too. Several times I tried to talk with her, but fear kept shutting me down. She seemed to be holding up better than I was. *Who's the coward now?*

Days turned into weeks. When three weeks had gone by and I hadn't heard anything more from Asher or Samuel, Mom sat me down to ask a tough question. "Baby," she said, reaching for my hand. "Sweetheart, do you think...it's been three weeks since we heard anything. Do you think...we ought to postpone the wedding?" I couldn't, I didn't want to think about the wedding not taking place, about cancelling it, about Asher not coming home. "*Baby*, I'm not saying we should cancel, just postpone. The wedding is..."

"Nine weeks, five days away," I whispered. "Mom, I can't talk about this right now." Standing, I swiftly went to my room and locked the door. Trembling, I sunk to the floor, the panic and the pain coming. I'd been trying to hold them off for so long. Mom's question, innocently asked, opened the floodgates.

Asher-

Asher woke with a start, his eyes straining against the pitch black of his cell. He was pretty sure he'd been here ten days, *maybe not*. It was hard to keep track. Once or twice, he'd heard screaming echoing from somewhere else in the area—to his knowledge, he'd been captured alone.

The informant had betrayed him.

Which meant he'd been on the right track.

It meant the information he'd already obtained and submitted would prove helpful. The unit should be able to accomplish their goal and someone would be able to find him. Hopefully before he was executed.

Asher's captors had worked on him, off and on, for several days, trying to gather information about who he was and who he worked for.

Even though his captors were Arab, they must know some German, because as he'd been refusing to give his name, refusing to speak at all, he'd suddenly remembered Kate and Scotty laughing over that ridiculous *Three Amigos* movie and couldn't help but chuckle.

The six guards had stopped, quietly observing him. Asher caught the leader's eye—and wondering if he wasn't becoming delirious—said in perfect German, "You son-of-a-motherless-goat."

When the guard nearest him backhanded Asher across the mouth, he'd laughed. That beating lasted for hours. When he'd passed out, they'd doused him with ice water to revive him and began again, vomiting blood after they'd returned him to his cell.

Asher was sure his ribs were broken. Every muscle in his body was angry and voicing it, but that was easily ignored. In the quiet recesses of his mind, he envisioned Kate. He could almost hear her voice; smell the fragrance coming off her skin. Seeing her kept him sane. It kept him focused, drove him to live, to fight.

Asher heard the sound again; a silent scraping noise reached his ears. He listened intently trying to pinpoint it. It had been three days since he'd last been fed, and hunger pains racked his midsection. He figured the bleeding had stopped, but it was hard to tell without light. Asher couldn't hear anything now except the pounding of his own heart.

Yesterday, at least he thought it had been yesterday; it may have been the day before, they'd dragged him from his cell. He'd been hung from a thick wooden beam by chains wrapped around his wrists. Then, just for fun, they'd sliced his biceps with a razorblade and poured alcohol on the wounds. A few days before that, they'd stuck a pick in his thigh several times. At least the alcohol would kill any infection, he'd thought with grim humor. Asher lost track of how many beatings they'd given him.

The sound came to him again, closer now. *I'm not imagining things.* Asher listened intently. It sounded like fabric brushing against a brick wall. The walls of his cell were brick.

He wasn't moving, but somebody outside his cell was. Whoever he was he was moving stealthily. Asher figured it could be one of the guards coming to get him, but they usually came in groups of four or five, and they made a lot more noise. It could be a rival faction trying to move into the territory. He'd rather not be stuck in the middle of that fight, but maybe he could use their conflict to his advantage and escape.

As silently as possible, Asher rolled to his knees, his injuries screaming, his body shaking with the strain. The cell was not tall enough to allow him to stand, but he didn't want to face whoever was moving in on him from his back. Fighting the pain and nausea, he gritted his teeth and regulated his breathing, silencing it.

Suddenly Asher heard something that made his heart skip a beat. A new sound came to him; the sound of a pigeon quietly cooing. Once. Twice. Blinking, he wondered if he *was* imagining things.

No, there it was again. Asher tried licking his lips, to make an identical sound; it was low and a little off. He waited. Then he heard it again—the sound of help.

Samuel had found him.

Asher-

Asher's knee bounced in agitation, causing the wounds in his thigh to throb. He was seated at a desk writing his debrief. He'd spent eleven days in captivity. The medic had released him two days ago, after spending five days in the infirmary. His stitches were holding and his ribs were wrapped. He'd been severely bruised and dehydrated. He still limped slightly when he walked. Two fingers on his right hand were broken. His nose was broken. His right eye was swollen shut. But the thing that caused him the most pain and discomfort was his heart. He was *desperate* to hear Kate's voice, to let her know he was alright, alive, and coming home, but he wasn't permitted to call until he was stateside. Samuel had been forbidden from making any kind of contact either.

When Asher was finally released, General Goldstein had given them strict orders to simply *go* home, not to call *anyone*, to remain *silent*. In frustration, Samuel and Asher caught a connecting flight from New York to Salt Lake City, then another up to Cody. The clock on the dash read 3:37 in cool blue numbers when they pulled into the ranch driveway.

Asher sat for a moment or two in the passenger seat, and simply stared at the house. All the lights were off except those on the porch.

He stared at Kate's darkened window, and was filled with such a powerful rush of emotion he wasn't sure if he could even stand. He waited until he had himself well in hand before carefully getting out. Samuel quietly waited with him.

Asher silently let himself into the house. Slowly, he made his way down the hall to his room to stow his bag before going up to Kate's room. He'd never been in her room before, but he knew where it was, and he was *not* waiting until morning to see her.

Asher opened his bedroom door and stopped; his heart slammed against his chest and the room began to spin. The blinds were open, the moon full and glowing brightly; from the light filtering in through the window, he was able to see clearly.

Kate lay curled on her side in the middle of his bed. She wore one of his sweatshirts; her arms were wrapped around his pillow; her cheeks streaked with dried tears. Asher silently dropped to his knees beside the bed, careful not to bump it. Trembling, his eyes stung with unshed tears and he couldn't seem to catch his breath.

For several moments he simply watched her. Her lips were slightly parted and as he listened to the sound of her breathing, thought it the most precious, most beautiful sound he'd ever heard.

He knew he wanted to spend the rest of his life hearing *that* sound and was fervently thankful he'd been given the opportunity. Asher didn't know what he was doing, but suddenly he found his hands clasped tightly in front of him, his face lifted upwards. The words he spoke he hadn't known he'd meant to say, but suddenly they were pouring from his mouth in whispered sincerity.

"God...I want...to thank You. I don't really know how to do this, but...I know I owe my life to You. So, You can have it. I know I need You in my life. I need Kate in my life. So, I repent and ask You to forgive what and who I was in the past and make a new man out of me. One who is worthy of her and worthy of You. Amen."

Kate-

I'm not sure what woke me, but I blinked to get the sleep from my eyes. Wiping a hand across my face, I felt the evidence from the tears I hadn't known I'd been crying. Sleep had been difficult to come by tonight; I was restless, more so than usual. Giving in to a sudden thirst, I'd decided to come downstairs for a drink. After guzzling a glass of water, I'd padded softly down the hall into Ash's room. Pulling one of his sweatshirts from the closet, I'd slipped it over my head. It still held enough of his scent to make my head swim and my lips tremble.

Sinking onto the bed, I'd wrapped my arms around his pillow, and prayed with abandon, pleading with God to bring him home. Sleep finally caught me while I was praying. I felt a little guilty about that, though the Lord knew how exhausted I'd been.

Some slight noise behind me caught my attention, and I rolled to see what it was. My heart stopped, clenching painfully in my chest. I couldn't breathe, my lungs wouldn't work. Asher was kneeling next to the bed, tears in his eyes. I don't know who moved first, but suddenly I was in his arms, my face pressed against his neck. "Is this a dream?" I whispered, clinging to him, terrified it was. Too many times to count, I'd woken, thinking he'd been home, only to find I'd been wrong.

"*No*, love, I'm really and truly here." I began to cry in earnest, sobs wracking my body. Asher lifted me with a grunt, then settled onto the bed with me on his lap. He held me tightly until the crying stopped and I was able to breathe again. He kissed my cheek, my forehead, his hands brushed softly over my hair; his fingers trailed along my neck.

"You're *home*," I said against his chest. "You're really home. I've been so scared."

"I know. I'm *so sorry*, love. But it's over now. The job is finished. I've already had my final debrief. I never have to go back. I *never* have to leave again."

Squeezing him tightly, I saw him flinch, heard him groan under his breath. "Are you *hurt*? What happened to you?" For the first time, I noticed the yellowish color around his right eye. His nose had some discoloring too, and his lips had abrasions on them. There were stitches above his left eye near the hairline.

"I'm fine."

"I saw you flinch. What *happened?*" Asher was silent, though he regarded me closely. "Why won't you answer me?" Fear squeezed my heart.

"I'm not sure telling you would be a wise decision."

"Why not?" My voice shook a little.

"*Nothing* happened that I won't heal from."

I considered his words and felt the relief course through me. "If talking about it is upsetting to you, I understand, but I've just survived almost six weeks of not knowing if you were coming home or even alive. If I can survive *that*, I can survive your wounds, too." Carefully, I hugged him, not wanting to cause him further pain.

"I love you. More than my own life." Asher lowered his head, tenderly kissing me, his hand coming up to stroke along my cheekbone. White bandages were wrapped around the middle and ring fingers of his right hand. Carefully, I reached up, holding it to my face. Then I turned his hand over and kissed his palm, then his injured fingers.

"Where else did they hurt you?"

Asher remained silent. Leaning up, I kissed each injury on his face. He sat still, watching me with somber eyes. Turning in his lap, I sat astride him. Moving slowly, I unbuttoned his shirt and saw the tape binding his ribs. Gently, I eased his shirt off and saw the bandages around his arms, the bruises across his torso. Anger, fierce, deep anger, and pain flooded through me. Taking a steadying breath, I tried to contain my tears.

Looking up, I found his eyes on mine, strong emotion flickering in their blue depths. "Stitches?" I asked. He gave a single nod, his gaze still searching mine. "How many?"

"Fifteen." His voice was low, but steady.

I kissed his arms, his ribs, his torso. "Where else?"

Asher pointed to his thigh. "I'm not taking my pants off, so don't ask."

Chuckling quietly through a few more tears, I looked where he'd indicated. Then, taking a deep breath, I placed a kiss on my palm, touching where he'd indicated.

"Kate, what they did to me is nothing, *absolutely nothing*. I'm here with you and that's all that matters. I feel so good *here*," he said, placing my hand over his heart, "that I don't even notice the rest. None of it matters. *Only you.*"

Unable to speak, tears choking my throat, I allowed him to pull me close, allowed him to simply hold me. I hadn't intended to fall asleep, lying there with Asher, in his bed, but that's exactly what I did. At some point after I'd dozed off, Asher must have gotten up and moved to the chair in the corner.

Mom found us like that in the morning when she saw Asher's door open. I awoke to the sound of her cry, and sat up, feeling disoriented. She swooped down on us, and at first, I thought she was angry about where I'd spent the night, but instead she was crying.

"Jackson! *Jackson,* come quick!" she hollered from the doorway. "Asher's *home!*"

Asher tightened his grip as he sat up straighter. His eyes met mine with warm amusement; his mouth curved into my favorite grin. In the light of the morning, I could see his injuries much clearer, and it hit me again in full force how fortunate I was to have him home. Suddenly, we heard the bangs of slamming doors and pounding feet running down the stairs.

Asher's room became quite crowded as Dad, Calvin, then Samuel and Tiffy came in. The questions came in a flood of happy and shocked voices. "Why don't you freshen up and get dressed, while I explain things to your parents," Asher rumbled against my ear. At the thought of leaving him, of being separated even momentarily, my arms tightened convulsively, and he quickly lifted me into his arms, ignoring everyone else in the room. "*Kate.*" He pulled back, looking directly into my eyes. "I will be here when you're done. I promise."

My body trembled violently and I couldn't seem to control it. "I'm sorry; I'm not sure what's wrong with me. I think...it...hit me is all. You really *are* here."

"I really am *here*. And I'll *be* here. I'm not leaving."

Noting the silence in the background, I glanced over my shoulder and saw everyone had left us. I could hear their voices coming from down the hall. It sounded like Dad was on the phone to someone.

"Go on," Asher said, releasing me. "I need to clean up, too. I'll see you in a few minutes. Alright?"

"I love you." I hated leaving him even for a moment.

"I love you, too." With that, on trembling legs, I forced myself to move, to comply with his request. That was the fastest shower I'd ever taken.

The first couple of days after Asher returned kind of came and went in a fog. I don't remember a whole lot about what happened; I only seemed to notice Asher himself. At first, I was tense and anxious each time he was out of sight. Fearful all of this had been a dream, and I'd wake, and he'd be gone again.

By the time a week had passed, I'd begun to relax; I could breathe freely again. Candi had carried on the plans for the wedding without me, not that there was much left that needed to be done. Asher and I would be married in the church, just a small ceremony—close friends and family only. We'd agreed on our attendants before Asher had left. Gina would be my maid of honor, with Candi and Tiffy being bridesmaids. Asher'd asked Samuel to be his best man and Calvin and Cory would be groomsmen.

We met with the pastor of our church about two weeks before the wedding. Asher had met him before, as he'd gone to church with me and my family basically every Sunday since he'd been here. Our first counseling session turned out to be an emotional one.

Pastor Ryan asked Asher a question I should have asked him myself, and maybe I would have if I hadn't been subconsciously trying to avoid it. He asked Asher if he'd ever placed his trust in Jesus Christ. Pastor already knew about me; he'd baptized me when I was nine. He didn't know about Asher, however.

Before I could gather myself to look at Asher, to gauge his response, or to draw in breath to speak, I heard him say, "Yes actually; the night I got back." I looked at him so fast I think I gave myself whiplash. "Sorry I didn't mention it sooner; I just didn't know how to say it." He raised my hand to his lips, kissing my knuckles, letting his mouth linger briefly. Then he turned his gaze to Pastor and said, "You heard I had some trouble and had been missing for a while, right?"

Pastor nodded and Asher continued. "Well...after one of the...sessions my captors had with me—one in which I was beaten pretty severely, after they dragged me back to my cell...I kept thinking of Kate and how I needed to get back to her. I began remembering everything I could about her: Her smile, the sound of her laughter, the scent of her perfume, the way the sun blazed on her hair. One image came to mind like it was tattooed there with permanent ink."

Asher turned back to me, and of course I was crying; how could I not be? "You remember that first Sunday you allowed me to come to church with you?" I nodded. "I hadn't been to church since I was about seven and hadn't known what to expect. I remembered sitting there beside you, watching you, or at least trying to watch you in a way that didn't give me away—I was still trying to play it cool then." He chuckled, then continued. "The morning sun came through the window next to the bench we were sitting on..."

"Pew," I whispered. "It's called a pew."

"That's right." Asher grinned. "It *is* called a pew—I forgot. At any rate, I couldn't take my eyes off you. Even when we were supposed to be praying, and our heads were supposed to be down, I couldn't stop looking at you. You were and *are* so beautiful, but it was more than that. There was something, some look on your face; you were almost glowing. I didn't understand what that was at the time.

"I've never really talked with God before, but I found myself talking to Him that day in my cell. I made Him a deal. If He'd get me home to you, to spend the rest of my life with you, I'd repent and give myself to Him. I knew God was the only way to make me truly worthy of you. So that night when I came home, when I found you in my bed..." Pastor Ryan choked at hearing that and I felt the blush creep crimson across my face, but I couldn't look away from Asher. "I watched you sleep for a while, then I found myself on my knees and upheld my end of the bargain."

CHAPTER TWENTY-FOUR

And Now Forever

Kate-

Before I knew it, the wedding was only days away. Asher's parents would arrive tomorrow, and I was equally nervous and excited about the prospect of meeting them. Jaime and Sean were arriving later this afternoon.

Tiffy and Samuel surprised us all by coming home from an appointment with the justice of the peace about a week ago. They'd both been married before, and had already had a wedding, so decided between the two of them they could forego the event this time around. Samuel decided to relocate to Cody, seeing as how Tiffy loved it as much as she did.

My passport arrived for the honeymoon—we were going to Ireland—Asher was eager to share its beauty with me. First, we intended to make a couple stops before heading overseas. I thought Asher was simply *amazing* to have done this for me and was tickled pink when I found out. First, he'd made reservations for a private cabin up on the Olympic Peninsula in Washington State. We'd be there a week, then before flying out of Seattle to Ireland, we would meet up with Karen and Danny. Asher had spoken with their parents, and they'd in turn discussed things with the school to gain permission for us to pick them up and take them out to lunch. I got an email from Karen; she was screaming in excitement, using all caps and lots of exclamation points. She also told me she'd broken up with Max; she just hadn't felt he respected her. I offered many thanks for that bit of welcome news.

I'd had the final dress fitting and all the arrangements were made. At times, I felt like I'd stepped outside myself and was watching everything unfold from a different vantage point. There were moments when everything seemed so surreal. Several times, I pinched myself, simply to be certain I wasn't dreaming.

Most of Asher's injuries were healed. All his stitches were out and the bruising was gone. His ribs were still a little tender and he had to be careful when riding. Asher being Asher though, never admitted to pain and assured me he was always fine. It did no good to coddle him. It was only when I really searched his eyes that I caught a glimmer of discomfort. He pitched in with everything, despite my protests. He bucked hay, fixed fences, and herded cattle, just like the rest of us. I gave up trying to get him to take it easy and let his body fully heal. I simply tried to keep up with and help him as much as I could, when he let me that is.

The morning of the wedding dawned cool and crisp. I looked at the indoor thermometer and noted it read forty-two degrees outside. Chilly for this time of year. Shivering a little, I gratefully turned to the coffee pot. I'd just poured my cup when a pair of warm, strong arms wrapped around me, Asher pulling me in for a hug. "Good morning, beautiful." His voice rumbled enticingly, his breath tickling my skin.

Turning in his arms, I raised up to kiss him. He nuzzled my neck and gently kissed my shoulder, sending shivers through me. "I wish we were already in Forks, so I could lock the dang door, turn my phone off, and have my way with you."

I tried to laugh, but it came out way more breathless and agreeable than I'd intended. Instead, I simply held him closer and breathed him in, hoping to convey my sentiment.

An hour later, Candi arrived with Gina to whisk me and Tiffy off to the church to begin preparations. Mom would meet us there and Dad was coming later with my new in-laws. Samuel was bringing Cory, Ash, and Calvin.

Yesterday, the girls and I had gone to get manis and pedis—that was our bachelorette moment.

Candi did my makeup and hair, then, sooner than I anticipated, it was time to slip the dress on. It was sleeveless and had a medium train; I loved the way she'd designed the skirt. She'd sewn layers of white chiffon in patterns that resembled large, delicate flower petals. My hair was curled and pinned on top of my head, and I wore a beautiful diamond comb nestled in the curls, compliments of Asher's parents.

In no time at all, Mom was kissing me before being escorted to her seat. Then Dad and I were standing together in the foyer, waiting for the moment the doors would open and he'd walk me down the aisle, giving me to my future husband.

I took a calming breath. "Dad," I said. "I love you and Mom so much. Thanks for being the best parents a girl could have asked for."

Dad didn't answer, other than to tighten his grip on my hand, his breath becoming shaky. Calming himself, he got hold of his emotions, then leaned over, gently kissing my forehead. "Love you, sweetheart. You're the best part of your mom and me."

So many things stood out to me that day, things I remembered and relived in the days and weeks and even years to come. I remembered the faces of my loved ones in the audience. But I remembered Asher most of all. I couldn't imagine anything more beautiful than him. Once our gazes locked, I couldn't look away. He looked triumphant and primal and sexy, all at the same time. I didn't know if it was appropriate for him to look that way—we were in church after all.

When Dad placed my hand in Asher's, I had the warming feelings of home and safety rush through me. Our vows were simple. We promised each other, God, and our witnesses that we would love, honor, and obey the other until at death we were parted. Not sickness, health, wealth, or poverty would separate us.

Asher-

Kate was beautiful. Radiant. *Mine.* Asher watched as she visited with their guests during the reception. He'd had to choke back tears, standing at the front of the church, watching her walk down the aisle toward him. His knees had gone weak when he'd seen her. She was *his*. It took only a few short minutes for Kate to become his wife.

Asher checked his watch again; it was time; they would be leaving soon to catch their flight to Seattle. He began making his way toward her, his heart now racing with anticipation. He'd been imagining being with her all day and the suspense was killing him.

As Asher reached Kate, he laid a gentle hand on her back. She turned toward him and smiled. "Is it time?" Asher nodded, taking her hand in his. As he did, a calmness came over him. There would be no more separation, no more stopping, and no more holding himself in check. Knowing this gave him peace. He could wait; he had time. Asher intended to take his time. Now that Kate was really and truly *his,* he wouldn't be rushed; he meant to enjoy every moment with her.

Kate-

When the engine of the rental car shut off, I blinked my eyes, looking around. Everything was quiet, hushed; a quarter-moon peeked through the clouds, and I could barely discern the shape of a cabin through the windshield. Asher brushed gentle fingers across my cheek, and my heart slammed against my ribs. I turned towards him, leaning into his touch. He studied me, watching, gauging my responses. Finally, he opened his door and stepped out. Walking around to the trunk, he pulled our luggage out, then moved to my door, opening it for me.

Carefully, I stepped into the cool evening air. A brisk wind was blowing and I could smell the brine of the ocean. Asher took my hand, carrying our bags under his other arm. He set those down on the little stoop and unlocked our door; he set the bags down just inside. Nervous and excited all at the same time, I briefly wondered if all brides felt this way on their wedding nights. Bending, even though this wasn't our home, he lifted me, intent on carrying me over the threshold. Stepping inside, he gently kicking the door closed. He reached back with one hand, and I heard the click of the lock.

Asher stood in the middle of the little cabin, still holding me, as we looked around. Both of our eyes landed on the rustic king-sized log bed that sat against the wall. I knew when his gaze shifted to me. Slowly, he lowered my legs, allowing me to slide to my feet. He held me steady; his hands resting at my waist.

The heat, the pressure in his grip brought a shiver across my skin. I wasn't cold, but suddenly found myself trembling. I took a slow, steadying breath, every part of me wholly aware of him. After a moment, I looked up to find he was closely monitoring everything I did.

With lips slightly pursed and brows arched in thought, the look in his eyes, though considering, sent heat billowing through me, bringing on more shivers. Turning slowly, his hand grazed across my stomach as he moved to the fireplace. Soon the soothing sound of a crackling fire filled the room. When he turned back, my heart was already racing. Slowly, he approached, coming to a stop directly in front of me. Taking my hands in his, he raised them, kissing my fingers, massaging my palms. He then slid his hands along my wrists, to my elbows, over my shoulders to cup my face. Mine dropped, coming to rest at his hips, gripping the fabric there. Tilting my head back with thumbs hooked gently under my chin, I watched in anticipation as he lowered his mouth. Hesitantly, he tasted, nibbling my lips and my chin, along my jawline until I was trembling again, and barely able to stand. Then slowly, intentionally, still kissing me, he walked me backwards until I felt the bed against my thighs.

His mouth left mine, leisurely travelling my features, tasting my skin. Warm hands angled my face, his thumbs playing with my mouth, smearing my lips. He nuzzled my neck, slowly inhaling before letting his breath out again, a low groan escaping his throat. Gently, he pressed me back onto the bed. For a moment he stood there, staring, his eyes burning as they moved over me.

When Asher pulled out his cell phone and shut it off, my heart took off, racing, pounding, removing any doubts about what was about to happen. He tossed it on the chair beside the bed, then slowly un-buttoned and removed his shirt, letting it fall to the floor. Firelight played across his features, as he reached for me, making me shiver in anticipation. Bending, he rested one knee on the bed beside me, kissing me deeply, yet still unhurried. I struggled to be closer, tried pulling him to me, almost frantic in my efforts. My hands stroked everywhere I could reach, needing, simply *needing*.

Maybe it was because he knew we wouldn't have to stop this time and we wouldn't be interrupted, but Asher seemed determined to take his time.

"Ash...*please...*" My frustration obvious as that *tension* continued to build.

"*Shhhh...*" he rumbled against my throat, my shoulder. Gently, he took my hands in his, holding them captive, controlling the play. He settled beside me on the bed, one leg coming to rest heavily between mine. I felt his weight and reveled in it, wanting more. "We have all night and I intend to take my time with you. While I still have the ability to do so."

His breath tickled the skin of my shoulder as he kissed me there, unhurried, and purposeful. He brought my body to such an awakening. I couldn't think beyond all I was feeling, all I was *needing*. "You are *so* beautiful, Kate," he whispered, his mouth once more on mine. "So beautiful. I love you. And I'm never letting you go."

Asher absolutely took his time with me. Unequivocally refusing to be rushed, he stoked the fire between us so thoroughly, I was nearly burned to a cinder by the end.

It was breathtaking.

It was beautiful and glorious.

And so worth the wait.

THE END

(of this story, but read on)

If you enjoyed this romance, PLEASE consider leaving a review. With all my heart, thank you, and keep reading.

https://a.co/d/1Yvb6xg

Taking place approximately twenty-two years after Out of the Blue ends, Written in the Deep, book 2 in The Blues Avenue series is now available.

She should have seen it coming.

He should have known there was more to it.

Spanning from Wyoming to Ireland to Scotland and beyond, Written in the Deep has

it all. A swoony and protective Scotsman, an untamed cowgirl, meddling grandparents, suspense, mystery, and chemistry for miles.

Get your copy today!

https://a.co/d/dVZPw1Z

And be sure to read on for the bonus chapter, *The Newlyweds Next Door—An Outsider's Perspective.*

Acknowledgements

Where to begin? There are so many people to thank. First, I think I want to thank you, the Reader. Without you, *this,* writing stories, would be pointless. So, from the bottom of my heart, thank you. Thank you for picking up this book, for giving it and me a chance. I hope I've lived up to your expectations and delivered an engaging story.

Second, I must thank those who aided me in this endeavor. Those who beta read for me, who edited, who listened and let me run ideas past them. Thank you, Cari, Laura, Toni, Leona, Lindsay, Jeff, Reah, Kayla, Megan, Jack, and Anna, truly, I thank you for your feedback, insight, and encouragement. Thank you, Rachel, for ALWAYS taking the time to answer my questions—seriously, thank you. Special thanks to Kristin Vayden, for your guidance and sheer awesomeness...you're a lifesaver. And to Jena Brignola, thank you—thank you for capturing Kate and Asher on this beautiful cover. Absolute perfection.

Next, to my family, and my husband, William; guys, thank you for putting up with me, for accepting me when I need to be left alone to write. For the MOUNDS of books I have all over the place because I prefer things in print to digital. Thank you. I love you. I couldn't life without you all.

And finally, to The One Who makes ALL things possible, to my Lord and Savior, Jesus Christ, thank You for giving me this ability, this desire, and this passion. May You continue to bless me and may I continue to honor You.

About the author

A child of divorce and abuse, E. L. Irwin found escape in reading and writing. She's a self-described romantic-rebel who wears her heart on her sleeve and tends to shoot from the hip on subjects that matter. E.L. lives in the Pacific Northwest on a small farm with her husband, children, and four dogs. When not reading or writing romance, E.L. enjoys, riding horses, going for drives, tattoos, antique shopping, starry nights, the smell and sound of rain, a deep red wine, a smooth whisk(e)y, camping, bonfires, and hanging out with her horses, cows, chickens, ducks, and goats.

Photo by, Shilowe
Esminger

Author Note:

Dear Reader,

Again, I want to thank you for taking a chance on this story and its characters. I sincerely hope you enjoyed it. As an independently published author, I truly rely on reviews and word-of-mouth. So, please, would you leave a review? It doesn't have to be verbose, just a few simple words expressing your thoughts. Your honest review will help future readers decide if they want to take a chance on a new-to-them author. Here's a link for your convenience: https://a.co/d/1Yvb6xg

Don't forget to read on for a bonus chapter. And be sure to sign up for my newsletter for an additional bonus prequel chapter, featuring Kate and Asher BEFORE they met. Newsletter signup here: https://dl.bookfunnel.com/ybjyjnmdy7

Find out more about me and my books here: www.elirwin.com

Bonus Chapter

The Newlyweds Next Door—An Outsider's Perspective

Anne-

Logs snapped and spit in the fireplace as the wood settled. My eyes blinked dreamily, savoring the quiet peace after a full, busy day. My daughters and I had arrived yesterday at the Quileute Oceanside Resort in La Push, just a short drive from Forks, Washington for an extended weekend jaunt. They were both *huge* Twilight fans and this was our end of summer trip. These excursions were something the girls and I'd started taking four years ago. Just the three of us. No guys allowed.

Headlights briefly illuminated the room before shutting off, alerting me to the arrival of newcomers. I heard a door shut, then, not long after another one. Out of curiosity, probably because it was so late, I peeked out the window to see who our new neighbors were. It looked like a couple. The man seemed a virtual giant, though the woman didn't seem particularly short, herself. I blinked as he set their bags down on the tiny porch, then swept the woman into his arms and opened their cabin door.

Newlyweds, I figured. Or, perhaps they were simply on a romantic retreat together. They appeared happy, whoever they were. Something...something about them struck a thought within me. It wriggled lose and floated to the surface of my mind. Maybe it was the way the man had been *so* focused on the woman. The intentness. A smile crept across my mouth. I lifted my hand to my lips, a wistful sigh escaping; I missed my husband.

Closing the curtains, I turned my gaze back to the room, letting my eyes drift over the interior. The rough-cut log walls, the homey windows framed in deep forest green curtains. The simple, functional furniture. The framed photos of Native American art. My gaze shifted to the lone double bed against the back wall where Joanie and Liz were both sound asleep, quietly snoring. I'd taken the couch. I didn't mind; it wasn't terribly uncomfortable. I shifted, snuggling deeper into the blankets, and my feet gave a throbbing complaint. Sore from all the walking we did today. We'd covered every conceivable Twilight tourist attraction in the area.

I reached for the bag next to the couch, retrieving my lotion. Rubbing the stiffness and soreness from my tired feet, I massaged the moisturizer in, silently sighing as the tension and pain eased. If this *was* the couple's honeymoon...as interesting and beautiful as La Push was, I'd have thought they'd have maybe gone somewhere more exotic. Maybe funds were short? I guess it didn't really matter. What mattered was their relationship. Heaven knew Brian and I had struggled financially at first. Mexico was as exotic as we could afford then. We would celebrate twenty-five years this year. Money didn't a strong marriage make; I could definitely attest to that.

My eyes drooped; I needed sleep, but before turning in, rose and checked the locks on the doors, then banked the fire until it was more red embers than actual logs. I made sure the screen was securely in place before climbing back into my spot on the couch, pulling my blankets up, and was soon asleep.

The following day had us up early for more exploring. We drove into Port Angeles, because apparently that's where Edward had followed Bella, and where they'd had dinner. So, of course, we had to have dinner at Bella Italia, too. The stars in Joanie's and Liz's eyes was worth it, though. I loved seeing them this happy. We ventured into numerous stores there that claimed Twilight fame, and on the way back to La Push, drove up to Rialto Beach and walked the coastline there. With our constant activity, our weekend seemed to fly by. On our last day, Liz awoke first. She had the tiny coffee maker going before the rest of us even had our eyes open. By the time I was awake, both she and her sister had showered and dressed. Soon I was up and joined them for a foggy, chilly walk down the beach. We scratched our names in the sand, and found interesting rocks and shells. We sat and took pictures and talked about our plans for the coming school year. By the time we made it back to the cabin, the fog had begun to lift and the sun was peeking through high, drifting clouds.

After freshening up from our outing, we made brunch, just the odds and ends we had left over from the weekend, and took it out to the deck at the back of our little cabin. We ate in silence, simply enjoying the warm sunshine. Several seagulls spied us and moved closer in hopes of getting scraps. We entertained ourselves tossing food into the air, marveling at their aerial acrobatics. We'd been out there close to twenty minutes, when I caught movement from the corner of my eye. Turning ever so slightly, I saw a woman step from within the cabin next to ours. The wind caught at her over-sized sweatshirt that hung to about mid-thigh on her bare legs. The material ruffled slightly in the breeze; her hair lifting in disarray. Three days ago they'd arrived, and this was the first I'd seen of them. Definitely newlyweds, I decided.

She said something over her shoulder to someone out of sight, then moved to the edge of the decking and leaned against the railing. She inhaled deeply; her face lifted to the sky. A man, the giant one I'd noted a few nights ago, stepped out. He wore sweatpants, the matching bottoms to her shirt. The chill didn't seem to bother him. Not at all. In fact, it didn't look as though much would have bothered this guy. He moved to her, caging her against the rail from behind. I couldn't seem to look away. It wasn't voyeurism. It wasn't. But something about them held me captive. The look on the woman's face, maybe? Such relaxation, such *satisfaction* on her features. A unique awareness. She held the look of a woman who'd been well and truly loved. Who'd had her eyes opened and had thoroughly enjoyed the doing.

The man leaned down, his mouth against her neck. Such blatant chemistry between them. My heart clenched. It had been a *long* time since I'd felt what was clearly written all over her face. Her head tipped back, resting against him. Her eyes were closed now, her mouth curving upwards, even as it opened in what had to be a silent noise of welcome. It had been many, many years. I didn't regret my children. Not at all. But I did miss *that*. That closeness, that connection my husband and I'd had. As I watched them, somewhere in the back of my mind, I was grateful I was wearing sunglasses; they hid the direction of my gaze, as well as my thoughts. I wanted that with my husband again. We'd grown distant over the years. Not intentionally, just always busy. Between the girls' cheer and Steven's baseball, and work, it seemed we were always being pulled in different directions.

A thought formed. An idea. A plan. Would Brian agree? The kids were definitely old enough to be left alone for a long weekend. And my parents could always check on them. As I pondered the logistics of my plan, Joanie gasped. I turned, and found her hands over her mouth. "*Omgosh*, I think...that dude looks like Asher Fitzpatrick. Which would make that Kate—I read they just got married."

"No way. Seriously?" Liz spun in her chair.

"Liz! Turn back around!" Joanie snapped. Liz glared at her sister, then took out her cellphone and changed the camera direction for a selfie. She snapped a picture over her shoulder, then blew the image up to study the couple closer.

"It *IS* him!" Liz gasped. "Omgosh, that's him. And that's her."

"This is so romantic. Look at them."

"Girls, stop it." I admonished, knowing full-well *I'd* just been staring. "You can't just take pictures of them. It's an invasion of privacy. I forbid you from showing that picture to *anyone*."

"But, Mom!" Joanie whined, almost desperately.

"No. Delete it now. Delete it from your trash bin, too."

Liz griped as she did what she was told, and Joanie pondered, "Maybe we could get an autograph, or something?"

"You may *not* knock on their door, but if you happen to catch them outside—not now, and preferably when they have more clothing on—then, you may ask."

"Maybe we can give them the rest of our firewood. That would be neighborly." Liz flicked her eyebrows conspiratorially, and grinned.

"That's fine, but not right now. If they come outside later, you may." I left them sitting there to keep watch and went inside to make a couple phone calls, chuckling under my breath as I did. *Obviously, money wasn't the issue for this couple.* No, something else brought them here. Whatever the reason, they seemed thoroughly happy, and I smiled. An hour later, after all the preparations had been made, I was dialing my cell again.

"Brian?" I said when my husband answered. "How're things? You missing us?" I listened to his reply, and smiled at the assurance in his voice. "Hey," My heart pounded. "I need you to clear your calendar next month. The 24th through the 27th. I'm...taking you somewhere; just the two of us." He was quiet a moment, then agreed, saying he was looking forward to it. He tried to get me to reveal more of my plan. My heart smiled at his antics. I was hopeful. And though I'd most likely never get the chance to thank them—and how would I word that if I could—I was fervently thankful to the couple next door. Asher and Kate. Maybe someday they'd know how their love touched the soul of a stranger.